ROUGH COPY

A novel by

Pearl Kastran Ahnen

PublishAmerica
Baltimore

Hardcover 978-1-4560-6176-0
Softcover 978-1-4560-6604-8
PUBLISHED BY PUBLISHAMERICA, LLLP
www.publishamerica.com
Baltimore

Printed in the United States of America

Author's notes:

Rough Copy in newspaper jargon is when a reporter writes the first or virgin draft of a newspaper article.

For Diana —
Thank you
You are great!
Pearl Kastran Ahnen
8-11-11

Dedicated to my children, Steve and Deneen, and to the memory of my husband, Bill, who always told me to "Believe."

Acknowledgements

I am grateful to my friends, librarians, creative writing teachers and family for their generous advice. Thank you Loretta, editor at Publish America, for your time and thoughtfulness. I was fortunate to have the computer expertise of Penny Kramer, Sue Poolman and Jack Sheridan. A big thank you to Carolyn Owen who was with me from the very beginning, reading and checking various versions of this novel. And finally thank you to my children, Steve and Deneen, their spouses Chelle and Curtis, and my grandchildren, Jessica and Drew, their spouses Bryan and Jenna for their love and support. I am also grateful to Father Jim and Father Nick for their blessings. Thank you God for with your guidance, all things are possible.

INTRODUCTION

AFTER
Detroit Metro Airport, Spring, 1990

He scared the hell out of me when I met him. I was six at the time. It was a dark and stormy morning. True, no cliché intended. A member of the National Guards driving a jeep braved one of the worst storms in Michigan to take us — my mother, Claudia Kali, a newspaper reporter and me — to her office at the Liemus Press. Her boss, Neil Liemus, publisher, demanded all his employees be on the job in spite of the weather. With one phone call to the governor and his political clout he got the National Guards to pick up the staff. The Liemus Press never missed a deadline!

After battling snow-clogged streets, we got to the office and rushed into the ad room. My mother plunked me down on a stool, gave me some colored pencils and newsprint and turned me toward a drawing board. "Jamie, create some ads, honey," she said. "I'll be back soon." Then she dashed off to the editorial department. While one of the graphic artists helped me with my designs, this tall man with a wild head of white hair and a smoldering cigar stuck in his mouth glared at the graphic artist. "What's this kid doing in my ad department?" Without waiting for an answer, he scowled at me, "Get out kid, now!"

Terrified, I burst into tears, scrambled down from the stool and raced into the hallway seeking my mother. That was my first encounter with Neil Liemus. Why am I thinking about him now? It's because my plane just touched down at Metro Airport. I've returned to Michigan after several years. You see, I "ran away" from Michigan after I received my degree from Detroit University. I had to get out, needed to—. Now I work for a Los Angeles newspaper as a graphic artist and came to Detroit on business. You might say I'm in the family business since my mother was a newspaper reporter. I didn't know it then, but at the time my mother led two lives.

At Metro Airport, I picked up the Detroit Dispatch, the local newspaper, as I watched the airport carousel spew out baggage. I flipped through and this third page headline hit me—LIEMUS PRESS BUILDING—HISTORIC MUSEUM? The article said that in the Michigan town of Pierre Corners, a group of citizens were in the process of raising funds to save and restore the Liemus Press building and eventually create a museum. The 1920 building was of classic, Gothic design and located on Main Street in the center of historic Pierre Corners. And next to the article was an old photo of my mother and Neil Liemus when she won the Michigan Press Association award. I gazed at her face, mine is a mirror image same shoulder length hair, same shape of eyes, large, only mine are green like my father's, small nose, full lips. The article quoted the group leader, "There are good memories here that have to be preserved for generations to come. Neil Liemus left a great legacy to the city and we plan to preserve it and create an historical museum in this building."

"Great legacy! Great lies!" I blurted out. My outburst surprised the woman standing next to me. I gave her a weak smile and said, "Sorry." But the article really got to me. The Liemus Press that they think they know is based on lies. I debated going to my hotel first but in the end I changed my mind. I hailed a taxi. Clutching my handbag and rolling my luggage to the curb, I climbed into the cab. "Pierre Corners, Main Street," I directed the cab driver. Riding along with the window open, I caught the polluted smells of the Detroit River and the fresh scents of spring flowers and trees on my way to Pierre Corners.

Twenty minutes later the driver dropped me off at the front door of the Liemus Press building only to discover the door was padlocked.

The huge windows, flanking the door, were boarded up. I wasn't surprised. Of course the building would be locked up. And I lacked the skills and tools for lock picking. So I walked to the corner coffee shop thinking a good cup of coffee would give me some ideas as to how to get into the building. Strange, that coffee shop was still in business after all these years, although several of the stores on Main Street were vacant and boarded up. Pierre Corners had lost its glory, now it was a "yesterday" town.

At the coffee shop door, I looked back and saw a group approaching the Press building. The woman leading the group held a key. I backtracked, pumping myself up for the confrontation with the group, getting my energy level up. But the Press door was opened by the woman when I got there. So, I strolled through the door just behind the last person in the group without a problem.

I had mixed feelings when I walked through the Press lobby, feelings of anger and a chilling feeling of fear. I saw the circular desk in the center of the lobby, dusty, cob webs clinging to the switchboard and I visualized Neil Liemus with a fistful of copy, barking orders. Broken glass and old newspapers littered the floor. I knew personally that the Liemus Press history was filled with corruption of power, mental abuse and a secret that shattered a trio of lives. These were NOT "good memories" to be preserved for generations to come. I know, I lived through those memories. It began for me in 1960.

PART ONE
CLAUDIA KALI

CHAPTER ONE

Pierre Corners, 1960

If Claudia Kali hadn't seen the ad for a reporter's job in the Liemus Press things might have turned out differently. Might have. And if she hadn't telephoned the Press yesterday she wouldn't be sitting in her old Ford now, staring at a scrap of paper. But she did see the ad and she did make that call. There was no real reason why she shouldn't have answered that ad. Then why had her hand trembled when she placed the phone back on the kitchen counter? And why had she felt Alex's anger even before he spoke?

"I told you not to call!"

"I had to—," she began.

"Had to? The only things you have to do are take care of Jamie and this house. Understood? Maybe I'll have to teach you another lesson." He folded his arms across his massive chest. "Let's stop playing games."

Claudia didn't answer. There was no point. It could lead to —. Taking a deep breath, brushing back her auburn hair, she said, "What's happened to us, Alex? My God, what's happened to you?" The nape of her neck was damp; she held her hands to keep them from trembling. There weren't anymore words left in her. Somehow the sickness began with Alex when their daughter, Jamie was born. Everything had changed.

"Nothing's happened to me!" He grabbed Claudia's wrist. "Nothing—you hear?'

Claudia didn't move. Then Alex twisted her arm. "Please don't," she said.

He released her arm. "When are you going to learn?" He raced out of the house slamming the door after him.

Now in the car, Claudia folded the scrap of paper and shoved it into her purse. Yes, she had learned. She had learned about Alex after being married to him for more than six years and finally she was going to do something about it, no matter what, she would be free of Alex. She would take Jamie and be free.

She hugged herself as though she were cold, sitting in their old Ford, but she wasn't cold. Quickly she tucked some stray hair into her navy felt hat, pulling the soft brim low over her forehead to hide the bruise, from a few days ago. No more bruises she told herself. No more!

No matter what, she'd get this job. She'd take Jamie and leave. Then she parked on the curb near the newspaper office and watched the traffic on Main Street. Opening the window a crack brought a whiff of cold air into the car. Claudia wrinkled her nose. It's from the river, she thought, and it smells like dead fish. The Detroit River, the conduit of Pierre Corners, its usual polluted gray, now was shrouded by low clouds. On a sunny day you could see clear across the river to Windsor, Canada. Strange as it seems, Windsor was south of Detroit. But it wasn't sunny today; it was a cold, overcast November day. There was only a mile visibility with Windsor hiding behind clouds. All Claudia could see was the dock at the foot of Main Street and the outline of the Liemus Press dispatch boat tied to it. Two men pulled bundles of newspapers from the deck and loaded them onto a waiting truck.

After watching them for a while, Claudia shifted her gaze to the rearview mirror and tilted it downward. Her own face appeared, slightly flushed, her brown eyes squinting. She grabbed the amber beads that dangled from the mirror and slid them into her jacket pocket. Her father's worry beads from Greece. They brought her luck.

14

Well, what are you going to do, sit in this car all morning? she asked her reflection in the mirror. NO! Now is the time.

This morning after Alex had left for the car dealership, she rushed Jamie through her cold cereal, bundled her up in her warm coat against the cold November wind and walked with her to their next door neighbor, where she would wait until it was time to go to school and return later to wait for Claudia.

Now Claudia watched other mothers' children standing at the traffic light behind crossing guards outstretched arms. Then her gaze fell on the Liemus Press building. It was the largest and oldest building on Main Street, taking up most of the block. Two windows flanked the entrance's carved oak doors. An antique press and a scale model of the newspaper's first dispatch boat were displayed in one window. In the other window was an oil painting of Neil Liemus, owner and publisher of the Liemus Press. The artist had captured the publisher's dark eyes, his immaculately groomed white hair, and his imposing presence. Even from a distance, Claudia felt the portrait's eyes staring at her. Neil Liemus stood posed at his desk, a brass elephant paper weight in his hand.

There was little traffic as she dashed across the street and walked into the Press. Above the doors was an orange sign with black lettering—THE LIEMUS PRESS. When she walked through the doors, she found herself in the lobby. To her right, was a long counter where you could get a subscription or place a want ad. Behind the counter, sitting at one of the desks was a thin red head in a pink sweater and skirt. She pecked away at a typewriter, while the tip of her tongue poked from the corner of her mouth.

In the center of the lobby was the circular desk of the receptionist-telephone operator, whose ample body strained under a tight grey sweater and skirt. Claudia slowed her steps, not wanting to be conspicuous. She felt over dressed in her best suit, a navy wool, and white silk blouse. In a soft voice, the operator asked, "May I help you?" Claudia nodded, "I have an appointment with Mr. Lucavate. I'm Claudia Kali."

"Claudia Kali?" The operator repeated, sweeping her gaze from

Claudia's hat to her shoes. "Just a minute," she said answering a blinking light on the switchboard. "Liemus Press," she said into the headset. A minute later her index finger searched through her appointment book. "Ah, yes, Claudia Kali. You're early, that's good. Mr. Lucavate's office is the first one on the left down the hall. You'll see his name on the door."

Claudia walked down the hallway in the direction she had pointed. She hugged her purse and the folder with her resume and copies of her news articles.

Richard Lucavate's eyes were on her as she tapped on his opened door. He waved her in while he paced his office, a phone cradled between his chin and shoulder. With the stub of an amputated thumb he flipped through a stack of papers on his roll top desk. He motioned for her to sit down.

Into the receiver he said, "Okay, Yiannis, I'll get back with you later. Your half page ad is going in tomorrow." Then he sank into a swivel chair. He glanced at his pocket watch, fiddled with the stem, and then turned his full attention to Claudia.

"Claudia Kali?" Without waiting for her to reply, he said, "You're early, good."

At first glance, Richard Lucavate was not imposing, though his features added up to something not easily forgotten. His height barely topped Claudia's five-foot six, and his body was sturdy but lean. His straight brown hair grew above a high forehead, his

blue eyes were intense behind horn-rimmed glasses, and his short beard was neatly trimmed.

"See you brought your string book." He motioned to the folder in her hand. "Can you spell? So you want to work for us?"

"Yes, I can spell, and yes, I want to work for the Liemus Press." She searched in her folder for her resume.

With complete naturalness, he took her resume and her string book and flipped through it. "Ah, you've done some features for the News and Free Press."

"Yes."

"Tell me a little about yourself," he said. He leaned over to fill a cup from an electric coffee pot that sat on a bookcase behind his desk. "Coffee?" He held up the cup.

"No, thanks." Then she began, haltingly at first, putting memories into words.

She told him about working for the university newspaper, about doing free lance features for the Detroit Free Press and News.

"Your string book and resume are fine. You worked for the university newspaper, eh?"

"Yes, and once I interviewed a frog in the lab."

Straight faced he asked. "Was he a good subject?"

"No, he croaked a lot."

He stroked his beard and grinned. "We're going to get along fine. I like someone with a sense of humor."

"I got it from my father. He was Mike Belos."

"Mike Belos was your father?"

Claudia nodded.

"I remember that name, that story, about a killing—"

"Yes," said Claudia. When she closed her eyes she still could see him, her father, a tall rugged man, sandy hair, soft hazel eyes. Over the years, she'd had this strange half-waking dream. She was running, running. In the dream she felt a cold wind stinging her face, and heard him call her nickname, Kukla, which meant "doll" in Greek. She never reached him in time—and he was killed, clutching his amber beads. Even when she was awake the horrible nightmare lingered on.

"Someone killed my father and got away with it. The system doesn't work, does it?"

Richard Lucavate nodded, stroked his beard and encouraged her, stirring his coffee with a spoon, yet always listening. "Sometimes it does. Seems to me it was a front page story—accidental death, but it was murder, plain and simple."

Murder, plain and simple. The starkness of the words surprised Claudia. After five years she could still feel the sense of shock and outrage that her father had died that way, his life snuffed out in an instant. With an effort, she pushed back the memory, forced the past back where it belonged.

17

Now she looked at Richard. "Yes," she said her face pale.

"I'm sorry," he said. Then briskly, "Yes, we need a reporter—someone who is tuned into these times—this year of 1960— that people are calling a new beginning. We're getting a new young president—John F Kennedy—next year. We shall see if he can turn the country around. But now, let's find you a typewriter, and see what you can do with these." He reached over and dug into a pile of publicity releases, letters and news releases stacked in a wire basket.

Why had she gone on and on talking about her father? Her fingers found the amber bead in her pocket. Yes, she liked this eccentric man. But there was something she could not tell anyone, not even Richard Lucavate, something that she could not put into words—and it was about Alex— Then she remembered his parting words, "Go for the damn interview. But that doesn't change anything around here, understand? I have a sucker waiting to buy a new car, so I can't be bothered with you now. We'll talk later." Then Claudia touched the brim of her hat hiding the bruise. Suddenly Alex's face appeared in her mind. She shook her head. Mustn't think of him. Richard's voice brought her back. "Hummm let me see. Yes, maybe this release will do," he said.

Claudia glanced around his office. There was a plaque on the wall. It was a Kiwanis award citing the Press, and there was a certificate from the Pierre Corners Jaycees. The certificate recognized Richard as founder of the chapter and he now was a "ruptured rooster." To the left of the certificate, hung a gold frame. It held five playing cards, the ace, king, queen, jack and ten of spades, spread in a fan.

"Here, think you can make something of this garbage?" He handed her a news release from the pile.

"I'll try," she said glancing at it. "They've misspelled campaign, or maybe it's a typo."

"If my memory is correct," he said, polishing his glasses with newsprint, and taking the release from her, "That person can't spell, write or make a good cup of coffee, for that matter. All we can expect is rough copy from him, even though he gets the big bucks as a PR man for a major Detroit corporation. Come on, follow me."

As he led her out of the office, his pocket watch alarm went off. He nodded and turned off the alarm. Had he timed her interview? Claudia wondered. They walked into a huge room with a hardwood floor. There was a sense of controlled chaos here. Stacks of newspapers, notebooks and page proofs were piled high against one wall; some doughnuts spilled out of a white bakery bag onto a table next to an old green file cabinet. A coffee pot perked nearby. Black bound volumes lay on the floor near a pile of newspapers. Although it was November, a wood-blade ceiling fan stirred the musty air.

There were two rows of desks, occupied by two men and two women. One wall of the room was covered with bronze plaques, certificates and awards. Two other walls were paneled in knotty pine. Against the remaining wall were several metal file cabinets flanking large windows facing an alley and a parking lot.

Richard's thin arm guided a path around the cluttered desks. The clang of telephones and the clatter of typewriters never ceased and competed with the nervous anticipation that swelled in Claudia's breast. She hunched deeper in the collar of her jacket, trying to disappear as she felt a pair of hostile blue eyes staring at her. They belonged to a long-limbed woman who looked at her from the desk where she was perched. She wore an elegant but outdated dress of burnt orange wool. Her long legs were crossed.

Richard turned to Claudia. "Claudia, meet Valley LaPorte."

"Welcome—I think," Valley said.

"Hello."

Then Valley slid off the desk. "If you'll excuse me, I've got to interview the owner of a bull dog, and I hope that damn dog is chained to a good strong post. I've got this man to thank for this gem of an assignment. I wouldn't exactly call it front page stuff."

"He's a prize dog," Richard said. "Act nice. And don't forget the school board meeting this afternoon."

"I won't if the bull doesn't eat me. Anything else sir?" She saluted Richard and fled the room.

"She's not too fond of dogs," he said to Claudia. Then Richard raised a pica ruler and rapped on the desk. "People, I need a typewriter for this young lady."

"Will this Underwood do?" The voice and the man were overpowering. He plopped the typewriter on a cluttered desk, first sweeping the clutter away with one movement of his hand. "Welcome aboard, I'm Bernie," he said. He stuck his hand out. Bernie towered over Claudia. He was a tall, muscle-bound, balding man.

"Hi, I'm Claudia Kali."

He winked. Then he turned to Richard. "We've got another emergency."

"Emergency?"

"Yeah, in less than an hour, I've had six calls, all asking for the Goddess of Night. Do you know where she is?"

"Hell, I don't even know WHO she is, and care less." He stroked his beard. "Must be a full moon, that's when the loonies come out of the woodwork."

"Don't you think I'd better check it out?"

"Stick to your police beat."

"You're the boss," said Bernie.

"Glad you remembered."

Claudia's eyes caught a man moving toward them. She recognized him from his pictures in the Press. He was Urho Liemus, the publisher's son. She'd seen photos of him and his wife, Dora, in the society section of the Press and on the sport pages at the annual golf tournament sponsored by the Press. Urho, a fistful of ads in his hands, walked up to Claudia. "I'm Urho Liemus. You must be Claudia Kali. Richard told me your interview was scheduled for today." His hazel eyes studied her. Not knowing what else to do, Claudia stammered, "Y- Yes."

"Go ahead, jump right in Urho, and don't wait for me to introduce you to the young lady."

"You take too long. Besides we don't stand on formalities, not here. We're one big happy family,"

"Certainly," said Richard and guided Claudia to the vacant desk where Bernie had placed the old Underwood typewriter. Then he handed her several news releases. "Here, see if you can make some sense out of these releases." He taped his pica ruler on the desk.

"That's right," said Urho. "Get her on the releases, pronto. We've got a deadline."

Claudia looked at him. His comments puzzled her—deadline? What did he mean? Wasn't this an interview?

Urho brushed passed her and quickly left the room.

"His manners need improving," Richard said. "I'm afraid you'll have to get used to him. He's in charge of advertising, but he lacks the social graces."

Claudia said nothing but found herself glancing at Urho as he dashed off. His thick blond hair touched the collar of his white shirt. He was tall, over six feet, and had the built of an athlete. Must be all that tennis and golf, thought Claudia. She had read about his feats in both sports. Finally she turned her attention to the typewriter and the pile of news releases patiently waiting for her.

Richard noted her gaze. "Think you can handle that batch?"

"Yes."

He took out his pocket watch and set the alarm. "Good."

He's going to time me, again, she thought. Then she grinned.

* * *

The sound of the hall clock striking twelve startled Claudia. She had promised her neighbor that she would be back by noon, when Jamie would be returning from a half-day of school.

"Going to lunch?" Bernie asked, slipping into his trench coat and sinking with a sigh of relief into the chair next to her desk. He pulled on his leather gloves. "You can join me. I'm going to the corner diner. Foods lousy, but the coffee's great."

"Lunch? No, I didn't realize it was so late. I-I've got to see Mr. Lucavate." She glanced at the stack of articles she'd written. Some of them were gone. When did that happen?

"Well, you'd better hurry. He leaves at 12:20 sharp. No ifs, ands or buts about it." Bernie carefully patted the thin strands of hair covering his bald spot, and then winked.

Claudia managed to squeeze through the crowd going to lunch. Panting, the news releases clutched in her hand, she knocked on

Richard's closed door. What if I don't get the job? she thought.

She had visions of Richard jumping out of his office, rapping her knuckles with his pica metal ruler and telling her she didn't fit into the big happy Liemus Press family, not at all.

He must be in his office! But she could not burst in. The slim redhead passed by her and gave her a blank stare. Was Richard in his office? She knocked again. The door was opened by Urho, his half-lidded hazel eyes gazed at her. Clearly she was the intruder, she thought. "Is Mr. Lucavate in?" she asked.

Urho stood his ground, staring at her with those eyes. "Yeah, he's in. Been waiting for you. Finished those releases? Don't forget we have a deadline." Not waiting for her reply, he grinned and walked away.

Richard was right behind him. "Come in," he motioned to Claudia. Well, are you going to lunch?"

"Lunch? No, I didn't realize it was so late. I have to get home. I lost track of time. I'm sorry."

"Don't be sorry. You write a good story. I shipped some of them down to our plant in Detroit." He smiled. "They'll be in tomorrow's paper. You can take the rest of the day off. Didn't mean to keep you so long, but you were on a roll, and we were on deadline. See you in the morning—8:30 sharp. He checked his watch. Got to run."

"Thank you, but I don't understand."

"What's to understand? You're hired. Will talk salary tomorrow," he said grabbing his tan trench coat. "Catch you tomorrow." And then he winked.

Do all the men wink in this strange place? Claudia wondered as she walked to the main lobby and past the telephone operator, who lifted her eyebrows in a quizzical stare,

"Did you get the job?"

Claudia nodded.

"Great," said the operator. She didn't sound that pleased.

Twenty minutes later Claudia drove into her driveway. Her heels kicked up gravel as she raced to the back door. The sun peeked through dense clouds, giving a promise of a bitter cold night. She noticed the dealership's Thunderbird in the garage. Alex was home early. She let herself into the house, closed the door and Jamie rushed to her and gave her a hug. "Mommy, mommy," she cried. "Daddy picked me up."

"I see, honey, I'm sorry I'm late," Claudia hugged her daughter. Then she faced Alex.

"What took you so damn long?" Alex asked.

"The interview – it took longer than I thought." She put her hat on the kitchen table, smoothed her bangs over the bruise. "I got the job."

"So you got the stupid job. How much are they paying you?"

"I don't know."

He came toward her. "You don't know? How stupid is that?" She backed away. He kept coming, slowly, relentlessly. Her back to the table, she considered running, running out the door, out of this life with him. She was no match for Alex, and she knew it. "Want another souvenir, like that? He brushed the bangs away from her forehead. "I don't have time for this crap. I've got cars to sell. Where did you put the Ford keys so I can get out of the driveway?"

Claudia thought this couldn't be the same Alex she met in college. The one who had pulled her into a dark corner at Detroit University and kissed her. She was a kid then, crazy in love. And how they had joked and laughed. And how when he introduced himself he said he was once Alex Kalieskowski but had his name legally changed to Kali when he got back from Korea. "They used to call me 'alphabet soup' in the Army," he said. "None of that now," he added. He was fun and kind then.

But soon after Jamie was born she found herself driving to Woodoaks Hospital with a fractured jaw and an eye swollen shut. And how she had sworn that night that, that would be the last time Alex would touch her. She'd leave him, take her baby and leave him. That was more than four years ago.

Now facing him she said. "I don't know where the keys are—"

"You don't know?" He watched her, as if she had nothing to do with him. "The keys remember?"

"I — I—" Then she saw them under the table.

He followed her gaze, scooped up the keys and raced out, slamming the door after him.

Claudia's hand shook, but she was determined to get control. Jamie had watched what had happened. She was huddled in a corner, teary eyed. Claudia scooped her in her arms. "It's okay, baby, it's okay."

CHAPTER 2

Richard rapped on the door before letting himself into Neil's office. In fact it looked more like a designer's show room. The afternoon sun shone on the oak paneled walls. An orange and blue oriental rug covered the hardwood floor. The carpet was so plush; Richard's shoes were lost in it as he walked across the room and sank into a brown leather chair. He faced Neil seated behind a mahogany desk.

In greeting Richard, Neil twisted his lips into one of those ugly smiles that he did so well. "Well, how did the interview go?" As always he puffed on a premium cigar, his eyes focused on a brass paperweight, in the shape of an elephant. He picked up the paperweight, inspected it, balancing it in one hand, then the other. It was one of his collections of elephants. They were everywhere in this room, as book ends, paperweights, ash trays and doorknobs.

A huge brass elephant stood guard at the door. All the elephants' trunks were up. It was a good luck sign, Neil told visitors. A wall of windows, draped in nylon sheers, looked out onto Main Street.

The adjoining room was a luxurious bedroom, carpeted in orange wool. A mammoth bed took over much of the room. Next to the bedroom were a dressing room and a bathroom.

Also on the fourth floor was the boardroom. A bare, barn-like area with none of the decorator's touches. It was used for staff meetings.

"The interview went fine. We've got a new reporter," said Richard, tossing Claudia's resume on the desk. "She can spell."

Neil scanned the resume. Mmmmm, Claudia Kali, what kind of a name is that?" While he waited for an answer he turned his cigar slowly in pursed lips and blew a smoke cloud toward the ceiling.

"What do you mean?"

Neil turned his chair. He was sixty-two years old, with penetrating brown eyes and neatly combed white hair. His gray flannel suit fit perfectly on his tall frame. "You know what I mean. I'm Finnish, and damn proud of it, and your folks were Italian, right? What is she?"

I didn't know that made any difference. She is highly qualified. But if it does, her father was Mike Belos."

"Mike Belos? The man that was killed in his restaurant? What was it some five years ago? I still remember the story. Some said it was murder. Yes, he was Greek, wasn't he?" asked Neil.

Richard nodded.

"Well, that's a good thing. Greek, huh? We'll have to introduce her to old Yiannis. Plan an interview. Maybe we'll get bigger ads from him. He's got it, that's for sure."

"Just talked to him. We've got a half page ad in tomorrow's paper, and he's considering a full page for Sunday's edition.

"Good, that old bastard's got more money than—but never mind."

Richard glanced at his pocket watch.

Neil raised his eyebrows. "Am I keeping you? Is that damn alarm going to go off?"

"Even if it does, we have a problem."

"A problem?"

"Yes, it's Valley, drunk again. After this morning's interview about the pit bull, she must have stopped off at a bar. She came back to the office stinko. Freda drove her home. We have to fire her," Richard said.

Neil reached for the brass elephant paperweight and slammed it down on his desk with such force that it marred the smooth surface of the mahogany. "After that talk I had with her last week, after my warning!"

Richard sat back and lighted a cigarette with his Zippo, then crossed his legs and waited.

"Valley stays," Neil said.

Richard's face flushed. "How can I expect the rest of the staff to toe the mark if we have to shut our eyes at Valley's drunken antics?"

"I said she stays—end of discussion."

Richard's cigarette hung from his lips. And at that instant, his pocket watch alarm went off. He leapt to his feet. "I've got to go."

"Damn, why do you let that thing rule your life?"

"Listen, this THING is my life, sets my life in order." He held the pocket watch in his hand examining it closely. The case was worn from many years of constant use. He glanced at the face and slid it back into his pocket, all in one swift motion.

"So, in almost fifteen years of trying, I haven't weaned you away from your watch, and your fucking obsession with it. Old Yiannis and I have a bet that you'll go to your grave with that damn watch in your hands."

Richard leaned over to jab out his cigarette butt in the brass ashtray on Neil's desk. He knew that Yiannis Miteas, Pierre Corner's biggest building contractor and Neil's poker crony, had never indicated anything but irritation over Richard's watch fetish.

"And who do you think will win?" asked Richard.

"Probably you. You'll see both of us six feet under," Neil said. "Now, get out of here. I'm busy. Urho's due here any minute with the ad dummies for tomorrow's edition."

Neil frowned. Urho, his son and heir. For decades Neil had possessed the eye for identifying good ads, good newspaper makeup, and now Neil had passed it onto his son, Urho. He was thankful for that, but there was a time when Urho didn't want to get into the newspaper business, he wanted to pursue the life of an artist. Grant you, he was good. When he got home from Korea, Neil straightened him out. An artist! Bull shit!

"Well, I'd better get out of here," said Richard, snapping Neil out of his reverie.

Neil said nothing.

When Richard closed the door after him, Neil walked to the windows and gazed down on Main Street. What both of them had left unsaid was that Valley had been viewed at one time as Richard's assistant. But that promotion never materialized. No, never. Now both Neil and Richard knew that Valley no longer had it. But only Neil knew why he could not fire her.

Finally he walked to his desk and sat down, his tall frame slipping effortlessly into the high-backed leather chair. He smoothed his short white hair, needlessly, because it was impeccably in place. He took a swallow of black coffee from a ceramic mug. It was his fifth cup that day.

Valley, Valley, he thought. He reached back in his memory to the time they met. Was it 1929? So long ago? In a time when women had bobbed their hair, Valley's hair was long, silky blonde, falling to her waist.

When Neil and Valley met, she was engaged to David LaPorte, heir to the French land baron fortune. At that time, Neil was a struggling dispatcher for the Detroit Times. The moment he saw her, he was overwhelmed by her—her deep blue eyes, her bright red lipstick, her long blonde hair, her shapely body, her exotic perfume. Just smelling her scent excited him.

Now he leaned against the desk, folded his arms in front of him, and looked at the coffee mug. He closed his eyes and pinched the bridge of his nose. There was a knock. He knew it was Urho. "Come in." He gazed out the window.

Urho walked in, "Got the ads."

It was only then when Neil turned and faced his son, he knew Urho had something on his mind, other than ads.

"What's the matter, son?"

Urho stood before his father's desk. "Saw Valley spread out in the lounge, dead drunk! Talked Freda into driving her home. I don't know why we keep that woman—that drunk on the pay roll."

"We keep her because I say so—besides you're here to show me the ad layouts, not to talk about Valley. Understood?"

"Yes." With quick movements Urho pulled layouts and ads from a large manila envelope and spread them out on Neil's desk. Silently Neil examined them and used a red pencil to OK the ones he approved. Then he said, "I tend to lose my temper when I have to deal with Valley. We go back a long way." Neil continued. "Hell, when I was hawking papers for the Times, she was engaged to a very wealthy man—later married him. Now that the tables are turned, I don't want to toss her out on the street, drunk or sober. And you should be one to talk. I've seen you blotto a few times."

Urho shrugged. "I could have gone the other way, drugs I mean, like some of my buddies in Korea. It was plentiful there, but it tore the guts out of them. So I took to the bottle, no pain, just trying to erase rotten memories of that hell war, or what did President Truman call it, a police action?"

"Yes, police action. But we all have them, damn memories, I mean. Even those of us who didn't see action in that hell war, as you call it."

"And now you're getting on my case, cause I drink now and then. Never on the job, you've noticed."

"I'm not on your case. It's just that Richard was here bitching about Valley and when you started in on her—it was too much." Neil wiped his face with his handkerchief as if he could wipe off the frustration with one stroke.

"Richard was complaining too?"

Neil nodded. "You know he doesn't like drinking anything stronger than coffee."

Strange, it was his obsession with a good cup of coffee that brought him to the Liemus Press.

Urho grinned. He threw his hands into the air and rolled his eyes in comical disbelief. "No, not that story again! I've heard it a hundred times."

Ignoring him, Neil went on and retold the story of how Richard had traveled from Grand Rapids by Greyhound on his way to Detroit. And if the bus hadn't stopped in Pierre Corners, and if Richard hadn't walked into the corner dinner for that cup of coffee, he'd probably be with the Free Press or News right now.

`Urho sat back in his chair and nodded, waiting for the rest of the story.

"It was November 14, 1944," Neil said.

"November 13," Urho corrected.

"Yes, you're right it was the thirteenth. And that skinny son of a bitch was looking for a job. He had the ability, no doubt about that, and the makings of a fine editor. It probably helped that he was down to his last ten bucks when he walked into my office."

"Don't forget about the thumb."

"Don't interrupt," said Neil. He glanced at Urho. They were so different, yet so alike. Urho wasn't a talker, and didn't have Neil's interests—antiques, politics, telescoping, priceless elephant statues, women and the Liemus Press.

As far as Neil could tell, Urho didn't care about anything, except his foolish art work. He didn't even care about his wife, Dora. Dora, oh how she reminded Neil of a young Valley.

"The thumb," prompted Urho.

"The thumb?" Neil looked at his son and grinned sheepishly. "Sorry, I was thinking about something else. You mean the lack of a thumb. Ah, I'm tired o talking about that man. Let's get these ads wrapped up. I want to get out of here."

"What?"

"You heard me, hell, remember I own the damn paper and –." The sound of the telephone interrupted him. Neil turned and looked at it.

"Aren't you going to answer it?'

"No, I know who it is."

The ringing continued.

"Well, I'll get out of your way." Urho gathered the red-penciled ads and stacked them in the envelope. As he closed the door after him, Neil picked up the phone and listened.

"Hello, Neil? Answer me, damn you!" The voice was muffled, the words slurred. "Say something, Neil!"

"Yes, Valley, it's me," Neil finally said. "Why don't you sleep it off? I'll see you in the morning." He hung up. It rang again and continued to ring as he walked out of the office.

Neil worked the ignition in his red Jaguar and didn't look back as he eased out of the Press parking lot, and then turned left without the turn signal on. On Main Street, cars flashed by—vans, pick-ups, trucks, sedans. Finally Neil turned on the Island causeway, the one he had built, his own bridge to the Island, private access to his home.

The call from Valley had spoiled his day. He didn't want to think about her. He was going home to his mansion. Damn that woman! He was still thinking about her when he stormed into the oval room in the tower and slammed the door after him.

Mounted on a brass stand, facing a wall of windows was a forty-power telescope. He adjusted the lens and looked though it. His land, as far as the eye could see. His land! He'd earned it, by God. So what if he had stopped along the way to smell the roses? So what if women were attracted to him?

Greta, his wife, was no good at pleasing him. But he was tied to her- with that agreement she forced him into a long time ago. Greta, that bitch! Although she did have a head for business and used it negotiating land deals for the Liemus Press Corporation, she was lousy in bed.

He adjusted the telescope, leaned forward and frowned as he spotted something in the lens. The cottage, the riverfront cottage. Damn, why must everything bring back stories of her? Why? Slowly he walked to the marble table and surveyed the three telephones on it – one red, one blue, one white.

Neil had devised a system many years ago. The red phone was for emergency calls; the blue one for calls to Richard, the Press attorney and staff calls the white one for personal calls.

The blue one was the one Neil used the most. It wasn't unusual for him to call a reporter at two or three in the morning to cover a breaking story. It was not an intrusion on the reporter's life, he would say. It was their job to be on call twenty-four hours a day.

Neil looked at his watch. Four o'clock. Dinner wouldn't be for another three hours. Then he reached for the white phone, rapidly dialed a number, one he knew from memory, waited and finally said, "Hello, Valley."

CHAPTER 3

"Say kid, how long have you been working here, a month?" Valley asked perched on her desk.

"Going on six weeks," Claudia replied. "Why?"

"So they asked the new kid on the block to drive me home. Right?" Claudia looked up from her typewriter.

"It was you, wasn't it?"

Claudia heard the tension in Valley's voice. Yesterday Richard had thrown his car keys on Claudia's desk and asked her to drive Valley home. Now Valley appeared sober and didn't seem to have a hangover. Her face did not have the after-the-binge paleness. Her eyes were bright and clear. She wore an expensive but old brown tweed suit. She didn't even smell of liquor as she had yesterday.

"Did I babble?" Valley asked. "Did I say something I shouldn't have?"

"No, not at all. In fact, as soon as I got you in the car, you fell asleep."

"Asleep or passed out? You're something else, Claudia."

Valley smiled and reached for a cigarette from her pack. "You have that look—about you, new, fresh."

"I'm new all right, but I don't think fresh." In less than two months Claudia and Valley had become friends. In the past few weeks, Claudia had learned a great deal about the newspaper business from Valley. Not only the basics but the ins and outs of writing for the

Liemus Press. She even discovered the secret of her temperamental old Underwood typewriter. All it needed was some sweet talk and a new ribbon.

"How fresh did you say I was?" Claudia grinned.

"Fresh and sassy," Valley said. "I owe you one kid. Let's get out of here. The newsprint smell is getting to me. I need to experience the smell of raw meat cooking and greasy fries. It's time for lunch." She stubbed out her cigarette in the coffee mug. "How about a lousy lunch but some terrific coffee?"

"Perfect," Claudia said.

Valley uncrossed her legs and hopped off the desk top. Her nose wrinkled. "See I told you the smell was getting to me. That damn fan doesn't seem to do much good." She looked up at the wood-blade fan. "Hungry? Let's beat the crowd."

She herded Claudia out of the office, never glancing at the others who watched them as they bundled into their coats and walked out into the lobby.

In minutes they were in the diner. The wet chill outside had penetrated to Claudia's bones through her thin coat. She shivered as they entered the warm restaurant. Once seated in the back, near the kitchen she caught the smell of frying onions and chicken soup. In one corner a jukebox blared out Elvis singing "Blue Suede Shoes." Valley got the attention of the harried waitress as she scurried around the diner. She took their orders of hamburgers and coffee. Then Valley sat back in the booth, reached for a cigarette from a pack and said, "All right kid, tell me everything, and I mean everything." Then she tossed back her head and laughed. "Don't leave anything out. I'll know if you do." Now she looked serious.

Claudia didn't know what to do, didn't know if she could take this woman seriously. In the past, they only talked about the office and their jobs. Should she tell her? Where should she begin? Sure, she'd tell her the truth, but she'd never tell her about Alex. Yes, right now she needed someone to talk to, someone who would listen. So she took a deep breath and plunged in.

"My father was the most important person in my life. Then he was killed."

"Holy cow! What do you mean, Claudia?"

"My father was Mike Belos. It happened in his restaurant—"

"Hey, I remember that—it was a front page story in the Press. Something about a man repeatedly bashing the owner on the head with a pop bottle and he fell and hit his head on a stool or something."

"Yes, that's right. And when I got there minutes later—I saw the ambulance pulling away. He was dead. If I had gotten there sooner, it might not have happened. Police reports say the man was drunk and out of control. And he walked away from that, can you believe it? Walked away."

"I'm sorry kid. Valley reached for Claudia's hand. "What did your mother do?"

"She tried to run the restaurant, no experience. It was too much for her. Finally she sold it at a loss and moved to Chicago. She never got over my father's death. She wanted to get out of Michigan, wanted to erase those horrible memories. But she couldn't. Her life wasn't exactly what she had planned, but whose life is?"

"Maybe you're right."

Claudia went on to tell Valley that she was married to Alex at the time and expecting Jamie, so they remained in Pierre Corners. Before her mother left for Chicago, they had a long talk and Claudia suspected that her mother blamed her for her father's death."

"Why? For God's sake why?" Valley asked

"I was late getting to the restaurant that day. If I had been there, things might have turned out differently. My father would be alive today. Anyway, that's what my mother thinks."

"It doesn't seem fair," Valley said. Then she asked Claudia how she met her husband. "I saw him once when he came in to pick you up. He's a handsome devil."

"Handsome?" Claudia stirred her coffee. Valley concentrated on her hamburger, squirting catsup on it, removing the circle of onion and placing it on the plate.

Yes, he was handsome, but Claudia didn't view him as handsome now. Still Valley's comments activated her memory of Alex and how they met at Detroit University. He had been standing in front of her locker, trying to work the combination. His green eyes challenged her. "Why doesn't this stupid lock work?"

"Maybe it's because you are trying to break into my locker," she had said.

When she finally convinced him he was at the wrong locker (his was on the second floor), he wouldn't leave until she promised to join him for coffee after classes. Then they introduced each other. "We'll meet here, at my locker," Alex said.

"It's my locker, remember?" They both laughed.

Later sipping coffee in the cafeteria, he told her he was a Korean War veteran going to college on the G.I. Bill.

Now she felt the same old resentments, the same old anger, dragged up year after year, with nothing totally forgotten. Their first heated quarrel came after Jamie was born, the time he was gone all night.

And through Valley's eyes she could see Alex, tall and handsome. And those afternoons that they shared at the coffee shop on campus had been another life. Alex drinking endless cups of coffee, holding her hand, talking about their future. She was going to write for the Detroit News or Free Press and he was going to own a car dealership. And how he had rushed her into marriage. A year later, after Jamie was born the nightmare began.

Valley said, "So your daughter is gifted?"

"What?" Claudia asked. "Must have been daydreaming. Yes, she wants to be an artist. But I've talked enough. It's your turn now."

The jukebox played another Elvis song, "That's all Right Mama."

"What's this, show and tell time?" Valley asked. She let her eyes close briefly and rubbed her forehead. "See, just the thought of talking about myself gives me a headache. Or it could be that jukebox. It has two volumes, loud and blaring." Then she laughed. "Okay, kid, want to hear my story? It can be told in one sentence. Neil Liemus owns me body and soul." Then she rubbed her forehead again. "Believe that, and I'll tell you another good one." And then she caught her breath and began to cough. "Damn smoke."

Claudia sensed that Valley was about to say something important. But she didn't press her to continue. Maybe another time.

* * *

At the weekly staff meeting after lunch, Richard waited for Valley to sit down before he tapped his metal pica ruler on the long board room table. It was his signal to start the meeting. He scanned the room while he ran the stub of a thumb over his beard.

Dominating the room was the long, scarred, stained table. Although Neil had hired an interior decorator for his office, the board room got the cast offs from other departments.

Valley called the conference room the 'crap room" because of the atmosphere and the comments made at the weekly staff meetings. She had also nicknamed Neil's office suite the "penthouse". Making a late entry, Valley took her time sitting down at Richard's right. She sat away from the table, an unlit cigarette dangling from her right hand, and stared at the large photo of Neil hanging on the far wall. Windows, with shades rolled up flanked the photo. Stacked beneath the windows were old copies of the Liemus Press, their front page a pale orange. That's another story Valley told Claudia.

Orange was Neil's favorite color. Orange and elephants... Neil swore by them. They brought him good luck, he said.

An automatic coffee pot spewed steam. The aroma of coffee masked the stench of old wood and mildew newspapers. On the table were envelopes, engravings, page proofs and galley proofs.

"People, let's see. Are we all here?" Richard asked.

"Tessie is on assignment, and Clyde is taking pictures of the new Christmas fantasy display at the arena," Urho said.

"Right," Richard said. The photos were the first thing he took out of the envelopes. They were clean, black and white shots. "For starters, it's no longer necessary to have our negatives double burned. Just tell the engraver the exact size of the photo." He held a glossy in one hand and his pica ruler in the other. "And when you reduce the glossy, don't forget we're using 34 ems now for three columns. Also try to make headline fit. Count, count, damnit it! Also think dirty!

"What does that mean?" Claudia asked. Then she saw Bernie blush. "You're talking about my headline, right? The one that slipped by last week about 'MILL MAKES OFFER TO SCREW COMPANY' I know I goofed."

"Bingo! It slipped by everyone, even eagle-eyed Liemus."

"I'll never forget our classic," Bernie began. "Remember—'PRESIDENT'S BALLS SWING OUT'? Ouch! That sure made the society section a must read." He winked at Valley.

"Shut up,"

"That was a long time ago," Richard added. "But I repeat, every writer must think dirty when it comes to heads, suspect everything." Richard stroked his beard.

"An old copy editor in Grand Rapids told me and I'll never forget it—'Even if your mother tells you she loves you, check it out.'"

"My mother loves me, I checked," Bernie said.

"Bullshit Bernie. You don't have a mother. You were found under a rock."

Valley laughed. "It had to have been a giant rock."

"Don't let them get you down Bernie," Urho said.

Bernie gnawed on his lower lip. "It's a fact, I did have a mother. Even Himself knew her."

Everyone at the Press called Neil "Himself". Although when Bernie told her about it he didn't know the reason. But he suspected that Valley hung that moniker on him. Claudia knew she would never call Neil by that name; he would always be Mr. Liemus to her, the one who used a red pen to okay ads, and a purple pencil to edit.

During her first two weeks at the Liemus Press, Claudia's copy had been covered with purple marks. Richard had said the extensive editing was not unusual for a new reporter's copy. Some day, he added, Claudia's copy would be clean and perhaps Neil would be consulting her about in-depth front page articles.

Sure, that will be the day, Claudia thought as she pushed her chair away from the scarred, old table. She didn't want to get another pair of nylons snagged. She knew that Valley had complained to Neil about that and wanted the table sanded. He didn't think it was necessary.

Now Valley's hand trembled as she reached for some paper. She searched in her purse for a pencil.

Claudia offered her one.

"Thanks kid," she said and began to cough, the same hacking cough. Then she jumped as Richard rapped the table with his metal pica ruler. He paused, looked at Valley. "Better switch to another brand of cigarettes." Then turning to Urho, "How's the new boat schedule?" While Urho talked about the schedule, Claudia recalled what Valley had told her about the dispatch boats and how they made daily runs from Neil's printing plant in Detroit to Pierre Corners. When the Detroit River iced over in mid-January and the Press boats were in dry dock, trucks took over. When the Press wasn't

using the boats during season, Neil leased them. Always trying to make a buck, Valley had said.

Claudia knew the meeting was about to end when Bernie started cleaning his old pipe. He had changed his brand of tobacco, and the aroma of rum and honey was not unpleasant. Valley reached for another cigarette, stubbing out the butt in a bent metal ashtray. Richard tossed some papers on the table.

"Here are the assignments," he said reaching for his pica ruler.

Claudia held her breath, expecting the familiar sound of metal on the table. Instead he pointed the ruler at her, "Claudia, you're handling the school board meetings from now on."

She glanced at her assignment sheet, "Yes, I see, but isn't that Valley's beat?"

Valley looked at her, opened her mouth to speak, but said nothing. Bernie, still cleaning his pipe, turned and winked at Claudia. Urho stood and walked to the windows looking down on Main Street. Snow flakes stuck to the panes."Damn, it's my beat!" Valley finally said. "What are you going to stick me with, more stupid dog stories?"

"We've got a new format, Valley," Richard said, his finger forming a tent. "For the time being Claudia will cover all school board and city council meetings. We want to lighten your load, gal, understand?" He spoke as one would to a child. At the Press, Richard's job was to coordinate the news department and act as liaison between news and advertising. In practice, Richard was as solitary as a lone wolf in the forest. He reported to Neil, who cared only that the copy was accurate and grammatically correct, and that the paper was making a profit.

Valley's face flushed. She silently puffed on her cigarette.

Urho walked to Valley, put his hand on her shoulder. "Let's give the new kid on the block a chance at those boring meetings."

"Shit," Valley said.

"Now, none of that, this is an editorial meeting not a bar," Urho said. "Claudia needs the experience." His hazel eyes darted from Valley to Claudia. He was in Claudia's line of vision. There was something different in that look, Claudia thought. And then Urho smiled at her, when Claudia returned the smile, there was uneasiness inside her.

Valley had told her that many women found Urho attractive, just like his father. Although Urho was married to Dora, it was a non marriage. Urho had met Dora in California while he was in the Army hospital recuperating. She was a volunteer. It was a short courtship. Neil objected to the marriage. Urho had to recover from his wounds, not get married in such a rush, he had told his son. However, Urho married Dora and brought her back to Pierre Corners.

Now Urho glanced at Claudia. "You'll do a good job, I'm sure." Claudia was affected by his off-hand remark. This man, with his hazel eyes hooded with shadows, was always in control, seemed to have it all together. He was moving through life and knew what he wanted and how to get it. It was a contrast to Alex, who had none of that, who had only bottled-up anger and hate.

CHAPTER 4

Greta Liemus pushed aside the curtains, unlatched the doors leading to the balcony, and shoved them open. She could feel the night air on her hand and drew it in wet and cold. It's a black night, she thought. An hour before midnight and Greta knew she was going to spend another night alone in bed. She moved around the bedroom, sipping scotch and water from a large tumbler. She was tired of sleeping alone. And then she took a deep swallow of her drink.

Perhaps she was only admitting to her despair, or perhaps this was her way of getting even with Neil, her husband. The trouble may have been in part her doing. The trouble she had been having with her marriage. But the truth was that even in her first flush of their marriage, she suffered an inadequacy, as some people suffer who were near sighted or hard of hearing.

So she supposed that the answer to this regrettable situation lay not only with her, but with Neil. And she had to get some answers. She had to get them fast. She was a full partner, if not in the marriage, at least in the corporation. She could pull the levers when, and if she chose.

And in that instant she was in the hallway, walking rapidly to the tower room, past their newly-acquired Dali three-eyed woman. In spite of her height, Greta appeared fragile and small in her black silk robe. The white lace collar fell softly around her long neck. Tiny pearl buttons marched down the length of her robe, ending at the floor length hemline. She had a fine profile, with a well shaped nose, full lips, deep set eyes and a neck that curved like a swan's. Her blonde hair was piled loosely on her head and held back by two antique tortoise-shell combs.

He's in the tower room looking through that damn telescope, she thought. Maybe focusing on that riverfront cottage. Then the first searing memory of that cottage resurfaced. No, she mustn't think about that, no! She opened the tower door and walked up to Neil, saw his strong back. Her eyes were riveted on him, his small action of dropping his hand in his pocket, taking out the silver case that held his cigars, and extracting one. Then biting off the tip of his cigar and spitting it out in an ashtray. He reached for the elephant lighter on the marble table and ignited it with one press of his thumb. Then turning, he glanced at Greta, but didn't say a word.

Then he leaned forward, rotating the cigar to light it evenly, and over the sound of the wind hitting the tower windows, Greta heard the sip, sip of his pull on the cigar and watched the flame flare up. She shivered, involuntarily. "Neil, I have to say that –."

And then the red telephone rang. Must be an emergency, she thought. She looked out the wide expanse of windows, black, black, a black night.

"Yes, chief," Neil said into the mouthpiece, then covered it and turned to Greta. "It's the police chief. Something about a tunnel near the cottage."

Greta nodded. He didn't have to elaborate. She knew the cottage. There was no need for words on her part. So there was silence for some time, a solemn silence, the silence of someone listening to a concert. And now Neil became forceful. Greta received the merest glance of his dark eyes. "Yes, chief," he said into the receiver. "The tunnel must go back to those rum-running days in the 1930s. Can't see how everyone could have missed it. Oh, it was well hidden, eh? I want an exclusive on this. Understand? Don't call the News or Free Press. Okay? I owe you. I'm going to send someone down right away, within the hour. I know it's late, but a photographer and reporter will be there pronto. Thanks chief." In rapid succession he called Richard,

Bernie and Clyde, the staff photographer, and barked his orders to them. Only after his last call did he turn his attention to Greta, who was fixing herself another drink at the bar.

"They've found a tunnel near the cottage," Neil began.

"So what?"

"Don't be like that," Neil said in his dry voice. "I started out on the river. Don't forget we have this place on the Island. My castle! I had to kiss ass and eat shit to get here. And I have to keep ahead of those Detroit rags, get the news before them. Eat fucking shit!"

"Please, must you." She walked to the fireplace, looked at the flaming logs.

"Language too rough for your delicate ears? And what are you doing here? It isn't often I have the pleasure of your company."

She hesitated, but finally said. "It's about Urho and Dora. It's about—."

"Damn it woman, spit it out."

She took a deep swallow of her drink.

"And cut out the booze, you know you can't handle it. What's that your third, fourth drink?"

"Who's counting?" What's the use? She had learned a long time ago, Neil only listened when she talked about money, land developments, and making a profit on their stock holdings. So she drained the glass and began pouring herself another drink, double scotch, this time, and a bit of ice.

"I'm waiting," Neil said.

Greta took her time, sipped slowly from her fresh drink. Let him wait. Then she blurted it out. "I think Urho (stumbling over his name) and Dora are getting a divorce. That name Urho, so strange. I know it's for a Finnish hero. Well, anyway that dinner we planned for them—Urho called me and said to skip it. I don't know what to do."

"Divorce? Nonsense, you are just imagining things. As for the dinner, no we won't skip it. I'll talk to Urho tomorrow morning. Now about my son's name, yes, Urho is for a Finnish hero, and I expected my son to be a hero. But he has disappointed me. Well, maybe not always, he was a hero in the Korean War.

And besides we don't get to see Dora enough, even if they live a stone's throw away. That's it, end of discussion. I'm busy." He flicked the long ash of his cigar into a marble ashtray. A small elephant replica was poised on its rim.

"No, it's not the end of the discussion. I'm not a child."

"You're certainly are acting like one. You're stoned, besides. Do you want to become another Valley?"

"And why not?" she shot back. She thought dully that she was drunk already. Neil was right. But she wouldn't give him the satisfaction of knowing her condition. She was not conscious of the wind whistling through the trees or the crackle of the wood in the fireplace. It was a cold winter night but she didn't feel it, didn't sense it. She laughed. "Pretend I'm Valley." She poured herself another drink with the exaggerated care of one who feels her coordination slipping. Then she settled back in the soft leather chair. Valley, the bitch. She had fought her from the beginning. Even when Neil was working at the Times and they were planning their marriage, he'd slip away to see that bitch. But Neil had been so handsome. She had been so in love. They were married in the summer of 1929.

Neil had convinced her to withdraw all her savings so that he could buy a bankrupt newspaper in Pierre Corners. They moved into a three-room flat above the newspaper office. Neil started rebuilding, and named the newspaper, The Liemus Press.

She kept her job as classified ad supervisor at the Detroit Times. They needed the money to build the Liemus Press. And Neil also had a part-time job on the Detroit River; a job Greta was unaware of, a job that generated money for the Liemus Press. One day when Greta returned to their flat after working overtime, she found Neil and Valley in bed.

Now Greta's face flushed, she cried, "Valley, that bitch, that whore!"

"Watch your mouth."

"No!" And then she looked out the windows and it was snowing, the snow swirling, the sky revolving, all whirling, whirling, whirling. "Neil, I've had enough of your—."

Once again the shrill ringing of the phone, the blue one this time, interrupted her. Neil spat out, "Shut up, Greta." Then he reached for the phone. "Yes, Richard, what's up? ... I agree, we need full coverage on the tunnel story. Maybe a feature, a woman's angle."

Neil put his hand over the mouthpiece. "Greta, get the hell out of here. I'm busy. You've had enough, sleep it off."

Greta held her breath, and then with all the dignity she could muster, she eased herself out of the chair. Careful, she thought. She did not look at Neil, instead she looked out the window, the snow and the sky had stopped whirling. Greta raised her right hand, pointing a finger at him. "Go screw yourself!" Then she staggered out of the tower room.

CHAPTER 5

"No, Pa don't hit me. I didn't mean to kill—." Alex moaned in his sleep as he lay beside Claudia. She opened her eyes. At first she tried to ignore his nightmares, but she could not. She bit her lips and tried to reach out to him. But she couldn't touch, soothe him, wake him. She couldn't. She shivered. What's the use? She couldn't sleep. Finally she slipped out of bed and reached for her robe near the bedside rocking chair. She listened, Alex's breathing was normal. The nightmare had passed.

She walked to the window, hugging her robe to her, her eyes scanning the street.

Street lights cast a hazy glow as the snow flakes fell, Christmas wreaths gleamed in some doorways. The cloudless sky was black except for a sliver of a moon. She turned and sat in the rocking chair, studying the walnut dresser, the antique one they had bought at an estate sale years ago.

Now bits and pieces of memory came to surface. But coupled with the memory was a sense of loss. It had been the dresser that made things happen. Alex and Claudia had skipped afternoon classes to go to the old mansion. Once there they both fell in love with the old dresser, with its beveled mirror. They pooled their money and bought it. It was their first piece of furniture. They spent many hours stripping and sanding it until it glowed, a mellow golden brown.

She went to the dresser and touched the old wood, felt its warmth.

She hesitated at the dresser, tightened the cord on her robe and went to the window, opened it. The cold air seared her lungs as she gulped in short breaths. A violent shudder made her hug her arms around her body. Carefully she closed the window, hesitated and then deliberately walked to the rocking chair. She ran her hand down the soft lap blanket, and then glanced at Alex. His features, strong, handsome, his hair, thick, black. What was the matter with her? What was she doing? Now she could see that he was shuddering, sweating. Was he cold? Somehow Alex had changed since she had started working at the Press, changed for the better. Could this change last? It was almost like when they had first meet in college. Smiling at each other, secret lover smiles.

She remembered their first year of marriage.

Did she want that feeling again? Yes. His embraces, his love? Yes. She remembered the anticipation was exquisite. She had been giddy with his kisses. She had been excited with their lovemaking, his hands on her breast, her body. Now she lingered over those thoughts of their lost love, the touch of him. She now felt desperate and ashamed. And then the phone rang. The sound seemed to explode in the quiet of the bedroom. Claudia jumped. Quickly she reached for the phone.

"Don't answer it," Alex said. "Probably a crank call." He rubbed his eyes, stretched.

"I've go to, it might be an emergency. It might be my mother."

He glanced at the alarm clock on the night stand. "Hell, it's two in the morning!"

"I've got to answer it." She clutched the receiver, willing her voice to sound normal. "Hello."

"Claudia, I want you at the riverfront on Biddle Avenue in thirty minutes," the voice ordered.

"Who is this?" But Claudia knew it was Neil. She put her hand over the mouthpiece and said. "It's Mr. Liemus."

"Tell him to go to hell. Doesn't he know it's two in the morning?"

"Alex, please, he might hear you."

"I don't give a shit."

Then Neil barked into the phone. "Listen, Bernie will pick you up in half an hour. Be ready."

"It's two in the morning, Mr. Liemus." She could visualize the frown on his face.

"I don't care if it's four in the morning, or high noon. There is a story breaking and I want you to cover it. Understand?"

"Yes sir." When she hung up she was trembling. "Damn you, Mr. Liemus!"

"You're not going," Alex said. It wasn't a statement, it was an order. His green eyes held hers. He grabbed her arm.

"Alex, please you're hurting me."

"Too bad."

Suddenly Claudia was aware of this different Alex. Where was the other one? Had she been dreaming these past few weeks—where was the changed Alex, the easy going Alex, the nice Alex? She could still hear her mother saying when she brought him home "A Korean War veteran, too? He's a nice young man. He'll make a good husband."

Alex quickly released Claudia's arm. She hesitated a moment in the bedroom, then slowly walked to the bathroom, pausing a moment to look back at him. Alex stood beside the bed. He took a step toward her. She backed away into the bathroom and shut the door. Sooner or later, I'll be able to cope, she thought. It's only a matter of time. Do I really believe that? She wondered.

The light caught the premature silver strands in Alex's black hair. Under dark brows, his green eyes were fixed on her as she reentered the bedroom. As he tucked in his flannel shirt into his pants, his eyes never left her. "We'll settle this later.

Then she heard a car pull into their driveway.

A few minutes later while Claudia struggled into her red wool coat, the door bell rang announcing Bernie's arrival. It rang again. Grabbing her purse and her gloves, she hurried toward the door, forcing herself to be calm. She reminded herself that during her last few months at the Press, Neil had not called her once for an evening assignment.

So this is what it's going to be like, working at the Press, Claudia thought. Pierre Corners was Neil's town and Neil wanted his writers on call twenty-four hours, seven days a week. Well, he had established the rules and for now she'd had to play the game using his rules. For now.

She watched as Alex opened the door. Bernie came in, stomping his feet on the entrance mat, shaking his head, removing his cap, patting gently the strands of hair over his bald spot. "Brrrrrr. It must be zero out there." He removed his leather gloves. "But it sure makes a pretty picture, like a Christmas card. Better bundle up, Claudia. I don't think the heater works in Clyde's car." He looked at Alex. "How're you doing?"

Alex glared. "That old bastard cracks the whip and you all jump, right?"

Bernie Schmidt smiled; Claudia knew that Bernie was a decorated hero who had fought in Iwo Jima during the Second World War. Did he sense trouble in this house? she wondered. Then his smile became even broader and his eyes showed genuine amusement. "Yes, this is a hell of a way to spend a cold December night. I could think of a million better things to do. But when Himself calls, we obey. Or as you put it, we jump. What can I say?"

"You can tell him to go to hell."

"Nothing would please me more, but I need the job. And I like it, the job I mean."

Very smooth, Bernie, Claudia thought as she reached into the hall closet for her red stocking cap and pulled it down over her ears. "I'm getting dressed for the North Pole." She glanced over and studied Bernie's profile. His features, though a shade too large, too irregular, were immensely gentle.

"Don't forget your notebook," Bernie said.

"Got it right here," Claudia said patting her purse. Then she turned and kissed Alex, deliberately, in front of Bernie. See? This is a family, a loving family. That's what she wanted to convey to the world. "We won't be long," she said to Alex.

He didn't respond, just closed the door after them.

Bernie guided Claudia down the walk. He opened the back door of Clyde's old Chevy and she slipped in. Bernie was right, it was cold in the car, the heater was really broken. Clyde nodded as she got in. He was in a sullen mood. Claudia shivered in the back seat. The two men in front were silent. Clyde turned the car onto River Street and the crispness of the icy river assaulted them as it came into view, heaving in the stark, cold night.

CHAPTER 6

Ever since Neil's two-o'clock morning call, Alex and Claudia had not spoken. When she returned that night, she moved a cot into Jamie's room and slept there. The next day her story about the riverfront tunnel was ripped apart by Neil and an in-depth interview from an old "river rat" was cut out. This angered Claudia because she had spent an hour freezing in a riverfront shack interviewing that old man.

He had rambled on about the tunnel and the cottage. "Sure, I know about the tunnel," the old man had said. "Listen little lady did you know that in the 1930s bootleggers fixed up the tunnel to store booze that they had gotten from Canada? See, Prohibition was just in the United States. Way back before you were born little lady, he said.

He wiped his runny nose with a dirty rag and went on. "See, that rich fellow, David LaPorte, owned the cottage. Too bad he drowned. That Detroit River is deep." His old eyes scanned the dark water.

Now Claudia stood looking at the water in her bathtub circling down the drain. As she dried herself she turned and faced the full length mirror on the back of the bathroom door. Flush from the hot shower, her skin glowed. Steam clouded the mirror. Too thin, too tense, she thought looking at her body. Then she turned away from the mirror, opened the door to the bedroom and rummaged through her closet, selecting a green sweater and skirt. How quickly she had adapted to the Press dress code of sweater and skirt. The unwritten code didn't bother her—what did bother her was the purple pencil

Neil used to mark her stories. She grew angry even now thinking about what he had done to her tunnel story. Neil had slashed it. How could he? The only satisfaction she got was that it got second lead on the front page. But was it her story or Neil's?

At the dresser, she picked up her worry beads and stuffed them in her skirt pocket. Later as she left the house, with Jamie in tow, Claudia convinced herself that she must not let her guard down, that she must continue with her plans, and in the meantime deal with Alex and not make any "waves." How long could she live like this? He had crawled into her life, disguised as a lover, and smashed it. Now she looked down at her daughter, Jamie, her green eyes so much like her father's. Yes, she is going to take her and run away, far, far away and live a life without fear, without pain. Dreams come true, don't they?

Jamie interrupted her reverie. "Mama, are you coming home early? We have to put up the Christmas tree. And I want to put the angel on top. Daddy will lift me, right?"

"Yes honey. Now you listen to Mrs. Dixon." They were at their neighbor's door. She kissed her. Mrs. Dixon was waiting for them at the open door.

Claudia glanced at her watch. She had to get to work at hour earlier today for a Christmas breakfast. Neil, as always, was being different. Instead of a traditional Christmas party, he had mandated that the Press employees attend a breakfast at the corner diner. Was he going to take attendance? Claudia wondered.

Although Claudia was early, she wasn't the first one in the news room. The usual chaos prevailed. A sprig of mistletoe was clipped to Tessie Warden's long red hair. And instead of her favorite color pink, she wore a red sweater and skirt. She was draping orange paper chains on a small spruce tree that sat next to the coffee pot. When she spotted Claudia, she shouted, "Merry! Merry."

"Same to you," replied Claudia. It would take Tessie to come up with a strange holiday greeting, thought Claudia. Earlier Bernie had filled her in on Tessie, who was the youngest reporter at the Press. Nineteen, she was hired straight out of high school by Neil, personally. It must have been the red hair, thought Claudia, because she certainly could not put together a decent story. Then Claudia thought about the purple marks on her copy and smiled. Tessie's duties included writing obituaries, photo sizing, and counting story inches. Her desk was the neatest in the news room. A ceramic Santa Claus was on it now Bernie had stuck one of his old cigars in Santa's mouth.

In a wire basket to the left of Santa was a neat pile of sized photos. After putting the last orange paper chain on the tree, Tessie relaxed at her desk, filing her long red nails. Valley who sat opposite Tessie, finished typing a news story and pulled it out of her typewriter with a flourish. "30! The end! Claudia are you ready for the famous Press Christmas breakfast?"

"I'm ready and hungry."

"Let's go kid."

Minutes later the two women were pushing through a crowd at the corner diner.

Inching their way to the back, where a banquet table had been set up. The jukebox played Bing Crosby's rendition of "Silver Bells." A banner strung across the ceiling read—LIEMUS PRESS CHRISTMAS BREAKFAST. A smiling Santa face was on each paper napkin and tiny silver bells were at each place setting.

"See?" said Valley pointing to the bells and Santa faces, "No expense spared. Himself goes all out!"

Richard and Urho were seated at the head of the table. Most of the staff was already there when Claudia and Valley squeezed between the tables and found places at the far end of the long table. That's when Richard stood up and removed his watch from his vest pocket.

Waving her hand to get his attention, Valley said, "Come on Richard, give us a break. Put that damn watch back in your pocket."

Holding fast to his timepiece, Richard said, "You're late, Valley."

"So, sue me. But I've got a good excuse. Just finished a hot story about Santa making out with one of his elves—female I think, but you never know." She winked at Clyde, the photographer who sat across from her. He frowned.

Valley made a face and lighted a cigarette. She leaned over to Bernie, who sat next to her, and whispered, "Just trying to shock the boss."

Bernie snorted. "That'll be the day."

"Where's the food?" Claudia asked. "I'm hungry."

"Patience, my child," Bernie said. While they waited, Bernie filled her in about the Christmas breakfast tradition. It had been Greta's idea. She decided that a breakfast was better than an office party where people got drunk. Both Neil and Richard agreed, and a tradition began. Richard was especially in favor of the breakfast since he didn't drink anything stronger than coffee—diner coffee at that.

"Sounds like a good idea," Claudia said, when Bernie had finished. "But where is Mr. Liemus or Mrs. Liemus since it was her idea?" The jukebox was playing Gene Autry's version of "Rudolph the Red Nosed Reindeer."

"Mrs. Liemus just came to the first one," Bernie said. "Himself has never been to one, not even the first one."

Valley added, "But number one son is always here. Did I ever tell you about the time Urho did a sketch of me? Still have the sketch, not bad."

Bernie said, "I remember that, it was about six years ago and he did it on one of these." He picked up a paper napkin. "Can't believe you kept it."

"Ah, at last, here comes the food," Claudia said, as a waitress placed a plate of bacon and eggs in front of her. "I didn't know he was an artist. That's what my Jamie wants to be"

"Really? Well, Urho was serious about his painting at one time. But he threw out his paint brushes and easel a long time ago. His life is all advertising, these days," Valley said. "Too bad."

Bernie said, "Here we are, good food, great company. Want me to get Clyde over here to take our picture?" He poured himself another cup of coffee.

"No, Tessie seems to have him wrapped up. But from what I've heard, she's not his type," Valley said.

"My, My," began Bernie. "Valley, you're really gunning for him, aren't you?"

"Shut up!"

Claudia glanced over and saw Clyde in an animated conversation with Tessie. He certainly was young and handsome, but a bundle of contradictions. He was tall, with a sharp wit, but always a mystery to Claudia. He had moved to Michigan from West Virginia, held down several jobs before the Press. Her was an artist with the camera, and had won a few awards with his photos.

"What?" Bernie eyed Valley.

"You heard me, Baldy, shut up!"

"Valley!" Bernie said. The jukebox volume was up and Crosby's "White Christmas" was on. When a waitress placed eggs, bacon and biscuits in front of Bernie, he dived into it. Valley squashed her cigarette in the middle of her eggs. "Take this crap away," she ordered.

"What are you doing? I could have eaten that," Bernie said. "Think of the starving Armenians. Besides, it's Christmas. All is right with the world."

"Bullshit!" Valley said.

Claudia could feel her face getting hot. What's happening? she thought. She knew Valley was sober, so what was her problem? She remained silent, ate her breakfast and waited. Then she heard metal hitting a water glass and looked up to seek Urho standing, a knife and glass in his hand. "Welcome to the Liemus Press Christmas breakfast," he began. "Neil sends his greetings, but he couldn't be here. I'll have to do." He smiled.

"Hell, he never makes it," Valley said. Bernie hushed her, while Urho outlined the plans for the new year—1961. A waitress slipped a check at each plate.

"What's this?" asked Claudia.

"That's a surprise, kid. You didn't think Himself was going to pay for your breakfast? Did you? Everyone pays," Valley said.

"This is the first time I've been to a pay-your way party. Dutch treat, right?" Claudia said as she dug into her purse for money to pay her bill.

* * *

Late that afternoon, Claudia sat alone in the news room except for the cleaning lady, who managed not to disturb the clutter on the various desks. She worked around them. Only Tessie's desk was neat.

Claudia couldn't imagine how she kept such an immaculate desk, considering she had to size and crop photos and clip news articles.

Claudia was waiting for the bus. The old Ford finally gave out and was in the car dealer's repair shop. She had decided to wait in the office instead of shivering on a street corner. She gazed at the cleaning lady dusting round the Christmas tree and thought about the Christmas breakfast. No one had a good word to say about it, yet everyone was there. Although he wasn't there, Claudia had the strange feeling that he presided over everything, including handing out the bills for the breakfast. She smiled.

An hour after the breakfast, Neil had come down to the news room to wish everyone a happy holiday. He deposited an orange envelope at each desk, sealed with an elephant crest. Tessie followed him carrying a large box filled with small containers of Sanders' chocolates. She gave one to each staff member.

"Last of the big spenders," Valley said after Neil left. She opened her box of chocolates and left it under the Christmas tree. Now Claudia looked at the empty box and the small Christmas tree strung with orange paper chains and suddenly was transported to another Christmas, another time. She closed her eyes and saw her father, his strong arms lifting her up, up to place the silver angel on the very top of the tree.

"Kukla, you are my angel!" he said, kissing her. And what had Claudia's mother said? "Don't spoil her with such foolishness. She is a child, not an angel."

Stop it, thought Claudia. It's almost 1961, stop dreaming, wake up.

"Happy New Year!" said a voice. Claudia turned and saw Urho, a coffee mug in his hand. But she suspected coffee was not what he was drinking. His face flushed, his hazel eyes bleary, he smiled. He took several sips from his cup and placed it on her desk with slow, exaggerated motions. Then he eased himself into the chair next to her. "Aren't you going to wish me a Happy New Year?"

Claudia smiled, feeling foolish. He was so tall, but not like Alex, leaner, more controlled muscles. Even in winter his hair looked sun bleached. "But it isn't New Year's yet. We still have Christmas to celebrate. New Year's is next week."

"Really? Guess, you're right. I don't recall seeing Guy Lombardo on the old tube. Never miss that giant silver ball crashing down into Times Square." He grinned. "So Happy Christmas then, or Merry, Merry as Tessie would say."

"Yes," Claudia said. Urho is drunk, she thought. But that was none of her business.

"What time is it?" he asked, confused.

"Almost time for my bus, Mr. Liemus."

"I'm Urho. Mr. Liemus is my father. I'm named after a great hero who lived in Finland." He looked at her. Now say it, Urho."

"Urho." Suddenly there was this insane thumping, deep down inside her.

"That's better. Didn't hurt, did it?" He drained his mug and lurched awkwardly to his feet. He walked to the bank of windows overlooking the alley. An alley in every sense of the word, but Pierre Corners' road commission called it a public access road.

Beyond the narrow road, lined with garbage cans, there were parking spaces, created when the road commission had torn down several old houses. Although the alley was paved, the parking lot was not. Now four teen-agers huddled in a car drinking beer. Beer cans flew from their open car windows at regular intervals. They sang Christmas carols in loud, off key voices.

"Shut up!" shouted an angry voice from a nearby house. "If you don't, I'll call the police."

"Call them!" one of the teens shouted back.

"Those kids know how to enjoy themselves and irritate the neighbors," Urho said.

"But they can't carry a tune," Claudia added.

Urho whirled around to face her, almost losing his balance then steadied himself, leaning against a file cabinet. "What did you think of the secret note?" he asked.

"Secret note? Oh, you mean the check for the breakfast?"

"No, not that cheap shot. Too cheap to buy his staff breakfast. But enough said. I'm talking about the note in the orange envelope, the one with the elephant seal on it. Remember?"

"Oh, I forgot about it."

"You are something else," he said. "Too dedicated for words."

What was she doing? Claudia thought. If the note was secret, should she be discussing it with Urho? "Okay, hang on. I think it's here somewhere. She rummaged through her desk drawer. "Ah, here it is. Shall I open it?"

Urho nodded.

Breaking the seal, Claudia found a note and a $20 bill. The note read:

> *"Please place this envelope and letter in your pocket or purse and take it home. DO NOT discard the note anywhere in the Press building. Also the amount of your bonus is confidential, between you and me. This information is definitely NOT a matter of discussion with anyone. It was signed,*
> *Happy Holidays, Neil Liemus"*

"I don't get it," Claudia said. "What if I do tell someone I got $20?"

"Off with your head,"

"Really?" she asked, going along with Urho's game.

Getting serious, almost sober, Urho said. "Another cheap shot from Himself. If you compare bonuses, off with your head!" He leaned over, so close to Claudia that she could smell his liquor breath, smell his spicy after shave. Then he paced, hands shoved into his pants' pockets, his face red with anger. "Some day I'm going to tell him—" Then one of the telephones in the news room rang. Claudia reached over and answered it.

"Yes, he's here." She handed the phone to Urho. "It's for you." Claudia knew it was Dora, Urho's wife. Her voice sounded strained. Claudia walked to the other side of the room, gazed out the windows. She didn't want to appear to be listening. She looked at her watch—5:15 p.m.

Urho picked up the receiver. "Yes, it's me, Dora. I'm busy. Don't have time to talk." He almost hung up on her, but thought better of it and listened. "Home? Where the hell is that? Yes, I agree, we can't go on like this much longer."

Claudia turned and saw that his eyes were on her. She walked over to the Christmas tree.

"No, Dora, we have nothing else to say to each other. What? No, I said!" He hung up and put the telephone back on the desk.

"Is everything all right?" Claudia asked and immediately hated herself for prying. It was none of her business.

"God no! Everything is all wrong." His face became a carefully arranged pale mask. Claudia could hear the strains of "Silent Night" from the parking lot.

"Where were we?" he asked. "That is when we were interrupted by that stupid call. Oh yes, the secret note." He brushed back his hair from his forehead.

"Is this an annual note?" she asked.

"Yes."

"I guess I'll have to find a safe place for them. Maybe in a bank vault." She laughed, trying to make a joke of it.

"Better still—cut the note up into little pieces and eat it. Maybe with catsup. What the hell are we talking about?" Urho asked. "We're getting as crazy as Himself. I've often been tempted to publish this insane note in the classified section in a bold box, in red ink."

"Orange ink," she suggested.

"Of course, what was I thinking."

Then they heard the roar of the bus as it turned the corner.

"Gotta run," she said.

"Happy New Year," he said.

CHAPTER 7

The Christmas breakfast was long forgotten at the Press. It certainly wasn't on Neil's mind as he paced the tower room in a fever of energy. It was April, a new month, a new year, 1961, and the beginning of a rush at the Press. No longer, as he had done earlier in his career, did he work at random, placing ads anywhere in the newspaper, placing articles and features that should have gone on front, buried inside.

Now he devoted himself to making sure the big paying ads were in prominent places and the important stories on front, with photos. In the past few months he had spent every day either in his penthouse office or in the tower room from dawn until dusk. His meals were brought to him, usually a roast beef sandwich, a salad, and a pot of coffee. He devoured everything standing up or at one of his phones barking orders. The Press was his life.

He had abdicated his interest in everything else to Greta, unfortunately that was the bargain they had struck long ago. The only satisfaction he had was that he knew she was a shrewd business woman. She handled all the land contract negotiations and carried on the correspondence with the land developers working on the first shopping center in Michigan, and it was going to be in Pierre Corners. Although the bank accounts were in Neil's name, the land was in Greta's. Long ago Greta had the leverage to demand more control— and she got it.

Now Neil was at the height of his power, and anything happening in

Washington touched him. His natural selfishness was only reinforced by the knowledge that he even pulled some strings in Lansing, in the Governor's mansion. He woke up each morning with an absolute need to rule his corner of the world.

As for the latest headlines in the New York Times proclaiming that the United States was in a new era of meteorology that was no concern to him. What was happening on Wall Street, was his major concern. And when he discovered that his printing plant in Detroit was down to one month's supply of newsprint, he was in a rage.

Greta, on the other hand, never lost touch with life and the Liemus investments. She understood everything that was going on and the Wall Street Journal was her bible.

Now Neil sipped on a cup of coffee in the tower room and thought about Greta. So what if she spent long weekends shopping in New York, or in the elite Birmingham, in Michigan? She still managed to work closely with the contractors building the shopping center in Pierre Corners—keeping track of its progress.

Now Greta walked into the tower room shortly before seven in the evening. She closed the door behind her and waved a sheet of paper in front of him to get his attention.

"Neil, listen to this. That electrician on the shopping center just gave us the latest bids. I think he's shaving some off the top for himself."

"Well, look into it. Isn't that your job? See what Yiannis has to say. He knows all the tradesmen. And besides, I don't tell you my problems at the Press. Get it done."

She stared at him for a while then abruptly changed her subject. "How does this sound for dinner? The cook and I decided on Entrecote of beef with natural sauce for the main course. Before that, of course, we'll have chilled vichyssoise, Urho's favorite. Then a salad of crisp romaine lettuce, endives, cucumbers and tomatoes. Cherry Pie, with cherries from our own trees, for dessert. The wine, California red, of course. How's that?"

"Why bother me with a stupid menu you've already decided on? What if I wanted steak? Get out woman can't you see I'm busy?"

"Neil, don't be like that—if you wanted steak—we'd have steak, simple as that. I want to make it special for Urho. They're coming for dinner, Urho and Dora."

"What about making it special for Dora?"

Greta ignored that remark. "I'm having yellow and white roses, from our garden, as a centerpiece. Then as an afterthought she said, "Besides, Dora doesn't care for food. She is as thin as a rail. I saw her earlier today biking, wearing thigh high white shorts and a skimpy halter. Can you imagine, and in April?"

"Bet she looked damn good." He looked at Greta and saw a tall woman in a flowing pale orange chiffon gown. Her tortoise combs held back her white blonde hair.

Without another word, head held high, Greta swept past him and to the bar and mixed herself a drink. "A little one before they come," she said. She glanced at her watch, "You'd better get dressed."

He sat behind his marble top desk, near the telescope. Page proofs, rough copy and galleys were scattered on the desk.

"Can't you see I'm busy? We've got a special edition and I've got to finish these proofs. I'll be ready soon enough. If I'm not, YOU entertain them. They backed out on enough of our dinner invitations. What makes you think they'll show up this time?"

"I don't know."

Neil glanced up at the circle of windows. It was a dark, balmy night, a sliver of a moon, no stars. He could hear the faint whisper of the Detroit River almost smell its musty odor.

* * *

No more than a mile away, Urho looked at that same river through his library window, a drink in his hand, relaxed. Urho's house was neither as luxurious as his father's, nor as flamboyant, but was decorated in better taste, that's what Urho's thought as he surveyed the library. All the leather bound books, with titles in gold leaf, lined the huge oak book cases. Not one elephant statue or ash tray in sight. The two chairs by the window were covered in a soft tan leather. The remainder of the room's furnishings, a huge couch and two other arm chairs, were covered in the same leather. The drapes at the large window and French doors leading to a deck were sheer silk print, blush and yellow roses. Urho decorated this room. Standing facing the window, he did not see Dora enter the room. He stood staring into his glass of scotch.

Dora sank back into one of the chairs. "Getting an early start on the drinking, aren't you?"

"What's it to you?"

"You drink enough for both of us."

"Shut up!"

"What happened to the man I married, the soldier?"

Urho drained his glass. "Listen, I don't want to talk now. We're expected at my parents for dinner. So shut up, please."

"Certainly." She smiled.

He thought as he looked at her. That smile, the same smile she used when he had been a patient in the Army hospital in California. She had been a volunteer aide. What happened? Then they talked about so much, their future. He was going to marry her and take her home to Michigan, watch the Detroit Tigers baseball team, shop in Downtown Detroit, at Hudson's, go on the Bob-Lo Boat, visit Belle Isle and especially live on his island, yes, truly it was his father's island, but in his mind, it was all his.

Once out of the hospital, he spent more time in her apartment than at camp. Three months into their affair, she got pregnant. Then they were married. Two months later, before his discharge, she miscarried. They both were devastated. Their marriage began to crumble when Dora told him she didn't want to go through that again. She didn't want the pain, the sorrow. She didn't want children. They lived a non-marriage.

Now Urho looked at his wife as she walked past him and out of the room.

"Coming?" she asked.

Yes, he had to do something about this non-marriage.

* * *

Greta allowed one round of drinks for everyone in the library, and then, on a signal from the butler, she called them into the dining room,

62

telling them to bring their glasses with them.

An hour later, savoring his wine, Neil placed his napkin by his dinner plate. "Everything was delicious, a wonderful meal."

"Especially the cherry pie," Urho said.

Then Greta suggested they have their coffee on the patio. The night was dark, cloudless, and the stars had come out, like sequins scattered onto a midnight blue velvet blanket. They relaxed on white wicker chairs. A huge stone elephant, trunk up, stood guard at the far end of the slate patio. There was a faint breeze from the river.

"Now let's get down to some serious drinking," Neil said. He brought out a bottle of bourbon and a bucket of ice. Greta and Dora declined Neil's offer and settled for coffee.

Once Neil had assured himself that he had everyone's attention, he began. "I was searching through my grandmother's trunk the other day and I found a unique piece of jewelry. Ah, but I'm getting ahead of my story, I'd better start at the beginning. The trunk had been shipped to me from Finland. I sold the family home there. But you know that, and the new owner was thoughtful enough to send me my family's personal things, all in this trunk."

"What about the unique jewelry?" Dora asked, her curiosity aroused.

"You see, my dear, Finland is my homeland, well almost. I was born in Michigan, in the upper peninsula, but my parents were Finns. I can remember as a nine-year old going to Finland with my parents. He frowned. "We went to persuade Grandma to come back to the states with us. But no, she would have none of that. She wanted to die in the old country, as she put it."

"But the jewelry?" Dora asked.

"Ah, yes the jewelry. Well, it's a piece made of human hair, a delicate brooch, made of my grandmother's golden hair, when she was young of course. It is twisted and braided to form flowers and set on a 24 caret gold background. Priceless! Come with me Dora and I'll show it to you," Neil said. He stood up and offered his arm to her. "If you and Urho will excuse us," he said to Greta. Neil looked at Dora and his jaw tightened. Yes, he was drawn to her, so much like the young Valley. Was he being a silly old fool? Or did he catch that look in Dora's eye? He knew that look, had seen it on other women that were attracted to him. A surprising number were intrigued and even excited by him through the years, excited by the man, excited by his profession, publisher of a daily newspaper. Unconsciously, they thought they could live his life, vicariously. Their fantasy was similar to those young women who followed celebrities, because they were convinced that the celebrity's life would rub off on them. Foolish women. But Dora was different, her look was different.

At the foot of the wide circular staircase, carpeted in thick orange wool, Neil turned to Dora.

"Lead the way," she said.

"I intend to."

A few minutes later they were sitting side by side on a green velvet love seat in the Green Room, the old trunk open in front of them. For the first time that evening they were awkward with each other.

"Here's the brooch," he said, handing it to her. It was small and oval. The tiny roses were a golden hue.

"My, it's so—so beautiful!"

"Let me pin it on you."

"No, please don't. She stood up."

He stood beside her. He felt slightly light-headed, must be the wine, the bourbon. In just these few hours with her, he had felt something, something different. He had never been unsure of himself with any woman. How could this young thing, even with all her blonde loveliness, make him feel weak-kneed? He could easily imagine her in his arms. And then he looked at her and thought that she was probably thinking the same thing. He returned the brooch to the trunk and picked up a handmade knit shawl, of orange and brown wool.

"See all these beautiful things, old, precious."

"Yes," she said and hugged herself.

"Are you cold?" he asked. "That's a lovely dress." He wrapped the shawl around her shoulders, covering the thin satin shoulder straps of her white silk gown.

"Better?"

She nodded and held the shawl close to her.

"We'd better get back," he said.

"Thank you for showing me the brooch," she said as she removed the shawl and put it back in the trunk. "I'm not cold anymore."

At the door, he asked, "Doing anything tomorrow?"

"No."

"Good, what would you like to do? With me, of course."

"Whatever you say."

He thought for a minute, brushed his immaculate white hair with one hand. "Shall we make a day of it, start early?"

"Yes, why not?"

"We'll begin with brunch. I'll pick you up about ten. I know a cozy coffee shop on the Island, the Old Mariners. Heard of it?"

"Yes, but I've never been there."

He kissed her lightly on the lips. "Tomorrow, then."

Then speaking softly but with a more serious note in his voice. "You know I'm never going to let you go." And then he closed the door after them.

They kissed again in the hallway, viewed only by Dali's exotic woman. Dora traced the deep furrows on his forehead with her fingertips. "I'll erase those frown lines."

"Dora," he whispered. Then he kissed her again, desperately. When he turned, he saw Greta watching them from the end of the great hall. "You bastard!" Greta cried and then turned and quickly descended the wide staircase. Neil caught up with her his words running together. "What the hell are you doing here? Spying on us? Dora is our daughter-in-law. It was just a friendly kiss."

"Was it?"

"Yes, damn, you don't understand."

"Oh, yes I do."

CHAPTER 8

"Claudia Kali, call the operator! Claudia Kali, call the operator!"

Claudia, checking the galley proofs in the advertising department, heard the page. She reached for a phone on the nearest drawing board and dialed the operator, "Freda, what's up? This is Claudia."

"Better get to the penthouse on the double. Himself wants you fast. That old Greek, Yiannis Mitias, is with him. Must be about that interview you're doing about him."

"Must be. I'm on my way." She turned and faced Bernie, who had bellied up to the drawing board, a pipe stuck in his mouth. "How do you like the new paint job in here? Himself got a painter who just finished doing a battle ship and had some paint left over. Battle ship grey!"

"Not bad," she joked. Sorry, haven't got time to chit chat, Himself just had me paged. And when he calls, you know what I do?"

"Jump?"

"Yep, I just ask how high? But as for the ad room, I love the posters of Hawaii, Alaska, Japan. Adds a neat touch."

"You know how he got them?"

"By twisting the travel agent's arm?"

"Bingo!"

"Gotta go," Claudia said glancing at her reflection in the glass door. Hair okay, make-up okay, everything's fine. Can't do anything about that tired feeling, though. Exhausted from yet another sleepless night, she raced to the elevator. Yes, last night was another one of those nights with Alex. Now at the penthouse door, Claudia remembered what Richard had told her about Yiannis Mitias, a self made man, to use the time worn phrase—but he made it big! She blinked several times, adjusted her blue sweater, felt in her skirt pocket for her amber beads, took a deep breath and knocked softly.

"Come in," Neil said.

Claudia walked in and stood before his desk. Neil sat behind it with a mug of coffee in his hand. The desk was stacked with galley proofs, page proofs, photos and letters. Across form Neil, Richard slouched in a chair, fingering his watch. He looked up when she walked to Neil's desk and Claudia felt each hair bristle on the nape of her neck. She knew this was a big assignment, and she knew Richard wanted her to do it, although at first Neil objected.

"Ah, here she is. Sit down, Claudia," Neil said.

Unconsciously she reached in her pocket and pulled out her amber beads. "Thank you."

Before Neil could say anything, Yiannis got up. He had been sitting next to Richard. "Are those worry beads?" he asked.

His abruptness startled Claudia. "Yes, they were my father's. They are like my security blanket. I hold them for luck or when I panic." Why did she say that? she thought.

"Which is it now?" Yiannis asked.

"Both."

Yiannis laughed. Richard grinned. Only Neil frowned, sitting at his desk. Claudia knew she shouldn't have said that last remark. What was the matter with her?

Neil got up. "Yiannis, didn't you tell me that the Greeks use those beads instead of head shrinkers?"

"Cheaper, too," Yiannis added.

"You would say that, enough of this nonsense. Yiannis I want you to meet the newest member of our staff, Claudia Kali. Her father was Mike Belos. Remember?"

"Ah, yes, I knew Mike, a tragedy, his death. I'm sorry Claudia."

Claudia was silent, she just nodded.

To make her feel at ease, Yiannis said, "Claudia? A strange name for a Greek woman, most of them are called Helen, Mary, Anna, Sophie. Right?"

Now Claudia was relaxed. She ran the tip of her forefinger over the worry beads, slowly, back and forth, back and forth.

"Tell me Claudia how you got your name. Let's hear your story," Yiannis said.

"I'll make it brief," she began. My name comes from Greek mythology. Have you heard of the daughters of Themis?"

"Of course—the three fates, Klotho, Laachesis and Atropos. And you, yes, you were named for Klotho, and your parents used Claudia as your American name, so the other children would not make fun of you. Right? But they should have spelled Claudia with a K, there is no C in the Greek alphabet."

"Well, they thought about it, but went with a C, instead," she said. "You're right about the kids. When I used to tell them my real name is Klotho, yes they laughed."

"Children are cruel, sometimes." Yiannis said. "Of course, you know that the three fates determine our destiny. They use their sharp shears to cut the thread of human destiny, whenever they please. Your name, how clever, going back to Greek mythology."

Richard, stroking his beard, said, "Too bad I don't have more time to read Greek mythology. That story is fascinating."

"Your job is editing the Press, and don't you forget it," Neil said. He lighted a cigar with the elephant shaped gold lighter on his desk. Then blew a smoke cloud toward the bank of windows. "By the way, my son's Urho's name is from Finnish mythology. But enough! Let's get down to business.

"Yes, business," Yiannis agreed. He paused to brush some invisible lint from the lapel of his black wool suit, and straightened his vibrant purple and yellow tie. "Enough about your name, young lady. I understand you are going to do a news story about me, for the Liemus Press. Yes?" His dark brown eyes, almost black, gazed at her. Do you have lots of paper to write on? It's going to be a long story."

"We're on deadline," Neil reminded Claudia.

The slight smile on the old Greek's face vanished, and his deep brown eyes darkened. "I understand. Can you write fast, Claudia?"

This time Richard laughed out loud. "Neil, don't try to pressure Yiannis. It won't work."

Neil ignored his remark. "You two can work in the board room." And with this comment he ushered them into the room. "Don't forget, write fast, Claudia," he said in parting.

Settled in the board room, Yiannis began his story. As a young man, just off the boat from the Greek island of Ikaria, he had decided what kind of person he was going to become. He was going to be rich! He paused and smiled at Claudia. Yes, strong, tough and rich. His mind returned to the present, he fingered his tie.

"Claudia, I had a humble beginning, poor, ignorant of the English language, alone. But I had plans, big plans. Started shinning shoes in Detroit's Greektown. Then by luck was hired onto a construction crew. I managed to save my money and eventually had my own crew, young Greeks right off the boat from my island. And that's how it began. I helped those Greeks and they helped me. We were like a family, still are, to this very day."

Claudia took notes while Yiannis talked. She was fascinated with his story, although she had heard it from her father many times. Yiannis was one of the few Greeks that did not go into the food business— that is restaurants or markets.

Finally Yiannis pushed back his chair. "I think you have enough information. I have a business to run. And I too have deadlines, that is if I want to stay in business." He laughed. Then he took her hand in his. "My dear Claudia, hang on to those worry beads your father left you. At times you will need them. And young lady, also believe in your dreams. Ah, but you know that already, don't you?'

She nodded

"Well then, Adio, as the Greeks say." He left the room.

"Good bye," Claudia said, gathering up her notes.

* * *

An hour later with a first draft of Yiannis' story in her hand, she walked into Richard's office.

"That was fast," Richard said, taking her copy.

"It's only a rough copy. It still needs some work. I just want to make sure I'm going in the right direction."

"Okay, I'll look it over. By the way, I wouldn't have thought to ask you about your name, your Greek name I mean. From mythology, right?"

"Yes."

"Someday ask Urho to tell you about his name. You have something in common."

Claudia merely nodded.

Richard added, "Yiannis is something else, isn't he? An all-around guy, rich, but concerned about people. He has half of his Greek village working for him. And he paid their passage to get them here, a good man."

"I agree," Claudia said.

"While I was growing up in Grand Rapids, we had to worry about survival. There was the great depression. Then in the 1940s, the great war, and another kind of survival, life and death. And in the 1950s what was it? Yes, the great recession." Richard checked his timepiece against the old clock on the wall in his office. "That clock is a minute fast. But where was I?"

"The great recession," Claudia said.

"Yes, mmm, I don't have a crystal ball but let's see we are in the 1960s what great will that bring? I know the young are itching to start life—and they will call themselves—?"

"Does it have to start with great?" Claudia asked.

"Don't want to spoil the series I started, eh?"

"The great generation, no that doesn't sound right." Claudia said. "How about the Now Generation?"

"Not bad. God what will those kids do with all that power? Blow it up in smoke?"

"I'm glad my daughter is too young for the Now Generation. What will the 1970s bring? I can't imagine the 1970s—too far into the future," Claudia said.

"Is it? It's tomorrow," Richard said.

"You sound like you can see in the future."

Richard looked at her, slowly stroking his beard. "Of course I can. Didn't you know?"

"Now I do."

"And speaking of tomorrow, I've got work to do. So have you."

Back in the newsroom, Claudia saw Valley, eyes blood shot, head bent over her typewriter, her nose almost touching the carriage bar. Her expensive but out-dated wrinkled green jacked was open to reveal a white silk blouse. Claudia knew she had spent her lunch hour drinking. Now she was babbling to the typewriter. She lifted her head from the keyboard, saw Claudia, and made a face. "Hi kid, met the rich Greek?"

"Yes."

"Was Himself his usual gracious self? I bet he reminded you we were on deadline."

"Yes, again," Claudia said.

"Listen don't kid a kidder. I know him backwards and forwards. And because of him, I in this sorry state, and I'm not talking about Michigan."

"Valley, don't say that. What did he do?"

"Never mind. It's what I let him do to me."

"What do you mean?"

"I mean I can't hide from him. He's everywhere. Do you know how long I've known that bastard?"

"Don't, someone will hear you." Claudia imagined that the walls in the newsroom were wired. Maybe they weren't, but somehow, someone was getting information to Himself. Claudia knew that for a fact.

Valley didn't respond. She just stared at her typewriter. Claudia wanted to hear more about Neil. But this wasn't the place for a confidential conversation.

Valley turned to Claudia. "Kid, it bothers me. He thinks I'm a nothing. I'm a person too. I'm alive, right? I knew him when, even before that stupid wife of his, Greta. And I'm not about to let him forget it."

Claudia pulled up a chair and sat next to her. "Want some coffee or tea?" she suggested. She signaled Clyde, who was coming into the newsroom.

"Hell no," Valley said.

"Hi, what's up?" Clyde asked. His camera was slung over his shoulder. Claudia knew that the camera was Clyde's pride. There was something sensuous about the way he carried it. It showed in his freckled face.

"Nothing's up, dog face. Go away," Valley said.

"I was only asking, to be polite. My Mamma taught me manners," Clyde mumbled walking away, a frown on his face.

"What's gotten into you?" Claudia asked. "That was mean. I motioned him over to get us some coffee."

"Listen I don't want him around me. He can't even zip up his fly half the time. I can get my own coffee. I can take care of myself— ever since David died." Tears fell from her red-rimmed eyes. She rubbed them with closed fists. "God, why did he die?"

Then in a hoarse voice, "I'm ashamed of what I did to him. He was a sweet guy—messed up—but sweet. I was young, foolish, selfish. Name it, I did it. Now it makes me sick to think of the mess I made of my life."

"Valley, don't torture yourself. You can't go back. It's over," Claudia said.

Valley covered her face with her hands and sobbed.

Claudia put her hand on Valley's shoulder. "Please don't." She felt helpless. How could she comfort her friend?

Finally Valley lifted her head and said, "That Neil, that son of a bitch!"

CHAPTER 9

"You got four big ones! Damn, you fell in shit and came out smelling like a rose," Neil said. "And that's more than I can say about this dump. Smells like the Detroit Tigers' locker room after they've lost a game."

Bernie laughed. "What did I tell you? This is my night!"

Another Tuesday night and Neil, Bernie, Richard and anyone else they could persuade to join them converged at the Pierre Corners Press Club for some serious poker. The Press Club, despite its high sounding name, was the small gym of the Knights of Columbus Hall, a few blocks from the Press building.

Richard pushed back from the poker table, coffee mug in hand, and gazed at his poker cronies. Besides Neil and Bernie, there was Yiannis and Clyde. Smoke was thick. Bernie chewed on his pipe, while Neil smoked one of his Cuban cigars. Clyde nursed a Budweiser. "Small crowd tonight," he said.

"Couldn't round up anyone else with money," Bernie said.

"And you ain't taking mine," Clyde said.

Two ashtrays overflowed with butts. Poker chips were in piles in front of the men, the largest pile in front of Bernie. He fondled some of the chips and grinned. " It's my lucky night."

Neil ignored him and refilled his glass from a half-empty bottle of whiskey. Overhead a bulb, with a green shade, illuminated the poker table. "Shut up. Let's play cards," Neil barked.

Richard walked over to a perking coffee pot near a locker and refilled his mug. He looked at Neil. He had played poker with Neil for more years than he cared to remember. And those who played with Neil had to play by his rules. There was an urgency there, a drive, a dedication. Just like there was in Neil's life, in Neil's work. Now Richard looked at Neil as he sank deeper in his chair. Age had caught up with Neil, scratching deep lines from his nose to the corners of his mouth.

Poker is a just a game, thought Richard. And he played it like he wrote and edited, straight and down the middle. He knew every play, recording every move and every possibility or probability and analyzing his opponents' hands.

Glancing at Neil he said, "You know gambling is as inherent in man as his affinity with the opposite sex."

Clyde rolled his eyes, "Not that again."

Neil scolded, "We're playing poker, Richard, not offering rules to live by."

"Queens open," Yiannis said.

Clyde plunked down some chips. Neil matched the bet and raised it. Richard frowned, said nothing. Yiannis matched it. Reluctantly Bernie saw the raise.

"I'll sweeten that," Neil said, throwing in five chips.

Yiannis hesitated, finally matched it.

Neil turned up a pair of tens and three odd face cards. Yiannis had a flush, queen high. He scooped up his winnings and piled them in neat rows in front of him. "That's better," he said.

"Hey, what is this?" Neil asked. "If Bernie isn't raking it in, you are, Yiannis." His eyes met Yiannis, and his hand went up to smooth his perfectly groomed white hair.

Yiannis grinned. "All's fair in poker."

"Hold on," Neil said. "This isn't just poker, this is SERIOUS poker." He drained his glass and set it down with a thump. Then he refilled it, drinking slower this time. "Deal, deal!"

Richard dealt and talked. "If all the money that was won and lost in Press Clubs all over the country was pooled, it could pay off the national debt. They can have laws—but they can no more rid the world of games of chance than they can stop the sun from rising."

"Shut up, Richard, and play your hand," Neil said. Then he turned abruptly when he heard a knock at the door. "Doors open, come on in."

The men watched as a tall, thin, elderly man shook his wet umbrella. His entrance came with a crack of thunder—making it a grand entrance into the smoky, smelly gym. Matthew Dolson shut out the rain when he closed the door. Richard looked at him and winked. "Come on Matt, join the fun. We need some fresh money."

Matt grinned, exaggerating the deep creases in his face. A soft brown felt hat dripped with rain. His gray mustache was trimmed in an inverted V with the ends hanging over the corner of his mouth. He ducked to avoid a hanging exercise rope and worked his way to the table, removing his hat and shaking it. Finally he squinted through the smoke at the four men sitting around the table.

"Make yourself comfortable," Richard said, nodding to a chair in the corner. Matt scooped up the chair from against the wall and placed it beside Richard. "When you sit at this table, you've got to play poker," Richard said.

"I'll pass. You'll have to make an exception for an old friend," Matt said. "Can we talk?" he asked Neil.

"Yeah, let's talk maybe a break will change my luck." Neil pushed his chair away from the table. "What brings you here, Mr. Schoolteacher, especially in this downpour?"

"Don't tell us, let me guess," Richard said, sipping from his coffee mug. "It's about those gifted kids, right? Matt, won't you ever learn? People aren't interested in those egg heads—too smart for their own good. The public wants to hear about bad kids, kids who kill—kids who steal—kids who burn down houses."

"That's not true," Matt said, on the defensive.

"I'm sorry, but it is true."

"I have a new approach," Matt said.

"What's your new twist?" Neil asked.

"I know," Clyde began. "It's about a gifted kid who robs a bank, then burns it down." He grinned and ran his fingers through his cropped red hair.

"Stick to your picture taking, Clyde. That was way out of line," Bernie said. He grabbed Clyde's arm.

"Let go, man, like to break my arm?" Clyde cried.

"I'll break more than that. Let's hear Matt's idea."

Richard eyed Matt. He knew his struggle to raise funds for a gifted school. Richard had heard Matt's story often enough. As a child, Matt showed signs of being gifted, but his teachers were threatened by him. He was too smart. An orphan, Matt was raised by an aunt who also was a teacher. But she recognized his gift and convinced him that he could be anything he chose, and he chose teaching. Richard smiled at the old teacher. What was his idea? He knew Matt had nothing going for him but a brain that worked overtime. "Well, spill it Matt," Richard said.

Matt began slowly. "It's a dream, but one that can come true. You two can help me," He glanced at Neil and Richard.

"I'm flush out of money," Neil said, showing his empty pockets.

"I don't want your money. I want much more. I want space in your newspaper. My plan is to build a school for the gifted, right here in Pierre Corners. And we can get funding from Ford Foundation, Mott —name it, we can get it, with your help. I just need some publicity. Or should I go to the Detroit News or Free Press?"

Neil grunted. He filled his glass with whiskey and cursed when it brimmed over and slopped onto the table. "Don't threaten me with the competition. Take your damn story to the News or Free Press."

"Now, Neil," Richard began. "We'll see what we can do. I'll get Valley on it. She knows the education beat."

"Valley ain't about to give up her romance with the bottle to write about the gifted," Bernie said.

"She'll do it," Richard said.

"Wanna bet?" Clyde said.

"Damn right she'll do it," Neil said.

"I see we are in agreement, gentlemen. Thank you. I won't halt your poker game another minute. Is tomorrow all right? I can be in early to talk to Ms. LaPorte. How about nine?"

"Nine is fine," Richard said. "Thanks for stopping by. Sorry we can't talk you into going a hand with us."

"See you tomorrow." Matt walked toward the door, moving quickly. He opened his umbrella before stepping out into the rainy night.

"Bernie, who appointed you Pope?" Richard asked. "Why did you mention Valley's drinking? Matt has his own problems keeping those high school kids in line, now that he's principal." Richard scratched his beard.

"Sorry," Bernie said, sucking on his old pipe, which he hadn't bothered to fill with tobacco.

"What about the old gal? I never heard the whole story," Clyde said.

"It's a long story," Richard began, reaching for his timepiece. He spoke low, just giving the facts, like the good reporter he was. From time to time he refilled his coffee cup. "Valley met David La Porte in college. It was a high class Catholic college in northwest Detroit. He came from a wealthy French family. I don't know about Valley's family. But she wasn't hurting either, financially, that is. David's great-great grandfather owned most of the riverfront area. Pierre Corners is named after him—General Pierre LaPorte. But David died penniless. His body was found in the Detroit River, not too far from his boat.

All I know is that one day he went fishing, alone, and the next day he was dead. Funny, he was a strong swimmer. It was 1929—right after the stock market crash. He lost a fortune in that disaster. Bad investments, bad stocks, who knows?"

"Whee! So that's the old gal's story," said Clyde. He belched and a stench of liquor rolled up into Richard's face. Richard pushed his chair back, away from Clyde. He looked at the freckled face of the photographer. What did this half-drunk 24-year old know about fortunes, or lost fortunes for that matter?

Yiannis began, "This David, Valley's husband. I don't understand. He should have played his cards differently. At least he should have held onto his land, at all cost."

Neil glared at him, but remained silent. He held his cards close to his chest. His deep brown eyes did not move from the cards.

"She never remarried?" Yiannis asked.

"No," Richard began. "After she went through what little money was left, she started working at the Press. Right, Neil?"

Neil grunted and nodded. "Let's play cards, damnit!" His voice filled the musty room like an explosion. "I don't want to hear any more about that woman."

"I've got an idea," Bernie said. "Why not give the story to Tessie, instead of Valley? She could cover it. She doesn't seem to have anything else covered." Bernie grinned. He sucked on his pipe. He had put some tobacco in it and the aroma of rum and honey engulfed him.

"What the hell does that mean?" Neil asked.

"We all know she doesn't wear a bra. But that's no big deal, get my drift? But in the last week she's been coming to work pants less. Maybe she's going to moon somebody. Last week when she sat on my desk, I could see all the way to China."

"What? I'll get to the bottom of this," Richard said.

"And a nice round bottom it is," Bernie howled.

Clyde's face reddened.

Richard frowned, "People, are we going to finish this hand? Or are we going to talk about Tessie's ass?"

CHAPTER 10

Matt, carrying a large cardboard box, poked his head into Richard's office. Here I am—ready to go."

Richard, his horn-rimmed glasses on top of his head, sat at the roll top desk, sorting the day's mail. Automatically he discarded some press releases in a metal waste basket, as he paper clipped others to their envelopes and deposited them into a wire basket on his desk.

"Good morning, Matt. I'll be with you in a minute," Richard said. "Coffee?"

"Nope, had my caffeine at the diner, earlier."

Richard sat back in his chair, reached for his pocket watch and said, "You're three minutes late."

Matt grinned and shook his head. "You and that damn watch."

Richard ignored his remark. He put the watch up to his ear. "Works, fine," he said to himself. Then he glanced at the large box. "Plan to have us write a book on the gifted? Sit down, old friend. And I've got good news, Valley's been on the wagon for a week. Sober, she'll write a terrific story."

"That is good news," Matt said.

Richard smiled. He had known Matt a long time. In fact, Matt was the first person Richard met in Pierre Corners, other than the Press staff. A teacher then, he made it a point to come to the Press office and introduce himself to the new editor. Richard's friendship with Matt began that day.

Richard said, "Mind if I look into your box?"

"Help yourself."

Minutes later, Richard said, "Yes, you do have enough for a book, maybe two. Matt, we can't devote more than one feature article to the gifted. We don't have the space."

"I thought—I thought, maybe a series, perhaps a three-part series? There's plenty of information and I can supply Miss LaPorte with more—interviews, experiences, etc."

""Series?" Richard smiled. He leaned back and sipped from his mug. "We discussed one article—uno—one, understand?"

"Must have got by me last night," Matt said. He hunched forward in his chair, forearms resting on his knees. With his right hand he brushed his mustache. "It will make a great series, Richard."

Out of the corner of his eye Richard saw a brass paperweight fly through the air past his open door. "What the hell?" he said. Both men jumped to their feet. Richard's chair went over with a thump. He raced to the door to see that the paperweight had narrowly missed Clyde. "That ole lady is crazy," Clyde shouted, eyes bulging. "She almost killed me!" A metal pica ruler came flying by, grazing Clyde's shoulder. "She's nuts."

Richard picked up the ruler and ran to the newsroom. What's going on here?" He found Tessie and Valley shouting at each other. Valley a glue pot in one hand, and a long steel letter opener in the other, pushed toward Tessie. "You bitch," Valley cried. "I'll show you." She lunged toward Tessie.

"Damn," Richard cried, pushing through the crowd that had gathered in the newsroom. The typewriters were silent, the phones went unanswered. Matt, close behind Richard, said, "My word, what's going on?"

Clyde volunteered, "That crazy Valley started it. She threw the first punch."

In the meantime Valley screamed, "I'll leave my mark on you, you bitch." She brandished the pointed letter opener at Tessie.

"For God's sakes get that away from her," Richard said to Clyde who was near Valley.

"YOU get it away from her. I'm not ready to die," Clyde said.

Valley moved in closer. Tessie cried, "Get away from me, you drunk. You belong in a padded cell." She backed into her desk, knocking the neat pile of counted copy to the floor.

"Break it up ladies," Richard shouted. "Valley give me that damn letter opener before you hurt someone."

"Like hell I will!" Valley raced after Tessie, cornering her against the file cabinets. She lowered the letter opener until it was inches from Tessie's face. Tessie screamed and covered her face with her hands. Valley laughed. Tessie sank to the floor in a dead faint—the letter opener made its mark on the file cabinet—a gash in the metal.

"Got her!" Valley screamed hysterically.

"See if Tessie is all right, Clyde. Valley give me that letter opener." Richard twisted the letter opener from Valley's grasp. He quickly tucked it into his pocket. Then he grabbed Valley's arm. Finally he turned to the crowd that had gathered in the newsroom. "Show's over, get back to work people."

"You're hurting me," Valley cried, looking at his hand where it held fast to her arm.

"Too bad," Richard said. "That was way out of line Valley. What's got into you?"

Valley sullen, did not answer.

Spotting Bernie in the crowd, Richard said. "See if Tessie is all right. And get me a chair for Valley."

"Tessie is fine. She just fainted. Clyde got her some water and took her to the lounge."

Taking all this in was Matt, standing beside the file cabinets, a frown deepening the creases in his face.

Suddenly George Novak, the short, stocky ad man, burst into the newsroom through the back door, pushing through the crowd. "What's happening? Can I give anyone a hand?" he asked.

"Valley's flipped," Clyde said.

Seated in the chair with Richard and Bernie hovering over her, Valley covered her eyes with trembling hands. Sun poured through the bare windows. Cars jockeyed for positions in the parking lot, horns blared. Valley put her hands to her ears.

"Stop that damn noise, stop that damn sun. They're in the sun, coming after me. Those ugly bugs. Stop them!" She shielded her eyes. "Oh God! Stop those bugs from crawling on me!" Arms waving, she rose and the chair came crashing down. "Those fucking bugs!" She raced to a corner and hid near the filing cabinets, her face to the wall. "God, help me!"

"Maybe we'd better call the cops," George said.

"Naw, she's all right, just seeing things," Bernie said. He went to her put a comforting arm around her.

"Get your hands off me," she cried.

"Damn you, Valley. I'm trying to help you."

"Go to hell! Oh Jesus, they're back, on my arms, my neck." She scratched at her arms and neck. "The whole damn place is crawling with them."

Unobserved, Clyde recorded Valley's antics with his Cannon. His muscled arms moved frantically as he clicked, clicked the shutter.

"Enough of that, put the camera away," Richard said.

"No, no. Take my picture," Valley chanted, lifting her skirt, exposing her legs up to her thighs. "Maybe the bugs will go away if stupid takes my picture."

"Get out of here, Clyde," Richard ordered. Clyde sprinted down the hallway, pushing his way through the throng in the newsroom and raced out the back door into his car parked in the alley.

Bernie righted the chair. "Here, sit down Valley." She looked at him. "Bernie, I think you scared those damn bugs away." She laughed. The telephones never ceased ringing. The crowd had thinned out. Reporters started to pound their typewriters. Valley sat in the chair quietly observing. Then the back door opened and a police sergeant pushed his way through the thinning crowd. Finally he came face to face with Richard.

"What's the problem, Richard?"

"Valley's a little under the weather, if you know what I mean," Richard said leaning close to the officer, a hulking figure in a blue uniform.

"She just has to sleep it off," Bernie said, moving closer, standing toe to toe with the sergeant.

Valley stared at them. "Say fellows, is it party time?" With shaking hands she undid the first three buttons of her silk blouse. She crossed her legs, lifting her skirt. Her blonde hair fell down over her face, her blue eyes, red-rimmed. "Well?" Suddenly she lunged at the sergeant.

That's the way he described the incident to the police chief later. One minute Valley was sitting there, quiet like, head bowed, and then she pounced on him. Her long body fell upon him, knocking him down, driving out his breath and a frantic mouth sought his, a wet tongue forced his lips open.

"Hey!" He managed to gasp. And it took all of Bernie's and Richard's strength to free the sergeant from Valley's grasp.

Bernie and Richard held Valley and the officer managed to slip out from under her. Red-faced he rose, brushed off his uniform and looked at Valley, who was grinning. "You're quite a kisser," Valley said.

"Valley, behave!" Richard said.

Valley flopped in the chair, eyes closed against the bright glare of the sun coming in through the back windows. She breathed deeply. "Beautiful," she said. "Just what I needed. Now those damn bugs are all gone." Her blonde hair fell softly down her cheeks. Her face was a picture of bliss.

"Sorry," Richard said, nodding to the officer.

"No problem. She caught me off guard. If everything is under control, I'll move along. Oh, and I won't file a complaint—I mean about—."

"We know what you mean," Bernie said. "Not a peep from us."

"I think we can manage her now," Richard said. "Bernie will take her home."

"I will? I've got a deadline to meet, remember? And my stories are only in rough copy."

"I can drive her home," the sergeant said. "There's a wire mesh screen behind the driver. But someone will have to sit in the back with her, unless I cuff her."

"Good idea," Richard said. "And Bernie you go with her. As for your rough copy, it's cleaner than some reporter's final draft." Then turning to Valley, "Come on ole gal, you're going home."

With Bernie's help he eased Valley into the squad car. The sergeant raced around to the driver's side. Richard said to Bernie, "She'll be fine, once she sleeps. And she was doing so good. Not a drop for a week. What happened?"

"Richard, as a non-drinker you don't know the score. When boozers quit, that's when they start seeing things, bugs, purple elephants, you name it," Bernie said as he got into the back seat with Valley.

"So that's the story," Richard said when he closed the car door. "See you later, Bernie."

"Are we going to a party?" Valley asked as the squad car left the curb.

Back in the newsroom Richard searched for Matt and found his old friend in his office. "Sorry about this," Richard said. He sighed. "We have a problem with her. She's getting out of control. We'll have to do something, and soon. And I swear to you Matt, she's been sober for more than a week."

"I understand. We have almost the same problem in the high school—with some students. Although it's drinking and driving in this case—more deadly."

Richard sank into his chair. "I know." He stroked his beard. "Matt, we'll get Valley on the gifted story as soon as she's able." That was a lie on Richard's part. He had no intention of giving Valley the story. But he had to say something to his old friend.

Matt rose and both men shook hands. "I'll wait for your call," Matt said. Minutes later Richard walked to the elevator, his destination the Penthouse. He looked at his watch, it was 23 minutes after the hour. Did all this happen in twenty minutes? Nervously he pressed the up button. The elevator doors sprung open and Neil walked out, his teeth clenched on a cigar, a stack of galley proofs in his hand. Richard looked at him. Had he heard? Under his bushy eyebrows, Neil's dark eyes were alert, his white hair, as usual, immaculate.

"Richard, have you seen these galleys? Full of typos!"

"Yes," he said falling in step alongside Neil. "Getting a new proofreader tomorrow."

"We'd better," Neil said. "Can't stand these typos getting into the Press," he said glancing sideways at Richard. "You look like hell."

They walked side by side down the hall to Richard's office. Richard was always amazed at what a big man Neil was, yet he moved smoothly. Just like his son, Urho, Richard thought. But Urho had another quality, something else, maybe it was in his compassion. Yes, that was it. It certainly was not in Neil's face, not at all.

"Well, what's the matter?" Neil asked. "What's eating you?"

"Huh?"

"There is something, I can see by your face."

"Yes, something came up. We have to talk." Richard said.

"Sounds important."

The men walked into Richard's office. He immediately reached for the coffee pot and poured himself a cup. Then waving the cup in Neil's direction, he asked. "Coffee?"

"No, just had some."

The sound of the hall clock striking the half hour caused Richard to reach for his timepiece. He checked it. "That clock is two minutes slow."

"Damn it, Richard. The hell with the clock. What's going on?"

CHAPTER 11

George Novack sat at a battered desk at the end of the ad room. The desk was on a two-foot high platform that made it possible for him to see over the artists' drafting boards. He got up and walked to the edge of the platform when he saw Claudia coming. He stood with his hands on his hips, his normal stance. His gentle brown eyes were planted in a face with sharp, hard features.

"Claudia, what's happening with Valley?"

"I just got off the phone with her. What has it been three days? She's sick of staying home, but Richard doesn't want her back, not yet."

"The broad is clean. I saw her yesterday, sober as a judge," George said. "Those bugs she saw was part of the program, I mean to get sober."

"Oh?" Claudia smiled. Wish I could visit her. But with my tight schedule, work and getting home to pick up my daughter, Jamie, I can't do it."

"That's tough. You also missed the big show with Valley," George said.

"Yes, I was at city hall, on an early assignment. I got here just to see Valley in the squad car. It must have been something."

"We're calling it the letter opener caper," George said. Then he looked around the ad room. "These gray walls don't do much for my complexion. In fact, I feel like wearing stripes, prison stripes." Then he grinned. "I bet the Goddess of Night put Neil up to painting the walls gray."

"Nope, she's too busy looking for aliens from Mars. Bernie got a call from her yesterday."

"Really? What did she have to say?"

Claudia didn't have a chance to reply, Tessie burst in on their conversation. "Claudia, there you are. Richard wants us in his office, pronto."

"Okay, lead the way," Claudia said. Following the slim redhead, she couldn't help notice her golden tan. Yes, it was the middle of July and the temperature had been in the 90s most of the month. But when does she find time to sit in the sun? It must be those outdoor assignments Tessie wangled from Richard. But does she go out on assignments in a halter top? Claudia smiled at the thought. True the hot weather brought on some crazy stunts from the community, including the "sharing the shower" caper. But level-headed Richard did not assign such outrageous stories to the staff. Claudia knew that Tessie would covet that assignment. She also knew that this was Tessie's stepping stone job. She wanted to work in New York for a fashion magazine, like Vogue.

Now in Richard's office, Claudia watched as Tessie melted into a chair, adjusting her pose and Claudia wondered if she was trying to see what effect she had on Richard. Then Tessie wet her red lips, cocked her head and spoke in a throaty whisper, "Richard—you wanted to—." That was Tessie's style. She tended to leave sentences unfinished, as if she had absolutely no idea where her thoughts were taking her.

"Yes. Sit down, Claudia. I want to talk to both of you."

Claudia sat in a chair opposite Richard, glancing at the large box at his feet filled to overflowing with brochures and notes.

"See this pile of information, data, etc., whatever?" He pointed to the box. "Matt Dawson wants us to use it to do a feature about the gifted, and a proposed school for the gifted, to be built in Pierre Corners."

"Really? I mean—." Tessie began.

"You want both of us to work on the feature?" Claudia asked.

"Well, that's not what I had in mind." Richard stroked his beard with the stub of his thumb. "Claudia, I want you to write the story. And I want you (he pointed to Tessie) to go with Clyde. While he's snapping the pictures of the gifted studying, playing, whatever, you make sure you get their names and spelled correctly. You will also write the captions."

"Check names, write captions. That's Clyde's job, I won't do it!" She scowled at the orange rug at her feet, as if she were trying to wither it.

"Settle down, Tessie. This is important in the whole scheme of things," Richard said. "Besides you have your hands full now with counting copy, reading galleys, cropping art, writing obits—name it—you do it. And do it well. We can't afford to have you involved in a long investigative story—no sir! We need you with the photos, the windows of the Press. Without photographs, we have a nothing newspaper. We need you to make sure the captions are right, and that all those names are spelled right. You're good at that—."

"Really?" Richard's remarks brought a smile to Tessie's face.

"Yes, really." Then Richard pulled out his timepiece and said, "If my watch is right, and it hasn't failed me in many years, Matt should be here in about six minutes. Well, ladies, that's it. I told Matt where he can find you, Claudia. And after talking with him, set up some pictures assignments and give them to Clyde."

"What am I – to —" Tessie began.

"As of now, check with Claudia. She's heading this assignment, code name Gifted. And Claudia, I don't want to see you until you have something decent to show me. Clean rough copy. Does that make sense?"

"No." Claudia smiled.

Richard grinned. "It doesn't?"

Tessie frowned. "What? Take orders from Claudia? What the—." She stormed out of the office.

"Maybe I'd better talk to her," Claudia said.

"No. Leave her alone to sulk for a while. It will do her good. Besides

Matt should be here any minute." As Richard glanced at his watch, Matt poked his head in the door. "Someone mention my name?"

"Ah, there's my old friend." Richard introduces Matt to Claudia. They spent a few minutes going over the box of notes and brochures. Then Richard said, "Instead of chit-chatting in my office and taking up my valuable time, why don't you take the young lady to lunch?"

"My pleasure," Matt said.

"Thank you." Claudia turned and walked out of Richard's office. "We're going to the diner?"

"Fine with me," Matt said.

"Enjoy your lunch. And Matt, I think we have a winner in this gifted story."

"Story? I thought it was going to be a three-part series. Isn't that what you said?"

"Oh, did I?"

* * *

After a quick lunch where Claudia and the old educator got acquainted, Matt walked her back to the Press office. He sat in a chair beside her desk as Claudia began the task of sorting through the box of material—cataloging various pamphlets, memos and brochures, taking notes, making folders. A special folder contained photos and data about several local gifted children. One in particular caught Claudia's eye. A blond youngster about four years old. Matt had told her, the child had taught himself Latin and Spanish.

"That's Bradley. I mentioned him at lunch."

"Yes, from your notes, it seems he's also quite a science buff. Amazing." She returned Bradley's photo to the file. "He's one of our neglected valuable resources."

"Certainly he is, and it's a sorry state we're in where we can't enrich and encourage these little brains." Claudia met Matt's eyes and a spark of shared respect registered between them.

Matt said, "I'm an old man and an old fashioned school teacher. Before I die, I want to show the world the gifted and their great potential. Care to hear my story?"

"Yes!" Claudia was mesmerized by this old educator.

"Well, my maiden aunt, who also was my guardian, encouraged me to study. I was an orphan. Would you believe I was nineteen when I started to teach? In those days you didn't need a college degree. But I went to Michigan Normal College in Lansing and earned my teacher's certificate, later got a degree at the University of Michigan, in Ann Arbor. Along the way I married my Martha, a fine woman, gentle and kind. But she had one flaw."

"Oh?"

"Yes, she was a compulsive joiner. And when there wasn't a group to join, she organized one. Did you know she was the founder of the Pierre Corners Garden Club? And the Red Cross chapter here, the Literary Guild, the Presbyterian Church's women's society and during the depression she was a member of the WPA board. We didn't have any children, Martha's clubs were her children. God rest her soul." He was quiet for a while. Then he said, "This school for the gifted will be dedicated to her. I know I'm way ahead of myself. We haven't even told the public about my plans. We haven't even raised one dollar."

Claudia nodded. "It's your dream. We all have dreams." She glanced out the back window, into the alley-parking lot. The afternoon sun had slipped past the shadow of the maple tree where Matt had parked his old Chevy. Now the light streamed through the window, over Claudia's shoulder. As she looked out the window, she smiled. "Yes, we'll get that school built. And Jamie will be the first to enroll."

"Yes, she will." Matt gathered his notebooks, preparing to leave. "Just call me if you have any questions. Leave a message with my secretary if I'm out."

"I will. Thanks." Then the telephone on Bernie's desk rang and Claudia jumped. Bernie reached for the phone and said, "It's probably the Goddess of Night. There is always something sinister about her rings, right Claudia?"

"Right." But Claudia knew that her nervousness was a symptom of something else, a mental disorder that she called the "I don't deserve this job or this plum assignment." Subconsciously she was afraid that God would take this away from her if he noticed. Then the sledge hammer would fall. Everything would be smashed, everything. No! No! She had to stop feeling sorry for herself. It wasn't luck. Luck had nothing to do with it. It was because she was a good reporter. She must not let these doubts take over. She deserved this job, this plum assignment. She earned it with her hard work.

The next day was a cloudless one. The morning light had that particular quality found only in Michigan and only on certain days in the summer. It was hot, even for July, and it gave you the feeling that at any moment the sky would open up to reveal another world beyond.

Claudia spent the morning at her typewriter working on a rough copy of the gifted story. Most mornings Claudia researched her stories, but she had compiled a batch of notes from yesterday's interview with Matt that had to be put in logical order. And no matter how agitated she was when she came into the newsroom in the morning because of Alex, she was always completely relaxed when she sat at her typewriter.

It was a few minutes before Claudia noticed Richard standing beside her desk, sipping coffee from a mug. When she looked up, he grinned, his blue eyes bright behind his horn rimmed glasses. He set his mug on her desk. Claudia knew he had had a rough time during Valley's letter opener incident, but he always seemed to bounce back, ready for the good things in life. Now he said, "That's what I like about you. You get right into an assignment. By the way, Matt talked me into making it a three-part series. The first will go into this Sunday's magazine supplement."

"Really? That's great." Somehow Claudia's amber beads which had been on her desk, found their way into her hand.

"Worried about something?"

"No—it's just the beads have become a habit. And this story—I mean this series is important."

"Yes, and if I didn't think you could handle it, I wouldn't have given you the assignment. You did a fine job on the tunnel story— even if Neil did pencil out some of it. Got on the front page, didn't it?"

Claudia nodded. She hadn't questioned him then and she wasn't about to question him now. So she quickly changed the subject. "George tells me that Valley is fine. Plans to get back to work soon."

He nodded. He was silent and she could hear the clatter of the typewriters, the ringing of the phones, the hum of the ceiling fan, overhead. She glanced over at Bernie and saw him make a face as he talked with the Goddess of Night on the phone. George walked into the newsroom, followed by two other admen, all laughing at one of George's jokes.

Claudia sighed. "I've never really understood Valley. Although we're friends, she's never told me much about herself, only the bare bones. But I can understand that—I've never told her my deep dark secret." Then she laughed.

"You don't have a deep dark secret," Richard said. "I'll bet my life on that—but I've wasted enough of your time. Back to work. Or I'll crack the whip."

That's when Claudia dropped the amber beads. Richard picked them up and held them in his hands, as if weighing them. "Magic beads?" Then he put them in Claudia's palm and walked away.

Claudia tucked the beads into her skirt pocket and walked to the lounge. When she stepped into the hallway she saw a half-dozen admen and reporters, familiar faces, and nodded to them. Freda was at the switchboard, clipping ads from yesterday's Press and plugging in calls. In between, she munched on a jelly doughnut. She grinned at Claudia. "You're the center of attention because of the gifted series."

Claudia smiled. "Flattery will get you anywhere. Want another doughnut?"

"Sure, only kidding."

Finally Claudia was in the lounge. Good she needed a cup of coffee. She got her coffee, sank in a chair and sighed.

Suddenly Tessie burst into the room, removed her pumps and plopped herself onto the sofa, her long legs stretched out. Tessie looked at Claudia and shook her head.

"So, I'm to report to you? Do you want to be called Captain or Major?" She saluted .

"I'm sick of this class system—it stinks—it—."

"Listen Tessie, it's not my doing. Tell me why did you want this story?"

"Because I'm tired of clipping stories—cropping photos—doing nerd's work—it's boring—it-s—" She stared at her painted toenails.

"Boring? No, it's what cub reporters do—to make it. How old are you? Eighteen? Fresh out of high school? I paid my dues, went to college, worked on the college newspapers, did free lance for the News and Free Press."

"So what? I don't want to hear your sad story, Claudia. Just because you went the long way—doesn't mean I have to—." She smiled thinly. "Besides, what have you got on Richard? I see the way he happens to stroll by your desk and —."

In that instant Claudia wanted to lean over and slap her face, back and forth, back and forth until it took the color of her flaming hair. With an effort she pushed back that urge, forced it back where it belonged. Then she said, " I don't have anything on Richard. I just do my job and mind my own business."

"Really? And you think I don't mind my own business?"

"Yes, you're a busy body." Claudia picked up her coffee and walked to the window, her back to Tessie. She found her worry beads in her pocket and held them, fingered them. Outside the leaves on the maple were bright green. A few clouds tracked across the turquoise sky. The sunlight was the color of ripe corn. In the parking lot a couple laughed and chatted as they climbed out of a red Ford, and farther down, on the waterfront, the Press dispatch boat pulled into the dock and men started loading rolls of newsprint bound for the Detroit plant.

Then Claudia turned and looked at Tessie. The wall clock struck five. Tessie jumped from the couch. "Listen, don't count on Richard. Even king pins fall."

"What?"

"You heard me." Tessie rushed toward the door, red hair flying, gold bangle bracelets jangling. "Gotta run. Have a top assignments—writing cut lines—before I leave this dump for the day. But mark my words, Richard's days are numbered. I have it on good authority and I—." She giggled as she fled the room.

Claudia stood for a while staring out the window. The very thought of the Press without Richard stunned her. Then she focused on the parking lot filled with people getting into their cars. They were going places, doing things. She didn't want to start for home, not yet, but there was nowhere else to go. And then for the second time that day, she dropped her amber beads.

CHAPTER 12

Claudia let herself into the house, turned on the entranceway light, closed and locked the door. She switched on the living room lamps as well. She was alone. Alex said he would be late. Jamie was in Chicago for the summer visiting her grandmother. Claudia wasn't hungry so she made herself a pot of tea.

An hour later, in her long cotton robe, sipping tea, she stared out the living room windows. After such a bright sunny day, it had turned into a rainy night and it was good to be home. She became aware of how much harder the rain was coming down even in the hour since she'd been home. The first rain in months and it was a downpour.

Claudia shook her head. The newspaper business was a disaster. Was Tessie telling the truth about Richard? Did she know something? Richard wasn't aware of the power play behind his back—if what Tessie said proved to be true. A disaster! And what about Valley, who found answers at the bottom of a vodka bottle? And what about her, not only was her job at the Press in jeopardy but her whole life. Deep down she was thankful for one thing, her beautiful daughter. Oh, how she missed her. Two weeks ago Alex had driven Jamie to Chicago to spend the summer with grandma. From the phone calls Claudia and Alex received, Jamie was having a good time and the visit was doing wonders for Jamie and Claudia's mother.

Now Claudia glanced at an old copy of the Press and saw her tunnel story on the front page. That story was the start of another problem in her life. Alex is jealous, jealous of my success, Claudia thought. He can't endure even the small name she was making for herself in the newspaper world. Whenever he sees her byline on the front page, he belittles it. "Big deal! You're writing garbage." He'd become a master at debasing her work.

Claudia thought—My life is becoming a battleground and I don't know what the war is all about. Take Jamie and run, run far away from him.

Then the child in Claudia crouched down and rocked in the rocking chair. She imagined she was in her father's arms. She hugged herself. Yes, her father told her stories at night, he gave her small gifts, he embraced her, he called her Kukla. He disappeared from her life, forever.

No, he is still part of her life! But she didn't do that one thing for him. She hadn't saved him. She was too late. It had been raining—a bad thunderstorm—and she got there too late, too late. And what had her father said to her as a child about thunderstorms? "It's raining outside, Kukla. But the sun is shining in our hearts." She wanted to believe that, especially now.

She turned when she heard Alex coming into the room. She didn't speak. Instead she reached into the pocket of her robe and fingered the amber beads. Finally she got to her feet, reluctantly. Time to come back to the real world, she thought. Her face slipped back into worried lines as she walked to the back of the house, into the kitchen. Her father's words echoed in her mind, "Kukla, the sun is in our hearts."

When Alex saw her, he lashed out. "What kind of a wife are you? I come home from work, and no dinner?" He looked at her. "You're daydreaming. Wake up. I got a promotion. But you could care less. Who wants to know that I'm assistant manager of the dealership? Shit! I'm talking to the damn walls."

His eyes were hard and cold and seemed to be fastened to hers by an invisible wire, a strong wire that would not break. Neither of them could look away.

And then the ring of the telephone broke into the silence. By the time she got to the phone to answer it, she was in no condition to give a calm and cheerful response to Jamie, for it was Jamie calling. The events of the past few minutes had affected her far more profoundly than she had thought at first so she handed the phone to Alex.

Instantly Alex's mood changed, right before her eyes. He smiled into the receiver. "How are you honey? And how is Grandma? Good. So besides your drawings, Grandma is taking you to art galleries and the museums."

Then he turned the phone over to Claudia. "She wants to talk to you." He opened the refrigerator and took out a beer.

As Claudia took the phone she thought—Stay calm, just stay calm. She stood with her back to him. Struggling to maintain her composure, she turned and faced him. She said into the receiver, "I'm glad you're having a good time with Grandma. I miss you very much, darling." She closed her eyes, even managed a smile. "Jamie, I miss you more than you know. I wish I could take you in my arms right now, hug you, kiss you. I love you too much." They chatted for a while, about Jamie's adventures in Chicago. It felt good to hear her daughter giggle, laugh. Yes, she was having a good time with her grandmother. Claudia's mood changed became brighter, while talking to her daughter. Finally after a long, cheerful conversation, she said, "Good bye my darling. See you soon."

* * *

Later, while Claudia finished the dishes, Alex, sitting at the kitchen table, put down the sports' pages and drank his beer. In a sober voice, he said. "Can we talk?"

She sighed and sank into a chair. "Okay." She wondered what they would talk about. About his promotion? She knew that his dream was to own a dealership. Maybe, just maybe, then things would change.

"I heard the way you talked to Jamie, the way a parent should talk to a child. Not the way my bastard father talked to me. My old man whipped me with a leather strap if I so much as opened my mouth. He didn't talk to me, he beat me."

"Alex, I'm sorry. I didn't know. Try to forget him."

"Listen, that's why I never talked about him. I tried to forget him, but he keeps crawling back into my life. Forget him? He was in my mind when I fought in Korea. He's everywhere." Then there was a silence. Alex drank his beer.

Claudia waited for him to continue. She did not act surprised at this sudden opening up after all these years. Maybe, it will change now, for the better, she thought. Alex's green eyes gave nothing away. He shifted his body in the chair, tapped his fingers on the table, took another swallow of beer.

Claudia knew she should not probe. Just encourage him to talk, she thought. It was obvious that Alex needed someone to listen to him.

Finally she said, "Alex, if you want to talk about him and your mother—." Then she immediately knew that she had gone to the heart of the matter much too quickly. Alex was not ready to talk about that part of his life, and he pretended not to hear her question.

Alex said, "What bothers me is the way I'm screwing up my life. No! He's screwing up my life. When we met in college, I was happy, I thought things would change. I thought he'd leave me alone. But he didn't. He's dead, yes, but he hasn't left me."

Claudia nodded. She felt that Alex wanted to talk about his father, wanted to get rid of the poison that had been building up in his mind, tearing at his heart for all these years, but he was only able to let it out a little at a time. This was a start.

Slamming down his beer bottle on the table, jolted Claudia out of her reverie. He said, "Sometimes I wish I were dead!"

"Don't say that, don't. Maybe if we talked, really talked." She knew this was the time to encourage him.

"Talk? I wasn't brought up that way. When I was a kid, you were seen, not heard. And I expected the worst—not once in a while—but every day. Beatings, beatings. He left me to die in an alley. Can you believe that? It was because of what I did to —."

Claudia nodded. She knew she mustn't do anything to stop this conversation. Alex pushed his chair back, rose and walked to the refrigerator for another beer.

"He treated me worst than a dog—left me to die—and if someone hadn't found me. I would have died. I should have died—instead of—

her." Alex was angry now.

"Who?"

Alex's mood had changed. He was filled with icy rage that made his eyes look like two steel rods. When she looked into those eyes she could not suppress a shiver. Alex glowered at her. She felt like the accused at a murder trial. She would not have been terribly surprised if Alex had pounced on her, shook her, charged her with murder.

Instead he rose from his chair, stood over her, looked down at her with unconcealed rage. What had she said to make him change? Who was this 'her' he spoke of? Why was he so angry? She looked at him unwaveringly until he turned from her and began to pace.

Finally she said, "What are you talking about? Please tell me. Why do you do this to yourself, to us? What made you change—so suddenly? Please, Alex—."

"Shut up!"

"What?"

Alex stopped pacing, stood in front of her, glared down at her like an angry god on Mr. Olympus. "Shut up! She's dead, understand? Dead and I killed her." And in an instant he was out the back door, slamming it after him.

CHAPTER 13

COLD!

Claudia was wearing a green wool sweater and skirt, not a light wool, but not heavy enough to ward off a January chill. She hugged herself and shivered. The lobby was as cold as a morgue. And with the door opening and closing, bringing in more blasts of frigid air, she felt like a penguin at the South Pole. Bernie had told her it was a practice at the Press not to turn the thermostat above 60 during the winter months.. One of Neil's economy measures. She vowed that tomorrow she was going to bring in an electric heater. Her cold fingers searched through the main file cabinet behind the counter in the lobby. Then she saw Freda wink at her from across the lobby as she answered a call at the switchboard. "Another complaint—an ad was wrong," Freda said.

"What else is new?" Claudia made a face and hugged herself as the door opened bringing in another cold blast. From her vantage point at the file cabinet she could see the maples on Main Street. They too were bent over and shivering from the Michigan wind.

Since last month, when Neil had laid off three clerks, reporters not only worked in the newsroom, but also did a good share of the filing. Freda also had additional clipping and filing. Freda complained to Claudia. It's not that she minded the original plan to do a little clipping and filing when the clerks were behind, but now she did most of it. And Claudia knew that Freda was peeved because it cut down on her listening to other's conversation on the line. Before she was burdened with the extra file work, she spent her time listening. She knew more about what was happening at the Press than even Neil or Richard did.

Now Freda was caught up with her filing and clipping, and since there was a lull at the switchboard, she pulled out a well worn paperback romance novel and rapidly turned to a bookmark. Her eyes raced across the page and found where she had left off, and now she was oblivious to the customers leaning against the front counter waiting to place their want ads in tomorrow's paper.

With her free hand she searched under the switchboard for the bakery bag filled with jelly doughnuts. Still concentrating on the book, she bit into a doughnut.

"What are you reading?" Claudia asked. She leaned over Freda's switchboard oasis.

"Another romance, and I'm at the sexy part now. Listen to this—. Melinda is about to get screwed, pardon my French."

Claudia laughed.

Freda began to read—'When Melinda scraped her nails down the side of Sir Gregory's face, he threw back his head and howled with lust. At that instant, he was pure animal, without conscience, thinking only of his need, his pleasure. When the ache within him became so intense, he grabbed Melinda, ripped off her bodice, tore her long skirt and undergarments and mounted her, feeling the urgent release in her. Finally, as she lay limp in his arms, moaning, he kissed her lips gently, held her close to him. All the rage was gone, flushed from his body. Then Melinda fainted in his arms.'

"Hot stuff, eh?" Freda asked, dropping her jelly doughnut. It landed in her lap. She blushed. "That Melinda sure gets around. In the last chapter, she had a go around with Sir Anthony." Then Freda saw a light flashing on her switchboard. "Yes sir?"

It was Urho. "Yes, Claudia is here. Yes." She turned to Claudia. That was Urho. He wants to know how you're doing with the water plant research."

"Got everything. I think." She patted the folder in her arms. She hoped she had found all the records she needed. Urho was getting started early on his homework. The millage election isn't until April. Glancing at the folders Claudia could only conclude that Urho must be up to his armpits in water, land developments and out-county water supplies, getting ready for the election.

When Neil made up his mind to push something through, he pulled out all stops. This time he wanted the millage to pass and he wanted his land considered for the new water plant. And what Neil wants, Neil gets, thought Claudia. If it wasn't one thing, it was another. First all that fuss about the gifted series. Then the hundreds of letters that had poured in lauding the series and supporting the proposed gifted school. Who knows, maybe there will be a school someday? Who knows, maybe someday I'll get a raise? Dream on Claudia.

Now Claudia was in the ad room. With the files in one hand, she searched with the other in her skirt pocket for her amber beads. Yes, they were there. Then she managed to squeeze between the drafting boards and nodded to a graphic artist working on a full-page ad. A small radio on the counter was on and strains of Judy Garland singing "Over the Rainbow" filled the room. Claudia hummed along. She always made a point to look at the posters in the ad room, instead of the walls, because the gray walls depressed her. Three ad men had gathered around a huge drawing of a thermometer posted on the wall, marking the ad men's progress in another promotion. Claudia looked at the names and numbers. As usual, George Novack was at the top. She wondered how he did it. Must be all those jokes he tells.

Now she was outside Urho's office. It was a corner of the ad room that had been enclosed by glass. A screen of heavy green silk draperies blocked her view. She tapped lightly on the glass door. Ordinarily the drapes would be open. Something must be up, Claudia thought.

"Come in." Claudia stepped into a well-appointed office, a sharp contrast from the gray ad room. Three sides of the room were glass, with the rich silk green draperies. The remaining wall was paneled in walnut. A Monet and a Picasso hung on the wall, each painting, spotlighted.

Urho was seated at his desk—a French piece that Greta had picked up in Paris. Claudia placed the folder on his desk.

"Here's all I've been able to dig up."

"Good. I'll look them over, and try to fill in the holes."

She glanced around the room. Then as an afterthought she said, "See that George is winning. How does he do it?"

Urho looked up from the folder, "He doesn't spend his time in the ad room. He hustles, makes contacts. That's how he does it." He returned to the folder. "I'll check to see if we need anything else. Thank you, Claudia."

And with that remark he dismissed her. He didn't have time for light conversation. He was wrapped up in his own thoughts. Even before Claudia closed the door, he was on the phone, quoting bids, reading charts, checking reports

In the background Urho could hear the music coming from the ad room. Have to get this ad finished. Before Neil starts screaming for it, Urho thought. Slowly he rubbed the back of his neck. He was exhausted. Every bone in his body ached; every joint seemed enflamed. Every muscle felt as if it had been put through a blender at high speed. Emotional strain could have the same effect as strenuous physical labor. Isn't that what his doctor has been telling him?

He was also jumpy, much too tense to be able to go through this file that Claudia had compiled. Damn that Dora! Damn her to hell! Damn that note. Every time the phone rang, he jumped. And when there was a long period of silence, he sensed something sinister in the silence. His nerves were worn thinner than the knees of a devoted worshipper.

The best cure he had ever found for nervous tension was—but he mustn't think about booze. He was trying to quit, wasn't he? He was taking Richard's advice. Didn't Richard often say that booze was for the weak, the weak brained. Yes, he was going to quit. A half hour later when he was just beginning to study the water output files, the door to his office opened. "Hello," Dora said.

Urho put down the files and stared at her. Dora was one of a vanishing breed. During the past two decades, in response to fashion and advertising, the American woman had indulged in a frenzy of imitating Paris fashions. But Dora had successfully bucked the trend. She didn't dress as Paris dedicated. She set her own style and did it well. She had nothing more to offer the world of fashion than her stunning looks and her outstanding figure.

Now she wore a severe, man-tailored suit of mauve wool that accented her curves. A silk scarf of hand screened violets was folded softly at the neckline. The heirloom hair pin Neil had given her was fastened to the scarf. Matching suede pumps completed her ensemble. Her long sun-streaked blonde hair was now coiled in a braid and piled atop her head. She wore a faint scent of flower fragrance.

Urho rose, "What are you doing here? I've got a deadline to meet."

"I know, but I must talk to you."

He sank back into the brown leather chair, remembering that it was this chair that Dora had picked when he was redecorating the office. He was still feeling outrage, but his anger died as he watched her pull up a chair and sit across from him. These last few days had been terrible for him. Then his thoughts turned to that note which linked Dora to his Neil, his father. He reached for the crystal elephant paperweight on his desk. He held it, weighed it, wrapped his hands around it, tighter, tighter. So the battle has begun, he thought.

"What do you want to talk about, the note?" Urho asked and knew by the look in her eyes that he had gone to the heart of the matter. He knew she was not ready to talk about the note because she didn't speak for a long time. She stared at the paperweight in his hands as she might have stared at a crystal ball.

"What?" she finally said.

"You heard me." An odd little quiver went through him, and he recognized it was one of relief. But how could he feel relief? He walked to the marble counter where a coffee pot sat and filled a mug. The look that crossed Dora's face when he walked past her made Urho smile. He could read her thoughts so clearly, now. She lowered her eyelids, then her eyes flashed open wide.

"Urho, you haven't changed from the wreck of a G.I. I met in the Army hospital." Then she rose, circled the desk slowly. He turned his chair to face her. She came closer. "I want a divorce."

He didn't answer her immediately. He remembered those eyes, how they fascinated him in the hospital, when they first met. Strange, he thought, when Neil had learned he was going to marry Dora, he had objected, strongly, so had Greta. But they were married anyway by an Army chaplain. Urho got his discharge and his marriage license on the same day.

And when Dora flatly told him she didn't want any children after her painful miscarriage, their marriage became a shamble. In the end, Urho gave up his dream to study art in New York and accepted Neil's offer as advertising director at the Press. He had put his dream on hold. By the time he realized he had made a bad bargain by returning to Michigan and the Press, it was too late.

"I want a divorce, too, but on my own terms," he said. He sat back in his chair, comfortable now. He wondered if other men, other husbands had the urge he had now—to grab his wife by the shoulders and shake her until her brains rattled, her eyeballs rolled up into her head, and her screams for mercy were heard throughout the building. He didn't do it. But he thought about it as she walked away from him and sat down, knees crossed.

She looked at him. "Nobody every stopped me from getting what I wanted on MY terms." Slowly, deliberately, she fingered the pin Neil had given her, the human hair brooch. She threw Urho a wild, angry look.

For a moment he could only stare at her. Then he reached in his desk drawer and pulled out the note. He had kept it in the desk, under lock. He read, "My dearest Dora, The moments we steal to be together are all that I live for. You are my heart, my soul, my love—." Then Urho placed the note in front of her on his desk. She did not reach for it. Instead a flush came to her cheeks she drew her mouth into a thin, tight line. He had never seen her so tense.

"You're not serious—that's just a silly note, a scrap of paper." She grabbed the note. She smiled, and if it hadn't been for the faintly lifted eyebrows, he might have been inclined to believe her.

"You know how Neil flirts. You're his son, you know." She threw the note on the desk. "It's nothing."

"Yes, I know. Nothing. Especially about the part where he says he wants to marry you." He took the note and put it back in the desk drawer. Suddenly he felt sorry for her. He could not forgive her, but they were no longer enemies. He wanted out, out of this marriage, this sham. He looked at her. She looked radiant, but her appearance no longer affected him. He said, "Be honest with your self. Try it. For the first time in your life, stop lying. I know what's been going on between you and Neil. God, he's my father!"

She was angry now. "Shut up you bastard! What do you know? What do you know about life, about love?" Nervously she fingered the brooch.

Finally Urho said, "I've seen it coming. We haven't been able to make this work for how long? Since that miscarriage, since you said no children, period. And now I want out!" He reached for a cigarette from a pack on his desk, put it in his mouth and touched a match to it. He could smell her special perfume even from where he sat, but it was nothing, nothing.

She smiled, "Well, we agree on something, don't we?"

He shrugged. "To use an old phrase—there is no love lost between us." But his thoughts flew to California, when there was an urgent love, a love they shared, uncontrollable, consuming.

"I'm moving out today," she said. "I'm going to Reno. You'll hear from my lawyer."

"In spite of it all, I'm sorry," he said.

"I'm not. I'm glad, happy!" She laughed wildly and to Urho's astonishment she grabbed the crystal elephant paperweight and flung it across the room. It struck the Monet, making a fine tear in it, and fell to the deep green pile carpeting. In the encounter the elephant's tusk shattered.

For a moment he could only stare at her. "Get out of here!"

She laughed. "I'm going, don't worry." Her eyes were enormous.

He felt the rush of blood to his face, felt the trembling inside him. She was telling HIM she was getting a divorce? How did things get twisted around? Then some of the tension left him. "I said get out of here."

Slowly she walked to the door and let herself out.

CHAPTER 14

"Let's get down to business. I've got all the plans and charts," Neil said, closing the door behind him with his foot. Richard followed close behind. "We're almost set on the special millage election even though it's in April—more than three month away. Have to be prepared and it gives us plenty of time to make sure it goes my way," Neil said.

"As I recall, the presidential election didn't go your way," Richard said.

"I don't want to talk about that. So Nixon lost. It was almost too close to call. Old Joe Kennedy's son squeaked into the presidency. Now we have to contend with the Democrats after so many good years with Eisenhower."

"Guess you've forgotten the recession in '58."

"Shut up, Richard." Neil dropped the charts and plans on his desk and walked to the bar at the far corner of his office. He glanced at his watch, a twenty-dollar gold piece was the face, and said, "It's happy hour somewhere in the world." Actually it was 1:30

"What can I fix you, Richard? A martini, some fine scotch on the rocks, or my good bourbon, straight up?" He grinned as he filled his glass with scotch and a few ice cubes.

"Coffee, black," Richard said. I'm not in the mood for your jokes.

Neil poured him a mug of coffee from the electric pot on the bar and handed it to him. It had been a strange few months for Neil, alternating between moments of unbearable happiness with Dora and hours of frustration with Greta. After that day with Dora that started with brunch at the Inn, and ended in a four-star hotel in Detroit, he fully realized the all consuming desire he had for Dora. It was a frantic need. He snapped out of his reverie when Richard said, "And don't doctor up my coffee, please."

Neil ignored him. He was too happy this afternoon to let Richard's remark bother him. He had talked to Dora this morning. She was in Reno getting her divorce. Things couldn't be going better for him. And as for Richard, he had plans for him, plans that Richard might not approve of—but what the hell. Neil took a swallow of his drink and looked around. Damn, he felt good! He patted the huge brass elephant at the door, and ambled to his desk, drink in hand.

Now Richard stood at the wide expanse of windows, staring out at the drizzling rainy day. "Rotten weather," he said, sipping his coffee. "What are you drinking, Neil?"

"Coke," he said. Then he grinned.

"Fat chance." Richard tugged at his beard. "Damn this weather."

"What do you expect, it's Michigan. Forget about it. It will change soon enough. We've got plans to complete. I've got Yiannis working on the water plant plans. It's about time Pierre Corners got its own water system. No more dry spells, depending on Detroit for water. Say didn't old Henry Ford have his own water system in his mansion in Dearborn? And his own electrical power, too?"

"Yes, he was a genius."

"Well, we can do it. Last summer was the last straw, when we had to beg Detroit for every drop. And the ultimate was Detroit directing us here in Pierre Corners with no watering the lawn days, and no shower days. That was the limit!"

"Yiannis and you have a solid plan. Now it's up to the voters," Richard said.

"Sure it is. With our out-county water intakes and treatment facilities in Pierre Corners, we'll be all set. And the engineers I hired to investigate clean water supplies nearby, we're home free."

Two weeks into the study, an engineer discovered a stream of clean water in the Detroit River on the Canadian side of the channel opposite the mouth of the Pierre Corners River. Further investigation proved that a proposed intake could be installed and a tunnel could be dug to land in Pierre Corners.

Bernie wrote the initial stories about the proposed water plant to inform the citizens of Pierre Corners of the water project. Neil's job had been to convince the mayor and council members to put a millage proposal on the ballot in April to finance the water system. After countless meetings, the proposal was set for the April ballot.

Why was Neil interested in the proposal? Was it because he was a concerned citizen? Was it because he was publisher of the Liemus Press? Or was it because the proposed water system would be built on Press Corporation land?

Neil scanned some galley proofs on his desk. "That new proof reader is working out, haven't found any typos in Bernie's water system story."

"I know. She's a top grammarian and speller. Got her right out of the University of Michigan. Matt clued me in on her. A journalism major. She was one of Matt's students in high school," Richard said.

"I see we are still getting mail on that gifted series. Claudia did an adequate job," Neil said.

"Adequate?" It was a terrific series. Matt said he's got some concrete offers from the Ford and Mott foundations to help fund a gifted school because of Claudia's series. I've sent the series to the Michigan Press Association Competition. She has a very good chance of winning it."

"You seem so sure," Neil said.

"I'm as sure as you are about getting that millage passed."

"Damn right I'm sure!" Neil put one of his premium cigars in his mouth. He was at the bar, refilling his glass. "I'm the one that started the ball rolling. I don't want to depend on Detroit for water. Not after that runaround they gave us last summer. We have the Detroit River at our doorstep and we depend on another city for water? It doesn't make sense." He emphasized his words by shaking his cigar in Richard's face.

"We weren't the only ones hurting. The other suburbs had a

shortage, too," Richard said.

"Yes, they did, except Wyandotte, the city with smarts. That city not only has its own water system, but its own gas and power companies. That's what I want for Pierre Corners. And this millage is the first step." He sank into his leather chair. "Yes, this is my town. I've got big stakes in it." Outside the rain continued to fall. Richard got up and said, "I've got a deadline, remember?"

Neil merely nodded, lost in thought. The door closed behind Richard.

My town, my new life, Neil thought. When Dora returns from Reno with her divorce, his problems would be almost solved. Now Neil had to retrace what he was going to do about Greta.

Since Urho found that note, that note that started everything tumbling down, he had avoided his son. At times Neil regretted having written that impulsive note, writing about his love for Dora.

Round and round his thoughts turned. What was he going to do about Greta? She was a problem, a big hurdle. After that hallway incident when she had come upon them kissing, things changed. Following her first outburst, she never mentioned the incident. That was very unlike her. She was one to speak out, explode, argue, but no, not a word. What was she planning? Not good, her silence, not good at all.

Yes, Dora's divorce brought its own sense of unreality. That Dora was thirty to his sixty-three was not reassuring. The newness of this love overwhelmed him. This was different, not like the others, the one-night stands. Why did Dora remind him of a young Valley? Why— he caught his breath every time he saw Dora. The first time they made love, he almost lost his mind. She was incredible.

As for Greta, she is an impossible woman. He never really loved her. She was only a means to an end. The end was getting out of the Detroit Times and into his own newspaper. And it was with her savings, that he got the Press. He had struck a bargain with her—and then another—and then another. They were locked together in many pacts. But he would free himself from her and soon. He would get his divorce. He knew some clever lawyers. He still felt dazed and unable to resist the avalanche of thoughts that crowded his mind when the phone rang. He grabbed it on the second ring, "Liemus, here."

"Neil darling, Neil, my love." It was Dora.

His face flushed. "This is a surprise, my dear. I didn't expect another call from you today. But I'm glad you called. I miss you."

"I miss you too, very much."

"I'm making plans for us," he began. "I'm going to talk to Greta about the divorce. It's going to be messy—but don't worry, I'll get it."

"Oh, Neil. I'm so happy. You are what I've always wanted in a husband."

He held fast to the phone. Was he getting paranoid? Did he detect something in her voice? Nonsense—it's nothing. "I'll see you soon. I love you," he said.

Yes, soon. I'm counting the days."

"Goodbye my darling." He hung up and reached for a handkerchief to wipe his flushed face. He must make a decision. And now! He was going to Reno, tomorrow. He picked up the phone and dialed the airport.

CHAPTER 15

As soon as Claudia picked up the phone, she knew it wasn't going to be her day. Except for Bernie, she was the only one in the newsroom. A heart-shaped apple cake, which Freda had baked and donated to the staff to celebrate Valentine's Day, was on the coffee table next to the file cabinet. Bernie leaned against a file case and bit into a slice of cake, sprinkled with cinnamon and sugar.

Claudia held her hand over the mouthpiece and whispered, "Bernie, it's the Goddess of Night." Waving the weather report in front of his face, she said, "There's going to be a full moon tomorrow. The Goddess is ahead of schedule."

Bernie rolled his eyes, looked up to the ceiling and said, "Why me, God?" Then to Claudia, "Tell her I'm out. Tell her I'm dead! You talk to her."

"Sorry, I told her you were in. Besides, it's her 'outer space aliens are after me' day." She handed the phone to Bernie. "And I can't talk to her, I've got another problem with Matt and his gifted children. Now he wants me to write a book about them. He said I could do it in my spare time. Want to trade?"

"Nope." Bernie said, gulped his coffee, finished his cake and grabbed the phone. "Goddess, how goes it with you on this beautiful day? It's Valentine's Day, you know." He patted the strand of hair covering his bald spot. Then into the mouthpiece, "Are these the same little green men from Mars that visited you last month? No?" He sat at his desk doodling on copy paper and the Goddess screamed into the phone. "Okay, calm down. Damn it to hell, how did those purple creatures get your address? Oh, they're coming in through the toilet bowl? Amazing!" He shifted his weight and scribbled something on the paper and passed the note to Claudia. It said—'Still want to trade? I'll take those brainy kids for these purple aliens in the toilet. Deal?'

Claudia read the note, grinned and shook her head. She could hear the Goddess screaming at Bernie—" They are all in the toilet, no, I think just the baby ones are in the toilet. The big ones are in my bathtub. They have those beady eyes and are wearing silver helmets. I think the captain of the crew is in there too. His helmet has gold stars on it. What am I going to do, Bernie. Please help me."

"Okay, I'll do my best. Got that special flashlight I gave you last month. Well, beam it at those little ones first in the toilet."

After a few minutes the Goddess returned to the phone, screaming. "It's not working, Bernie. Shit, it's not working!"

"Damn, Goddess, you've shattered my ear drums. I'm getting a headache. I know what you forgot to do. You have to turn around three times, remember? Flash the beam on the ceiling first, and say, 'Aliens, go home, and then aim it at those pesky purple people."

"Oh yeah, I forgot," the Goddess said. "Let me see—turn—three times. Go home—and then zap those bastards! Bernie, it's working! They're going right down the toilet and right down the drain. God love you, Bernie. Thanks a bunch. Good bye."

"No problem, any time," Bernie said. He hung up and went back to the coffee table for some more cake. He finished another slice, wiped his hands across his mouth and went back to his desk. "That crazy lady. If the Goddess calls again, I'm not in, got it?" He looked at Claudia.

"Got it."

Bernie then began his morning ritual of lighting his old pipe—first packing the tobacco, the same mixture of rum and honey, and finally lighting it and sending clouds of smoke throughout the newsroom. That's when Tessie and Clyde came in. Tessie made a face. "Not that old smelly pipe again. Can't you at least wait until we've all had our cof—?" Then she sneezed.

"Nope."

Tessie pulled a handkerchief from her pocket and covered her mouth. She walked to the coffee table and sliced a piece of cake for herself. "That Freda sure can bake. I bet she baked one for the office and one just for herself when she gets home."

Clyde laughed. "Cut me a big slice, please."

Since the gifted children series, Tessie and Clyde had unofficially become a team. In spite of the teamwork, Clyde just tolerated her. He didn't want anything to interfere with his photography. He was serious about it and had won several competitions while working at the Press, and he wasn't about to have Tessie spoil his art work, because that's what he called his photos.

When Richard teamed Tessie and Clyde with the photo assignments going with the gifted series, Claudia thought maybe Richard was getting soft, or else he was partial to young women with red hair. Claudia knew that at first Clyde was peeved with the assignment teaming him with Tessie. He complained to Claudia enough times. Claudia told him straight out that the person he should complain to was Neil. But Clyde never did. He was just blowing off steam and complaining to everyone except Neil.

Washing down his cake with some coffee, Clyde glanced at the 'wall of honor' as the staff called it, the one wall in the newsroom devoted to awards and plaques earned by the Press staff. His eyes fell on the most recent honor, a first-place photography award he won from the Michigan Media Council. Claudia followed his gaze.

"Congratulations, again," she said.

"Thanks. Too bad they don't give cash, just plaques. You can't eat a plaque."

"That's true. But awards are good for the ego—and the soul. Sometimes they're better than cash," Claudia said.

"Some day your name will be on one of those awards, Claudia."

"Sure. And some day I'll write that book about the gifted—the one Matt has been bugging me about."

"So write it!" Clyde said and ambled out the back door. Tessie

114

followed him.

"No, Tessie, this is my assignment. I won't need you." Clyde said.

"Oh?" Tessie retreated into the newsroom and walked to her desk.

Clyde almost collided with George and Richard, who were deep into a conversation as they strolled through the back door.

"And jokes are what make the world go round," George said.

"Don't you mean, jokes sell ads?"

"Guess you're right, Richard. People like to laugh."

"But work pays the bills," Richard said.

"So you're saying that I should cut the crap and get to work?"

"No. You said that. I'm saying that your jokes sell ads. Don't ever stop telling jokes George. They've made you the top man here at the Press." Richard removed his horn-rimmed glasses and put them on the top of his head.

"Thanks for the kind words," George said and walked toward the ad room.

Richard spotted Claudia. "I want a word with you, young lady. Come into my office."

"Now, what have I done?"

Right behind her was Urho, a smile on his face. "You've done something and it's time to pay the piper."

The three of them walked into Richard's office. Richard stared briefly at the playing cards encased in a gold frame.

"Why didn't you frame the whole deck?" Claudia.

Both men laughed. Urho then said, "Richard why didn't you frame two decks?"

"Enough jokes," Richard said. "Those cards represent a royal flush in poker, and they are mighty hard to come by." He fished for a cigarette in his drawer, found a crumpled pack, drew one out, and lit it. Then replacing his glasses, he looked closely at the gold frame.

"What's a royal flush?" she asked.

"Tell her, or shall I?" Urho said.

"You do the honors, Urho. I have other things to tell Claudia."

"I know. Well, Claudia, about this royal flush. It's a once in a lifetime deal, and my father almost had a heart attack when Richard pulled this one off. It was during a usual Tuesday night poker game at the Press Club. It had been a close game with Neil winning most of the pots. Then Richard was dealt a royal flush."

"I treasure that moment and the look on Neil's face, but I especially treasure the $500 pot I won that night." Richard grinned.

"That's something," Claudia said.

"Something hell! I can now put a '30' on my life and die happy," Richard said.

"That's another thing I wondered about, the '30'. Why do we put '30' at the end of our stories?" She also wondered about Richard's lonely existence, the Press and poker—his entire life. Somehow her amber beads found their way from her sweater pocket into her hands. She held them, unconsciously, and then they slipped from her grasp. Both Urho and she reached for them as they fell to the floor. Their hands touched and the beads slid to the floor. Their eyes met. Why was her heart beating so fast? An awkward moment, that's all. She brushed thoughts of him away. Yes, just an awkward moment. Then Urho scooped up the amber beads and handed them to her. He smiled. "Slippery beads, right?"

"Thank you," she said and quickly slipped them into her sweater pocket.

Richard eyed them both, cleared his throat and began, "About the '30'—it goes way back—to the telegraphers. They would sign off for the night with that code number—30. Later, the printers latched onto it—using two hyphens for 30 and that meant the end of the message. Then reporters adopted it."

"So, that's the story. I'm learning all the trade secrets. This is a fascinating business."

"Fascinating, yes," Urho said.

"I'm glad you both think so." Richard pulled out a letter from his wire basket and handed it to Claudia. "Read this."

"You want me to rewrite this news release?"

"No, read the damn letter," Richard said.

"Now, Richard, don't get nasty," Urho said. "By the way, Claudia, congratulations!"

116

"Really, for what?"

Urho and Richard grinned. "Read the damn letter," they both said.

The letterhead said, "Michigan Press Association." Claudia raced through the greeting and the first paragraph. Then she read—"We are proud to announce that Claudia Kali won first place state-wide for her series on the gifted child in the daily newspaper category."

"Wha—?" began Claudia.

"Congratulations, again," Richard said, and gave her a hug.

"My turn?" Urho asked, and embraced Claudia, who held her arms awkwardly to her side. Her face flushed. Her heart began to race again.

Urho looked at her for a moment and then said, "I've got to run. Deadlines are staring me in the face." And with that remark he rushed out of the office.

Richard began, "The awards ceremony is in April in Lansing. I'll go with you. You'll receive a plaque and $500."

"Really? I can't believe it. My first award! Clyde and I were kidding about awards just a few minutes ago."

"I like the way you said that—first award, because there will be more," Richard said.

"I—I—," Claudia stammered.

"I have a gift for you," Richard said. "It's standard practice to give new reporters a dictionary. You got yours, right?"

Claudia nodded.

"Well, here is another book, more important than a dictionary." He reached into the top drawer of his desk and pulled out a Bible. "Here is you source book. But, I'm sure you're no stranger to the Bible. This is for the office put it in your desk." He leaned back into his swivel chair. He said, "I'm not a religious person. But the Bible is more than religion—it's about life—about the world. I've found many an answer in this Book."

"Book means Bible in Greek, did you know that?" Claudia began. "Listen to this," she began, as she thumbed through the Bible. "Therefore judge nothing before the time until the Lord comes, who both will bring to light the hidden things of darkness and will make manifest the counsels of the heart." She closed the Book. "Strange,

I should go to that passage in Corinthians. My father's parents came from Corinth."

"No, it's not strange. I believe it was meant for you to find that paragraph. Here, let me see that—yes, hidden things of darkness. There are so many hidden things in our lives—so many secrets." He handed her the Bible.

"Yes, there are. Thank you."

"My pleasure," he said and rapped his desk with his metal pica ruler.

She said looking at the ruler, "I've always wanted to ask you about your pica ruler. Do you measure progress with that?"

"No, sorry to disappoint you. I just measure copy and use it to crop photos. Also this ruler is my attention grabber. Bet you don't see a metal ruler without thinking of me, right?"

"Right." As Claudia got up to leave, she faced a woman framed in the doorway. She was tall, slim, and wore a black mink coat. Her hair was even blonder than Valley's and had been cut fashionably short, close to her head. Two tortoise shell combs held the short hair in place.

This, of course, was Greta Liemus. Claudia recognized her immediately. She had seen enough photos of her around the Press. Valley had warned Claudia about Greta's biting tongue.

"She cuts like a razor," Valley had said.

Richard greeted Greta warmly, and then introduced Claudia to her. "Oh, yes, you're the one who wrote the series on the gifted." But her expression held no warmth and her pale blue eyes dismissed her quickly. Obviously Claudia wasn't up to Greta's standards, and for a moment Claudia felt like a child being shooed off to her room. Her back stiffened. So, she did not live up to Greta's standards. But did she want to? Perhaps Greta needs to live up to my standards, Claudia thought as she started to leave Richard's office.

"Richard, I've got to talk to you, alone," Greta said eying Claudia.

"I was just leaving," Claudia said.

"Good." Greta said.

Claudia quickly stepped into the hallway and walked rapidly to the newsroom. She must have been standing open-mouthed against the file cabinet, because Bernie walked over and put his arms around her. "Caught you," he said. "By the look on your face, you must have just seen the Dragon Lady." He pulled out his waterproof pouch and slowly filled his pipe with tobacco. "I've seen that expression—open-mouthed , shock, bleary eyes. It happens every time someone meets the Dragon Lady for the first time."

"She's— she's overpowering. She's —."

"Cold, freezing cold," finished Bernie.

"Oh no, I didn't mean that—."

"Yes, you did. And I can guess why she's here to talk to Richard. She sure took her sweet time. It started when Neil took off for Reno a few months ago. That was a deliberate slap in the face to Greta. That's when he also moved out of the mansion, bag and baggage, into the penthouse. Well, that was the last straw. Haven't seen hide nor hair of the other woman, who shall remain nameless. Heard tell though that Himself has set her up in a fine apartment in New York. That accounts for his frequent weekend trips to the Big Apple. Enough said. Man, doesn't this sound like a soap opera? Tune in tomorrow—to Pierre Corners, and watch 'As the Town Turns'. More data on the 11 o'clock news." Bernie laughed.

Claudia smiled. "Bernie, stop it." They continued to stand by the file cabinets, making the crowd leaving for lunch walk around them. Claudia felt comfortable talking to Bernie, this hulk of a man, who was only vain about his bald spot and was forever patting the thin strands of hair over to cover it.

"I've got some news," Claudia said. She grinned. "No, it's not about the Dragon Lady. Richard just told me I took first place in the Michigan Press Association competition for the gifted child series. I'm happy."

"And you should be. Congratulations." He walked to the wall of honor. "Let's put your award right at the top, next to Urho's advertising award. Okay?"

"It's not for me to say." Claudia could feel the blood rush to her face.

"Can I treat you to lunch, to celebrate?"

"Thanks, no. But I'd like a rain check." Claudia spotted Valley at her desk, drinking from a green mouthwash bottle.

"You don't want to mess with Valley now," warned Bernie, his eyes following Claudia's. He reached for his raincoat and walked toward the back door. "Sure I can't talk you into lunch, now?"

"Another time." Claudia could see Valley watching her. She deliberately took another swallow from the bottle. Ever since the open affair between Neil and Dora, Valley was trying to drink herself into a stupor on a daily basis. And she was succeeding. Now she slumped into her chair, head lowered, hands on the old Remington, eyes shut. She wore the same outdated orange dress she had worn the first day Claudia had come into the newsroom. When was that— 1960? Now it was February, 1962.She walked to Valley's desk, leaned over and whispered, "Are you okay?"

Valley's blue eyes flashed open. "I'm okay. It's just that the whole damn world is rotten. Do you hear me?"

CHAPTER 16

After dialing the switchboard and informing Freda he was leaving for the day, Neil left his office, walked to his penthouse suite, tossed his suit jacket onto a chair, undressed, showered, and put on brown corduroy slacks and a plaid flannel shirt. He threw on his fur-lined leather jacket and in a matter of minutes was out of the Press building and walking the two blocks to the Pierre Tavern and Inn. He shivered, pulled up his collar, searched in his pockets for his leather gloves and slipped them on. Mid-March and it was in the low 20s. The weather forecasters had predicted a snow storm. Was it three years ago, we had a wild blizzard on St. Patrick's Day? thought Neil.

The usual five-o'clock happy hour crowd was already there, sipping their drinks. The Pierre Tavern and Inn—often called the Tavern by the regulars, was a vanishing idea in the 1960s—an ordinary neighborhood bar. Maybe a bit more than the ordinary, because on weekends, the Tavern featured "name" acts, usually entertainers who were either on the way up or on the way down in show business. They were put up in the old restored French village inn next to the tavern. The Tavern had nothing more to offer than pleasantly low lighting, comfortable bar stools, a postage-size stage and dance floor, Harry, a top notch bartender, great chili and hamburgers served from a clean kitchen and ample drinks at reasonable prices.

Above all it was not a topless bar with a naked child-woman wiggling her hips and ass in a dime size stage. Thank God for that,

121

thought Neil, motioning the bartender for a refill.

As a bonus there were the week end floor shows. Last week, the attraction had been Sally Rand and her Fans. Sally Rand had introduced her famous fan dance act at the 1933 Chicago World's Fair. Now almost thirty years later, she was still billed as the dancer that shocked the World's Fair crowds. But her press agent was discreet, he didn't mention the year.

Next week Rudy Vallee would be the star attraction. Neil was looking forward to listening to this crooner, who was popular even before Bing Crosby. Vallee and his megaphone went way back to the 1920s. Neil believed that entertainers were like generals, they didn't die, no, they just faded away. Where in the world did the Tavern dig up those relics? Oh well, that's show business. Why can't the Tavern get Sinatra or Elvis? wondered Neil.

Sipping his scotch and water at the bar, Neil watched the crowd. It was a mix of Pierre Corners old timers, solid citizens, businessmen, and some young people, clerks, bank tellers, ad men and reporters from the Press and off duty policemen.

Harry, the bartender, dimpled chin and thick gray hair, used a rag to wipe off the bar and set up some fresh drinks for the crowd. He glanced at Neil at the end of the bar, nursing his drink. "Anything else you want, Mr. Liemus?"

"Yes, Harry, now that you asked. I want to be forty, win the Pulitzer Prize, and a week in Paris with— never mind," Neil said and took a swallow of his scotch and water.

"Okay, but what will you settle for –now?"

"One of those famous Tavern hamburgers, the works."

"That I can do, sir."

"And freshen up this scotch."

"Coming up."

Neil nodded glumly. His broad face seemed to sag into a melancholy mask. Damn, how he missed her, his Dora. If he didn't see her soon he'd burst. A month since he'd seen her last. Who could he talk to about his feelings? He certainly couldn't engage in an intimate conversation about his life with the bartender—and certainly not with Richard, and definitely not with his son, Urho. That would lead to bloodshed. Yet it was obvious that he needed someone to listen to him. Dora, where are you? He took a long pull of his scotch. Then Harry set the steaming hamburger in front of him.

"Another scotch coming up," the bartender said.

"Good." Neil wanted to talk about Dora, wanted to get rid of this feeling that had been building up in him and eating at his heart for a long time, but he couldn't.

After the bartender left, Neil ate silently, listening to those around him. Finally he joined their conversation and for a little while forgot about Dora and enjoyed their company.

It was almost midnight and Neil was getting drunk. He tossed his jacket on the bar stool and unbuttoned the top buttons of his flannel shirt. He kept constantly running his fingers through his hair. He glared at the mayor through blood shot eyes. His face was flushed. "Damn it, that water millage must pass!" He slurred some of his words.

"Now, Neil, don't get on your high horse," said the mayor, whose florid complexion matched Neil's. "That election isn't until next month, April. We've got time."

The closer Neil got to being completely smashed, the louder he became. When he motioned Harry, the bartender over for another scotch, Harry said, "I'm not sure that's a good idea. Look, Mr. Liemus want me to call you a cab to get you home to the Island? It's getting late."

The mayor said, "I can drive you to the Island."

"You're just as drunk as I am," Neil said. He laughed. "Besides, I'm not going to the Island, I'm living at the Press now. I can walk home from here, just two blocks." Neil made a point to stress each word, carefully. "I planned to get drunk, sopping drunk. But I'm not too drunk to walk home." And then he struggled with his jacket and staggered out the door. The short walk in the storm had sobered him. Now in his penthouse, he undressed and jumped into the shower. That's what I need, a bracing shower, he thought. Fresh from the shower, a brisk rubdown with a towel, he then slipped into pajama bottoms. Finally he pulled back the draperies to his panoramic window and watched the storm, the snow piling in huge mounds, the wind wiping the icy branches.

He murmured to himself, "That's a bitch of a storm. Better get some sleep. I feel lousy." As soon as his head hit the pillow, Neil was snoring peacefully.

Hours later, the squeal of brakes woke him from a deep sleep. Was he dreaming?

Quickly he turned on the lamp on his nightstand—glanced at the clock—4 o'clock. Then he glanced down Main Street. In the dim light cast by the street lamps he saw a solitary taxi parked in front of the Press. He wondered what fool would be driving in this hell of a storm?

The taxi driver got out and went to the passenger side of the car, opened the door. A woman, with a suitcase, stepped out. She jumped over the snow bank and using a key let herself into the Press building, as the taxi drove away. Neil grabbed his robe and raced for the elevator. When he reached the first floor lobby, he rushed out of the elevator. She ran toward him. "Neil, Neil!" she cried, breathlessly and kissed him, her arms around his neck.

"My darling, Dora. It is really you? I've been going crazy. I've been so hungry for you—." He kissed her, little kisses on her cheeks, her eyelids, her nose, her ears. Then he wrapped her in his arms, kissed her on the lips, long, lingering. And suddenly they were in the Press lobby all shaky-voiced, teary-eyed, hugging and kissing. He would not, he vowed there in the lobby, risk the unbearably sad and depressing feeling of letting her go, ever! He had been lonely for too long.

Catching his breath, he said, "Let me look at you." He saw a tall, slim woman, wrapped in an amber alpaca storm coat, her feet covered in tan leather boots, her long blonde hair pushed under a tan wool beret. Neil's red-rimmed eyes grew watery, and for

a moment he looked as if he were about to cry. But he blinked rapidly. In a voice choking with happiness, he said, "Let's fuck."

"You publishers have a way with words." Dora smiled.

* * *

Back in the penthouse suite, Dora dropped her coat on the bed. "I've so much to tell you. How much I missed you—how dreadful it was in New York without you—how I planned to surprise you with this visit. But honestly Neil, I didn't bring this storm." She rambled on, talking, breathless, eyes sparkling, cheeks flushed from the cold wind.

Neil, still not believing his good fortune, was content to nod in agreement, and touch her, caress her, stroke her hair, her face, kiss her lips. He didn't say a word. He was too happy. Perhaps if he spoke— the spell would be broken and she would disappear.

I missed you so, Neil. I'm so happy I'm here."

And then Neil did believe it was real, and did believe his good fortune. He said, "Take your clothes off. Let's make love, is that better?

In a few minutes she was naked beside him in bed. The wind howled, the snow made patterns on the glass, the clouds hung low and ominously, while Neil felt Dora's feather light touch on his body. Her fingers seemed to reach his very nerve endings lying just under the surface of his skin. He shuddered and closed his eyes, giving himself up to her sensual touch, to the scent of her rising from her body. He touched her breasts, then he brushed them lightly with his lips. Then he filled his mouth with them, until she lay on the pillow gasping.

It began to snow harder, harder, the wind beating against the glass. He kissed her gently at first—then brutally, and his excitement overpowered him. He wanted her so much. He needed her so much. He cried out. "Dora, Dora!" He felt slightly light-headed, not from the scotch but from being so close to her. So much time had passed since he'd allowed himself to be touched and possessed in this way, since he'd shared in this way. How could he have let so much time pass? He leaned over and kissed her again and again. She opened her mouth to him . He pulled back and looked at her, put his hand against her face as if he were touching fine porcelain. "I love you."

"I love you, too, Neil." She leaned back and he leaned into her, still kissing her. He stroked her soft throat with his fingertips. Dora put his hand on her thighs. He sensed her excitement and his fingers traveled from her thighs, leaving cool trails on her warm skin. She put her arms around him and slid down on the bed and pulled him on top of her. She kissed him hard, crushing her lips against his.

"Now, now!" he cried.

"No, not yet—darling," she said. "Get off me and turn over on your stomach."

"Why?" he grumbled. He could not bear another minute of this— not another minute. Then she began stroking—fine delicate finger strokes, tingling strokes, on his neck, his shoulders, his back, his buttocks, his thighs, his legs, his feet, his toes. Maddening, tender, feather-light touches.

"Oh my God!" he cried.

The wind pounded on the glass. The draperies were open. "Do you want me to draw the draperies?" Dora asked.

"Damn the draperies!"

Dora laughed. "Come to Mama. My baby, come here."

Goose bumps popped up on Neil's body.

"Now!" she said. And then he was in her, and he felt her quake in great tremors. The spasms he had suppressed for so long, the spasms he denied himself for so long were finally released and they overtook him, shook him, like the storm raging outside and he cried out. "My Dora, my Dora!"

Later they lay in each others' arms and kissed, gentle kisses. It was extraordinary good and right. It was something they should do again and again, tonight and always, he thought. Could he? He reached for her and she moved into his embrace.

The next morning Neil awoke to the drone of snow plows. He looked out the window and whistled softly. "What a bitch!" Quickly he slipped into his pajama pants and reached for the phone on the nightstand dialed the weather bureau. Then he looked over at Dora. Lazily she stretched and opened her eyes. His hand pressed on the receiver, he said, "Good morning, darling. It looks like we're snowed in."

"Goody." She pulled back the blanket and walked naked to the wide expanse of windows, lifted her arms above her head and stretched wide, yawning. "What a beautiful, snow white day." She stood in front of the windows, naked, feet apart, head thrown back, mouth open in a yawn, arms raised. Neil reached over and threw a robe over her body. "Put this on, you'll catch cold. Besides—" He grinned and looked down. "You're getting me excited—and I've got work to do."

Dora winked at him and opened her robe for a second. "Want a peek?"

"Can't play right now—business calls." Then he dialed the weather bureau. After getting the day's forecast, he hung up. "Damn them to hell. We're snowed in, and this storm doesn't seem to be letting up."

"What are you going to do?"

"We've got a paper to get out. I'm a cantankerous old bastard and not entirely admirable. But as long as the Press and the truth are my weapons, I don't mind calling in a few markers. The governor owes me. And I don't mind waking up that fool." Immediately he dialed the governor's mansion in Lansing. After a brief talk with the governor, who assured Neil that the National Guards would be at his disposal, that he could rely on the Guards to supply him with jeeps and other four-wheel vehicles, and the men to drive them, and that anything else Neil needed would be available, Neil thanked the governor and hung up.

"That's the way to get things done. Go to the top. I'd have gone to the president, if necessary, even if he is a Democrat," Neil said. "Now, let's get ready. It's going to be a busy day. Turn on the radio and see what they have to say about the storm."

"Okay. Want to share my shower?" Dora asked.

"No. I'm going to shower first." In less than ten minutes, Neil was out of the bathroom, showered, shaved and dressed.

Dora had made some coffee in the compact kitchen. She carried her cup to the window and watched the storm. The radio announcer said: "We are urging all residents to stay home unless they are members of emergency, medical or utility units. Schools, banks and stores in Detroit and the surrounding suburbs are closed. A complete storm up date will be broadcast every fifteen minutes...."

"Turn that thing off. I've heard enough. The Press will be publishing soon. As soon as the jeeps come from the National Guards, I'm going to have them pick up my people and bring them down here. Also, I'm sending some of those jeeps to my Detroit plant—to pick up galleys. The Press has never missed a deadline, and it's not about to today."

"You're serious, aren't you, Neil?"

"Damn right!" He was all too aware of her searching eyes. He wasn't too pleased with his emotions being so easily read. Did she know what she was doing to him? Instantly he reached out and pulled her to him. He untied the robe and felt her cool, soft skin. Then his voice, husky, he said, "I love you. You being here has made all the difference in the world to me. Last night was—."

"I know." She kissed him. "And we're going to get married, aren't we?"

And then his office telephone rang. "Damn," he said. Quickly he walked to his desk. "Hello. Yes, Richard, we're operating full steam. I'll send a jeep to get you as soon as they get here. We've got the National Guards at our disposal. How did I manage? The governor owes me. See you soon."

Dora's laugh had a wicked sound as Neil hung up. "You're really missing out. Here, you could have had me all to yourself – and you chose to put your silly newspaper out. Oh well, my loss is the newspaper's gain." She kissed Neil passionately. "Will that hold you for a while?"

"You're beautiful," Neil sighed.

In a sudden change of mood, Dora said "Now back to business. You've got to get the Press out. And I can't help. Do you think one of those jeeps can give me a lift to the Pierre Inn? I know it's only two blocks, but I don't think I can navigate it in this storm."

"You can have the first jeep."

And when the jeeps arrived a half-hour later, Dora dressed in her storm coat waited at the elevator with Neil. Before she stepped into the down elevator Neil kissed her. He frowned.

"Don't look so worried. I'll be all right. Think of tonight. We'll be in a quaint little inn—just you and me in our lovely room."

128

He grinned. "Get some sleep. You didn't get much last night." In the sharper light of morning her hair appeared sun streaked. She didn't speak, just smiled.

Neil reacted to her smile with awe. "You're stunning, absolutely stunning."

"I know."

* * *

She rode the elevator to the first floor, alone and in pensive silence. As she crossed the main lobby of the Press with its bright orange carpeting, it was like a flash of sunset against the dark paneled walls. And from the twin lobby windows, she saw Main Street cloaked in white. Three jeeps were parked in front of the Press, having dropped off Press employees. She found Freda at the switchboard, and two women on the phones at the classified counter. Freda smiled at Dora. "I think we broke a record last night," Freda said.

"Yes, I think we did." Dora smiled.

"And if it weren't for those jeeps, I'd be snug as a bug in my bed this very minute. Mr. Liemus knows how to get things done."

"Yes, he does."

Then Richard walked to the switchboard and leaned against the counter. When Dora looked at his grave, unsmiling face, she realized that his expression was sympathetic; perhaps less critical than it might have been. During her exchange with Freda, he must have been weighing their conversation. Yes, Richard was a difficult man to understand. But that's what makes him interesting. He isn't easily read.

Richard said, "Dora what a surprise to see you here. I thought you were in New York."

"I was, but I missed Pierre Corners too much. I had to come back, hadn't counted on this storm. Any port in a storm though, as the old saying goes." She wanted to sound light.

Well then, why don't you stay at the Press? You don't want to tackle that storm." He motioned to Main Street. "Must be a few feet of snow out there."

She hesitated, her concern for Neil, and then what would Urho say if he saw her here—now? "I'd like to—but."

"Then stay, at least until the streets are plowed."

And then Richard's understanding surprised her. "On second thought, maybe you're right. We're going to be very busy here."

"Yes, and I've got a jeep waiting for me," Dora said, rushing to the door. And then she saw Urho at the door. It didn't matter, she told herself. She must not panic or she would spoil every future moment of her life with Neil. She must learn to accept the situation, strange as it was, without falling apart. She fumbled with her gloves, and finally shoved them into her pocket.

Urho asked, "What the hell are you doing here?"

"It's none of your business." She pulled out her gloves. This time she managed to fit her gloves, calmly, smoothing the kid over every finger and finally over her palms.

"This place IS my business!" he said.

And Dora remembered the flow of power that Urho managed to summon when he was angry.

"Get out of here!" he said. His voice was ominously low. "There's a jeep out front, get in it." He looked at her and once again she saw the burning in his eyes. They were banked fires but angry fires.

"You have no right to give me orders." False words, she thought, even as she spoke them. Yes, Urho had changed. She moved her gloved hand, and suddenly Urho grabbed it. His mouth tightened as his hand covered hers. Then he let go, allowing her hand to drop, as if the touch of it had disgusted him.

Without another glance in his direction, Dora walked out the front door and got into a jeep, her alpaca coat sweeping about her.

CHAPTER 17

At eight-thirty that morning as Claudia stood in the kitchen drinking her orange juice and staring out the window at the havoc the storm had created, the telephone rang. It was Richard. "Claudia, we're sending a jeep after you. The Press is operating today."

"What? Everything is shut down in Pierre Corners and Detroit. That's the latest I heard on the radio."

"I know. But Neil doesn't want to miss a Press run. He heard that both the News and Free Press aren't publishing. It seems like Detroit was the worst hit. And besides Neil has the governor's assurance that we can use all the National Guards manpower we need to get an edition out. So the word is GO!"

"How much time do I have to get ready? Alex didn't go to the dealership, can't get the car out of the garage. He's doing some bookkeeping now. You're really serious aren't you?"

"Yes, I'm serious. And you've got a half-hour. The jeep will pick you up at nine."

Just a half-hour, thought Claudia. Then she glanced at Jamie eating her oatmeal. "Mama, the radio said no school today. But I'd better study anyway and do some drawings. Can we study together?"

"Believe it or not honey, I have to work today. Maybe Daddy can help you. He's not going to work. There's too much snow in front of the garage."

Since their talk a few months ago, Alex had changed, for the better.

Claudia believed he needed to talk more about what happened to him as a child. He needed to talk more about her—. His father had blamed him for her death. There were many questions she needed to ask Alex. She had to pick the right time. Now Jamie brought her back with a plea. "First I want to make a big snowman. And Daddy can help me."

"We'll see." Claudia was constantly amazed at her daughter. She had so much talent as an artist, and so young. When she talked with Jamie, it was as if she were conversing with an adult, a small adult. Claudia smiled. Yes, her Jamie was smart. She had a gift. Matt better hurry up and build that Gifted School, so Jamie could get the schooling she deserved, because Jamie had one of the brightest and most innovative minds in her class.

And finally Claudia thought about the book Matt wanted her to write the book about gifted children. It could be a big step in the right direction for her. Yes, she'd do it. It was a promise she had made to Matt and herself. She'd be honest and thorough, a full complete story about the gifted. What would Alex think about it? Would he support her? Or would his hot temper flare up? No matter what, she'd write that book, it was a promise she would keep.

"When are you going to work?" Jamie asked.

"Soon. I must have sensed it, because I dressed for work this morning. Or maybe it was just habit or ESP."

"What's ESP?" Jamie asked.

"It's complicated. I'll explain that another time, promise. Now, I've got to find my boots."

"They're on the back steps. I'll get them."

Claudia thanked her daughter when she returned with the boots. Jamie had grown into a serious six-year old, soon to be seven. No more playing with dolls. She seemed to exist only for school, books, and her drawing. She looked at Jamie and saw Alex's green eyes, Alex's square jaw.

Alex walked into the kitchen, a note pad in his hand. "What's happening?"

"I'm going to work. Richard is sending a jeep to pick me up. Can you believe that?"

"That Liemus must be crazy. Everything is shut down tight. Even the Free Press and News aren't operating. What's he trying to prove?"

"I don't know. Maybe he thinks there should be one daily newspaper publishing.

Alex leaned forward, frowning, raising one fist and shaking it. When he spoke he snarled, "Damn, when are you going to put your family first?"

"It's not that Alex. My family is always first. But I can't say no to Richard. Not after all he has done for me. Not after he assigned me the gifted story and all those other front page stories. I can't let him down."

"But you can let us down."

"That's not fair."

"Well, if you're going to work, so am I. You'd better take Jamie with you."

"What? You've made up your mind to shovel your car out of the garage and go to the dealership—just like that?"

"Just like that."

The sound of the jeep's horn ended their conversation. "Jamie, get dressed, you're coming with me to the Press."

"I am? Great!"

In less than fifteen minutes the jeep deposited Claudia and Jamie in front of the Press building. From her vantage point at the switchboard, Freda was the first to greet them. "What do you think of this? Are we at the North Pole or what?" Then she glanced at Jamie. "And is that little one going to write the front page story for the Press?"

Jamie giggled. "Sure."

"I'd better get her on it right away. Have to check with Richard first," joked Claudia. That's when Urho came out of the advertising department. "No," he said.

Claudia held her breath. Suddenly her heart began to pound. Why was this happening when she saw him? "No?" she repeated.

"No, Jamie is going to work in the advertising department." He grinned.

"I am?" Jamie smiled.

"She has a terrific sense of design and color," Claudia said. Of course, you're assigning her a color ad, right?" Claudia smiled and went along with the game.

"She's that good?" Urho's hazel eyes regarded Jamie warily. "Let's see if we can find a drawing board for you young lady. "Follow me."

Claudia and Jamie did, and in a matter of minutes Urho had Jamie situated in a corner of the ad room with a graphic artist helping her. . Supplied with pencils, newsprint drawing paper and rulers, she was already sketching her first design, a delicate rose for a perfume ad. Jamie was involved in her work and didn't notice when Urho and Claudia walked out of the room and into the lobby. Several jeeps had deposited more reporters and ad men. Urho turned and faced Claudia. "What a mess. Can you believe this?" he asked.

"Yes, the storm is terrible," Claudia said.

"I don't mean the storm, but never mind. This day started all wrong for me." He fumbled in his jacket for a cigarette, removed one from his pack and then snapped his Zippo lighter, holding the cigarette close to it. After a few puffs he changed the subject.

"Jamie resembles you, especially her eyes."

"No, not the eyes, she has her father's eyes."

"Oh? I suppose I saw the resemblance at first glance, it's the smile in her eyes, not the color. But she has the eyes of an artist, and you of a writer."

"Really? I never heard that before."

"I just made it up." Then he grinned, trying to make things light. "But I should say an author's eyes, while I'm making things up. How is the so-called gifted book?"

"It's a big project, bigger than I thought. Even with all the material Matt's given me, there's a great deal of research involved. The other day I interviewed six gifted children."

"Don't forget Jamie." They had reached the newsroom and he stubbed out his cigarette in one of the elephant ashtrays on the file cabinet. In spite of the storm, someone had managed to bring in a coffee cake. Claudia guessed it was Freda. Clyde was at the coffee pot, sipping from his mug and nibbling on a slice of coffee cake. He tipped his cup to Claudia in greeting.

"Don't eat all the coffee cake," Urho warned. "We've got a hungry crew coming in. Bernie's been out for hours covering the storm. The least we can do is save him a piece of cake."

Clyde said, "I haven't been sitting around, just got back from the fire department, went on a wild run with them. Some old warehouse was blazing on the riverfront. Got some shots of that and then took more shots of the storm and what it's done to Pierre Corners."

"Good," Urho said, and left the newsroom.

Claudia walked to her desk, and when she saw Valley with Richard, she braced herself for another of Valley's stormy outbursts. Bet she gave the jeep driver hell when he stopped to pick her up, Claudia thought.

But Valley, dressed in another of her vintage wardrobe, an emerald green wool suit, was reminiscing with Richard about storm stories of the past. She waved her coffee mug at Richard. Claudia was sure that there was just coffee in the mug this time, because Valley appeared alert.

"Just like old times, eh?" Valley said. "Richard, this reminds me of the storm of '48. Remember that one? It was a beauty—snowed three days."

"Nope, it was a week," Richard corrected. "And it took a week to shovel us out, with the National Guards help, again!" Then he pulled out his watch from his vest pocket, checked it with the wall clock, nodded, and slipped it back into his pocket.

Claudia wondered how Richard managed to look so fresh in all this confusion—wearing a crisp white shirt, a gray suit with a vest, too?

"Used dog sleds, didn't we?" Valley asked.

"Yes, we did."

"And don't forget those St. Bernard dogs with their goodie kegs." Valley laughed.

"No, Valley, that was another time, another storm." Richard winked at Claudia. "Let's not get Claudia confused."

"Nothing can confuse me, not now. I've seen everything. The National Guards picking me up? How about that for starters? By the way, Richard, I brought along a new art designer, small of statue, but brilliant."

"Ah, so you brought Jamie with you."

"Hope you don't mind. She's in the ad room."

"No problem. Now we've got to get down to business. Just got word that the bureaucrats in Lansing are fighting over who's getting the snow-removal contract. It probably will be the one with the most markers."

"Markers?" Claudia asked and then her phone rang. "Wonder who's got a hot story for us on this cold, stormy morning?"

CHAPTER 18

Since his affair with Dora, Neil was acutely conscious of the brevity of life. He didn't want to waste one precious day, one precious hour away from her, and he felt every minute he spent bogged down in the water facility proposal was definitely minutes wasted.

Of course, he would receive an enormous amount of money for the Press Corporation land, and the site of the water facility, but he already had all the money he would ever need. He had thought briefly of having Urho take on the water facility project. But he immediately turned the idea down. Their relationship since Dora's divorce had not been amiable, not even cordial. It was strictly business, and they avoided each other whenever possible.

In five weeks the ground breaking for the water facility and he'll be there, of course. Yes, the millage passed yesterday. Neil knew it would, and he had Clyde take a photo of the mayor at the polls, that ran on the front page of today's paper. Now he scanned the front page. Yes, a clean front page. He knew his job was made easier by two factors—Richard and Urho. But Richard had to go. He was not in Neil's future plans. Neil thought that Richard was getting too power hungry. No, it wasn't his imagination. He knew about the meeting Richard had with Greta. What had she told him? Richard was sticking his nose where he had no business sticking it.

Richard also was getting too mouthy. He had ranted and raved at last month's staff meeting about the recent budget cuts and layoffs. Richard had said that the editorial department was seriously understaffed. His exact comments at the staff meeting were, "The Press was all screwed up and dissipated by a publisher that was doing everything else but publish a newspaper." It was met with mixed reaction by the staff.

Neil had heard rumors that Richard was thinking of bringing the Newspaper Guild union into the Press. Things were getting out of hand. Neil knew that the union wanted in, but he had stopped advances in the past, and wasn't about to give in to the union, now.

There was Greta and Urho, now Richard and the union. But he could handle Richard. Neil leaned back in his chair, pleased with himself. He'd fix that bastard's wagon. Now he swiveled around to look out the window at Main Street. Yes, April in Pierre Corners was a nice time of year, he thought.

He had accomplished quite a lot in the past six months. And getting the millage passed was the high point. After the water facility was built, then he could spend more time on the things he enjoyed: being with Dora, sailing his boat, and indulging in a occasional week in New York or Las Vegas. But he'd have to come to some agreement with Urho and soon. Yes, he was doing a good job handling the advertising department. There was more he'd have to do. He'd have to have a long talk with his son, and not about Dora. He was his son, damn!

Where is that Yiannis? Neil looked at his watch. He did say three. He got up from his chair and went to the bar, put ice in a glass, and added a generous measure of scotch. He had taken only a sip of the drink when the telephone rang. "Yes? Send him right up. I've been waiting for him." Neil sighed. He glanced at his watch, ten minutes late. That old Greek must be losing his touch. He never was late. In a matter of minutes there was a light tap at his door.

"Come in."

In greeting Neil, Yiannis said, "The millage was approved. Also I like the photo of the mayor at the polls on the front page. It's a very nice touch." He sank into the leather chair opposite Neil, leaned over and dropped a folder on his desk. "Here are the drawings for the proposed water facility. I consulted with your men from New York.

They had a few good ideas." Yiannis smiled.

"More than a few. Can I get you a drink—scotch—bourbon?"

"No. Too early in the day for me."

Neil looked in the folder. "Are you sure this proposed plant can produce nine million gallons of water a day?"

"Certainly, more if necessary."

"I don't want any more dry spells—like we had last summer—and no more depending on Detroit. I've even prepared my speech for the ground breaking."

"You're sure the mayor won't mind?"

"Damn the mayor!" Neil said, placing a cigar in his mouth. "I'm the one who started the ball rolling on the millage. And the Press owns the land." He emphasized his words by shaking his cigar in Yiannis' direction.

"How much time do you need to build this thing?" Neil shoved the folder toward Yiannis.

"Hard to say—depends on my contractors—depends on the suppliers. I won't tell you a date and then not have it completed by that date. But if all goes according to schedule—we're looking at— maybe six months."

"Not good enough. You're talking November. You must slice off some time."

"I'll do my best I always do. My word is my reputation."

"I know—I know." Slumped in his chair, staring wistfully at the glass of scotch on his desk, afraid that Yiannis was about to tell him something that would disturb his complacency even more, Neil decided that a bit of gruffness might speed the conversation along. "I know about your reputation. That's why I hired you. And I know you'll do your best. But sometimes best is not good enough. I have to have dates. I'm a newspaperman, I deal in deadlines. Understand?"

Yiannis looked at him. "Yes, I understand. I have to make some inquiries, then I'll give you some dates. I'm not in the newspaper business, but I too work on deadlines." With this he got up. "I have things to do, Neil. This meeting is over as far as I'm concerned. Good day." He closed the door softly after him.

Evidently, overseeing the completion of a water facility in Pierre Corners was not going to be as short and easy a job as Neil had thought. Who did that Greek think he was? He had deadlines? He didn't know the meaning of deadlines. Now that they were understaffed at the Press, he had his hands full. Then Neil reached for his phone and dialed Richard's office. "Richard? Listen I've been thinking about that award ceremony in Lansing. Yes, the one you and Claudia plan to attend tomorrow. Forget it! Yes, I mean it! I can't afford to have both of you gone on a busy day. You know we're shorthanded. Call the Michigan Press Association, give them our regrets and tell them to send us the plaque and check. What? That's an order, Richard."

Richard shouted his reply over the phone, "Neil, this is too much! I won't stand for it—I—."

And that's when Neil hung up the phone.

PART TWO
ALEX KALI

CHAPTER 19

After work, Claudia boarded the bus on the corner, but she wasn't going home. Jamie was at the local community center and Claudia had promised she would meet her there. The center was only two blocks from their house. The walk home will do me good. What a day this has been, thought Claudia. First her old car breaking down and then, what? Through the bus window she watched the fog roll along the Detroit River. It was getting denser by the minute. Then she thought about Richard and his strange behavior. Richard, who never closed his office door, had not only closed it today but also locked it. When she stopped by to talk to him about the trip to Lansing tomorrow, she had to knock twice before she could get in. Finally he opened the door, a frown on his face. She said, "Just wanted to check on when we're leaving for Lansing tomorrow."

"What? You mean the awards ceremony?" He glanced at his watch. "We should get an early start. How about nine?"

"Fine. See you tomorrow." Richard made a point of locking the door after her. Strange, thought Claudia. And there was something about his expression, something about his eyes— or was it all her imagination? Did she see things that weren't there? What was happening to her? Maybe living two lives was making her paranoid. Two lives—one at the Press and the one with Alex.

For the past nine years she had this fear that she would die as her father died; trying to hold off a monster that was after her. Her father had died when the monster struck. Like father, like daughter?

The next stop Claudia got off. When she turned the corner she saw Jamie sitting on the steps of the community center. Claudia's stomach began to growl with hunger, and she remembered that she hadn't eaten lunch. She had been too nervous to eat—thinking about tomorrow's award ceremony. Then thoughts of dinner came to mind. What was she going to fix? No much in the refrigerator or cupboards, she thought. It's going to be tuna casserole, not exactly Alex's favorite dish. Now she spotted Jamie.

"Mom, Mom, do you know what the teacher said about my drawing?"

"Yes, excellent! She said you were a born artist. But why the sad face, honey?"

"Gee, I can't fool you. Didn't I look sad enough?"

"Nope. Enough games, young lady. We have to get home and make dinner."

"You're right, she liked my drawing. Held it up for all the class to see. What's for dinner?"

"Tuna casserole."

"Oh no, Daddy doesn't like that."

"Well, that's all we have in the house."

"Race you home," Jamie said. "Maybe we can get home before it rains." She looked up. "It's too foggy to see the sky."

"Where do you get all that energy? "Don't get too far ahead of me. Yes, it does look like April showers."

"Bring May flowers," Jamie said.

In less than ten minutes Jamie was in her room putting her drawings away and Claudia was in the kitchen opening up a can of tuna. "Bring your drawings in here, honey. I'd like to see them again."

And that's how Alex found them a half hour later. The aroma of tuna and macaroni baking in the oven filled the kitchen. Alex flung himself into a chair without taking off his damp raincoat, out of breath. He clenched his hand into a fist and pounded the table. "A nut almost slid into the side of my car. Why do they let those crazies on the road? He said the road was slippery—as if I didn't know that.

What did he expect in this pouring rain?" He bent over to remove his wet rubber boots.

"Hi, Daddy, see my new drawings?" Jamie giggled.

"Keep it down will you? I've had a bitch of a day, lost two car sales. Two— that I've been working on for a week. And then this bastard almost runs into me."

"Alex, please. Must you use that language?" Claudia looked at him. She suspected that he had been drinking. He often stopped at the bar near the dealership before coming home. She got to her feet and crossed over to the stove, opened the oven and with a large wooden spoon stirred the casserole.

Alex watched her. "Not that crap, again!"

A shudder went through Claudia, working across her shoulders then down along her spine. Her hand continued stirring the casserole.

"Mom, tell him about—." Jamie's mouth tightened; her hands folded narrow pleats into her cotton dress. She bit down on her lower lip. Finally she said, "Daddy, Mom's going to Lansing tomorrow to get an award."

"What's she taking about?"

There was a tension coming from Claudia when she turned to face him. "I told you. Remember? I'm going to Lansing to pick up my award for the series about the Gifted."

He walked to the refrigerator and got himself a beer. "So—big deal. Does that mean more money?'

"Yes, there's a check with the plaque. I think it's $500."

"Peanuts."

"It's something. I'm going with Richard."

"You're not going anywhere with Richard." He finished his beer. He wiped his mouth with the back of his hand.

"Sure she is," Jamie said. Her look was as dark as her father's. Her green eyes glared at him.

"Shut up and get out of here before I smack you."

Jamie fled to her room in tears.

Claudia didn't look at him. She returned to the stove, got two pot holders and took the bubbling casserole from the oven, placing it on the counter. A sharp crash of thunder filled the room. Claudia said, "I'm going to Lansing."

"You're not going anywhere."

Then Claudia made the mistake of saying, "You're jealous of my work—jealous of this award." That's when Jamie came back into the kitchen.

Alex's back toward them, he reached in the cupboard and took out a fifth of whiskey. Opening it, he then held the bottle to his lips and the brown liquid streamed down his throat. He saw Jamie. Tearfully she pleaded. "Daddy, please don't—."

"Didn't I tell you to get the hell out of here?" And with the back of his hand he slapped Jamie across the face and sent her sprawling on the floor. Tears spilling from her eyes, she held her injured cheek and ran to her room.

A violent shiver of revulsion snapped through Claudia as she realized what Alex had done. He had never struck Jamie—never, until now.

"Why did you do that? You're drunk."

"Listen bitch. Don't call me drunk." He grabbed her arm.

Claudia could hear her heart beating although she stood very still. "Take your hand off me."

Alex let her go, swept his arm across the counter and the casserole came crashing to the floor—tuna, macaroni and pieces of glass at Claudia's feet.

"That for your tuna casserole!" He grabbed her and slammed her up against the wall. The back of her head hit the plaster with a sharp crack, and she struggled to remain above the darkness that seeped in behind her eyes. He clutched her throat with his left hand, pinned her in place and then slapped the side of her head, back and forth, back and forth. She must not faint! She must not! Then slowly, deliberately she lifted her knee and slammed in into his groin. His eyes went wild he let out a high-pitched yelp. Claudia kicked him again. His face was suddenly as white as the refrigerator he collided into. He looked down at himself in astonishment.

Claudia did not wait for his expression of amazement to change into agony and anger. Run—run—run. Outside the thunder cracked and lightning streaked through the windows turning the curtains a bloody red. She bolted for the back door. She had to get out of this house. She could hear Alex's groans and curses and clumsy movements, wondering if he had sufficient strength to overtake her.

"You bitch!" Holding himself with one hand, he lashed out at her, grabbed the front of her blouse. She wrenched away from his grasp, and he was left holding a portion of her blouse. Claudia's shoulders were covered ridiculously by the blouse's long sleeves. The amber beads in her pocket spilled on the floor. She backed away, her breasts heaving. She knew it was now possible for him to kill her and the thought made her gag with horror. She reached up, tried to claw, scratch, rip at his eyes. He pulled her down to the floor. "If you make a move, I'll kill you." His eyes were fastened on hers.

He licked his lips. "Do you understand?" His voice was deep and it did not waver. "It was a neat trick, kicking me in the balls. Where did you learn that, bitch?"

Claudia moaned. "Please."

"I'll have you begging." His eyes were still hard and cold. "Now I'll teach you a lesson, a good one. So I'm jealous, am I?" He punched her, in her face, her chest, bringing tears to her eyes again and again. He had pinned her right hand behind her. It was beginning to go numb. With her left hand she scratched his face. It bled. Alex seized her wrist, squeezing and twisting it, bending it back. Claudia cried out in agony. She said, "I wish you were dead—dead."

He grinned and squeezed harder.

With a great effort she fought off the darkness that threatened her. She couldn't move. Her chest was painfully bruised. Her mouth was dry and sour. Their breathing seemed to fill the room like the wind, yet she could detect the ticking of the kitchen clock. She groaned— "Die, die!"

"Want me dead, do you?" He twisted her arm again. Claudia cried out. And then in the distance she heard Alex's voice—"Don't pull that fainting shit on me."

* * *

Hours later Claudia lifted her head and carefully looked around the kitchen. From where she was lying on the floor, she could see the pieces of glass, the macaroni and tuna splattered on the floor, and her amber beads. Slowly she raised herself to her feet by sliding her back against the wall behind her. And at last, she was standing, held up by the wall.

Gasping, shaking and panting, she clung to the walls, making her way to a chair. She fell into it. And then she looked at the overturned planter and the soil and aloe plant on the table. Her eyes scanned the room, saw the empty whiskey bottle on the counter, smelled its strong odor. Finally she eased out of the chair and began to shuffle groggily to the bathroom, gently holding her left side.

Bending over the wash basin, she splashed cold water on her face and looked into the mirror—bruised skin, bloodshot eyes, a dark puffy ring under the left eye, possible broken ribs and her wrist hung at an odd angle. Was that broken too? She could not stop shaking, the pain was unbearable.

Then her thoughts flew to Jamie. Where was Jamie? What had he done to her? Suddenly her body was racked with spasms, and finally she turned and vomited into the basin. She bent far over and retched, ugly sounds coming from her, and then she fainted.

When she woke, Alex was standing over her.

"Don't hit me, don't."

"I'm taking you to the hospital. You fell down the stairs, understand?" He looked sober now. "If you say anything else—I'll kill you." He lifted her into his arms and it was as if she was underwater and could not swim. She struggled to breathe and then darkness. Fight, fight! Her life was a battleground—a secret one. Only she knew of the battles, and Alex. There were invisible bars around her. She was trapped!

Alex dressed her and carried her to the car.

CHAPTER 20

Jamie wasn't a cry baby. She had tried so hard not to cry at school. During recess when all the kids were at the playground, she hid in the girls' lavatory and couldn't stop crying. She didn't want the other kids to think she was a baby. She wasn't.

That morning her teacher had asked her if there was anything the matter. She said no. She said she had a cold, that's why her eyes were red. But the feeling was in there, deep inside her, a scared, worried feeling. She was worried for her Mom who was in the hospital. Scared of Daddy who would be home when she got there. The thought of yesterday made Jamie's breath come faster. At times she couldn't breathe at all, her chest began to heave. She gulped down air.

Alone in the girls' lavatory, she thought. I can't go home. I've got to stop crying. But she couldn't. Daddy had hit her, had knocked her down. That was the first time he had ever hit her. And then he punched Mom, again and again. She couldn't make Daddy stop. She couldn't. She was afraid, so she ran and hid in her closet, shut her eyes tight, put her hands over her ears, and prayed. That's where her father had found her the next morning. He said, "Get up and get ready for school."

At the breakfast table she had gathered enough courage to ask, "Where's Mom?"

"She's in the hospital. She'll be okay."

That's when Jamie closed her eyes and let out a mournful wail. She sobbed and shook and gasped for breath.

"Shut up!" Alex said. "I said she would be all right."

Jamie leaped from her chair, grabbed her coat and lunch and raced out the door.

* * *

After school, Jamie walked home alone. She pushed open the back door and saw him sitting at the kitchen table a water glass filled with whiskey in his hand. The copper pots were back on the wall. The kitchen floor was clean— not a trace of last night's disaster. Then she looked at her father and her breathing got fast again. She must not think of last night, she must try to think of something else.

Alex said, "I told you to go next door. I'm going out and I won't return for a while." His voice sounded strained.

Jamie tried to swallow, "All right." She put a thumb into her mouth, it was so comforting.

"Don't do that. You're not a baby!"

Quickly she removed the guilty thumb and hid it in the folds of her cotton dress.

"That's better. Now get your things together. You're going next door and you're staying there overnight."

* * *

Minutes later Alex frowned as he watched his daughter walk to the neighbor's house. It was hard to imagine that at one time Jamie had been a happy baby. He could still remember vividly the feelings of that night, the night Jamie was born. That's when the nightmares began. Was that a sign for him? Alex brooded over that question while he sat in the kitchen, poured himself another drink. He tried to remember what the nightmares had been about, but he could not. That wasn't unusual. Most nights since Jamie's birth he suffered through horrible dreams from which he'd wake in terror, heart pounding, and mouth dry. He had to escape Pa. Pa was causing those nightmares.

Alex grew up in a rat and roach infested flat in one of Detroit's slum area. Even now, even here in Pierre Corners, in his kitchen, he could close his eyes and see every detail of that long ago place—mice in his bed, cockroaches on the kitchen table. He could still see in his mind's eye the mice. As a child, Alex dreaded falling asleep because that's when the mice found refuge in his thin blanket and crawled on his legs, over his body. Even now, when darkness came and he was in the bedroom he began to imagine those creatures crawling on him, skittering over his body, on his legs, on his face. And yet, the bedroom had been a haven from his father's beatings. The shabby bedroom had been his escape from his father's fists. His father would say, "You're bad Alex. You killed her. You have to be punished!" He was terrified of this man. Suddenly Alex wailed, "Claudia, he made me do it. Pa made me do it to you. He called you a bitch, he beat you. Claudia, it wasn't me."

Alex was back in his childhood surroundings. The dreary flat came to life, the old scuffed furniture, the peeling wallpaper, the torn linoleum, the cockroaches coming through the walls, crawling over the bread and cheese on the kitchen table. Suddenly in Alex's vision, his father entered the room. "Pa, you never forgave me. And you never took me to the cemetery—never to see her grave—never put flowers on it—never."

Now Alex didn't bother with a glass. He put the whiskey bottle to his lips, closed his eyes, tilted his head back, and gulped down the liquor. He felt dizzy. He lay with his face on his arms on the table. By two o'clock in the morning, Alex was asleep.

Something woke him. Was it his imagination or did something slither over his arm and on his face? It went for his mouth. He pressed his lips together. He brushed frantically at his face, but he couldn't shake it off. Finally, no, there was nothing, nothing. He shuddered.

"Claudia, I'll fix everything. You'll see, things will be different, better, I promise. I'll fix that son of a bitch, that father." He staggered across the room. When he got to the bedroom, he collapsed on the bed. Hours later, he woke from another bad dream. He was sweating, shuddering, clutching the blanket with one hand and punching the pillow with the other. He gasped. At first he didn't know where he was. He sat up, felt the bed with one hand, squinted at the clock on the nightstand—eleven o'clock, an hour before noon. Gradually he oriented himself. He tried to remember what day it was, where Claudia was, where Jamie was. Finally he got out of bed, raised the shades, went into the bathroom and showered. Then he remembered—Claudia was in the hospital. He must call her, go to her. He had to tell her something important. Quickly he dialed the hospital number, asked for Claudia's room. He finally heard her voice. "Claudia, are you alone?"

"No, I'm not. Richard is here from the office."

"Listen, and listen good don't tell anyone about what happened. It was an accident, you fell down the stairs. Understand?"

"Yes, I understand."

"I'm having Jamie stay next door until you get back. Do you know when you're coming home?"

"No, I don't. The doctor hasn't said."

"Well find out, I'll try to get there later."

"All right," Claudia hung up the phone. Richard got up from the bedside chair and said. "Claudia, I'd better get going. I just wanted to show you the plaque you won. It's going right at the top on our wall of honor." He grinned. "And I want to give you this check."

"Thank you

"That was quite a nasty accident. A couple of broken ribs, too?"

"Yes."

"Well, I'll get out of here and let you get some rest. Take care," he said as he closed the door after him.

At six o'clock that evening Alex backed out of the dealership parking lot. Two blocks later when he turned off Main Street, he saw Woodoaks Hospital ahead. It looked unreal, like a mirage in the setting sun. The rambling building the stately oaks and foundation-hugging shrubs did not look as garish as he remembered it. It was the newest building in Pierre Corners—one of Yiannis Miteas' construction projects.. That Greek's got his finger in every pie, thought Alex. In its own way, the hospital was rather elegant.

Minutes later in the hospital room he glanced at a nurse at Claudia's bedside. "Time for your pill," the nurse said. Her uniform strained over her buxom figure. She gave Claudia a pill and a glass of water. Then she turned when she saw Alex. "Don't stay too long and tire her. She needs rest." The nurse closed he door softly as she left.

"I'm not tired," Claudia said to Alex.

"Listen – I can go no big deal. You didn't tell anyone about—?"

"No, I didn't." And then the telephone rang. She reached for it and said, "Hello."

"What is it?" she asked. "Yes, I told you when you were here, just after Richard came. Yes, that's what happened. I fell down the stairs."

Alex watched Claudia. He moved from the window and sat in the chair next to her bed. He saw her close her eyes, listening. He glanced at the roses on her nightstand.

Finally Claudia said into the receiver. "I'm sorry, I have to hang up. Someone is here, now. Goodbye." She placed the phone back on the nightstand and gathered the sheet around her, pulled it up about her shoulders. She was shivering.

"Who was that?" Alex asked.

"Valley."

"What did that drunk want?"

"Nothing."

"I don't think so. She was trying to get information from you about the accident, wasn't she? And who got you those roses?"

"The news staff."

"Are you sure it wasn't your boss' son?"

"What are you talking about?"

"Has he been here?"

"No."

He paced the small room, looked out the window. "What did Valley really want? She was after something, wasn't she?"

"Yes, yes. But I didn't tell her anything."

"Good, I want you home by tomorrow."

She stared at him, shut her eyes opened her mouth to speak. Finally, she said, "Home? I don't think so."

"What the hell are you talking about?"

She took a deep breath. "When I get out of this hospital, I'm not coming home. I'm taking Jamie and leaving. I don't want you starting on Jamie—the way you started on —. I'm leaving."

"Like hell you are." He stared at her for a moment. "Over my dead body."

And then the door flew open and John Nikropolus said, "Did I hear someone mention dead body? I'm just the man for you." He walked in and smiled at Claudia and Alex. He was the owner of Nikropolus Funeral Home on Monroe Street, in Detroit's Greektown. "Little brother," said the tall barrel-chested man as he gave Alex a bear hug. He then leaned over and kissed Claudia on the cheek and ceremoniously presented her with a long stemmed red rose wrapped in green tissue paper. "For you, Kukla," he said using her nickname.

Claudia could hear the concern in John's voice and see the compassion in his eyes as he looked at her, bruised and bandaged.

"You might have had a dead body—me," Alex began. "The other day during that storm, a crazy man almost rammed into my car."

"Had he been drinking? There's a lot of that going on. A car is a deadly weapon in a drunk's hands." Then John turned to Claudia. "Looks like you had quite a fall. I went to the dealership and one of the guys told me of you're accident. I'm very sorry."

"Thank you for the rose and for being here."

He stroked his thick black mustache. "No problem." He smiled an easy warm smile.

Alex glanced from Claudia to John. He knew that John was a fun–loving man but he seemed to feel that his public image as funeral director had to be sober and serious at all times. Claudia reached over for John's hand. John raised her hand to his lips and gently kissed it.

"Hey, watch that!" Alex said with a grin. "Some bedside manner you have."

"Aren't we brothers? Listen kid, if I hadn't dug you out of that cardboard box in the alley many years ago, we wouldn't be family. And God knows where you'd be today. Besides I wanted to see Claudia smile. She has a beautiful smile,"

Claudia smiled again and placed her hand on John's arm. "It's sweet of you to say that John."

An hour later while the two men were deep in conversation and

154

Claudia lay listlessly in bed, the closing chimes sounded in the hospital.

"They're playing our song, brother," John said.

"We'd better make tracks."

"Well, I'll leave you two alone for a second," John said, as he hugged Claudia. At the door he said, "See you soon. Alex, take care of this lovely young lady."

Alex nodded.

Meanwhile as the main entrance doors of the hospital swung open automatically, Urho rushed through them, glancing at his watch. He had only minutes to see Claudia before visiting hours ended. Then he heard the closing bell chime. He clutched a small bouquet of violets, wrapped in tissue paper, and raced down the corridor. His head down, coat collar up semi-hiding his face, he hurried to her room. Down the hospital hallway, Alex strolled to the main entrance. Unaware of each other, the two men crossed each other's path. Both were deep in thought. Alex raced out into the night heading for the parking lot.

Moments later, Urho walked into Claudia's room. He placed the violets beside her and smiled. "Hope you're feeling better. And then on an impulse, he bent over and kissed her gently on the lips.

"Oh!" Claudia's eyes lit.

"I can't stay, just heard the closing chimes. But I had to see that you were all right. I know you didn't fall. Then with a hint of anger in his voice, he said, "You have to get away from that man and soon." He reached for her hand and held it. "Soon."

Claudia was silent. She just stared at Urho, tears welling in her eyes.

* * *

Later in his car, Alex brought the engine to life, dialed the radio, and sat for a while, staring at the flow of traffic out of the hospital parking lot. So she's going to leave me, he thought. Just let her try. He eased out of the parking lot onto Main Street and the cars flashed past in an endless stream.

Outside his window, the full moon shone. He felt as if the moon was shining through him. Sweat tricked down his forehead. He drove a short distance on Main Street—and in his mind his father's voice shouted, "You killed her. I'll teach you a lesson you'll never forget!"

"I didn't, honest Pa—I didn't!" Then suddenly a wild rage rose from deep within him. His eyes blazed with anger. He pressed down on the accelerator frantically, racing, racing. His hands trembled as he gripped the steering wheel.

"I'll fix everything, you'll see Claudia. It will be different. I promise. You can't leave me!" And speeding down Main Street, racing home, he said, "Pa, you son of a bitch, you screwed up my life!"

CHAPTER 21

What had started Neil on this economy crunch? Richard thought about Neil as he sat in his office on this hot afternoon. It's unusual weather for May. He mopped his forehead with his handkerchief, unbuttoned his shirt collar and removed his tie. No air conditioning, another edict from Neil. A small fan on Richard's desk slowly moved the air in the closed office. And this heat wasn't helping matters. Almost like last year, but thank God, there's water. He checked his pocket watch. The dispatcher was late again. Richard paced.

Even through the closed door, the sound of the newsroom's telephones and typewriters filtered through the walls. Finally Richard sat down at his desk and began sorting galley proofs. He was convinced that Neil's behavior wasn't normal. Of course, the source of this behavior was still unknown, but Richard believed that Neil was a deeply disturbed man. Richard leaned back in his swivel chair and mentally counted out the possible motives for this behavior.

The union? It wasn't a threat, and he knew Neil would never allow a union to get into the Press. Dora? She was still in New York, and Greta wasn't giving Neil the divorce he wanted. The water plant? It was moving along, ahead of schedule with Yiannis making the decisions. True to his word, Neil had spoken at the ground breaking.

Then Richard's mind went back to the union. Yes, that's when it all began. Neil even accused Richard of passing out the union bulletins that morning a month ago. He would never forget the look on Neil's face when he saw the bulletins on the desks of every reporter and ad man that Monday morning. That was the beginning. Neil swore he'd sell the Press first, rather than see a union come in.

Richard shook his head, stroked his beard. Neil would never sell the Press. It meant too much to him. He glanced at his watch, "Damn, where is that dispatcher?" A late dispatcher was just another problem that Richard didn't need at this time.

Lately Neil seemed to grab at anything to make Richard look bad. That's why Richard had made a practice of locking his office. Not that he had anything to hide. He knew that Neil was poised, ready to attack, and he wasn't going to give him any reason to, not if he could help it. During Neil's campaign against the union, and his bid to stymie the union's drive, he raised the threat of dismissal if anyone was discovered attending union meetings.

Richard wasn't worried. However, their easy, friendly business relationship was a thing of the past. They had a contract, binding and legal. More than the gentleman's agreement and hand shake they started out with so many years ago. Although Richard was not involved with the union, he knew that union meetings were being held secretly. Once, Bernie had mentioned the meetings, in his off hand, casual manner. The newsroom atmosphere during the first stages of the union's infiltration was like a battle camp. It was a battle that Neil fought with all his resources.

Richard unconsciously massaged the stub of his severed thumb. The lost thumb—his mind raced to that day in Grand Rapids, the print shop, the presses, his thumb cut off, his mother's tears, the pain. Then he heard a knock on his door. The dispatcher, in his usual Army fatigues, shirt open to the waist, Army boots. His olive green sweatband was damp, his face sullen, sweating. With one hand he wiped off his brow, with the other he handed Richard an envelope.

"What took so long?"

"The boats are running late, too many freighters on the river."

"Everything in here— galley proofs, page proofs, photos?"

"Sure, got it from the shop foreman, personally."

"With that get up, looks like a war is on," Richard said.

"Who knows? Have to be prepared. Don't forget there was a Sputnik orbiting the earth." Then he was off, running out the back door.

Richard walked to the elevator with the dispatch envelope under his arm. He had to face Neil, listen to his bitching.

"What was the holdup?" Neil asked as he carefully stripped the cellophane from his Havana cigar. He lighted it with a brass elephant lighter, blew a plume of smoke at the ceiling, and sat down.

Richard sat uncomfortably in the chair facing Neil and slid the dispatch envelope on the desk. "Same old excuses. The boats were backed up."

Neil frowned, chewed on his cigar, and glanced at Richard. Then quickly, painlessly, he said, "I'm selling the Press. Let the new owners fight with delays—fight with the union. I'm getting out. I've got a good offer, one I can't refuse."

Richard's blue eyes widened behind his horn-rimmed glasses. "What the hell are you talking about?" He fumbled for his pocket watch. "I don't like jokes, Neil."

Neil walked over to the bar, poured himself a measure of scotch—then turned and faced Richard. "It's no joke. A toast to a good sale," he said lifting his glass.

Richard sat numb in his chair, his eyes darting around the room. "Quit kidding."

"I'm serious. I told you I'd sell the Press if that damn union got a foothold."

"But the union hasn't gotten in—and I don't think it will. You're talking about your life—my life. You can't sell."

"I can do damn well what I please. I'm not getting any younger life is too damn short to waste any of it."

"Stop talking like that, you've got a lot of years ahead of you. And so do I."

Neil's face tightened. He shook his head and said in an angry voice. "The years go too fucking fast. There's no time at all. I want what time I have to spend my way. And that does not mean a union in MY paper, calling the shots."

"You're not making sense."

"I'm not? Well, maybe this will make sense. I have a surprise for you. See that contract on my desk, our contract? Well, it's worthless. Had my attorney go over it—the same one that set it up in the first place." Neil grinned. "That man knows his contracts, and knows how to make them work to my advantage. You're out Richard. I know you've been working with the union behind my back. I know!"

Richard stood. "My God, Neil, what are you saying? I know nothing about the union, you have my word. And, as for our contract, it's binding. All these years, Neil, remember?"

Neil reached over and picked up the contract and ripped it in pieces. "That's how binding it is, Richard."

"You bastard, you're not getting rid of me that fast."

"Richard, get the hell out of my building." Neil ran his fingers through his white mane, smoothing his immaculate hair. "I want your ass out of my office, now!"

"I'll fight. You can't get rid of me that easily." Richard shook a finger at him. His hand trembled.

"Face it you've outlived your usefulness at the Press. I'm selling the Press, and I don't want any dead wood to botch the deal." He looked at his watch. "I'm a busy man, got a paper to put out—for the time being—that is—so get the hell out of here."

Richard glared at Neil. Was he having a nightmare? This wasn't really happening. Then he said, "Mark my words, this is NOT over." And then he stormed out of Neil's office, slamming the door after him. In the elevator, an enraged Richard had only one thought. He wanted to kill Neil.

When Richard stepped out of the elevator he saw a tall, muscular policeman standing in front of his office. Richard's eyes lingered on the gun in the officer's holster. His neck ached, his mouth was dry. With the tip of his tongue he wet his lips. "What's going on officer?"

"Sorry, Mr. Lucavate, orders from Mr. Liemus."

"'What?" And then he saw the padlock on his office door. Suddenly he was out of control. He banged on the door, kicked it with a fury. How dare Neil do this! How dare he! The final insult was when Tessie and Clyde walked by and Clyde aimed his camera at Richard. "Make a good shot for tomorrow's front page," he said.

Tessie giggled.

"Get the hell out of my way," Richard said, pushing them.

"Watch it old man," Clyde said.

Gasping, shaking, cursing, Richard stumbled out the back door. That son of a bitch, that Neil, Richard thought, racing out to his car. He is not going to get away with this. I know too much, I know too many secrets.

* * *

Up in his penthouse, Neil watched from his back windows as Richard raced to his car. He gloated. He could not stand to have that short, bearded man in his building a second longer. Richard sold him out to the union. Neil sat behind his desk, confused. He should be feeling great, but a nervous stomach told him he wasn't. This was supposed to be one of his good days, one of his best days. He had gotten rid of the enemy, hadn't he? When would the happy times come? When? Damn, where was his Dora? He'd call her. She had to be here with him. What was she doing in New York?

But first things first! He'd have to finish this Richard business. He'd dictate a bulletin for the staff. He reached for his Dictaphone. "May 4, 1961—To all staff members: As you know we're not only are a newspaper, but a family. That means as a family we must project a budget, and as a newspaper, we must be solvent, show a profit, each and every month.

For the past three months we have NOT shown a profit. Not once. If we can't show a sales increase, either in advertising or circulation, we must cut expenses. That is where we stand now. We have begun an austerity program and I have taken a good hard look at each department to decide where immediate savings can be initiated. And also to decide where we can cut out staff.

Richard knows the situation and he has decided to take an early retirement, and I accepted his offer, of course with a feeling of personal regret. We go back a long way." Neil smiled, and continued dictating. "Effective this month we no longer will be the Orange Paper. Our costs are an additional $100 a ton for orange newsprint, and we can't afford it.

"And on another note, habitual tardiness and absenteeism will not be tolerated. If you can't come to work on time and can't be here every day, we can't afford you on our staff. Understood? My only regret is that in Richard I have lost a good company man, and a good friend in the business. The Press will never be the same without him."

Neil flicked off the Dictaphone and played back his message. He leaned back in his chair, crossed his hands behind his head, and smiled.

CHAPTER 22

Valley looked into her rear view mirror as she backed into a space in the parking lot behind the Press and saw Richard pull out of the lot, his tires squealing.

"What the hell?" she said. She rushed into the newsroom and demanded an explanation from Bernie. "What's happening? Richard drove off like a wild man."

Bernie wiped his brow with the back of his hand. "Hot as hell in here." Then he sighed. "Sit down, I'll tell you all about what happened to Richard."

"What?"

Then Bernie talked and Valley listened. She was a good listener it was both her blessing and her curse. Being a good listener was an asset to a reporter. It was Valley's business to listen attentively to all sorts of people. Now she listened as Bernie told her about Richard. Yesterday she had known nothing about Neil's plans to fire Richard, and now she knew almost everything. Actually it was more than she really cared to know.

Speaking so softly that Valley had to lean forward to hear him, Bernie said, "I don't know how in the hell Tessie knew about it, but she did. She was telling us the news at the very moment Neil fired Richard. By the way, your favorite police officer is guarding Richard's office. Remember, he was the one who drove you home?

Ignoring Bernie's last remark, Valley said, "Why did that bastard fire Richard?" She was furious. She ran her fingers through her long hair and then turned to Bernie. "I don't think we've heard the last of Richard. He'll be back, one way or the other."

"What does that mean?"

"I—I don't know." Valley sensed the awkwardness of this conversation. "Maybe the staff needs time to adjust to this situation. Maybe—."

"What are you talking about? Situation—bullshit. Richard was canned, booted out of the Press. Do you understand?'

"I understand."

"Well Valley, that isn't the half of it. We also have an important bulletin." He waved it in the air.

"From Himself?"

"No."

"Who's it from?"

"You've got a copy on your desk. Read it." And with this Bernie reached for his tobacco pouch and slowly filled his pipe.

"Okay," said Valley, pulling out the bulletin from its envelope. She began to read:

"The Liemus hatchet has struck. After more than 25 years of loyal service to the Press, Richard Lucavate has been fired. If Liemus can fire him, how secure are your jobs? Will you be next? The only protection you have is to join United Newspapers International (UNI). If you're a UNI member, the Press must have a solid reason before you can be released. Vote UNI into the Press before you get fired. Vote UNI and you will have job security. Richard was NOT an UNI member. Where is he today? Who will be next? YOU?"

Valley put the bulletin on her desk. "Where did this crap come from?"

"How do I know?" Bernie replied. "Hell, I don't know everything! The bulletin was on my desk when I got here this morning. I don't like this." Bernie frowned and gently patted the strands of hair over his bald spot.

"Himself won't stand for this," Valley said. "The union tried this a few years ago and got nowhere."

"I know." Bernie said.

Even before Neil's memo about Richard's retirement had reached the staff, the story of his dismissal had buzzed from desk to desk, department to department, office to office. But all Valley could think of was Claudia.

She had visited Claudia at the hospital yesterday, and from the bruises on her face, it did not look like she fell down the stairs. She knew a battered woman when she saw one because she'd written about them and seen them often enough. That bastard Alex had done that to Claudia.

Claudia was also on someone else's mind. As he read through and tore the union bulletin into pieces, Urho paced his office. He had to do something about Claudia. He would not allow that animal, that Alex, to beat her again. Not if he could help it. He belonged behind bars. Claudia had to be taken care of, and he was going to do it.

* * *

Off in the newsroom, Bernie leaned over Valley's desk. "Are you all right?"

"I'm all right." Valley threaded paper into her typewriter. But she was miserable. Why is this world so screwed up? Richard fired, Claudia in pain, living with a monster, a union attempting to come into the Press. It's enough to turn a gal back to drink, thought Valley. Then she smiled. She had been very good lately, staying away from the bottle. And it was all because of Claudia. Now it was her turn to help her friend.She heard Urho's steps before she saw him, before his quick strides reached them. There was a deep frown on his face.

"I've got a memo," Urho said. "I usually don't deliver them, but this is important."

"From the union?" Bernie asked. Then with a slow smile he said, "Only kidding."

"No, this one is from up stairs." He eyes shot to the ceiling, to his father's penthouse office.

"Now what?" Valley asked. She glanced at the memo.

"Holy Cow!" Bernie exclaimed. "Read this, on second thought don't read this. It's a sure fire way to get a heart attack."

"Shut up, Bernie, let me read," Valley said. And she picked up the memo.

"Protect your best interests. United Newspapers International will sink you. If UNI gets voted into the Press, you would not automatically keep the same wages and benefits you now enjoy. The wages and benefits you now take for granted would be subject to bargaining between the Press and UNI. In some cases your wages might be reduced.

And when the company and union do not agree, a strike occurs. While striking, your job security is nil and your earnings are ZERO. Your best job security is what you have now, but if the UNI gets in, all will change, and your job will be on the line."

It was signed Neil Liemus.

"That son of a bitch," Valley said.

"You don't mean that Valley. There's some reason in that bulletin. That's not just an old man talking," Urho said as he walked back to the ad room.

"He would say that. He's his son," Bernie said, pacing.

"So he is," Valley said. She watched Urho's back as he left the newsroom. The usual ringing of telephones and the clatter of typewriters continued. The old wooden fan hummed overhead. But Bernie and Valley at her desk had grown very quiet. "We've got to do something," Valley finally said.

"Soon," Bernie said.

Valley nodded. They were in a bizarre situation. Even though she could not understand everything that was happening, Valley knew there was danger ahead. She only wished she knew which door it would jump out of. Valley had the disturbing feeling that they were not moving fast enough, that they were overlooking something Important!

"Yeah, soon," Valley said.

A few minutes later, on her way back from the lounge, Tessie stopped at Valley's desk, but looked at Bernie. "Isn't this exciting, Bernie? These bulletins, the union business, everything!"

"Shut up!" Valley said. "Why don't you go home and put on some underwear?"

"Old lady, am I getting you excited?" Tessie smiled and strolled to her desk.

"Ladies quiet down. Remember the last time?" Bernie warned.

"She always starts it," Tessie said.

"I said shut up bitch! But why should I waste my time talking to a stupid redhead," Valley said.

Then the phone rang. The minute it rang Valley remembered that she hadn't called Claudia. It must be her. And then she heard Claudia's voice. Valley said, "Hi kid. Sorry I didn't call. Things have been happening around here, big things."

Valley listened to Claudia's reply. "Good, you'll be getting out soon?" Valley asked.

Claudia said, "Yes, the doctor says I can go home tomorrow. But— there is something I've go to ask you, Valley."

"Okay, what is it, kid?"

Claudia said, "I'm not going home. I'd like to stay with you for a while. Take Jamie and stay with you. I'm leaving Alex."

And that's when Valley felt the tightness working down her throat, a steady pressure against her windpipe. "Yeah, sure kid, you and Jamie can stay with me. No, it's no problem. I've got plenty of room."

Finally Claudia told her about Alex, and Valley felt anger pulling her voice tight and thin. "I understand, kid. That bastard I could kill him." Suddenly Valley did not know why she had said that. In the silence that followed, she could feel Claudia's physical hurt and her strained conversation.

"Don't worry kid. I'll see you tomorrow."

Then they made polite conversation, like two strangers being very careful not to say the wrong thing and not really certain what the wrong thing might be.

CHAPTER 23

Alex picked up a few pebbles on the dock and threw them out as far as he could without too much effort. After awhile, tiring of this, he leaned against a post. A lighted cigarette dangled from his lips. During the next twenty minutes Alex smoked several cigarettes. He closed his eyes and shook his head. What the hell was he doing here, on the dock, at dusk?

What a mess he had made of his life. He was thirty-three, still young, but he had never truly given much serious thought to his future, his marriage. Claudia, Jamie, weren't they his future, his life? It seemed only yesterday he was twenty-three, an ex-GI in college, but a decade was gone.

Alex stared at the shadows among shadows on the dock. He took a few steps toward the river, looked down into the water. Dangerous but fascinating, he thought. Suddenly his scalp seemed to crawl and then tighten; his heart began to pound, his mouth went dry, a shiver went up his spine.

Then he sat down on the edge of the dock, unconsciously seeking comfort, forgiveness. Already things seemed unreal, increasingly dreamlike. Was there actually peace in the water? Would his problems disappear in the water? Alex's muscles relaxed, his heart slowed as he leaned over the water-peaceful water. The threat of his father, which had seemed so strong, now in retrospect, was a phantom.

"Come on in," the river seemed to say.

Then silence.

"Come on."

He began to think he had been a fool all his life. John was right. He had dragged him out of an alley. Beaten by his father, he had run away, escaped while his father lay drunk. He was never going back. He was twelve he could make it on his own. He didn't want to live in that flat with rats. He didn't want to live with his father. And then, John found him.

Yes, John had saved his life. Days later when John's parents tried to locate Alex's father, he had vanished, left the state abandoned his son. And Alex was glad. He was free, free from the sudden outbursts of rage and anger and unbearable punishment. No more. No more!

"Come on in," coaxed the river.

Alex stretched out his arms, and as if in a trance said, "Such a big, big, beautiful river, my Detroit River." He said it with pride, as if he had created the river.

Claudia, you still don't understand, Alex thought. Don't leave me. I need you. I didn't hurt you. It was him, that bastard of a father. He beat us both, first me, then you Claudia. I wouldn't hurt you, wouldn't hurt my Jamie. No. never! He hurt you. He wants you to suffer because of her death. He made me suffer. And I didn't mean to kill her. I didn't!

Now, Alex knelt on the dock, looking down into the deep water. He was aware of muffled sounds of motors and boats in the darkness. "Pa is coming to get me. I must hide from him. He won't be satisfied with just beating me. He'll kill me this time."

"No, Pa," Alex screamed into the wind. "Don't beat me, don't beat Claudia don't beat Jamie!" A great hot anger was building up in Alex. "Damn you Pa, I'm going to get even. Yes, you won't beat me anymore!" He wrenched off his shoes, first the right, then the left, and threw them into the river. A yacht backed into the dock. Two laughing, happy couples were on deck. They waved their drinks at Alex. The yacht's propeller churned the water.

Suddenly Alex was in the water, bucking, thrashing, kicking, screaming! He tried to swim. He jerked back, raised one arm to protect his chest from the slashing propeller, screamed as it gouged his chest, crushing his strong body.

* * *

Alex's body was taken to the Nikropolus' Funeral Home. John was in the Acropolis Café across from the funeral home having his morning coffee when he saw the ambulance pull into his parking lot. He finished his coffee, quickly paid his bill and raced across the street in the rain, dodging the puddles. He was anxious to make sure everything was done right for his brother, Alex.

When the ambulance attendants spotted John, they wasted no time in removing the canvas clad body from the ambulance. They lifted the body effortlessly onto a gurney and wheeled it into John's embalming room in the funeral home's basement.

"I need a signature," said the taller of the two, handing John a yellow form. He looked out the window at the dark clouds. "It's May, time for flowers," said the ambulance attendant.

"Yeah, flowers," John said, closing the door after them. In a few minutes John unzipped the bag, and a guttural sound of horror burst from him as he saw the mutilated body. The handsome Alex was no more. He placed his hand on the cold metal table, sucked in his breath and said, "Dear God. What happened, brother?" John was a pale as one of his corpses as he tuned away. And then as gently as if he were speaking to an infant, "I'm sorry Alex. Sorry for the way your father screwed up your life. Sorry for this—." He could not go on. The rumble of thunder shook him. The lights in the sterile room went out for a moment. John flinched, a nervous flick of his head as he heard another roll of thunder.

Then he forced his eyes back to the table. It must be a closed casket. He knew that even with his tools, all his cosmetics, all his skills, he could not restore Alex. No. He would not allow Claudia and Jamie to see him—to see this—.

The ringing of the telephone seemed a strange sound in the room of the dead. He reached for it and said, "Nikropolus Funeral Home." He pulled a handkerchief from his pocket to wipe his damp brow. Then he heard her voice, hesitant, strained.

"John, this is Claudia." Was it only two days ago when he had visited her in the hospital? Through the window he saw the dark clouds and the rain. He felt a deep sadness. "Yes, Claudia."

"Take care of everything, John. You were his brother, his friend."

"Claudia, I can't believe what happened to him." There was silence at the other end. "The ambulance just left. He's here. The accident—it was horrible. It's not fair."

"Fair?"

"I mean he never was given a chance. His father—was a son of a bitch. Excuse me, Claudia, but he was." John's knuckles were white where he gripped the phone.

"When the police came to the hospital to tell me about the accident, I couldn't cry. I still can't cry."

He didn't ask her why. Instead he said, "Where's Jamie?"

"She's at my neighbor's house. She's okay."

"I'll take care of everything," John said. His voice had a note of command in it.

"It's too late now. But I think I understand him. We can't go back, can we?"

Somehow John had tied his handkerchief in knots. When did he do that? Then his words rushed out, "Yes, you're right. God, how I wish we could go back and right the wrong." Then he took a deep breath. "When we were in college, he wasn't the same kid I found in the alley, beaten, bleeding by that bastard, his father. And when he met you Claudia, I was certain that the old wounds had healed—that he had become a new person. But I was wrong, wasn't I?"

There was a silence on the other end. Finally she said. "Yes, John. He left too many things locked in his heart. There was too much anger in him."

Gently, slowly John untied the knots in his handkerchief, the phone cradled between his shoulder and chin. "Alex carried too many things to the grave with him."

Finally John said, "Alex's father blamed him for the death of his mother. She died giving birth to Alex. His father never forgave him." John shivered in the cold, sterile embalming room. "You know that

Alex fought in Korea, but you didn't know that's where his temper exploded, his bitterness increased. And after, he used his strength to fight back, to smother that temper, for a while. He believed he had been cheated in life, so he fought back, hurting the ones he loved, hurting you, Claudia."

"Yes," Claudia said. "When we met and fell in love, he was gentle, kind a good man. It was only after Jamie's birth that he changed. Too many memories, too much pain from the past. Now that it is too late, I think I understand."

"Claudia, there is something about the accident that I must tell you. Alex's face was—." John began

"John," Claudia interrupted. "I want you to do your best for your brother. I want an open casket."

"No—no, it's not possible," John began. Then in a calm professional voice, he said, "Yes, I will do my best for Alex."

PART THREE
URHO LIEMUS

CHAPTER 24

Claudia stood in her bedroom. She held clothing in each hand; her arms outstretched as though she were offering what she had to someone. She was rigid and motionless; then suddenly aware of the intrusion into her privacy she whirled around and faced her mother, Anna, and Jamie, her arms still outstretched.

She said in a barely controlled whisper, "Look." She was holding a pain of gray socks and a gray and white tie in one hand. In the other hand was a black pair of socks. On the bed was a gray suit, white shirt, boxer shorts and an undershirt. "Isn't this crazy?" She began to laugh. "I'm wondering if the socks should be gray or black." She brought both pairs up to her face and held them against her cheeks. "Silly me."

When Anna moved toward her, Claudia pulled away. "It's funny isn't it?"

Jamie rushed to her, hugged her. "Mom, please, don't."

"Come here child," Anna said to Jamie.

"I'm standing here trying to coordinate the clothes he is going to be buried in, make everything right for him for the last time." It was there again, that terrible feeling in the pit of her stomach. Her mouth opened but there was no sound. She bent over suddenly, clutching her stomach. Anna tried to catch her, ease her down onto the bed. Claudia pulled away. "Do you want me to sit on his suit?"

Claudia pulled herself up, showed the socks to Anna and said, "Which pair? Don't you think it's funny?"

"What color are his shoes?" Anna asked.

"Black."

"The black socks," Anna said.

"Of course." She nodded, moved to the walnut dresser and dropped the gray pair of socks into a drawer. Then she searched in the closet for his shoes. She held them up. "Need polishing."

"I'll polish them," Jamie said.

"Okay, honey." Claudia slumped against the closet door. Her fingers trembled as she dabbed at a smudge on one of the shoes.

"Claudia, are you all right?" her mother asked.

Claudia turned to her mother. Her face was devoid of all pretense, all masks. "I wished him dead. Many times."

"No, no you didn't," Anna said. "He was a good husband."

Claudia wanted to tell her mother about Alex, about the good husband. She wanted to get it all out, once and for all. It was the only way she'd ever free herself—from him. "Yes, I wished him dead!"

Silence filled the room. Finally Anna said, "Claudia, it's too much for you."

All Claudia said was, "Jamie where's the shoe polish?"

Minutes later the three were in the kitchen. Jamie had spread the want ads of the Press on the table and was polishing her father's shoes. When she finished she put them in a paper bag.

Then she went back into the bedroom with Claudia and Anna. Claudia began pulling Alex's clothes from the closet, folding them in piles. "I'm giving these to the Goodwill. The needy will appreciate his clothes."

"Yes," Anna said, clearing out his drawers. Jamie put the clothes in a large cardboard box.

"You don't want to keep anything?" Anna asked.

"No!" Claudia went to the bed, looked at the gray suit. Did I forget anything? Does everything match?"

"Everything is fine."

Then Jamie said, "Come on, let's go. The taxi is waiting."

But Claudia seemed reluctant to leave the bedroom. "You're sure I haven't forgotten anything?"

A half-hour later, they arrived at the Nikropolus Funeral Home in Greektown. John was there waiting for them. He made comforting conversation with them as he took Alex's clothes. Then he said to Claudia. "There was a call from Neil Liemus for you. You can use my office phone."

"Thanks." Once in John's office, Claudia dialed the Press' number and asked for Neil Liemus. His voice was tense. "Claudia, I know the funeral is tomorrow. I just wanted to know when you'll be back to work. I'd like you back, the day after the funeral. You know how understaffed we are."

"What? What?" was all a startled Claudia could say. Then she slammed the receiver down and rushed out of the office. "That bastard!"

* * *

Alex's funeral—was it last week? Claudia would never forget the moment she saw him in the casket. The expression on his face, or the face that John had constructed, was calm, serene. The green eyes forever shut. Why had she insisted on an open casket?

Claudia could still hear the wails that came from her mother sobbing at the coffin. But why couldn't she cry? Why couldn't she shed one tear for Alex?

The salesmen at the car dealership paid their respects. No one at the Press came to the funeral. Neil would not allow any time off on a work day, especially since they were understaffed.

Urho apologized for his father's rudeness when he came to the wake the night before the funeral. They talked for a short while. "Take some time off," he said. "I know you have things to take care of, family matters."

"Yes, thank you." she said. "My mother is here from Chicago, and we have things to do."

"I understand," he said and left shortly after.

Richard, Bernie and Valley also paid their respects, but only stayed minutes.

Yes, it was a week ago, thought Claudia, as she waited with Anna and Jamie for the taxi that would take Anna to the train station. Even during that week, Claudia did not really talk to Anna. She never told her about Alex. Another time, Claudia told herself. Yes, another time.

As the taxi pulled to the curb, Jamie looked out the window and held her grandmother's hand. "Please stay with us, please!"

"I can't stay honey. I must go back to Chicago. And it isn't as if Chicago is China. I'm only hours away. And in the summer you can come and stay with me. Remember the fun we had last summer? Besides it's only a month away."

"Yes, I remember."

Claudia watched her mother and daughter. She saw that look on Jamie's face, that secret look of pain. Would Jamie have that look always? She's young, she'd forget that look. She must because this is a new beginning.

Anna gathered Jamie in her arms. "My sweet Jamie, take care of yourself and your mother."

"I will!" Then Jamie began to cry.

"Hush." Anna said and kissed Jamie on both cheeks and held her until she quieted. After a while, Jamie was calm.

"That's my girl," Anna said.

Jamie rubbed her eyes with her fists. "I'm all right."

Anna dabbed at Jamie's cheeks with her lace handkerchief. "Sure you are."

Then the doorbell rang. "That's the taxi," Claudia said.

Anna grabbed her suitcase. "You're sure there is nothing else I can do for you?"

"I'm sure." Claudia said, hugging her mother. After Anna got into the cab, Jamie and Claudia waved good-bye.

* * *

When Claudia returned to work the next day, she was early. She wore the black dress, the mourning dress that Anna had bought for her. "You have to mourn Alex for forty days, wear black for forty days, it's a Greek tradition," Anna had said.

Now only Freda at the switchboard was there to greet her. "Glad you're back, Claudia. I'm sorry—about Alex." She got busy at the switchboard with incoming calls and gave Claudia a smile. "See you later." Claudia disappeared down the hallway to the newsroom. She stood at her desk and took a deep breath. She didn't know what alarmed her more—the knowledge that she had to make it on her own—or the strange feelings she had about Alex's death. Could she have helped him? No, he would not let her into his life, into his secret fears. Instead he had wanted to crush her, even kill her when his full anger took over.

But Claudia knew one thing for certain now. And that was she was on her own and had to plan for her future, plan for Jamie's future. And she had a secret weapon—the book on the gifted. She must finish it. Drawn like a magnet, she pulled out her desk drawer and found the folder with her notes and photos. This was the first folder Matthew had given her. She spread the notes and photos on her desk.

In the hallway she heard Valley's voice. "Welcome back, kid." She wore a green silk dress, with a white silk scarp knotted at the neck. It had a vintage look, and had obviously been high fashion a few seasons back. She gave Claudia a warm embrace and then looked at her at arm's length.

"Are you all right? I missed you."

"I missed you, too. And yes, I'm all right." Claudia noticed Valley's clear eyes, her speech, not slurred, her hair glistened

. "Valley, you look great!"

Valley beamed. "You might say I got a 'wake up call' because of Alex. I guess he taught me not to waste my time and wallow in booze. There is something to live for—out there. And I'm going to find it."

"I'm glad."

She studied Claudia. "We both have to get our acts together, kid."

"Who's getting their acts together?" asked Tessie as she entered the newsroom.

"Oh God, it's none of your damn business."

"I'm just asking." Tessie walked to her desk. "What's the big deal?"

Bernie came up to Claudia, his arms outstretched. "Welcome back." He gave her a hug.

For a moment she could not speak. She could feel her cheeks burning, her eyes stinging.

179

"Work, that's what you need," Bernie said. "Damn, I wish Richard were here."

"I do too," Claudia said. She was standing at her desk when Neil walked into the newsroom.

"So you finally decided to come back to work."

"What? Urho said I could take some time off."

"I know. Sometimes he oversteps his authority."

"You mean I should have come back to work the day after the funeral?" Claudia voice was raised. "Or maybe just as soon as his body was put in the ground. I have the strangest feeling that is when you wanted me back on the job."

"Now Claudia, don't—," Bernie said.

"No! Let her talk. I want to hear what she has to say," Neil said.

Claudia willed herself to maintain her composure. What Neil had said had made her extremely angry. When she turned to Neil at last, her face was flushed. "This is horrible! So if there is a death in the family, the good worker is expected to come back to work right after the funeral—the same day? Is that right?"

"No, not in every case," Neil said.

"Neil—." Bernie began.

"Shut up, Bernie. I'm talking to Claudia, trying to explain business to her, deadlines—." He was angry now. He towered over her.

"So, you expect them to come back to work, after the funeral?" Claudia was beyond anger now.

"If we are understaffed, as we certainly are now. And if there are important stories to cover and write." He looked down at her with unconcealed contempt. She realized that he was trying to stare her down, but she did not waver, and finally he turned away and began to pace.

"Young lady, you work for the Press. Why I could not afford for you to take time off to accept your award in Lansing. Damn, in any case you were in the hospital. We're understaffed. We need every writer and then some. Do you understand?"

Obviously convinced that Neil was the enemy, she sat down at her desk, and sighed. "I can't believe it."

"Believe it!" Neil said brusquely. "I've got a paper to run, I've got deadlines." And then he stalked out of the newsroom.

What had she done? She had talked back to Himself? She stood trembling at her desk. She had to get out of here—out of the newsroom. In a moment she ran out of the back door, Valley close behind her.

She leaned against the building taking deep breaths, trying to control her anger. "I still can't believe I did that—."

Valley said, "That Neil, that son of a bitch."

Claudia said, "Now I've done it. My first day back and if I'm not mistaken, I'm out of a job." She looked at her friend.

Valley glanced out into the parking lot, "Neil is sick—dangerous too."

Instantly Claudia turned to Valley. "No he's not sick, not dangerous. I'm to blame. I made him angry. And now he's going to fire me."

"You don't know what you're talking about. He won't fire you. You're a valuable part of the Press. I know that old bastard, known him for a long time."

How long Claudia stared at Valley, she could not tell Then Urho came out of the building and walked over to them. From his expression, Claudia suspected that he knew what had happened. He merely said, "Good morning, ladies."

Claudia wanted to run up to him and fling herself into his arms. She needed a friend, now. Hadn't he been kind to her? Didn't he go out of his way to talk with her?

Yes, he was her friend. But he was the publisher's son. Friend?

Urho held out his hand to her. "Claudia, I'm glad you're back. I'm sorry about Alex." He continued holding out his hand. Claudia did not take it. "Is something wrong?" he asked.

"Yes, just about everything," Claudia said.

"Talk some sense into her, will you Number One Son?" Valley said.

"Tell me about it." With a brief nod in Valley's direction, Urho turned toward Claudia.

"Go ahead, tell him," Valley said and walked back into the building.

"It's a long story," began Claudia. "And besides, I don't know if

I have a job. I don't think your father appreciated my crazy outburst, especially after my first day back."

"What do you mean?"

Then he hadn't heard. Claudia thought. So she spent the next few minutes telling him about the argument she had with Neil.

"I was afraid that would happen. He hasn't been himself, lately. Listen, you need a break from this place, you're coming with me."

For a moment Claudia looked at Urho. "What?"

"You heard me. We're getting away from this place."

Why was he so indescribably warm, gentle and friendly? Why was he concerned for her? She could tell from looking at him that he truly cared what happened to her.

She blinked in surprise. "Why are you doing this?"

"For God's sake, I've worked with you for some time, now. I hope we're friends. It's all right to be strong and independent but when you carry that burden and it gets too heavy—as I think it did this morning, you need someone—to say wait a minute—take a breather. I think that's what Valley was trying to say. And that's what I'm trying to do. You need a breather. We're going for a ride."

"What?"

"You heard me. Come on." He grabbed her arm. "You're coming with me."

Minutes later Claudia was in Urho's Thunderbird convertible.

"Where are we going?" she asked.

"To my island."

The road snaked back and forth after they crossed the bridge, with houses hugging the shoreline. Claudia leaned back into the leather seat and relaxed. "It's beautiful, your island," she said.

He nodded. "Yes. I can't understand why anyone would live anywhere else. I know some think we're crazy to live on the island, especially in the winter after a heavy snow."

"Well, we've been shut off in Pierre Corners after a heavy snow storm, remember?"

Urho laughed. "You're right. I'll never forget that great snow storm and the National Guards and the jeep convoy."

Claudia knew that he was trying to cheer her up. But she didn't want to talk—it was too pleasant and relaxing to sit in his car watching the sailboats on the Detroit River—not thinking about anything at all.

When the road turned, Claudia saw the peaked roof of the Old Mariner's Inn. Urho slowed down and turned into the Inn's parking lot. Minutes later they joined the crowd of people lining up for brunch. The sunny day had brought a large crowd into the Inn. Claudia caught the scent of coffee, pecan rolls, eggs and ham. Soon the hostess approached them. "Good morning, Mr. Liemus, a table by the window?"

"Yes, please," he said.

There was a magnificent view of the river from their table. Claudia saw the motor boats and sail boats, while a helicopter hummed overhead. Then she said, "Yesterday, I wasn't sure I wanted to come back to the Press."

Urho nodded. "I can identify with that feeling. I've had that thought, once or twice. I mean to chuck it all—stay here on the island and paint. And you, Claudia, should finish that book on the gifted. Do it. That's an order." He looked at her and smiled.

"The gifted book? Yes, I guess I should finish it. Somehow I see it as my way out, or a way into another area. I'm not making sense, am I?"

"Yes. I understand what you're talking about, what you're trying to do with your life. The Press is not your life. The book, and other books, that's what it's all about for you and your future."

Claudia nodded. "I have to think about my future, about Jamie's future. Things happen too quickly. Soon, I'll turn around and Jamie will be all grown up. I don't want to be working at the Press—then." She couldn't look at him. Tears burned behind her eyelids and she blinked furiously to keep them back.

"Now—now," Urho said and offered her his handkerchief.

"Thank you." She dabbed at her eyes with the handkerchief. "It's just that —." Before she could finish, a waitress in a blue and white sailor's outfit came toward them, menus under her arm. Claudia was glad to see her—glad to study the menu. Had she said too much to him? Finally she said to Urho, "Please order for me."

Urho nodded and then turned to the waitress, "We'll have coffee, scrambled eggs, bacon and whole wheat toast. How does that sound?" He turned to Claudia.

"Fine," Claudia said. The waitress left taking the menus with her and Claudia had nothing to hide behind. She glanced out the window, watched the white caps of the waves and the faces of the strollers on the wide deck. Above the deck, birds swooped and soared, enjoying the sunny spring day.

"Claudia?"

"Yes?"

"Come back. You seemed a million miles away. I look at you and I can see myself, months ago—ready to strike out—at anything- anyone. I think if Neil wasn't there this morning, it would have been someone else, maybe me." He smiled, took her hands. "You're angry and bitter. I know that you have been through a rough time, and I don't mean at the Press. Now that has ended and things will be better, I promise." He squeezed her hands and released them.

"Yes, things will change," she said. How could she tell him the hell that she had lived with Alex? No, she could not.

Urho glanced at her, picked up his fork and used it as a pointer. "One thing I'm certain of is that it takes time." And then in an instant he changed the subject. "All I know is now we are in a great inn, surrounded by happy people and good food. It's a beautiful spring day on the island. And all's right with the world." Then he winked.

Claudia smiled. "Right."

The waitress brought their order. For the time being they seemed like everyone else at the inn.

"Eat," Urho said. "You'll feel better. Once again he smiled.

CHAPTER 25

Claudia felt lazy on this Sunday morning in July. Lazy—lazy. I don't want to get out of bed. And I won't get out of bed, she thought, stretching her arms. Jamie was in Chicago with her grandmother, and from the telephone reports was having a good time. A grown-up child, wise beyond her years with an identification tag pinned to her dress, Jamie had taken the train to Chicago all by herself.

Yes, Claudia was going to stay in bed all day. Hide in bed. Too many things had happened at the Press. Valley was right. Neil did not fire her after her heated outburst. Now the entire staff was on overtime, with no additional pay. That was Neil's edict. And another disaster loomed on the horizon. Beginning next month, in August, salaries were being cut by ten per cent. Neil cited the downswing in the economy.

Neil would say to anyone or everyone within ear shot, "They should have elected Nixon, instead of that young upstart Kennedy. Nixon would have kept us solvent."

Perhaps Claudia could have coped with these things one at a time—but they came in bunches. She didn't want to get out of bed—ever! And as for her book on the gifted child it was on hold. If the truth were known she hadn't written one word since Alex died, almost three months ago. Matt still conferred wit her, encouraging her, but she couldn't concentrate, she couldn't write one word.

She lay in bed thinking about the book, about the Press, about

Jamie, about Urho. Yes, about Urho, that gentle man, who always went out of his way to talk with her, to encourage her, to make her laugh. She needed to laugh. Thinking of him made her smile. Then at eleven o'clock she got out of bed. Perhaps because of her strong convictions or from a stern resolve that she had to start the day, and not in bed! After a long leisurely shower and a steaming cup of coffee, she had sorted out all her problems and placed them in a neat pile marked, "hold."

After her second cup of coffee, she drummed her fingers on the kitchen table, looked out at the overcast sky. Not a typical July day. Well, had she solved all her problems? Had she decided what she was going to do with her life? Did she know who she really was now? Questions, and were the answers in the distance?

She was not going to allow this gloomy day to bother her. There was enough gloom at the Press. Pay cuts, no overtime pay, long hours, what next? Bernie and Valley spent many a lunch hour discussing the union. Was that the solution? Claudia didn't know. Bernie had said that the union would guarantee fair wages, good benefits, provide clout for negotiations with Neil to attain these results. Now Claudia was really confused. She could feel her muscles tightening in her neck, her shoulders, her back. She rubbed her neck. Too tense? Drink some more coffee.

"Just what I need," she said to the walls in the kitchen. There are bright lights in my life, she thought. There is Jamie. And, yes, there is Urho. Since their breakfast at the Old Mariners, they had become what? Friends? More than friends. She didn't want to think about that idea. Yes, friends.

She walked into the bedroom, coffee cup in her hand, and placed it on the walnut dresser. She rubbed her hand on the smooth surface. She looked into the beveled glass mirror. A memory tugged at her, a memory she didn't want to explore. A memory of Alex . That memory haunted her. It was almost an hour before she put it all together. She had made the bed and dusted the walnut dresser—and then it came to her. Stunned her.

No, not the memory itself, but the fact that when it happened, she was convinced it would turn her life around. And that she would never forget it. Now she dragged it out of the past. It was about Alex. What happened was this...

It was the day after her father's funeral. Claudia and Alex were having dinner at a restaurant in Greektown, Detroit. John was there. He had stopped by, bought them wine, and stayed to talk. Claudia barely touched her food. The lamb chops and rice pilaf remained on her plate, grew cold as the two men talked. Then John left and Alex said, "Claudia, stop blaming your self. It wasn't your fault."

"Yes, it was. I don't want to hear it wasn't my fault. If I hadn't been late getting there, he'd be alive today. He wanted so much out of life. He was so proud of the restaurant, of us, his family."

"Yes, I know." Alex let her talk.

Claudia remembered he was so kind, a different Alex. He had told her that she should not carry this guilt inside. Yet, he carried a guilt that eventually killed him. He told her that time would take care of the pain. And yet, his pain grew and grew, overtook him, destroyed him and almost killed her.

What else did she remember about that night? Yes, she remembered they walked to downtown Detroit, to Woodward Avenue, to the theatre district, to the park. It was a warm night and walking helped her that night.

Now, in the bedroom, tears filled Claudia's eyes. These were the tears she could not shed at Alex's funeral. Her life was shifting into another phase. How was she going to handle it? Somehow she was drawn to the window. She looked at the apple tree, the one Alex had planted. She glanced at the rose bushes, now heavy with blossoms, deep red, their fragrance carried by the wind into the bedroom. She stared at the patio, at the green and white lawn furniture, glistening in the rain. Then she shut her eyes, shut out the rainy day. Decisions, decisions, too many decisions. And that's when the door bell rang. Who could that be? Must be the newspaper boy, she thought. She grabbed some bills out of her purse, tucked her shirt into her slacks and glanced at her reflection in the dresser mirror. She walked to the front door, opened it.

"Hello," he said, standing on her doorstep, her Sunday newspaper in his hands, his hazel eyes smiling.

Claudia didn't know how to react. She stood there, silent.

"I wasn't sure you'd be pleased to see me. I mean, this is your day off—and—and, well, anyway here's your Sunday paper." Urho grinned. "I'm the new newspaper man."

Finally she said, "Thank you." She had never felt so awkward.

He didn't move. He stood in her doorway, sheltered from the rain.

She looked at him. "I'm sure you didn't come here from the island just to deliver my newspaper." Why was she so abrupt? "You're right. There is something else."

"What?"

"One question."

"Oh?"

"Will you have dinner with me, tomorrow, or the next day, or the—?"

"Well, I don't think I can."

"I see."

"I mean, I'd like to—."

"You would?"

"I don't have time to go out to dinner, these days."

"You don't?"

"I've got my book, and then there's Jamie. And my work at the Press."

"I understand."

"It was nice of you to ask me."

"Yes, I know your book is important and it will be great."

"Thank you."

"I'll see you at the Press, tomorrow," Urho said.

"Yes." She smiled.

He turned away. Before she closed the door a robin flew out of a tree and landed in front of him. He looked at the bird and then at Claudia. The bird sat pruning its feathers in the rain.

Urho spoke to the robin. "I shouldn't have given up, right?"

The robin responded with a peep.

"What have I got to lose? I'll try again."

He stepped up to the door and held Claudia's hand. "Am I that repulsive?"

"What?"

"Is it because Neil is my father?"

"I don't know."

"Or that the son of the boss is off limits?"

"It isn't that, no."

"Or maybe because I'm rich and live on the island."

Claudia smiled. "No, that isn't it."

"What's wrong with me?"

"Nothing's wrong with you."

"That's good you had me worried for a minute."

"I said no for one reason. I don't have the time."

"Claudia, even the mayor of Pierre Corners, the chairman of Ford Motor Company has time for dinner, even the president of the United States and the Queen of England. No one can be that busy."

"After what I've been through the last few months, I don't think I'd be the best company for dinner."

"If I wanted the best company, I'd have asked , let me see, yes, I'd ask Marilyn Monroe."

She smiled. "I'm sorry, I can't."

"Can't isn't in my vocabulary. If you don't believe me, ask Mr. Robin," Urho said.

"Mr. Robin?"

"He's that little creature enjoying the rain and our conversation. He's a new friend, right behind that tree. Mr. Robin tell Claudia she has to go to dinner with me."

The robin swooped up and circled them.

"Thank you, Mr. Robin. Oh, it's Chuck? Okay, thank you Chuck. And what will you do if she refuses again? I see."

"What did he say?" Claudia asked. "Will he peck me until I cry uncle?"

"Worse, he's going to call in his cousins, by the dozens, and they will attack you. Did you see Hitchcock's film, 'The Birds'? He said his attack will be worse."

She smiled. "Oh, no! Okay, okay, I give up."

Urho grinned. "Then it's tomorrow night at seven?

"Yes, if I don't have to work late."

"I'll see that you don't."

Urho shielded his eyes and looked at the trees. "Thank you, Mr. Robin, I mean Chuck, wherever you are. He flew away. Guess his work is done here."

Claudia laughed and watched Urho walk back to his car, whistling happily in the rain.

CHAPTER 26

Claudia could not remember another date that was as much fun as the one with Urho. She had worn a pale rose silk dress, with a halter top and a softly flowing skirt. A white silk shawl covered her shoulders. They passed an enjoyable hour driving to Detroit in his Thunderbird with a stop at Belle Isle where they got out at Scott's Fountain and spent time watching the rainbow colored water spray into a circular pool. A small tow-head boy sailed his toy boat in the pool while his parents sat nearby on a bench. Then Claudia and Urho spent an hour at the Isle Zoo, where the chattering monkeys made them laugh.

Later, Urho drove across the bridge to the Detroit Yacht Club. They sipped wine while sitting outdoors at a glass topped table and relaxed to the rhythmic drone of breaking waves on the river while an occasional sail boat drifted by.

Although Claudia had lived in Michigan most of her life, she had never been to the Yacht Club, never been to Belle Isle. It was all new to her. She felt like a wide-eyed tourist—or like a prisoner who had just finished serving a long sentence, most of it in solitary confinement. But it was not just where they went that made the evening special. None of it would have been half as exciting or as much fun if she'd been with someone other than Urho. He was so charming, so witty, so handsome.

After drinking two glasses of wine each, they were starving. "Let's go to Windsor, have dinner there," Urho suggested.

"Really?"

"Yes. I know a terrific place, Ship's Landing." In a matter of minutes they were crossing the Windsor tunnel and pulling into the restaurant.

"Yes, this is another place, that's new to me," Claudia said, as they entered the unpretentious restaurant on the waterfront.

"You don't get around much kid, do you?" Urho smiled.

They enjoyed a dinner of the freshest and tastiest seafood.

Urho tasted one of the shrimp in his cocktail. "Not bad, not bad at all. This is some place, isn't it?"

"I feel like a country bumpkin. All these places you've taken me to are so fantastic. My speed is Pierre Corners and maybe Greektown , in Detroit." Claudia glanced at Urho.

"I'll show you places of wonder. Eat up!"

They ate too much shrimp and then too much broiled trout, salad and baked potatoes. They drank too much wine. Considering how much they ate, Claudia thought it was amazing how much time they had to talk. Claudia wanted to hear Urho's thoughts on everything. First they explored their names.

"All I know is that Urho was a Finnish God or legend. I'm not too clear on that score. I only know that he was a terrific fighter and brave in battle. Of course, it's Finnish mythology," Urho said. "The name Claudia isn't so unusual, right?"

"Well, my real name, or I should say the name my father gave me is Greek and it's Klotho, she is one of the three fates in Greek mythology. They determine our destiny. So you'd better watch out." Claudia grinned.

"No kidding. I think my Finnish God could handle your Greek Klotho with one hand tied behind his back, so there."

They were having fun, Claudia thought. She hadn't experienced this in a very long time. They talked and laughed about everything, sports, movies, food, fashion, politics, religion, everything. They talked and talked as if they would be struck dumb by midnight, or their fairy godmother would whisk them away in a pumpkin carriage

192

drawn by six white mice. Claudia was intoxicated, not on the wine, but by Urho, his conversation, his nearness, his presence.

By the time he took her home and agreed to come in for a brandy, she was certain she was falling in love with him. She wanted him very much and the thought made her warm and tingly. She sensed that he wanted her. He sat on the couch, lit a cigarette, while she went for the brandy and some glasses, then the telephone rang. Claudia glanced at her watch.

"Why, it's almost eleven, who would be calling now?"

"Beats me," Urho said.

Claudia picked up the phone, "Hello? Oh, mother, how are you? Is something wrong? Is Jamie all right? It's almost eleven o'clock. Oh, it's only 9:45 in Chicago. I forgot about the time change."

Claudia winked at Urho who was enjoying his brandy. Then Claudia spoke to her mother. "Yes, put Jamie on. I miss her. Hi honey. I miss you. Are you having fun in Chicago with Gram? Good. Shouldn't you be in bed? Oh, you just came from a Disney movie. Great."

After a few minutes of conversations, Claudia said her goodbyes to her mother and Jamie. She placed the phone back on the desk.

Urho said, "If that phone rings again—."

"It won't." Claudia took the phone off the receiver.

He sat on the couch and sipped his brandy. With the other hand he crushed out his freshly lit cigarette and stood up. Claudia took a sip of her brandy and put it on the table. No matter how many times she saw him, she felt the breathless anticipation of a schoolgirl. Suddenly she bolted down her brandy. Her throat was burning. Then the burning gave way to a slight glow in her chest. She sipped a second brandy and it went down easier. She kept taking small slips. It was better than burning her throat with one big gulp. She felt giddy. It's the brandy, she thought.

With a slow smile, Urho held out his arms. "Come here," he said.

Claudia hesitated for a second, finally rushed to him.

Urho said, "I've been waiting to do this all evening." He kissed her gently, softly.

Later when they were locked in each other's arms on the couch in the cool dimness of the living room, Claudia said, "What are we doing?" And Urho's kiss silenced any other protests. "We're doing what comes naturally, as the old saying goes."

Claudia smiled. "You make me happy, and I don't think I've been this happy in a long, long time."

"Yes me too."

"But, that call from my mother made me think—about my past. You want to know something Urho?" You want to know about me, about my life, about Alex, and his death?" Tears welled in her eyes.

"Claudia, don't do this. That's in the past. This is now, and I'm here with you."

"I can't get him out of my mind. Do you understand? I did not cry at his funeral. I was glad that he died." She wiped at her eyes with the back of her hand then held her head up. "I wasn't going to tell that to anyone, especially you. I was afraid. I'm still afraid."

Urho held her close, "Don't be afraid. I'm here, now."

She took a deep breath, another sip of brandy and began. "I feel so lost— I have to talk about this, about him. Alex was a dead man long before he died, long before he jumped into the Detroit River. Ever since I knew him, he was filled with this anger, this hate growing inside him. It began when he was very young, and his bastard of a father beat him. Finally one day he ran away, but the anger, the pain inside him, was still there. It exploded when Jamie was born. Strange, can you believe that when we met in college, he was a different man, a loving man? And I did care for him, did love him."

"Don't torture yourself, Claudia."

Her dark hair surrounded her face, her skin picking up the rose color from her dress. Softly she asked, "Can you understand? I want to get it all out—my feelings for him."

"Yes, I can understand."

She sighed, her dark hair fell, covering her face then she parted it with her hands, like parting velvet curtains, and held her face up toward Urho. "Before I finish talking, you'll think I'm crazy, or that the life I led with Alex was crazy-insane. He didn't treat me right. He was a great pretender. Everyone loved him. At the dealership he was top man, always a joke or a smile. Yes, the great pretender. But at home, the mask came off, he was pure evil and I was his target. He beat me, Urho. I wound up in the hospital, the last time. And just before his death, he struck Jamie. Was he going to start on her? I would not allow that to happen, never. I was going to leave him when I got out of the hospital." She was sobbing now.

Urho leaned over and kissed her gently on the cheek. "Don't do this to yourself, honey, please." He kissed her on the eyes and then a long lingering kiss on the lips. He held her hands, put her fingers to his lips and kissed them. "It's in the past don't please, don't."

"I don't know why I went on about Alex. I don't care what others think, but I do care what you think. It matters very much to me what you think."

"I think you had a hell on earth with that man, or should I say bastard?" He cradled Claudia in his arms. "Forget it, forget about him."

She was silent for a moment, then she said, "Urho, I don't know what to do... I'm scared."

"You've nothing to be scared of ...now."

Hours later they stood at the front door saying their goodbyes. Then Urho said, "Saturday night. Will you have dinner with me?"

"Will I. . . oh wow. . . I mean, no." Claudia said.

"What?"

"What about Monday?"

"You mean the day after tomorrow Monday?" he repeated.

" Yes. Doing anything for dinner?"

"Oh, after putting the Press to bed, I'll probably have a TV dinner out of the freezer."

"Ugh!" she said.

"And maybe I'll have some of that ice cream that's been in the freezer for months, for dessert."

"Double ugh!"

"Then I'll wash it down with some week-old milk."

"You poor soul."

"That's the bachelor's life."

"I can't allow you to eat frozen food, stale ice cream and sour milk. Not when I can make a delicious salad and some lean lamb chops."

"Mmmmm, sounds delicious."

"And some wine, of course, and perhaps some Ouzo for dessert."

"Ouzo? Sounds like something from outer space."

"It's an after dinner drink. When you've had a glass you'll feel like you've landed on the moon."

"Great! I'm for some space travel. See you Monday, six-thirty." Then he held her close and kissed her. "Will that kiss hold you until Monday?"

She smiled. "Maybe." Then he leaned over and kissed her again, pinning her against the open door. "Mmmmm," she said and closed the door. And he was gone.

* * *

Later after sipping from a glass of warm milk, she fell into bed and was so exhausted that she slept soundly, something she hadn't done in a long time. Her dreams were a whirlwind. In her dream she was with Urho in his office at the Press. And suddenly they were naked and lying in each others arms on the green plush rug with the Monet painting looking down at them. The draperies in his office were closed, but they could hear the phones ringing and conversations in the ad room, where the graphic artists worked on their drawing boards and ad men made their pitches for advertisements on the phone. It was crazy! They laughed and made love there on the plush rug.

Her other dream was more like a nightmare. Alex's hands made sharp hard slapping sounds as he struck her face. He took a beer bottle and smashed it against the side of her head. Glass exploded beer and foam splashed over them. Suddenly Claudia woke with the sound of glass breaking. She turned on the lamp and saw the glass of milk she had placed on the night stand shattered on the floor beside her bed.

CHAPTER 27

Neil squinted across the lawn table, poured himself another scotch with a splash of water from the pitcher and for a moment watched the sailboats glide gracefully across the water, their sails moved by a western wind. A perfect Indian summer day in October, All's well in Pierre Corners, and Michigan, but what the hell are they doing in Washington? Sure, that young Kennedy is campaigning for re-election after getting us into a mess in Cuban waters and the Bay of Pigs. Neil's thoughts left deep frown lines on his forehead. He's too young to be president Neil finally concluded and turned his thoughts elsewhere.

Here he was on his island. For that is what Neil considered it—his island as he sat in a cushioned lawn chair at the water's edge. He frowned again. What was that Claudia up to, now? Was she being paid off by the union to spy, or by Richard? And why the hell was Urho interested in her? Whatever she had in mind would not do the Press or Urho any good. And that was for damn sure! He'd better watch her closely.

Then there was that book on the gifted she was writing. He'd made sure she was NOT working on it during Press time. Her Press assignments kept her too busy and besides Tessie watched her every movement for him. And his old friend, Matt wasn't any help. He dropped in often to talk to Claudia about the book and the proposed school. And how the hell did Matt talk Yiannis into drawing up plans for the proposed gifted school? Damn that Matt!

There was no getting away from them. Neil's thoughts kept going round and round and always came back to the same thing, the Press. That was his plight, because he had few confidantes. Of course, he could no longer confide in Greta, or even Urho for that matter. Richard as a confident was long gone. He'd switched to the other side. So Neil found himself with only one friend—Yiannis, only because he was a patient listener, never argued, and provided Neil with a sounding board to vent his anger and frustration.

It was building the water plant in Pierre Corners that brought Neil and Yiannis closer, and at the opening ceremony last week, Neil and Yiannis shared the podium with the mayor. Yiannis had been true to his word and brought the plant in a month ahead of schedule.

Now that the plant was running and bringing clean water into every home in Pierre Corners, Neil was considering selling the Press. But it was only words he mouthed, nothing serious, just words. Yes, that was the song-and-dance he gave Richard when he fired him. But instead, almost immediately, he began plotting an expansion of the Press and the demise of the union's threat—even before the union had made an attempt to organize the Press.

He leaned back in his chair, his fingers meeting behind his head. A kaleidoscopic series of events with Dora flashed through his mind and he smiled. His eyes closed, he daydreamed about Dora, how when they made love they became one body, one soul, one heart, in a way he had never been with any other woman. And he knew Dora felt it too, this unique bonding. They were physically and emotionally joined into a single being.

But somehow in his dream, Greta appeared. She was always there. Yes, he had confronted her, demanded a divorce, but she would not budge. Damn, why did he tie up his land holdings in her name? It was her suggestion, and at the time a good idea. Besides he had been too busy with the Press. Now he thought, maybe that was not such a good idea. Sure, they had struck a bargain many years ago, and she was a good manager of the land holdings. Greta was shrewd and had the legal clout to back her up, all nice and tidy, all drawn up by very expensive and competent attorneys.

Nevertheless he had to get Greta out of the picture. It would cost him, he knew that from the beginning. Now, Greta was gone for the time being. She had decided to take a short trip to New York City to buy a winter wardrobe and see some plays. She's gone, and he could return to his island for a few days. Damn he missed his home, his island. Greta, that miserable woman!

Neil thought, they both were in New York— Greta and Dora, but not together. Dora and Greta—Greta and Dora. His eyes closed against the sun, and finally in sleep. He awoke startled. He looked at his watch; it was one o'clock, time for lunch. Then he reached for his binoculars at his side and focused on a sail boat with red sails. Tiring of watching the boats, he set the binoculars down on the table, picked up his drink, and felt hands covering his eyes.

"Guess who?" Her voice was deep, throaty as he had remembered. He turned his head, put down his drink, and managed to grab both her wrists, holding them. She struggled.

"Caught you!"

She was breathing heavily, her cheeks flushed. "I'm glad you caught me," Dora said.

He said, barely containing his joy. "Mine, you're all mine." He rose, covered her face with kisses. "What a beautiful surprise!"

"Yes," she said, and they embraced. Finally he sat down and Dora dropped down beside him, sitting on the grass, her hands in his lap. His hands traveled to her face, paused for a moment at her lips, then moved upward to the scarf on her head. He unfastened it and her hair, loose, fell down around her shoulders.

"It's been too long," he said.

"I know. I had to see you—had to touch you," she said. She closed her eyes and laid her head in his lap. Neil stroked her long hair. For several minutes neither spoke. Then he shook her gently. "Darling, come sit next to me. It's damp on the grass." He patted the empty lawn chair. "God, I've missed you." She sat next to him. He leaned over and kissed her "Let me look at you. It's been so long."

She wore a yellow wraparound skirt and a white halter top, a yellow wool sweater was thrown over her shoulders. His eyes took her in, from her long, sun streaked hair, to her sandal feet.

He kissed her again, and it was like their first kiss in the mansion after he had given her his grandmother's hair brooch. Now he looked at the brooch fastened to her halter and his fingers traced the pattern. "I have a wonderful idea," he said. "Let's go sailing."

"Oh yes, let's."

Neil stared at her. "God, you're beautiful. With the sun behind you, you look like an angel."

"Thank you." Dora smiled.

"No, you look like honey, all gold, sun ripened."

"You make me sound like some kind of golden raisin. Want to taste?" she teased, getting up from the lawn chair.

Neil reached for her but she escaped his grasp.

"See? You can't catch me," she said. She raced to a tall oak and ran around it. Neil got up from the chair and chased her. Dora's long legs took giant strides, her blonde hair flew. She looked back, teasing, "Catch me, catch me."

Neil panting, breathing hard, exhausted, finally sat down beneath the oak. "I'm too old to play games."

She fell down beside him, laughing, kissing him. "My poor darling, you're not that old." She ruffled his white hair.

"Come here woman."

"Yes, yes."

He kissed her, his tongue found its way into her mouth. "God, you even taste like honey."

"I know." Arm in arm they walked to the screened gazebo. He reached for the phone on the white wicker desk and dialed the marina. "I plan to go sailing this afternoon. Please prepare the sailboat. Yes, in half an hour."

"Come," he said to Dora. "Let's take a walk." They spent the time waiting for his boat by walking about the estate, visiting the bird sanctuary, observing the exotic birds and feeding the ducks, squirrels and tame deer on the grounds, relishing this time they had together.

`Finally a signal from the dock told Neil that the boat was ready, and they walked down to the 30-foot sailboat. Two crewmen were on board. The older one had started the auxiliary engine. The other, a young man with a freckled face, handed Neil a clip board with a check list.

"Everything set?" Neil asked, glancing at the list.

"Yes sir."

"Fuel tank?"

"Full, sir."

The older man sounded the whistle briefly, testing it. The hatch covers were open to allow the engine and fuel tanks space to ventilate. Both men conferred with Neil, "There's a full picnic lunch on board, sir."

"Good."

"Champagne, too, sir," said the younger man.

"Excellent," Neil said.

"She's ready to sail, sir," said the older crewman.

"Thank you," Neil said. He helped Dora aboard. "Put on a life jacket, they're in the bow."

"Aye, aye, sir," Dora said, quickly slipping on a life jacket and giving him a salute.

"And untie those two bow lines. You're part of a working crew now, Dora."

"Yes, sir," she saluted again.

Neil was an expert sailor. He guided the sailboat cautiously into the channel at about five miles an hour, observing the 'no wake' signs in the water. Past the channel, he shut off the engine, raised the main sail and set his course into the wind. For the first half hour, Neil was at the tiller at all times. Dora sat at his side. Being a cautious sailor, he knew that to handle a sail boat required the highest caliber of seamanship. Finally he could relax, the boat was clear of traffic and glided past island estates, pine covered shores, gleaming rocks and sandy beaches.

For more than an hour, Neil at the tiller, Dora seated beside him, they were silent, watching the blue water find its way into several secluded inlets, inhabited by sea gulls.

"Let's pull into that inlet and have some lunch. I'm starving," Neil said.

"Aye, aye, skipper. How can I help? Want me to drop anchor or something?"

"Yes, you can drop something." Neil smiled. He lowered the sails as he approached the inlet and timed his turns into the wind, arriving at the mooring with little momentum. He headed into the wind until the boat came to a stop. As the boat gently began to drift backward he shouted, "Lower the anchor over the bow and feed the line slowly after it— slowly, now."

"What?"

"Here, let me show you. The anchor is heavy." They both lowered the anchor into the water, feeding out the line, keeping the tension on it, allowing the boat's bow to remain in the wind. Neil then expertly tied off the anchor line. "That should do it." He smiled. "We deserve a drink, don't you think?"

"Aye, aye, skipper. Race you below deck."

"No more races," Neil said.

Below deck Neil reached into the compact refrigerator for the champagne. With a flourish, he uncorked the bottle and poured two glasses. "To us," he said, holding his glass high.

"To us," she took a sip. "Here's to our future, Neil."

"Yes, to our future, my darling."

"When?"

"Soon, my Dora. Now slice the cheese. It looks delicious, and the bread—mmmmmgood. Smell it. Here's some fruit, apples, grapes, peaches." Yes, a well stocked galley."

"Neil, you know what bothers me?" Dora said nibbling on some grapes and cheese.

"What?"

"That we don't have enough time—together."

"We'll have our whole life—together."

"When?"

"I'm doing my best, darling. I'll get that divorce, and soon. Don't worry."

"I'm not getting any younger," she said.

He laughed, grabbed her and held her. "You are the youngest, sexiest woman I've ever seen, especially with that life jacket on."

She looked at him. "Is it safe to take this thing off?"

"Yes, that and everything else you have on." He rose to refill his empty glass and turned on the radio. The voice of Frank Sinatra singing "Embraceable You" filled the cabin. He joined her on the couch, kissed her lips gently. Then he gave a comical leer, showing white teeth, "I've got you in my power, pretty lady!"

Dora stared. "Don 't—don't say that, don't look like that , leering at me." She gulped her champagne and began to cough.

Neil tapped her on her back lightly. "Better?"

"Thanks. I'm sorry, but that look you gave me threw me. And all that talk about power. I want your love, and power has nothing to do with it, my darling."

"Oh, I thought power was the name of the game." Neil said. He took off his life jacket and unbuttoned his shirt collar. His fleshy neck, reddened, bulged free. "Why don't you make yourself comfortable?"

"Aye, aye, captain." She stood up and untied her wrap-around skirt. His gaze followed her every move. He watched as she untied her halter, brushing back her long hair. She turned, wearing only white lace and silk panties. She tossed her skirt and halter on the bed in the cabin's corner. Then she walked up to him, hands on hips, her head tilted to one side, her hair falling across her face and touching her breasts. "You like?"

"I like." Slowly he put the champagne glass down on the table. He touched her breasts and then gently his hands traveled down her tanned skin and pulled the lace and silk underpants down. "Take them off," he whispered.

"Help me."

"You're driving me crazy." Then he was holding her tightly, kissing her.

"Oh, Neil. When you kiss me there I want to scream."

They lay on the cabin bed in the soft light of a single lamp. He held her and kissed her eyelids, her nose, her ear lobes, and finally her lips.

He kissed her chin, her neck. He cupped her breasts, filled his hands with them.

And the gentle rhythmic movements of her hands on him made his skin tingle and sent shivers through him. "Neil, do you like this, and this and this?"

"Yes, yes." He went to his knees and caressed and kissed her body, her long slim legs. "Dora, my sweet, my love."

She parted her legs and he entered her. She had never felt so alive, as they became one, and she knew she would never be alone again, never. This must never stop, she thought, rising from one peak to another and another, going on forever and ever.

Afterwards, as they lay together beneath the silken sheets, he said, "My darling, I love you."

"I love you, too."

"Dora, you have changed my life, completely. I love you more than I thought I could ever love anyone."

"I need you Neil, I want you."

"You've got me!"

Later as he lay with his arms around Dora on the edge of sleep in the cabin, a sharp crash of waves hit the boat, rolled over the deck. A strange thought flashed through Neil's mind: The waves are cleansing. It's an omen. It's telling me that everything will be all right. But before he could explore that thought further, he fell off the edge of sleep

CHAPTER 28

Richard paced in his small cramped apartment. He'd better make that call, he thought. It was late November, 1963, and things were happening, not only in Pierre Corners, but in the nation, a sad nation. He reached for the phone and dialed the Liemus Press. "Valley? How are you old gal?" he asked.

"Richard, this is a surprise. As for how I am, just like everyone else in this country, torn apart. Our young president, dead! Can you believe it?"

"I know. What is happening to this crazy nation? A tragedy, he was a good man, young, but an intelligent man. I hear the Press staff walked out when they heard President Kennedy was shot in Dallas."

"Yes, we did. Some went to church, others to the diner, and others to the bar. Himself didn't like it, but too bad. He ranted and raved about deadlines. Can you believe that?"

"Yes, I can," Richard said. "And where did you go, Valley, to the bar?"

"Believe it or not I went to church with Claudia. It did me good to pray, not only for our dear president, and our nation, but for the Liemus Press. We are in a mess."

"I know," Richard said. He pulled a cigarette out of his pack and lighted it with his Zippo. Then he glanced at his pocket watch. "Is this a bad time for you Valley? Can we talk?"

"Sure, we can talk."

"Good, listen, I'm interested in setting up a meeting with you and a few others from the Press. I'm sure you'll find the topic interesting. Why don't we make it tonight, your place, about eight, is that all right?"

" It sounds fine to me."

After Richard's talk with Valley, he called Claudia, Bernie, Freda and George, the ad man. It was only after George had hung up that Richard allowed himself one small, brief smile of triumph. The meeting at Valley's tonight—it would be the first win. With a satisfied nod he slipped his watch into his pocket.

When Neil had fired him, the hardest thing Richard had even done in his life was to walk into union headquarters in downtown Detroit and tell them that he wanted to work with them to make the Press a union newspaper. Although he felt an impatience to organize the Press, install the union in it, his self-discipline and bred-in-the bone motivation were strong enough to make him pace his work, perfect his plan. A number of men at the union approved of him and his plan. Only John Butler, a union representative, had to be convinced that Richard's plan would work.

When they first met, Butler, a big man with a head of unruly red hair, had taken Richard aside and said, "I don't much like you, Lucavate. And I imagine you feel the same way about me. But I carry a lot of clout on the executive board of this union, and if you expect to get anything done, you better listen to me."

"Meaning what?" Richard had said.

"I just want to make it perfectly clear that you'll be on a short leash; I'll be looking over your shoulder every inch of the way until the Press is locked up. Clear?"

"I just want to do it right, make the Press a union newspaper."

"Good, that's what I want too."

Now Richard snuffed out his cigarette in an ash tray. That conversation was still vivid in his mind. He had mixed thoughts about being a union representative. Perhaps tonight's meeting at Valley's would provide the answers to some of the questions that had been bothering him as he wavered between the union and newspaper work.

The meeting had been narrowed down to just five –Valley, Claudia, Bernie, Freda and George. They'd get the message out to the rest, encourage them to demand an election authorized by the Michigan Labor Relations Board to make the Press a union newspaper. Did he forget anyone? Yes, certainly. He'd need Butler at the meeting. He'd better call him.

Picking Valley and her apartment was not by chance. Richard knew Valley and Neil went way back. She had some hold on Neil, Richard was certain of that. He knew that Valley and Neil had been lovers at one time. And then there was the tragic accident that killed Valley's husband. And always in the background, always in the shadows was Greta—watching, waiting. Greta was a shrewd, tough old broad, thought Richard.

What was the deal there? Why was Greta the key persons involved with the funding of the mall, with the Press Corporation land holdings? It puzzled Richard. He knew that the change came almost immediately after Urho's birth. Strange that Greta had chosen to go to New York to have the baby.

Urho, the son and heir, was propelled as a youngster into the newspaper business. Twelve years of the finest schools, private tutors, art lessons, the University of Michigan. Only the Korean conflict had interrupted the big plan Neil had for his son. He wanted to make his son in his image, thought Richard. He didn't succeed, Urho was his own man.

That's the phrase Neil used to describe his son, "his own man."

Well, he certainly had to prove it, if the rumors Richard had heard had any foundation. Neil was losing it. He'd heard that Neil was still living in the penthouse suite at the Press, and only went to the island when Greta left town. And more than once the police in Pierre Corners had found Neil wandering down Main Street at three, four in the morning, sometimes in his robe and pajamas. And then there was that mess with Dora. Neil was old enough to be her father. Richard's thoughts abruptly changed when he drove up to Valley's apartment.

When he glanced at the building where Valley lived, he was reminded of an old town house in Grand Rapids. Then as he walked

207

up the old walnut staircase, the image changed; he was certain he would find Valley entertaining in the equivalent of an old movie set, heavy furniture, lace curtains, candles everywhere.. Valley's door was open.

But the reality was more astonishing than interiors he had dreamed up. Valley's apartment was a four-page layout from Better Homes and Gardens, with a smart meld of antiques, modern and early American furnishings that gave the impression that an expensive decorator had a hand in it. Her Christmas tree, a giant spruce, loomed in a corner, a glitter of silver, everything silver, ornaments, tinsel and tiny white lights.

She must have hired a caterer, because a buffet table featured a spread of ham, chicken, shrimp, a variety of cheeses, pickles, carrot sticks, celery curls, and crackers. He could see a full bar had been set up in her black and white tiled kitchen.

Looking around and spotting John Butler deep in conversation with Bernie, he began to revise his opinion of him. Perhaps he underestimated this man. The two big men were near the Christmas tree.

It took him less than a minute to work his way through the room. Valley greeted him with martini in hand. "See, I had my Christmas tree put up early, even though it's not December yet. I wanted to bring a little cheer. Speaking of cheer, Richard, what can I get you to drink, vodka, brandy, Scotch?" She smiled as she teased him, knowing that he didn't drink.

"You know better than that, Valley, how about some black coffee?"

"Coming right up. How do you like my tree?"

"Fantastic!"

"Thanks, I'll get your coffee in a minute. Everybody's here except Claudia. She called and said she'd be late—something about a baby sitter."

Richard looked around him. He greeted Bernie and George, and looked in the kitchen to see Freda eating a sandwich. Lastly he nodded to Butler. He smiled. He knew that he had picked key Press people. He also knew that if he was going to start a revolution, he had the power here, in this room. Now he had to sell his idea to them. The chance to unionize the Press and stick it to that bastard Neil left him light headed with the sheer thrust of it, the power of it.

In the past, Richard had gone with his intuition and his intuition had paid off. If anyone had ever told Richard Lucavate, when he was associate publisher at the Liemus Press that one day he would round up key people of the Press to talk them into unionizing it, he would have been outraged.

The handful of people in Valley's apartment reflected the strength of the Press. Richard knew that for a fact and everything that was said tonight would reaffirm his commitment to the union. Richard would see to that before anyone walked out of the door.

Ten minutes later, while Richard sipped his coffee, Butler walked up to him. Butler said, "I know I've been giving you a bad time, but you've got to realize that we're playing hard ball now."

"I knew that from the start," Richard said.

"Mr. Lucavate—." Butler began. "Oh, hell, may I call you Dick, and you call me John? I don't think this gathering is a place for formality."

"My name is Richard."

"All right, Richard. I just have a feeling that you and I could do each other some good, even if it's just an exchange of information. And I know the union will benefit by having a powerful person— you—on its side."

Richard, pocket watch in hand, glanced at it. "I think we'd better call this meeting to order. We can't wait any longer for Claudia. I'll fill her in later."

"Right," Butler said. He picked up a green folder that he had laid on the coffee table. "I'm ready."

"Attention, people," began Richard. " I feel naked without my pica ruler, but let's settle down, we're going to start, now."

Butler removed some charts from the folder and passed them around.

Bernie, his old pipe filling the room with rum-honey tobacco aroma, glanced at the chart. "Is that big slice of the pie our cut?"

Butler nodded. "Yes, but that's only half of the story. Some of the things we'll bargain for on your behalf will include sick leave, job classifications, promotion within the company, retirement benefits, vacation pay, pensions, and much more. But first we have to concentrate on getting the union in, and that means an election. That's our main priority."

"How about discrimination?" Freda asked. She munched on a cracker. Several crackers with cheese on a plate rested in her lap.

"Sex discrimination?" Butler asked.

"No, fat discrimination." George said. He laughed out loud.

"Shut up!" Freda said. "I mean discrimination against those who join the union. Will we get fired if we join?"

"No, you can't. It's the law. But to make sure, we can include that stipulation in the contract."

Richard could see the relief on Freda's face.

"Thank you, I feel better now," Freda said.

"Don't thank me. Richard is the one you all should thank. You're damn lucky to have him in your corner." He smiled at Richard.

"I've heard about your problems at the Press," Butler said. "Old man Liemus isn't going to give us Brownie points for initiating the union vote. He's going to fight us all the way to the bank. We're starting from Zero! Sure, the Press is the best damn newspaper in the state, sure it's gotten tons of awards, more than any other publication. But who made it great? You all did!" He paused for a moment and then looked at them. "Sure the old man has threatened to sell the Press. But that's all it is, a threat to keep the union out. We're not buying it. And we've got an ace in the hole."

"What's that?" Bernie asked.

"We strike!"

"My God!" Freda said. She dropped her plate filled with crackers and cheese.

"What did you think?" Bernie eyed Freda. "This is hard ball we're playing."

"Strike, that'll be the day," George said.

"This is something we must consider," Richard said.

"What the hell are you talking about, strike. Shit!" Valley said, dazed.

"How many martinis have you had?" Butler asked.

"None of your business, big guy. This is my house and I can—."

"Valley for god's sake, lay off the booze," Richard said. "Get me some black coffee, and have some yourself. This is serious business."

"Oh, shut up!" Valley said and walked carefully to the kitchen.

"Should she be alone in the kitchen?" Bernie asked.

"I'll go," Freda said.

"People let's get back to our discussion," Richard said.

"Okay, so what about clout?" Bernie asked glancing at Butler.

"If you'll excuse me, John, I'll answer that question," Richard said. He walked to the Christmas tree, fingered a silver bell. The pine scent filled the room. "I'm getting clout. In case of a strike, and I don't expect one, I've got back up, and clout that will shut down the Press, that is if we strike. We'll get to the heart of the Press—the advertisers. And my clout will see that no one and I mean no one advertises in the Press, until the union gets in. I mean there won't even be a one-inch ad."

Bernie said, "You sound so sure of yourself." This clout must be damn impressive—must have a lot of influence in Pierre Corners."

Then Valley returned with a cup of coffee. She carefully placed it on the coffee table near Richard's chair. "Thank you," he said.

"No problem," she said. "And I didn't need a body guard in the kitchen either." She glared at Freda.

Freda began, "I didn't mean to—."

"Of course you did." She sank into the overstuffed chair.

Richard sighed, checked his pocket watch and said, "Back to the clout that you mentioned. In about fifteen minutes OUR clout will walk through that door."

Butler said, "Really?"

"Yes, John, and you have less than fifteen minutes to wrap up your presentation."

* * *

Fifteen minutes later while Butler was putting away his charts, pay scale graphs and literature, the door bell rang.

Bernie said, "I'll get it. Must be our clout, right?"

Richard smiled. "Maybe."

Bernie opened the door, "Why Yiannis, Matt, what the hell are you doing here?"

"Show them in, damn it!" Richard said. Just then his pocket watch alarm went off. "Right on time as usual." Then turning to those in the room he said, "People, may I present our clout."

"Clout, my ass, what can they do against Himself?" Valley asked.

"Believe it. These two men have Pierre Corners locked up," Richard said. "And Neil knows it. But he doesn't know that they are on our side."

The door bell rang again. Valley said, "I'll get it this time. Maybe more clout?"

She walked very carefully to the door, swung it open and looked into Claudia's face. "Well, come on in kid. The show is getting mighty exciting now."

PART FOUR
THE UNION

CHAPTER 29

By the third week of December, 1963, Valley had attended five union meetings. After the first meeting at her house, all she was conscious of was the rapid passage of time, one union meeting blurring into another, and another.

Now as she pecked away at a story, and tried to visualize the look on Neil's face when he had come down from the penthouse earlier raging and waving a letter he got from the Michigan Labor Relations Board announcing that the majority of the Press employees wanted a union election.

"Like hell they'll unionize the Press. Over my dead body."

Valley said, "That can be arranged, Neil."

"Go to hell, bitch!" He fled the advertising room and raced down the corridor to the elevator, and his retreat, his penthouse.

Hours later Tessie deposited a bulletin at every desk in the news room and advertising department. When she got to Valley's desk, Valley said, "What now, stupid?"

"It's a special memo from Himself. And don't call me stupid!"

As she picked up the memo Valley thought, things had been happening since those union meetings. George and Bernie had talked to all the Press employees stressing the good deal that the union would give them. Both men had made their point and the election scheduled for next week looked like it would be in the union's favor. Then Valley read the note: "The union or your job! It's your choice.

If the union is voted in, as God is my witness, there will be no Press. It's your choice. The union or your job!

It was signed "Neil Liemus, publisher."

Valley said, "That does it!" She raced to the elevator. In a matter of minutes she was in Neil's office, waving the note in his face. "Trying to scare us? What the hell does this mean?"

"I see it is working." He turned his chair abruptly away from her to face the windows. It was snowing. Valley wondered what he saw there, or what he avoided seeing. True he had a capacity for fury. He managed to anger her on an average of once a day. But she knew she gave him a few uncomfortable moments. Damn, she had loved him so much—once, so long ago.

Now Neil turned and faced her. "Well, what do you want?"

Valley shook her head. "Nothing." Then she paused, looked at him and said, "Everything!"

"What the hell does that mean?"

"Listen, Neil, I know you fired Richard. He didn't quit or take an early retirement as you said. But that's ancient history. What we're talking about now is union, and a fair shake for us employees. We want what every other newspaper in Michigan worth its salt has— meaning good wages, retirement, overtime pay, sick pay, insurance— and- and—." She was breathless and knew that Neil was getting irritated with her rambling, so she cut it short. "You can't keep the union out. Too many of us want it."

Neil was silent. He sat slumped in his chair, regarding her thoughtfully. "I'm going to damn well try to keep it out of my newspaper. But I want to ask one question, and I want an honest answer, okay?"

"Okay."

"Is Urho involved in this union business?"

Valley's eyes grew wide. "Why should he be? He's management."

"You didn't answer my question."

"I've told you all I know." She pressed her fingertips to her temple. She was tired, exhausted.

"A simple yes or no, that's all I want."

Abruptly Valley turned to walk out of the office.

Neil got up. "You always manage to skirt the issue, especially when it comes to Urho."

Valley could feel her face getting hot. Yes, he still could get to her, even after all these years, she thought. He still had it. He was an old fool, but he still had it. And he was flaunting it by having an affair with Urho's wife, Dora. No, his ex-wife, remember?

Quickly she shook her head. She had to clear her mind if she was going to bring Neil around to her way of thinking. She'd once been able to do it, but that was a long time ago. Finally she said, "No sense in talking to you." And she walked to the door.

"Oh, Sun Valley," he said, using his private nickname for her, which she loathed.

"Yes?" she replied, acidly. "And don't call me that."

"Forgive me. Just a slip into the past. But I did want to say that you and Urho have much in common."

"Shut up!" She slammed the door after her.

The phone in Neil's office rang. He let it ring several times before he grabbed the receiver. Valley paused at the closed door. She was angry. Why did he bring that up? Should she listen to his phone conversation? Maybe it will be useful. Then she heard, Neil's voice, loud and clear—"Liemus here." Then a pause, then "Yes, my Dora. How are you? How, good it is to hear your voice, darling."

Valley scanned the hallway, she was safe, no one in sight. Good! She continued listening at the door, listening to Neil's booming voice as he said, " I miss you very much my dear. Oh? You have good news?"

Valley wondered what Dora was up to now. That bitch!

Neil said, "I know what it is. You're coming back to Michigan. You've had it with New York."

Then a long pause—and finally Neil said, "Pregnant? God, are you sure? I'm so happy. I'm going to be a father, again. I can't believe it. Yes, you should stay in New York where the best obstetricians are."

Valley at the door, cursed under her breath. Her blue eyes became cynical. That old fool got Dora pregnant.

Finally Valley heard Neil say, "Good. That's what I wanted to hear. I love you. I'm taking the next plane out of here to be with you. You've made me very happy, my darling. Goodbye."

At that very moment Valley raced to the elevator and pushed the down button. Dora, pregnant! Downstairs in the newsroom, she hid behind a Detroit newspaper reading the latest news from Detroit about a report of a crime summit meeting held by the mayor and city council. She had to get her mind off Neil, off Dora, off the expected baby. They're having a baby, what a mess, she thought.

Valley flung her newspaper aside and it joined the Liemus Press on the cluttered newsroom floor. She said, "That stupid Detroit council, what we need is an ANTI-crime summit. Hell, we'll have a riot if this keeps up."

Claudia said, "It does look bad, doesn't it?"

"Sure it does." She went back to her half finished story in her typewriter.

"Too bad you're not with that Detroit newspaper, you'd set them straight." Claudia said that in jest but Valley took it for a fact.

"Damn right. I've got brains! Not like some of these gutless wizards."

"True," Claudia said. "Your tantrums don't bother me. I know you're just getting primed for the union election next week." Claudia winked.

"Yes." Valley didn't wink back. She was angry—angry with that call Neil got, angry with Dora and yes, now even angry with that unborn baby.

"Don't look so gloomy, the union will get in and there won't be a strike."

"I'm not worried about the union."

"Besides we've got all that clout." Claudia said. "But first things first, we have to get a fair contract."

Valley nodded and without a word went back to her story. She couldn't get Neil or Dora off her mind.

A week later on union election day, Valley was still in a foul mood. At the Press the Michigan Labor Relations Board representative had set up make-shift voting booths in the board room. The long board table had been pushed aside and two booths were put in the center of the room. As a vote of confidence Richard had persuaded Butler to select Valley to be the union's representative when the ballots were cast. Tessie was named by Neil to oversee the ballots for the Press.

All day long employees at the Press voted. At seven p.m. the counting began. In addition to Valley and Tessie there were two men from the relations board involved.

Valley was tired, dead tired. She had spent the day checking off names as employees filed by her to vote. She was in no mood to shuffle ballots. At nine o'clock all the ballots were counted and at a signal from the relations board representative, Valley and Bernie herded all the employees into the ad room. Tessie and the two relations board representatives were at the head of the room. Bernie and Valley were in the rear, near the door.

Claudia went up to Bernie, "What are we waiting for?"

"We're waiting for Urho. He represents management. You know that Neil wants no part of this election. He left for New York last week. He either had an important meeting, or he had the hots for Dora."

"Oh, shut up!" Valley said.

Bernie turned to Valley, "All kidding aside, I think you did a terrific job today at the election."

She leaned toward him. "You really think so?"

"Scout's honor." He raised his palm.

She said, "Listen, I worked my ass off for this union. I want to stick it to that bastard, Neil. I have my own private reasons."

"Do you?"

"Sure. Nervous, Bernie?"

"Nah, once Urho gets here and makes the announcement, we're home free."

"Here's number one son, now," Valley said.

A hush fell over the crowd as Urho walked into the ad room. In

219

ten minutes Urho had most of them seated, on desks, chairs, and they were all attentive.

"Ladies and Gentlemen," he began. "I want to thank you for participating in an orderly election. Well, shall we see what the results are?" He opened the envelope. The murmur from the crowd swelled. "Let's quiet down please," Urho said. "The results are as follows— fifty-five for the union, and twenty against. The Liemus Press is now a union shop. We will get together soon to draw up a contract. Congratulations." He shook hands with the union representatives, Bernie, Valley and Tessie. Then he left the room.

Clyde shouted, "We won! We're in business, now!" Somehow he had managed to scramble onto a desk. Now he was snapping pictures with his camera.

Copy paper flew into the air. Valley said, "This calls for a celebration." She hugged Claudia. Suddenly the room was filled with flying paper and paper airplanes. George blew up several balloons and tossed them in the air.

In the thick of the happy crowd, Valley motioned to Claudia. "Let's go to the diner. It's a mad house in here."

"I've got to make a call to Mrs. Dixon to see if Jamie got there. I'll meet you in the diner."

A few minutes later Valley spotted Claudia threading her way through the crowd in the diner to the back table where Valley presided. "Over here, kid. I saved you a seat. "Waitress, more coffee, here."

Sipping her coffee, Valley said, "We made it, kid. With the union behind us, the sky's the limit. We've stuck it to that old bastard, but good."

"I'm surprised at you, Valley," began Claudia. "I've never known you to gloat."

"Well, I'm gloating now. Once we get a decent contract, things will happen, good things. No more crap from Himself."

"Right on," George said, leaning over the table. "We're in the big league now."

"I'll drink to that," Claudia said, raising her coffee cup. "Hey, look who's coming in the diner."

"Well, what do you know? But he should be here, he's the man of the hour. He started the ball rolling. He had to be here to celebrate with us," Valley said. Then she motioned to him. "Richard, come back here, join us."

George rushed to meet him, put his arms around him and said, "We did it. We certainly did it!"

"That's what I heard. So it was a success. Great!"

"You did it Richard," Valley said.

"No. I beg to differ. YOU did it, all of you." Then he pulled out his timepiece, glanced at it."

"Are you going to time us?" Valley asked.

"Just a habit. Like Claudia has her worry beads, I've got my watch. Ah, I see she's got them in her hand."

"Caught me," Claudia said, her face flushed. "Yes, the beads are my security blanket. I even held them when I went into the booth to vote."

Richard smiled. "Brought you luck. Now that we've got the union in the Press, the risk is minimal. We'll get a good solid contract. Not from Neil—but I think Urho will give us a fair shake. I've heard rumors about Neil. Are they true?"

George said, "Search me, but as for a good contract, Amen to that. I can't see a strike in our future. We've got the union in, and we've got our secret clout. Remember?"

CHAPTER 30

Claudia was in a strange mood. Now she knew what it felt like to be split in two, right down the middle. Manic-depressive, is that what they call it? She was curled up on the couch in her living room. First the election, and then everyone celebrating at the diner—everything. Had she left it just a few hours ago? Too many things had happened. She couldn't sleep, although it was almost midnight.

For the past hour she had been sitting by the fireplace mesmerized by the flickering flames, sipping white wine and thinking about the Press, about Urho, about her future. She was a writer, a good one. She believed in the two principles of good reporting: anyone is capable of anything, and things are rarely what they seem.

But she had also learned since working at the Press, that journalism was a lousy profession. Men and women of talent, ability, imagination found work in the universities, industry, science—few in journalism Why? Maybe because it was a strange, confused often heart breaking profession. She knew it well.

Why was the newspaper business a back stabbing, dirty dealing world? Neil must know, he was a king pin for many years. Claudia knew that this business was just a temporary job for her. She did not want to make it her life's work. No. Never! What did she want to do with the rest of her life? First of all, she wanted happiness, love and success in her writing, books, of course. Is that asking for too much, God? No, just do it. Do it for yourself. Do it for Jamie. She glanced at Jamie's easel in the corner, her sketches hanging on the wall—the roses, the violets, Claudia's worry beads.

Then images began appearing in the flames, vivid images of Alex. He was leering at her. His fist was clenched. He was drunk, angry, cursing. He hit her hard, again and again. Claudia shook her head, took a deep breath. "No, no," she cried aloud. With an effort she banished the images. She jumped to her feet, reached for the wine bottle and poured herself another glass of wine. By the time she heard the doorbell ring she was in no condition to answer it calmly.

Finally she was standing in the foyer staring at her reflection in the long mirror. No make up, no fancy dress. Just an old red bathrobe, scuffed up slippers. Not a tempting invitation for anyone. "Now you're really thinking crazy. Stay calm," she said aloud. By the time she reached the front door, she had a grip on herself.

Claudia thought that it couldn't be anything serious. Jamie was asleep in her bed, and she had just talked to her mother on the phone. When she got to the door she said, "Who is it?"

"'It's Urho."

"Urho?" Quickly she unlatched the door and he appeared out of the night, a box under his arm. He looked at her for a moment and then embraced her, kissed her. It was the first time in days that they had been alone with each other. There was an awkward pause. "You okay?" he asked.

"Yes."

"I didn't want to scare you with this late visit. But I had to see you, talk to you."

"Come in. I was just having some wine, and looking into the fire, looking for my future. Can I get you a glass of wine?"

"Yes, thank you. Who's that on the radio? Ah yes, Sinatra." He placed the box on the coffee table.

She returned with the wine. "Yes, I've tuned into the all-night station that plays his records." After sitting quietly beside Urho in the darkness, staring at the fire, after listening to Sinatra, after sipping wine, Claudia found herself talking about the union and the election. She didn't realize she was going to open up to him about the union until she had already begun. She seemed to hear herself in mid-sentence, and then the words poured out. For half an hour she spoke continuously, pausing only for an occasional sip of wine, recalling the first union meeting at Valley's house, and succeeding meetings. When she closed her eyes she could see Richard, just as clear as she could see Urho now, here, sitting beside her.

Finally, she paused. Urho said, "I'm glad the union got voted in. We'll get a good contract, one that everyone will be happy with, and then we will be the happy family that I've talked about for so many years." He grinned.

Claudia smiled. "Happy family— I remember that's the first thing you said when Richard introduced us, the day I started at the Press."

"Yes. I remember— happy family. It was a joke then, but maybe we can make it happen, now. Almost forgot, I've got a present for you. It's a little late for Christmas. But just in time for 1964, a new and good year, I hope." He picked up the box.

"A present— I was wondering what was in that box."

"Here, open it." He kissed her gently.

She tore through the wrappings like a child opening a gift. She searched though the tissue and found a gold and black silk Japanese kimono. "My, it's beautiful!" The robe was embroidered in gold and silver threads. On the back was a gold dragon. Claudia burrowed her face in the silky softness. "It's so beautiful. Where did you get it?"

"I've had it a long time— bought it in Japan when I was on R & R after getting wounded in Korea. I packed it away, thinking I would give it to someone special. That was a long time ago." His eyes never left Claudia. He held her hand, and then lifted it to his lips and kissed it.

Then Claudia embraced him. She picked up the robe and threw it over her shoulders and danced around the room as Sinatra sang, "Strangers in the Night." "Oh, Urho, you make me so happy." She hugged him again, kissed him gently on the cheek.

"Yes," he said touching her cheek. "I'm absolutely happy too." He kissed her again and again. In the living room, with the fire blazing in the fireplace, they whispered their love to each other. And then he grabbed her and kissed her, long, hard.

She forgot how tired she had been. She forgot her aching muscles, and forgot everything in his embrace as they danced. They moved in a slow dance to Sinatra's love song. "Don't leave me," she said. "Don't ever leave me." So they danced entwined, swaying to the music.

"I love you," he said. "I can't help myself. I'm hooked."

"Hooked are you, on a writer, on an author?"

" Yes, I'm hooked on a beautiful woman, who just happens to be a writer, author. I'm addicted."

"Oh, Urho," she said, kissing him frantically. "What a couple of crazies we are."

"Crazies?"

"Yes." She held him close, would not free him from her embrace, pressing him to her. She ran her fingers up and down his strong back, his shoulders. Then she laughed.

"What's so funny?"

"This insane world is funny and we are two crazies. I took part in unionizing the Press and I'm kissing the son of the boss. Is that sane?"

"I don't know. But I hope it doesn't end with just kissing," he said pulling her down on the rug in front of the fire place. In the soft glow of the fire he held her and kissed her. For Claudia the world shrank to just sighs, sounds and sensations; the scent of him, the hiss of logs on the fire, the yellows and reds of the flames. She knew that what they had was special, powerful. They were physically and emotionally joined into one being. She knew this would last as long as they lived. She could trust him rely on him as she'd never been able to rely on another human being—and most of all she knew that she would never be afraid again.

In their love making when she lifted up to meet his thrust, she cried out his name, "Urho! Urho." Still later in the after glow, while they lay together on the rug staring into the flames, she said, "It's a miracle. Us, I mean. Do you believe in miracles?"

"Yes, I do darling." Then he wrapped the kimono around her. "Keep warm."

Much later when the fire had burned down to embers, Urho said,

"I'd better go. I don't want to, but soon Jamie will be up."

"And she'll say, 'What are you doing here? Going to have breakfast with us?'"

Urho turned to Claudia, "Then I'll stay."

"Sure, if you can make French toast." He smiled as they walked to the door. "See you tomorrow. Sorry can't make French toast," he said. He gave her a tender kiss. "Hope we can negotiate a fair contract. Then all would be right with the world. Hooray!"

"Shhh," she said. " We mustn't wake up Jamie."

Then in a stage whisper he said, "Maybe we can use Jamie at the Press. She's a good artist."

Claudia smiled. "Sure she is, now scat!"

* * *

During the next few months as contract negotiations waned, a cold war prevailed at the Press. With Richard no longer there and no longer Neil's scapegoat, Urho assumed the role. On one occasion Claudia and others on the staff witnessed the stormy outburst between father and son. Neil had barged into one of the news meetings gasping, shaking, cursing and lunged at Urho, grabbing him by the throat, shaking him, insisting that he was working 'behind his back' with the union. It took all of Bernie's strength to separate the two.

Claudia knew Urho coped as best as he could and realized that Neil now had difficulty staying in control. Problems, pressure, tension, Neil had thrived on them, once. Then he had made swift decisions when it concerned the Press. Now he wrestled with the smallest problem.

Also Tessie had started a rumor that Dora was pregnant. Unfounded, Claudia, suspected, because Urho had told her that Dora didn't want any children. "There were too many unwanted children in the world," Dora would say. But, Claudia had her suspicions. There were Neil's frequent trips to New York to see Dora. Of course, Claudia knew that Neil was obsessed with Dora. Neil's neurotic behavior seeped through the Press walls creating a depressing atmosphere.

Now on a sunny May morning, six months to the day when the union was voted in the Press, Claudia stood by her desk, fretting. It had been weeks since she'd written a paragraph on her gifted book.

Will she ever finish it? Claudia thought. The union and contract negotiations had occupied her as well as everyone else at the Press. Sometimes she couldn't even function as a reporter, submitting rough copy articles to Urho.

Now she watched as a cheerful Matt walked up to her desk. Abruptly he said, "I'm sixty-three years old. And I'm a damn good teacher, damn good principal."

"No doubt about that," Claudia said. She smiled. It was the first time she had smiled in days.

"I'm the best there is. Teaching not only is a profession, it's a mind opener. That's my work, opening minds—especially the gifted mind. Your book is one of the tools. We'll reach tens of thousands with it. My dream is to have it in every school in Michigan, every school in the United States."

"Wait a minute. It's not finished yet."

"It will be and soon." A mischievous grin appeared on his face. He reached over to the next desk and shook Bernie's hand. A cloud of smoke enveloped both of them.

"How are you doing, Matt? Hot enough for you today, this May day?"

"Nope. I'm ready for some really hot weather. Why in the summer of 1930 it reached 110."

"Before my time, old man," Bernie said.

Matt laughed and sat in the chair opposite Claudia's desk. "Yes, I imagine it was." Then he turned his attention to Claudia. "Of course you're aware that we've broken ground for the school? Yiannis chose an ideal site, overlooking the Detroit River. And most of those great oaks and maples will stand. I don't want a barren site. No bulldozing down the trees. I gave orders and Yiannis is in full agreement. He's following through." Matt grinned. "But you know all about it, you wrote the story about the new school's site."

Claudia said, "Yes I did. And I know why you're telling me all this. You're like a little kid, telling and retelling good news—happy news."

"You're wise to an old man's ways, aren't you?"

227

"Yes."

"Saw Richard today," he whispered. "But that's not why I'm here." There was a faint smile on his face. "Did you know I had clout? Enough of that—I've got something important to tell you."

"About your clout?" she whispered.

He chuckled. He reached in his suit pocket. In spite of the heat, Matt wore his usual blue wool suit. His eyes bright, he took her hand and placed a sheet of paper in it. From the letterhead she saw it was from the University of Michigan.

"The University of Michigan wants you," he said.

"They can have me—if the price is right."

Matt glanced around the news room. Then he turned to Claudia and whispered. "The university press wants to publish your book on the gifted."

"What?" Then Claudia read the letter. "But it's not finished."

"They bought it on the synopsis and the first ten chapters I sent them."

"That's great news! Are you sure? Thank you. I can't believe it. I'd better finish it, and soon," Claudia said.

That's not all the good news. My mission today is to cheer you up. You know about the school, and that it will be completed later this year. You know about the book contract. Now to celebrate I want to invite you to my fraternity's Masquerade Ball. It's this Saturday to celebrate the end of the term. I'm going as King Arthur. And will you be my Queen Guinevere? You've got six days to get ready."

"Queen Guinevere? Who will be Sir Lancelot?" she said.

"Have no idea. Besides we don't need him. He'd spoil the party. Run off with you." Matt smiled.

"Well, it sounds like fun. I will be Queen Guinevere to your King Arthur. We'll have our own Camelot, won't we?"

"Yes. But alas the Camelot in Washington has vanished, and so have the dreams for this nation with this war in Vietnam and the young people in an up roar. I'll be off now— back to the planning board for our gifted school." And with that, Matt left the news room and the Press building.

* * *

Where had the days gone? Claudia had hoped for a good night's sleep to wash away the confusion and the disorientation that had plagued her this past week. But now as she stood in front of the bedroom window basking on this sunny Saturday morning, she was no more in command of herself than she had been several days before when Matt had invited her to the ball. Too many things were happening—yes some were good, but some were bad. Her mind was writhing with chaotic thoughts and doubts, questions and fears Memories, good and bad tangled like snakes; mental images shifted and changed..

It had been a busy week for her. She had managed to find the perfect Queen Guinevere costume in an out-of-the way costume shop in Detroit. Just perfect, a shimmering silk, powder blue, the long sleeves and oval neckline trimmed in delicate lace. And her slippers were gold, not glass like Cinderella's. A beautiful gold crown completed her costume. She was pleased as she glanced at herself in the mirror imagining the gown she would be wearing that night. Then other thoughts began to crowd her mind, thoughts about the union. What are we going to do? she silently asked the mirror reflection. The reflection had nothing to say to her.

Then she heard Jamie's voice. And in an instant, the tall, dark haired ten-year old walked into the bedroom. "How about if I make breakfast?" she said.

Claudia said, "Great!" She hugged her daughter. "You're getting to be a big girl. Why you're almost as tall as I am."

"I am." Jamie beamed.

Minutes later in the kitchen, Jamie spread peanut butter and strawberry jam on toast. The smell of toast and frying eggs filled the room. Claudia poured the orange juice. "Mmmmmm, I love the way you make toast, eggs too," Claudia said, biting into a slice.

"My secret recipe. Why put just butter on toast? Peanut butter and jam are so much yummier."

And the mother and daughter talked, forgetting about time, spending a lazy Saturday morning in each other's company and enjoying it.

By late afternoon the sun had slipped behind a dark cloud and it had started to rain. Hours later when Matt rang the door bell, it was still raining. He wore a regal purple robe befitting a king and under it a gold and ivory fitted suit. On his head was a gold crown. He shook his practical black umbrella and set it open on the porch before going into the house.

Claudia greeted him with a low bow, appropriate for a king. "Your majesty," she said. The folds of her soft, silk blue gown surrounded her like a cloud. Claudia was truly queen of Camelot. She wore a pearl encrusted gold crown on her head.

"By George, is that you Claudia? You're a perfect queen, regal, beautiful." He tipped his crown. "I bow to you my queen." His plush purple robe swept the floor with a flourish.

Claudia beamed.

Then Jamie piped up. "No, King Arthur, she's not Claudia, but your queen."

"Yes, you are right, my dear. And a beautiful queen at that." He offered his arm to Claudia.

Jamie said, "You two are off to the ball, and I'm off to my baby sitter. But I don't call her my baby sitter, I'm not a baby. Mrs. Dixon is my friend and neighbor. Right, Mom? Oops, I mean Queen Guinevere."

* * *

A half-hour later, Matt and Claudia were caught in the crush at the entrance to the Michigan Union Building. Damp umbrellas were stacked in the entrance way. Matt led Claudia into the ballroom, festooned with garlands and streamers. Claudia gasped when she entered the room which had been transformed into a medieval summer garden with rose garlands, latticed arches and huge banners in deep purple, gold, vibrant red and royal blue. Couples danced to the music of a band seated on a flower-decked band stand.

Footmen in scarlet coats were stationed in the doorways. Matt gestured. "Look at the costumes. The fraternity board insisted everyone be in costume—and we've covered the spectrum, everything from Neptune's daughter to King Kong."

"But everyone is masked, except us," Claudia said.

"Almost forgot." Matt reached in his robe and pulled out two masks—a black velvet one and an ornate gold one encrusted with seed pearls and sequins. "A mask for my queen," he said presenting Claudia with the gold one.

"Thank you. Now I'm really in disguise."

He offered his hand and they walked to a small crowded bar in one corner of the room. ":What'll you have?" he asked.

"Surprise me. I'll wait here. There's too much of a crowd by the bar."

"Sure you'll be all right? Don't talk to strangers."

"I won't move a muscle until you return. Hurry."

Claudia leaned against one of the pillars and watched the dancers. It was make believe and she was caught up in it. Giant candelabras aglow with tapered candles sparkled and shimmered from every corner of the room. The couples dancing swayed and dipped to the music. Three Musketeers filed past Claudia in pursuit of an Indian maiden, who proceeded to hold them all captive. Finally the musketeer in the royal purple plumed hat and the Indian maiden glided to the dance floor.

Standing in the corner watching the dancers, Claudia smiled to herself when she remembered how Urho looked when he gave her the kimono. Maybe she should have worn the kimono and come as Madame Butterfly. Now she ran her fingers down the silk folds of her queen's gown. Suddenly an Army lieutenant in a black mask approached her. He was in full uniform, with several medals on his breast pocket. An officer's hat low over his forehead, and the black mask, covered most of his face.

"Lovely, queen, may I have this dance?" he asked. With a flourish, he touched his hat and bowed. He did not remove his hat.

"Sorry, I have instructions from King Arthur not to talk to strangers."

"We don't have to talk, just dance," the lieutenant said.

"Besides I was checking out the competition. Tarzan, Robin Hood, King Kong, King Neptune, and oh yes, King Arthur, are you any relation to King Arthur?"

"Maybe," she said.

He grabbed her arm. "Don't look now, but that old geezer King Arthur is making his way toward us."

When Matt approached them, he ignored the soldier and gave Claudia her drink. Then he said to the soldier, "Are you bothering my queen? I told her not to talk to strangers." With a wave of his hand, he said. "Now—be off—go away."

This time the soldier ignored Matt and looked at Claudia. "I'm not leaving until you dance with me. That's an official order." He grabbed her arm and led her to the dance floor.

"No! No!" she said in mock protest. "Then as he encircled her waist with his arm, she looked up into his face and saw smiling hazel eyes behind the black mask. His voice was slow now as he whispered into her ear. "Lieutenant Liemus at your service, how is my darling Claudia?"

"Urho, you fool. You certainly surprised me. Now I know why Matt didn't put up a fight when you swept me off to the dance floor. He was in on this, right?"

Urho grinned and nodded. "Come with me, I'm tired of dancing."

"Where are we going?"

"Not far." He led her to a secluded area in the courtyard, covered by a canopy. It was still raining. The air smelled of roses and freshly mowed grass. He took off his mask. Then he kissed her. Two shadows in the courtyard. "I wondered if my Army disguise was enough."

"Well, let's say, you almost fooled me. Your eyes were a give away." Then she kissed him on his eye lids. "Say, you didn't say anything about my regal gown. How do you like it?"

"You're beautiful as always." He kissed her gently on the lips. "Beautiful also in that kimono someone gave you, beautiful also when you take it off."

"Oh, so you like the kimono. Someone who loves me gave it to me."

"Anyone I know?" Urho asked.

CHAPTER 31

"Urho, it's your fault! You bastard," Neil said. He paced the length of his office. "You let the union get a foothold in the Press. Now, it's getting way out of hand. Those contract talks—they want too damn much." He shook a fist at Urho. "And that son of a bitch Richard's hooked up with the union. I knew it all along." His hand trembled as he reached for a cigar in his humidor. Then thinking better of it, he stopped short and closed the lid on the humidor.

"It's a fair contract," Urho said. "They just want some changes, changes that are long overdue."

"You're taking their side?"

"It's not a matter of sides, it's what's right. And if things continue as they have been for the last few months, I wouldn't be surprised if they pulled out and called a strike."

"Don't bullshit me, strike, eh?" Neil pushed the thought out of his mind. "Before that happens, I'll sell the whole ball of wax."

"You wouldn't do that."

"Wouldn't I?" Neil stopped pacing and stood behind his desk, slapping his hand on the contracts piled on it. He knew at the moment he had one advantage—the threat of selling the Press. "Here, read this damn contract." He sat behind his desk and looked at his son, his eyes impaling the younger man. This time when he reached for his humidor, he pulled out a Havana cigar, stripped off its wrapper and settled back to enjoy it. There was a momentary silence in the

233

office, the army of elephants frozen, their trunks up. Ivory statues, brass paperweights, silver, crystal, all mute. Only the soft whine of the air conditioner sliced the silence while Urho read the contract.

How strange, thought Neil, he was accustomed to making snap decisions when it came to the Press, yet he struggled with decisions in his private life. The essence of the problem, Neil realized, were his old recurring thoughts about personal guilt. Could he, years ago, with love and understanding have saved his relationship with his son? Should he have been a good father, instead of a good publisher? Couldn't he have been both? No! Even now he was not able to set in motion the ruthless machinery that would cause a final break. Urho's mother would not approve. That was the bargain he had struck with her many years ago, when Urho was born. He was always to remain Number One son.

And now his beloved Dora was going to have a baby. Perhaps a son. Where is she now that he needed her? But she had insisted on staying in New York, where the top obstetricians where. Yes, it was best, for both Dora and the baby. Greta still refused to give him a divorce. Why had so many problems surfaced to destroy him?

It was like the past. Yes, he was reliving his past. When he was a young man rum running across the Detroit River. He'd help load the boats with bootleg whiskey and gin from Canada and sell it to speakeasies on the river front. And then after, he'd meet Valley at the river front cottage—until David discovered them.

Now Neil watched his son involved in reading the lengthy contract. He thought, Why do we make the choices we do? Why do we make the same mistakes? Why had he married Greta instead of Valley? And now, why wouldn't Greta give him a divorce to marry Dora, his true love. The hell with Greta! The most important people in his life now were Dora and their unborn child. And then the telephone rang—the red one.

Urho looked up. "I'll take this contract with me. Looks like you have an important call." Urho walked quickly out of the office.

* * *

An hour later Neil was on board a plane headed for New York City.

The call had been from Dora's physician. She was in premature labor. Later, in the hospital, Dora's doctor talked with Neil. He said, "There is a bit of a risk, as there always is with premature births—for the mother and the baby. However, we are taking all precautions."

"Can I see her?"

"Certainly. She is in a private labor room." The doctor thrust his hands in the pockets of his green scrub gown.

From that moment on everything was a blur to Neil. He followed the doctor down a long corridor and into a room. And then he saw Dora in a bed. Without a moment's hesitation he ran to her, kissed her and embraced her. "Dora, my dearest."

"Neil?" She looked up at him. "I'm glad you're here darling. When they say labor they really mean torture." A small smile appeared on her drawn face. Her forehead was beaded with perspiration. Then suddenly a spasm overcame her. She shuddered. "Neil, oh, it hurts. Damn it!" The shades were drawn in the room and the overhead ceiling lights were on. Neil watched as the doctor talked to Dora. "Remember to breathe from your mouth, short pants, remember? Work with the contractions."

After the contraction, the doctor placed the bell of his stethoscope firmly above Dora's swollen navel and listened, moving the instrument across her body.

Neil watched and felt a pressure on his shoulders, down his back, consuming his entire body. He wanted to comfort Dora, wanted to help rid her of the pain—pain he had caused her. His fingers felt clumsy when he reached over to touch her, stroke her hand, pat her face, wipe her brow with a damp cloth, whispered words of love in hushed tones. Finally he reached for her hand—kissed it again and again. And when another pain overtook her, he was helpless. There was nothing he could do for her. "Please, God," he prayed.

Did her face appear tinged with blue? Was she having difficulty breathing?

"You're doing fine," the doctor said.

Dora's dry, cracked lips moved, but not a sound came from her; instead her body once again became rigid, her breathing labored.

"How long has she been in labor?" Neil asked.

The doctor looked at his watch, "Almost six hours. She didn't want me to call you right away. She wanted to surprise you when the baby was born. I thought it was important you be here with her now. This is not an ordinary birth. Of course, at first, we could not foresee any complications. But now, her blood pressure is high and there is evidence of a toxic condition."

"What does that mean? Will she be all right?" Neil asked. His voice was low, thin, frightened.

"We're doing all we can."

"What are you saying? What the hell are you talking about?"

"Oh God," moaned Dora.

The doctor quickly went to her. Her lips appeared blue to Neil. Dora was in great distress. Her breathing was shallow, labored.

"Help her, damn it!" Neil said.

Immediately the doctor signaled to the nurse and she walked up to Neil. "You'll have to leave now," she said.

Neil endured the long hours in the waiting room pacing, helped by periodic reports from the nurse who told him of Dora's progress.

Finally Neil slept fitfully on the couch in the waiting room. The arm chair was occupied by a young man chain smoking. Neil moaned every time he changed positions on the uncomfortable couch. In the morning the nurse walked up to him as he lay on the couch sleeping. She shook him gently. "Mr. Liemus, wake up."

Neil woke up and saw the nurse, black circles under her eyes and her white face matching her white uniform. In his dreams he heard Dora scream, tearing at him, and he felt through the fog of misery, an uncontrollable sadness. "What? Did I sleep through it?" he asked. "Is everything all right with my Dora and the baby?"

All the nurse said was, "The doctor will be here in a few minutes."

When the doctor entered the waiting room, he wiped his damp brow with his hand. Neil stared at him. He was not aware of the bright sunny day, outdoors, or the rose bushes beginning to bloom outside the hospital window, or the two boys outdoors racing by tossing a baseball.

"Yes, doctor?" He tried to read the doctor's face, examine it for any signs, any clues. "The baby, my baby—is it all right?"

"Yes, Mr. Liemus, you have a healthy baby girl."

"A daughter?"

"Yes."

"And she's all right?" Reeling back, Neil grabbed a chair. "Thank God. And my Dora is all right, too?" Even before the doctor spoke, Neil felt nauseated and dizzy. He wiped his brow with his handkerchief. "Damn! Tell me about Dora."

"Why don't you sit down, Mr. Liemus." He motioned to the couch. The young man in the waiting room stared at Neil and the doctor. Then he crushed his empty pack and tossed it into the wastebasket. He fumbled in his pockets for another cigarette in vain. Finally he left the room in search of a cigarette vending machine.

Now that they were alone, the doctor said, "And Mrs. Liemus—." The tenseness of his remark, the neutral quality of his normally pleasant voice, indicated to Neil that something was wrong.

"There were complications," the doctor said. "Some amniotic fluid got into her general circulation, resulting in an embolism." He reached for Neil's hand. "I'm sorry, but—she died."

"Died?" Neil felt as if someone had torn his heart out of his chest, twisted it round and round. "You liar! You son of a bitch." Neil grabbed the doctor by the throat. "What did you do to my Dora?" The doctor struggled to free himself, shouting. "Orderly!"

"Liar! Liar! She's not dead! She can't be dead."

An orderly and the nurse raced into the room. The nurse's white face appeared even whiter, even sadder. Finally the orderly released the doctor from Neil's grasp and guided Neil to a chair. "Please, sit down, sir."

Neil slumped into the chair like an old man. A feeling of weariness pressed down on him. Holding his head in his hands, he felt hot tears sting his face. He wasn't cold but could not stop shivering.

CHAPTER 32

Ghosts. Claudia didn't believe in ghosts. She had become a different person and lived a different life after Alex's death. What had happened when Alex was alive seemed so distant—another time, another life. It happened to another person, not to Claudia.

Although she did not believe in ghosts, she was certain that Neil did and he was haunted by Dora's ghost. Success and wealth should provide some protection against ghosts, Claudia thought. Yes, that was what one should expect from success and wealth.

In the weeks following Dora's death, Claudia knew that Neil grieved for her as he had never grieved for anyone. She also knew that it was Urho who pulled the family together. It was Urho who insisted that Neil move back to the Island mansion—enjoy the summer, sail his boat, fish, read, relax.

Urho had hired a nurse to take care of Leah, the baby. Claudia knew that a mourning Neil and a distraught Greta were in no condition to care for an infant. Urho didn't know if Greta resented the baby, but he did know that she never visited the nursery, never held little Leah. Neil and Greta were two troubled people and little Leah did not bring them together. If anything, they were further apart. Each day the baby grew stronger, Neil and Greta grew more distant. Things were changing at the Island mansion.

Things also were changing at the Press. Claudia spent an infuriating morning with Tessie, whose sole purpose in the news room was to

238

poke and pry and generally make her presence obnoxious. Tessie was singing the same tune; the union was not doing what it had promised for the Press employees.

Claudia made the mistake of trying to talk to Tessie. "Damn it, can't you see what the union is trying to do for us? And it's working. All you have to do is look at the tentative contract to see what it's bargaining for on our behalf. They are making things happen."

"Brilliant, just brilliant," began Tessie. "If that contract is so great, what's the hold up? Besides, I know that Himself won't stand for the union's funny stuff. He'll sell the Press, first."

The discussion went on and on, reducing Claudia to a white-faced furious woman.

When Tessie left on an assignment with Clyde, Claudia stormed out, headed for the diner.

In the afternoon, another catastrophic memo from Neil was passed around. In his hard, abrupt way, Neil stated that the union contract negotiations were not going as planned and he was seriously considering selling the Press. "You'll all be out of jobs because one stipulation I'm making in the sale is that former employees of the Press NOT be hired."

So Claudia was in a somewhat angry mood when she took the elevator to the penthouse office to talk to Urho. But the elevator ride cooled her disposition, and when she walked into the huge office with sun streaming through the wide expanse of windows, she began to relax. First she told Urho about her argument with Tessie. Then she pulled out the memo from her pocket. "Have you seen this?" she asked.

"Neil's latest about selling the Press?"

"Yes."

"I've seen it. Don't worry. It's nothing."

"Nothing? He threatened to sell the newspaper, and as a topper, he's going to tell the new owners to fire us? Nothing?"

Both were silent for a moment. He was seated behind the desk facing an angry Claudia. It was in fact, his father's desk, his father's office. Now he leaned forward and regarded her gravely. "Claudia,

I'm going to ask you a question. You don't have to answer it, but I hope you will. Do you consider Tessie a dangerous woman?"

"No problem, I can answer it honestly. Yes, Tessie is dangerous. She's a loose cannon. She's a gossip, a sneak. Quite frankly she scares me. She's unbalanced. When I see the damage Tessie is doing, I feel like packing and leaving the Press—going far, far away from this mess."

"You don't really mean that, about leaving, do you?"

"I don't know what I mean Urho. I'm so confused."

"If you leave the Press, I'm coming with you." Urho walked up to her, held her in his arms. "You know how I feel about you."

"You leave the Press? You're talking nonsense. You're putting me off about this memo that Neil sent us. This is also threatening, also damaging."

"No it isn't, Claudia. I have an announcement to make at the news meeting this afternoon. It will cover that memo, and it will clear everything up."

"What?"

"Trust me." And then he kissed her. "Trust me."

* * *

That afternoon Claudia was the first one to arrive at the news meeting. She opened the door to the vast room, stared at the huge scarred table, looked at the bundles of newspapers in one corner, and the pile of old photos on the floor. Maybe the union will redecorate this room, she thought. Or maybe just give it a good cleaning. Fat chance. She sat in her regular place, the second chair from the head of the table, and searched in her leather purse for a pencil. She shook her worry beads loose from a pocket mirror and glanced at her reflection. In an instant she pulled her hair back behind her ears, away from her face. That's better. Great! Her world was crashing down around her, and she was worried about how her hair looked, she thought. Then she retied the beige silk scarf around her neck, and it fell in soft folds down the front of her beige sweater. Beige sweater, beige skirt, beige wall. She was fading into the woodwork and maybe that's what she wanted to do today, she thought. She slipped her amber beads into her pocket as Bernie walked into the room. "How's it going, Claudia?" he asked concentrating on lighting his pipe, the aroma of honey and rum surrounding him. He plopped himself next to Claudia and immediately began gnawing his bottom lip, a sign of frustration, Claudia noted.

"I wish I knew how it was going."

Tessie strolled in, filing her long scarlet fingernails. She sat as far away as possible from Claudia and Bernie, not even acknowledging their presence. Clyde, his camera case slung over his shoulder, sat next to Tessie. Clyde wore his typical Army fatigues shirt and pants, with his favorite button, a red, white and blue one that said "Vietnam—Hell No, I won't Go!"

Valley and George came in arm-in-arm, Valley laughing outrageously at one of George's jokes. "George, you must have a million of them," Valley said.

"Almost."

Soon a crowd of people filled the room, representing every department—advertising, classified, editorial, sports, feature, display ads and circulation. Urho was the last one to arrive. He followed the Press attorney, a small man with thick eyeglasses and a shaggy mustache.

Bernie tapped his pipe in the metal ashtray. Valley, seated across from Claudia, was flushed. Clyde fiddled with his camera. The meeting opened when Urho rose to his feet. Without an explanation he began reading a headline from one of the Detroit newspapers: "Liemus Press Immobilized by Publisher's Illness?"

Urho slapped the paper down on the long table. "That's a lie. And we're going to sue."

"There's nothing to sue about," Bernie said with his customary bluntness. "That Detroit newspaper hasn't stated a fact. It just poses a question, and it's not malicious." Bernie's remark was casual, a take-it-or-leave it one. His hands were folded behind his head, his pipe in his mouth.

"It is malicious," Urho said. "Any fool can see that."

Bernie sighed. "All right, sue them." He picked up one of the newspapers spread out on the table. "One of the reasons I earn my salary at the Press is that I'm an expert on news."

Valley laughed.

"Go on expert," Urho said.

"Right now, my know how, tells me this is a hunting story. This story is out hunting and the Liemus Press is the game. Get my drift? Unless I miss my guess, this is a kind of story that will be picked up, so we'd best be prepared. By the way, is that what this meeting is all about?"

"No, I'll let you know in time. When Neil got back from New York, six weeks ago, he was in shock, torn up with grief following Dora's death. But he's not sick." Urho slammed his fist down on the Detroit newspaper. "He's not sick. He's fine, in good health."

Claudia knew that Urho was lying. On more than one occasion they had discussed his father's condition. Neil was sick, he was in a deep depression. Urho had even talked with doctors about his father.

So now Urho was telling the staff what it wanted to hear—that Neil Liemus, publisher of the Liemus Press, was in good health and able to negotiate a good contract. Unconsciously Claudia pulled her worry beads out of her pocket and held them. The cold amber felt good against her warm palm.

Now Urho looked over the people assembled at this meeting. He nodded to himself, took off his jacket and rolled up his shirt sleeves. Claudia glanced at him. Then her attention was drawn to Valley, who began to cough violently. George jumped up and got her a glass of water. "Better cut out the cigarettes," he said. Then he leaned across the table. "Come on Urho, what's the big news?" George was dressed in a fashionably tailored gray suit. He often told Claudia it was his "screw the advertisers" suit.

"She should cut out more than cigarettes," Tessie said with a pout. As usual she resembled a hooker on Twelfth Street in Detroit. Her red mini skirt hugged her thighs and the front of her low cut orange sweater was hidden by strands of orange and red beads. Her thick plaited red hair hung down her back.

Claudia glanced at the old wall clock which showed that the meeting had been going on for an hour. No, she thought. Why did she want time to stop for a few hours? Didn't she want to hear Urho's important announcement? Was a settlement reached? No, that wasn't it because the union would make that announcement. What could it be?

The wide curtain less windows reached out to her. August in Pierre Corners, a hot month, but a beautiful one with all the trees and flowers ablaze. Main Street, busy, with its traffic sending off a blast of horns. Bernie strolled to the windows.

"Sit down Bernie," Urho said. Then he turned to the attorney, "Let's have that envelope." The short man sifted through a handful of envelopes and finally handed Urho one.

"Urho said, "Thank you. Yes, that's the one."

Claudia turned her gaze from the window to Urho. His smile was a false one, and Claudia knew it. What was Urho trying to say to them?

"Okay, people, let's get down to business," Urho said. "Isn't that what Richard would say? Now, for the news."

Bernie sulked and cleaned out his pipe into the ashtray. Then he stuck the unlit pipe back in his mouth and glared at Urho.

George asked, "Are you going to tell us that Himself sold the Press?"

"Shut up," Valley said. "Let Number One son finish."

"Bullshit," muttered George under his breath.

Nervously Claudia fingered her beads. Why hadn't Urho told her beforehand? she thought.

"Have I got your attention, people?" Urho asked. Then he removed papers from the envelope. "This document records a transfer of ownership. As of today, I am the new owner and publisher of the Liemus Press."

Then Claudia dropped her amber beads and Clyde scrambled under the table to find them.

CHAPTER 33

Claudia strained under the heavy ropes that bound her to a chair. "I can't finish the book! I can't!" she cried.

"Can't," Alex leered at her, raised his whip and struck her across the back. She screamed and sat up in bed, her heart pounding, her head throbbing. She held her head in her hands and pressed her fingers to her temple. When were the nightmares going to end? When?

Quickly she turned on the lamp on the night stand, grabbed her red robe from the rocking chair and wrapped the robe around her shoulders. Only then did she glance at the alarm clock. It was five o'clock on a Sunday morning. She couldn't go back to sleep. Instead she got up and began to pace. After a while, she stopped and drew aside the heavy drapes, peered out. Snow was falling. It was a raw, cold morning with cutting wind that shook the windows. The half moon kept ducking behind clouds. Claudia shivered as she stood at the windows. She could see down to the end of the street. Christmas trees, forlorn, shorn of their glitter, were strewn at the curb waiting for rubbish pick up.

She thought that in a few days, another year –1965—and she hadn't finished the gifted book. The University of Michigan was getting impatient. And she was working without a contract at the Press. She needed to stop, sort things out, slow things down, just for an hour or two. But, no, noting stopped, nothing slowed down, for her or anyone. In her mind's eye, she saw Urho, she saw herself, off somewhere away from Pierre Corners, perhaps on an island, basking in the sun, carefree, loving. Stop dreaming, she thought. This is real this is life, stop dreaming this instant! She went to her desk, rummaged through the top drawer and pulled out the latest union bulletin. She had stored many union bulletins in this desk at home.

In the December, 1964 issue of the Union News, Butler's column had drawn a parallel between the Revolutionary War and the Press contract negotiations. Desperate as these two events may seem, Butler argued that the contract negotiations headed by Urho had much in common with British strategy during the Revolutionary War.

And of course, Butler was General Washington. In his article, he cited that at the beginning of the war, both sides believed in the orderly conduct of combat, following the war rules of order. But under General Washington's command and following his crossing of the Potomac, the entire situation changed and it was a "bloody-messy war." So be it, Butler wrote, now we have a "bloody-messy war" with the Liemus Press.

Claudia read Butler's closing remarks—"I predict the union will triumph just as General Washington did. We are in the midst of a revolution! How we handle it will measure what kind of people we are."

War? What is he talking about? Claudia thought, her mind confused. What was in her future? Working at the Press, or writing books? Mustn't think about that, mustn't make a decision now. She rolled a sheet of paper into her typewriter and began a new chapter on her gifted book. Three hours later, still at the typewriter, she pulled out a sheet of paper from her typewriter, crunched it into a ball and threw it into the wastebasket. Some had missed the wastebasket and were strewn all over the room.

"Garbage, I'm writing garbage," she said under her breath. Impulsively she snatched the manuscript pages from their box and tossed them in the air. "Garbage!" she cried.

The bedroom door opened. Jamie said, "Mom, what's going on in here? Looks like the blizzard came into your room." She picked up the typed pages and put them back into the box.

"I'm fed up with this book. I'll never finish it. I want—oh, I don't know what I want. Come here, honey. I need a hug, bad."

Jamie raced to her with outstretched arms. For a silent moment mother and daughter hugged. "I know you'll finish it. You've got to, it's our gifted book."

Claudia stroked her daughter's hair. "I wish I had your confidence, honey. As far as I'm concerned, at this moment, it's garbage."

"Maybe if you had something to eat, you'd feel better. And guess who's going to make breakfast?" Jamie smiled. "Me!"

"That's my girl." And then Claudia smiled and hugged her daughter. "Let's go honey."

* * *

In the afternoon, Claudia was in a better mood. She worked on the book for several hours. Jamie occupied her time by sketching winter scenes from the living room window. Mother and daughter sat at opposite ends of the room, Claudia with her typewriter propped up on a table, and Jamie with her easel set up in front of the picture window. A fire blazed in the fire place, while outdoors the wind howled and the storm continued.

"Looks like the storm we had when everything was shut down," began Jamie. "Everything except the Press, remember?"

"This isn't as bad. There are cars managing to drive down our street, and the wind isn't blowing as hard." Now Claudia flipped through her manuscript pages. Jamie had assembled them all neat and tidy in the box, but mixed in was the Union News. Once again Claudia glanced at Butler's column about the Revolutionary War. And now she knew she had to get some answers. Urho would have some answers. At no point did it occur to Claudia that Urho would NOT have answers. Maybe she was too impatient, too overenthusiastic, too much in a hurry. She wanted answers! New contracts take time. New books take time. New relationships take time. But her relationship with Urho was not new. She had loved him forever. Yes, she had to see Urho and now.

"I'm going out, Jamie. I'll call Mrs. Dixon and you can stay with her until I get back. Get ready."

"You're going out in this storm?"

"It's stopped a bit. And, I have to talk to Urho. It's very important."

* * *

Forty minutes later Claudia was following the narrow Island roads leading to Urho's house. Her gloved hands held the wheel, her eyes strained to see through the blurred, snow-streaked windshield. The windshield wipers swished and accumulated tiny mounds of snow at their corners. She swung her car into a side road leading into Urho's private drive. Swish, swish went the windshield wiper blades; mesmerizing her. She soon would be with Urho, talking to him, getting some answers. She opened the car window a crack to see and a blast of snow flakes hit her, sending shivers through her. The iron gate at the entrance to Urho's property was covered with snow. Small branches, beaten by the wind, had fallen. Was the gate locked? Was she seeing things, or was that Urho trudging through the snow? A red cardinal cried from a nearby tree and another answered. Claudia looked up and saw the scarlet birds against the bleak whiteness of the storm. Then Urho was there. He opened her car door, grabbed her, held her close, kissed her. Then he said, "It's snowing."

"Who needs it?" she asked, huddled in his embrace.

"Reindeers?"

Claudia grinned. "How did you know I was here?"

"Heard the car. Not too many cars on my drive in this storm, so I came out to investigate. Here, let me help you." He took her arm.

Minutes later they were in Urho's house. She followed him though the entrance way. He led her into his den. His hunting prints covered one of the paneled walls. In the floor to ceiling book case were his books, Hemingway, Fitzgerald, Forrester, Cronin, and Margaret Mitchell's "Gone with the Wind", all in rows. Off in one corner were skis, ski poles and Nikon camera. In another corner was a flagstone fireplace. The smell of burning logs warmed Claudia. She was learning more about Urho just from this room and the things in it. Who was Urho, really? A successful publisher—owner of the Liemus Press, or a man who liked to laugh, to tease, a man who loved her? She settled on the tan leather couch, still chilled from the drive.

Walking back to the couch after throwing another log on the fire,

Urho turned to Claudia who was hugging herself. "You're cold, aren't you darling?"

Claudia nodded.

"I'll fix that." He soon returned with two snifters of brandy and a plaid wool robe. "Here, put this on. And drink this. Dr. Urho's orders. It was crazy of you to come out in this weather.I could have driven to your house."

She took a sip. Her head felt stuffed and stupid. " I had to come, get out of that house. I was getting violent, throwing my manuscript around—and—."

"And what?"

"It started with a nightmare I had—about Alex. Everything went wrong today."

He turned to her, embraced her. "Those nightmares will end, in time." He kissed her gently.

With his touch, his words, she felt better. She was surprised at how safe she felt in his arms. For a while they stood like that, in each other's arms. After that she felt she had to tell him about Butler's latest column. Isn't that why she was here? She pulled the union news out of her pocket. "I thought you should see this, it's Butler's latest column."

He read it while pacing back and forth in front of the fireplace. "This doesn't make sense. The Revolutionary War, General Washington? Butler is crazy. I don't trust that man."

"What?"

"In fact, I don't trust anyone."

"Does that include me?" She smiled.

"Of course." He smiled back. "Do you trust me?"

"Not completely."

Urho continued his pacing, his hands thrust in his pockets. She let him mull over Butler's column for a few minutes. Then he said, "Right now I need all the friends I can get. These last few months since I've been publisher of the Press haven't been any picnic. Plus there's Neil, Greta and the baby, Leah. And now Butler, with this crap about this being a war. He's stalling on the contract negotiations. He wants to crush the Press, and me. He's pushing for a strike."

"No!" she said, shocked. "That isn't what he wants. He wants a fair contract."

"Like hell he does. I've offered the union the best, and Butler won't budge." He sat on the couch, close to Claudia.

"Tell me. What usually happens to men like Butler?" Claudia asked.

"I'm no authority, but I can read the signs, and usually men like Butler tend to self destruct. Few of them last more than five years. It's the pressure, and mostly they destroy themselves. And I certainly don't want him to drag us along, the Press and everyone when that happens."

"What do you think will really happen?"

He shrugged. "Right now I hope, and I'm working toward a good contract, in good faith, of course. I want something that everyone can live with, fair, honest. I don't know if Butler is on the same wave length. I'm guessing but I think he's out for a strike, at all cost."

Claudia sat thoughtfully sipping her brandy. She did not respond .

Urho glanced at her. "I think Butler is going round in wider, wider circles, just to prove to the staff that he is doing something. But he's just making waves, treading water, actually accomplishing nothing for the good."

"It's a mess, isn't it?" Claudia asked.

"Yes." Urho finally smiled. "Do you want to continue this depressing conversation, or do you—?" He leaned over to set his brandy snifter on the table. Then he reached out and touched her lightly, her face, her neck, and then slipped his hand under her sweater as if it were the most natural thing in the world.

"Don't start something you can't finish," she said. She pulled his head down and kissed him.

"I can finish," he said. Their eyes met and held in the semi-darkness—for a moment everything seemed suspended, like a film when the frames suddenly go into slow motion. Claudia put her head on Urho's chest. Almost absent-mindedly, he was stroking her hair. He lifted her chin. Their eyes were close. "You are beautiful," he said.

For a moment the room was very still. Claudia was leaning close, still staring into his eyes.

Urho said, "I find myself thinking of you all the time." He pulled her to him and kissed her on the lips, gently. "Tell me, Claudia, do you feel the same way about me? I have to know."

"Urho. I…Oh, Urho, I do care for you, I do love you. Do you love me?"

"Love, that's a very heavy word, and when I use it with you, it'll have to be for real, and forever." He lifted her face and his eyes were gentle. "Claudia, you are more beautiful every day." Then he took her in his arms and stroked her hair as if he were comforting a child. Suddenly Claudia flung herself into his arms. The robe around her shoulders fell off. He held her close and kissed her. And for the first time she understood the intimacy of their kiss. Their bodies were close. She pressed against him, wanting to become part of him, again and again.

* * *

Hours later they went into the kitchen. Urho prepared a light supper of cold roast beef, cheese, salad, fruit and wine. They brought their plates and wine into the den and ate in front of the fire place sitting cross-legged on a bearskin rug. For a time, they ate in silence.

Then Urho said, "You see, we are ideally suited, lovers and friends. You have beautiful eyes."

"What has that got to do with being lovers and friends?"

"Everything," he said.

"Tell me."

"Tell you what?"

"What I want to hear," she said

"I….I love you."

"Say it again, and don't hesitate this time."

"I love you, Claudia!" He kissed her then with an urgency, an excitement. "I don't want this to end. I want you forever and ever." He reached out and brushed her lashes with his. "That's a butterfly kiss," he said.

"I love it. Do it again." She closed her eyes. "Mmmmmm, butterfly kisses are delicious."

Then he hugged her, "You silly girl." For a while they just sat there, their arms around each other, gazing at the flames. Then she said, "I've got to go. It's getting late. Jamie is waiting for me at Mrs. Dixon's house." She looked out the window. "Thank God the storm is over."

"I want you to spend the night with me."

"Some day," she said.

"We will spend many, many nights together."

"Yes."

And I'll eat graham crackers in bed and we'll watch Johnny Carson," he said.

"Of course, and I'll wear a flannel nightgown and wear wooly socks, because my feet get cold."

"Of course, and we'll live happily ever after," he said.

CHAPTER 34

It was April 26, 1965, when a Detroit newspaper began a series on the Liemus Press, concentrating on the strung-out contract negotiations with the newspaper union. Then a Detroit newspaper investigative reporter dipped into the newspaper's morgue files and came up with startling information about Neil's past regarding his part in prohibition rum-running, hauling bootleg whiskey from Canada across the Detroit River. It was a front page story.

The morning the story came out, Neil was sitting on the edge of the couch in his tower room, hunched over, holding his face. Stringy white hair made a tent. An empty bottle was nestled in one of the cushions, a copy of the Detroit newspaper on the floor.

They know, he thought. The whole damn world knows. But they can't touch me. It was too long ago. And they can't prove a thing. They didn't mention the river front cottage, they didn't say anything about Valley, about David. "There's not a damn thing they can do about it!" Neil said aloud to no one in particular. He crouched back into the cushions of the couch, weeping. "Oh dear God!" He kept repeating those three words. Then his mind pushed back to that last time—to that last run to Canada, to that last time—before David died.

At the river front, David and Neil had dragged the boat to the shore and unloaded the whiskey and piled it in a shack leading to an underground tunnel near the cottage. It was dusk and they worked quickly and silently. Back in the cottage, Neil turned around and faced David. "What's eating you? You haven't made much sense all day," Neil said.

" I know." David said.

"What the hell do you know, rich boy? Is this excitement, this thrill getting to be old hat to you? I'm in this for the money, you know that, and you're in this for the thrill."

"That's not what I'm talking about."

"Listen, we have a deal, a gentleman's agreement partners."

David eyed Neil. "Partners with Valley, too?"

"Shit, you don't know what you're talking about."

"Don't I? I know what's been going on with you and Valley."

The next day David's body was found in the river. Afterwards, it was never definitely determined what really happened. David had been an excellent swimmer. But the police had called it accidental drowning.

* * *

Now when Urho walked into the tower room and saw his father huddled in the couch, he groaned. "Hell, you're something else, you are. Look at you."

Neil raised his head to stare at his son. He grabbed the newspaper. "What's this? They're digging, digging for more dirt. Soon they'll learn about Valley, about David, about the drowning. Valley, poor thing, was in a bind financially when David died. I helped her, hear? And I'm still helping her. It had to be. I had to keep it that way. It was a pact we had. Life sucked Valley in, or was it the booze, the smokes? Once she was very important to me, and to you, Urho. Hear?"

Urho said, "You're talking in circles. David, Valley, that's all in the past. This is the present. Straighten up, old man. You have to snap out of it, or else."

Turning away from Urho, Neil said. "Or else what? Go take a flying leap son, or should I say Number One Son as Valley so often calls you? I'm going to make my official last act as publisher of the Liemus Press. Watch me son." He grabbed the red phone from his desk, and tugged and pulled it until the cord was jerked loose from the wall. Then twirling it around his head, three, four, times, he flung it, toppling the telescope off its stand and sending the red phone flying like a bolt through the circular window, out into the blue, cloudless sky. Then he laughed.

Urho grabbed him. The fact that Urho was shaking him, trying to reason with him, struck him as being very funny. Neil swung around and embraced his son. He felt light headed, released from all responsibility after getting rid of the cursed red phone. Then he freed himself from Urho and danced around the room, using a metal pica ruler to send small ivory and crystal elephants crashing to the floor.

"I'm free! That damn red phone won't bug me ever again!"

"Stop it!" shouted Urho, grabbing Neil's hands. "Stop it! I'm going to have you put away if you don't stop."

"Go ahead." Neil yelled back. The thought of being put away only brought forth further laughter. "Be my guest, Number One son." And then with a sudden mood swing, Neil was solemn. "Nobody orders Neil Liemus around." He was close to his son, so close, he saw the brown flecks in his hazel eyes.

Then with an open palm, he slapped Urho, hard across the face. Urho didn't move. "That's for your disloyalty, son."

And all through this there were the sounds of motor boats racing on the river. The roar of the engines grew louder, and the stillness in the tower room grew deeper.

Urho rubbed the side of his face. "Father, you're losing your mind."

"No, I've found it. You're the one that's mad. Mad that I took Dora away from you. Mad that I have a child by her, my sweet little Leah. Dora? Dora? Where are you? Urho, you're no son of mine. Your mother was no good. I begged her…begged her to, but it was no use. Too many things were happening. And there was David, and then there wasn't David—." His fist clenched, he beat the wall until his knuckles were raw.

"And as for my old and trusted friend, Richard. He stole the Press from me. You're all in this together. Take my newspaper, I don't give a damn. I just want my Dora." He scanned the room, and with dazed eyes looked at Urho. "You son of a bitch. You and your mother are alike, out to get me."

Urho took his father's arm and led him out of the tower room. Neil's face clouded. For a moment he seemed close to tears. As Urho guided him out of the room, into the hallway, Neil's anger once again surfaced. "That bastard Richard and his union, they're sapping the blood out of me." His dark mood deepened, his eyes glazed, his expression became anxious.

Urho said, "Don't worry. Everything will be all right." They walked together down the hallway, lined with oils by Picasso and the exotic woman by Dali. "Is that woman smiling at me?" Neil asked.

Urho nodded. Only Urho's long strides and Neil's shuffling steps broke the silence. Where was he? Neil thought. He was lost and all around him stretched vastness and over head a giant crystal star shone, twinkling, twinkling. Finally he reached the circular stairway. He looked down and saw the vestibule below with the giant crystal star. No, it's not a star, it's a chandelier hanging from a brass chain.

He resorted to his old habit. He reached up and smoothed his white hair. Now he was ready to do downstairs. He grasped Urho's arm and braced his shoulder and back against the wall, near the railing. He bent his knees, taking small steps, like an old man, not releasing one foot until the other was firmly planted on the next step. Gripping Urho's arm, he allowed him to propel his body down the stairs.

In this way, the two men, father and son, slowly walked downstairs, where they reached the entrance way and the vestibule. At that time of day the vestibule was washed with bright sunlight.

Now Neil placed his hand flat against the beveled glass door and stared out. What's happening? He is Neil Liemus, publisher of the Liemus Press, the best damned newspaper in the state, right? he thought. Then who the hell is this old man who needed someone to help him walk down the stairs? He took a deep breath and allowed the warm sunlight to embrace him. Then he turned toward his enemy, Urho. Moving swiftly now, to catch his enemy unprepared, he lunged at Urho, beat him with his fists, beat him on the chest, on the face, in a steady rhythm, shifting from one foot to the other. And then something was shoved into Neil's face. It was Urho's fist, his enemy's fist. And then there was darkness.

* * *

Neil lay in bed in a private room of the mental wing of Woodoaks Hospital, the bright sunlight profiling him. He stared through a drugged dimness. He smoothed his hair and began to rise. Urho walked into the room.

"How are you father?"

Slowly Neil's eyes came up to focus on Urho and then he turned away. "You're no son of mine."

"Don't say that. I'm sure you don't mean it."

"Like hell I don't. What am I doing here?"

"Look at you? You're in no shape to go home. You need rest, you've got to pull yourself together. Time and the right medicine will help you."

Neil groaned. "Medicine? That's what you've been giving me—mixing up my mind, confusing me." Then he covered his face with his hands.

At that moment the door to the room opened softly. In walked Dr. Walter Steel, the psychiatrist. He was a brusque no-nonsense man, with a full head of wavy brown hair. His white lab jacket hung on his thin body. Nervously he pushed back his horn-rimmed glasses. He nodded to Urho and went quickly to his patient. Finally after examining Neil, he spoke for the first time. "Things are going as well as expected."

"When can he come home?" Urho asked.

"Not for a while, maybe a month, at the earliest. He's a very sick man," the doctor said, as if Neil were not in the room. "The name for his illness is psychoneurotic. We've started treatment which involves tranquilizers."

"Those damn pills are making me sick," Neil said.

The doctor ignored Neil. He turned to Urho. "Medication alone will not cure him. He is experiencing a state where his concentration is impaired and withdrawal follows."

"Is there anything we can do?"

"Well, some patients who are undergoing psychiatric treatment for severe depression like your father can benefit from occupational therapy." The doctor paused to remove his glasses and pinch the bridge of his nose. "The object is to help the patient develop new interests, instill self-confidence and guide logical thinking. "We're not at that point yet with your father."

"Why can't he be treated at home? We'd get a nurse to stay with him."

Dr. Steel shook his head.

CHAPTER 35

Neil's stay at Woodoaks Hospital was shorter than Dr. Steel had predicted. It lasted a total of sixteen days. During her daily visits to Neil's room, Greta came away with the frightening impression that he was getting worse. His condition had declined. He was in deep depression. New symptoms developed during those sixteen days, severe pain at the back of his head that sent him screaming into the hallway and sudden attacks of nausea that left him limp. To protect him from himself, Dr. Steel had prescribed a straight-jacket.

"We're doing everything we can," he said to Greta. "We're making him comfortable."

"Comfortable? By tying him up in a straight-jacket?" she asked. After that conversation Greta took Neil out of Woodoaks Hospital. It was May, 1965. She managed to have him admitted into an expensive sanitarium in Grosse Pointe, a wealthy suburb on the east side of Detroit. It was all done in a matter of hours. Greta had a busy schedule that day, and she could not afford the luxury of wasting even one hour.

After the morning at the sanitarium with Neil admitted and the afternoon filled with meetings regarding land contracts and holding companies, Greta was exhausted as she steered her Thunderbird toward the Island mansion. Now, she had another problem to deal with—

The first few months she had left well enough alone, and never visited the nursery. Urho had hired a capable nurse who attended to all the baby's needs. Greta wasn't to concern herself with the baby. She didn't want the responsibility. Yes, she was going to be smart this time. She wasn't going to fall into the same old trap—the one she had fallen into so many years ago. She was too old to be a mother. Why even the thought of a baby frightened her. It wasn't the same, not like when Urho was born.

She remembered when she first held Urho in her arms, coming home from New York. He was all eyes—all hazel eyes—laughing eyes. And it was Neil who insisted on calling him Urho. He was named for one of Finland's great heroes, Urho, the strong. That was an eternity ago. No. No! She would not. She could not go through that again. Dora's baby. How ironic. Leah should be her granddaughter. But instead she was – what? She is Neil's daughter, as Urho is Neil's son. Will it ever end? Greta, weary with her thoughts, slowly guided the Thunderbird into the three-car garage.

Briskly she walked down the long hallway, unaware of the eyes of the paintings following her, unaware of the erotic Dali woman. Neil had insisted on acquiring the best for his home—priceless paintings, art objects, furnishings, everything had to be the best. Greta nervously ran her fingers through her ash blonde hair, adjusted the tortoise-shell combs. She unfastened the top button of her blue silk blouse and then jammed her hands into her tailored blue wool jacket pockets. She was still attractive —still in control of her life.

She walked past the nursery and a small cry came from within, no louder than a kitten's mew. The nursery door was open a crack and Greta heard the nurse make cooing sounds to the baby. Finally after a moment in front of the door, Greta resigned herself to the inevitable. So, it had come to this, she thought. Greta face it, that baby is going to be a part of your life, whether you like or not. She went into the nursery. Suddenly silence enveloped the pastel room. Greta looked at the nurse and baby. Two heads going back and forth, eyes flickering. And then Greta looked, no stared at baby Leah—stared into her eyes, so much like Neil's velvet brown, so demanding.

And unbelievable as it seemed to Greta, the baby smiled at her, eyes bright, alert and inquiring. So much like Neil's, thought Greta.

And then the baby laughed, and lifted her tiny arms, in a gesture of friendship.

"I think she likes you, Mrs. Liemus," the nurse said. "Do you want to hold her?"

"Yes," Greta said, not even aware she had spoken.

* * *

Later when she opened the door to her bedroom, Greta pondered this problem that had resolved itself—Leah. What made her pick up the baby? What made her spend an hour playing with the child and enjoying it? She glanced at her reflection in the floor length mirror. In another age she would have been called old, ancient. Now as she looked in the mirror she saw a well-preserved, alert, intelligent exquisitely dressed woman with the complexion of a younger woman and a smile on her young-old face that she could not suppress.

Now as she changed into a long silk black robe, she allowed herself to remember, and at first it was a beloved thought about Neil. She saw herself walking arm-in-arm with him down Main Street, in Pierre Corners. He was smiling, coat rakishly open left hand inside his coat pocket, snapping the fingers of his right hand. The smile, the nod, the hot surge of blood as he grabbed her, held her in his arms. Then quickly kissing her for all the world to see on this sunny afternoon in May. What did she feel? She felt enormous pride. That was it—a pride for what they had accomplished together, young and in love— with a bright future ahead of them—as owners of a newspaper—The Liemus Press.

But what amazed her—what truly amazed her was her love for him, an all consuming love. It was the kind of love where she couldn't sleep, couldn't eat and thought about him constantly. At first when Neil asked her to marry him, she was thrilled. She loved him so much. Oh, it was something to come so close to his love, and yet not really attain it. Now she understood, completely—so close—

She sat on the velvet couch in the spacious bedroom that Neil never shared with her. She looked at the bed that Neil never slept in with her. Yes, there were others for him. First it was Valley—then, then, and finally Dora— to end with Dora, how ironic, to end with his son's ex-wife. Now this was the final blow, to leave as a reminder of their brief love, little Leah.

CHAPTER 36

Claudia never failed to read the obituary page of the Liemus Press. It was part of a reporter's job, and that was the first thing she did every morning when she got to the news room. She'd never written an obit, except for the required one of herself that every reporter writes when they are hired. It was Tessie's job to call all the funeral homes and get information for the obits, which she also wrote. She hated writing them—but she did.

Claudia spread the obit sheet out on her desk and read it. The obits were interesting, the names, ages, cause of death, occupations, survivors, and public service. Sometimes a photograph of the deceased accompanied the death notice.

"Find your obit, Claudia? Did I get your age right?" Tessie asked. She giggled.

"I won't even humor you by answering that question. That's an old chestnut. It was asked of Ben Franklin by one of his printer's devils when they were printing Poor Richard's Almanac."

"Really? My, aren't we informed."

Then Bruce, the Press dispatcher, barged into the news room with a briefcase full of galleys and page proofs. He made a point to say hello to everyone in the room. From his voice Claudia guessed he was being friendly, not the indifferent person he usually appeared to be. She watched as he went over to Clyde and Clyde poured him a cup of coffee and offered him one of Freda's muffins. He unzipped his leather jacket, revealing an Army khaki shirt and a Vietnam button pinned on it with the words 'Hell No, I won't go!.' To belie those words, Bruce was dressed for battle with his combat boots, khaki pants and his air force pilot's leather jacket.

Claudia was aware of the friendship between Clyde and Bruce. Both were interested in President Johnson and followed the president's every address, scanning news bulletins for information about the war. Now Claudia looked at the two young men and dismissed them, she had other things on her mind—important news, and she wanted to share the news with Urho. She had finished the book on the gifted and had given the manuscript to Matt last night. "This is going to Ann Arbor tomorrow," he said.

Urho would be pleased, she thought, as she dialed his number and asked to see him. She left her desk and walked past Clyde and Bruce on her way to the elevator and the penthouse. They were deep in conversation, but still nodded to her when she walked passed them. "How are the press boats running?" she asked Bruce.

"September is perfect weather for the boats and the traffic's good. There are less freighters to mess with. Get my drift?"

"Sure," Claudia said, heading for the elevator.

The door to the penthouse office was open and she let herself in. No matter how many times she was in this room she was overwhelmed by Neil's flamboyant taste—the orange décor, the elephant statues. The sheer draperies were pulled back and the room appeared suspended in space, all orange and glass. Nothing much had changed after Urho took over the office except for his two paintings. They were moved upstairs—the Picasso and the Monet. The fine tear on the Monet created when Dora threw a crystal paperweight at it had been mended by an expert and could not be detected. Claudia could still remember Urho's fury when he told her what Dora had done.

Now Urho sat behind his father's desk, fingering one of his father's crystal elephant paperweights. Since he had become publisher, Claudia noticed a new weariness in the set of his shoulders. He had confided to Claudia about Neil's illness. She was sworn to secrecy. Both Urho and Greta wanted it kept secret, at least until a contract had been reached with the union. But somehow Claudia suspected that Valley knew.

After she walked in, Urho made sure the door was closed. Then he took her in his arms and kissed her urgently. "Oh, I needed that," he said. "Now tell me, is there a problem?"

"No problem. Aren't you surprised? Guess that's all you've been getting lately, problems. This time I have good news. My gifted book is finished! Happy Day. I gave the manuscript to Matt last night. It's on its way to U of M at this very minute. I can't believe it."

"Great. Let's celebrate." Urho grinned.

Claudia smiled. She had succeeded in changing his mood. He had a worried expression on his face when she walked through the door, but now he was smiling. Then the telephone rang. He reached for it. "Urho Liemus here. Yes, yes, she's here." With a puzzled expression on his face he gave Claudia the phone. "It's for you."

"For me?"

Urho said, "I'm sure Freda knew you were coming up. She keeps track of everyone."

When Claudia took the phone she heard Matt's booming voice. "Claudia, got great news."

"You have?"

"Yes, can't wait to tell you."

"You can't?" She glanced at Urho and shrugged her shoulders.

Matt chuckled, "Very good news, my dear."

"You want me to guess, or are you eventually going to tell me."

"I'll tell you. But is Urho there?"

"Of course. This is his office and you just talked to him. Matt, are you all right?"

"Splendid."

"Then we must be playing some sort of game," Claudia said.

"No game. I've teased you long enough. We've got a publication date for the gifted book, and a handsome advance for you. I'm in Ann Arbor, just left U of M. How does September next year sound? One year from today. And the book is going to be distributed in every school in the United States."

"Matt, I can't believe it. It's – it's." In her excitement she dropped the phone. Urho picked it up and handed it to her. Then she laughed, held her hand over the receiver and told Urho the news. "I can't believe it, I can't believe it," she kept repeating into the phone.

Urho hugged her. "Great, my darling." He grinned.

Into the phone Claudia said, "You're not teasing me, Matt?"

"No, my dear, it's all true. But I'll let you get back to work. We'll celebrate later, when I get back."

"Celebrate? I'm already celebrating. Did I tell you this was my dream, and it's coming true? My impossible dream is coming true. Thank you. Thank you. Good bye. Thank You. Oops, I said that, didn't I ?" She hung up.

Urho kissed her again and again. They both were giddy with happiness locked in each other's arms. "Congratulations darling, I knew you'd do it. Things are certainly looking up." He looked into her eyes. "Yes, things are good. Now we just have to get a good contract for the Press. And then—and then—."

"And then?" she asked

"And then, my darling, the world is ours," he said.

* * *

Claudia was at home, curled up in the couch, eating pop corn and watching television. It was almost midnight and the final scenes of "It Happened One Night" the old classic movie starring Clark Gable was on TV. She pulled her red robe around her, fished into the pop corn bowl for the last kernels of pop corn, and weighed an important question in her mind. Should she make another batch of pop corn? Nope! She shouldn't, she decided, and stretched out on the couch to enjoy the rest of the movie. Then the telephone rang. At first her thoughts raced back to the days when Neil made midnight calls. She knew it wasn't him—he was in the hospital. Could it be her mother from Chicago? They had just visited over Labor Day. And she had telephoned Claudia yesterday. Something must be wrong— maybe an emergency. She picked up the phone.

"Claudia?"

"Yes, is that you Richard? What's the matter? You usually don't call me at midnight, must be important."

"It is important, Claudia. I'm sorry to call you so late. But I need your help. Didn't wake you up, did I?"

"No. I was watching an old Clark Gable movie."

"Ah yes, he was a classic actor, that Clark Gable. They don't make them like him anymore." Then abruptly changing the subject, he said, "I have a request to make, it's important."

"What is it? It's about the union, right?"

"Yes it's about the Press and contract negotiations, which I might add are going nowhere. We've got to build a fire under them."

What does that mean?"

"I think you know."

"You can't mean a strike vote. You can't be serious?"

"I'm afraid so," Richard said. "Butler and I agree, which is unusual to say the least. We have to consider the welfare of the employees at the Press. Urho, I'm sorry to say, has other things on his mind. We know about Neil, and his illness and hospitalization — breakdown, right?"

"I – don't know."

"That's okay. I'll accept that answer, but I know for sure. I think everyone knows. It's an open secret. I want to ask you a favor, Claudia."

"What?"

"We have to set up a meeting. I'd like to meet at your house."

"Oh?" Claudia's hands were trembling.

"Please say yes. We have to have a pre-strike meeting, and vote."

In the silence that followed, the tenseness drained out of Claudia. Strike, she didn't want to think about it. Picketing the Press? No! It must not happen. She wished she could run away—run away from the Press—run away from the strike.

"Claudia, are you still there?"

"Yes." She looked into the empty pop corn bowl. She watched the ghost like images on the television screen—Clark Gable, Claudette Colbert. She could not answer Richard.

"Then we can use your house for a meeting. Your basement is fine, plenty of room. I'll make some calls. Let's say, tomorrow at eight?"

"Tomorrow?"

"Yes, tomorrow. Get a grip on yourself. We had discussed striking as a final option, remember? Our tentative target date is December 7—Pearl Harbor Day. Right nice time to start a strike."

"Pearl Harbor Day?" She couldn't help herself. She seemed to be echoing Richard's words. Certainly the union had given the Press enough time. The balance sheet at the Press showed that it could well afford to give its employees a raise and a good contract.

Who was stalling? Should she believe Urho? He often said that Butler was a power hungry bastard who was bound to self destruct. Or should she believe Richard, who said that now it was time to act—to strike.

"It will be a short strike, I promise you," Richard said. "Don't forget we have the clout. And calling the strike just before Christmas will really paralyze the Press, because its big advertisers will pull out. The bottom line is money, it's always money. Don't forget the pre-Christmas advertising is 60 per cent of the Press' annual revenue. Are you listening, Claudia?"

"Yes," she said. Only then did she realize how thorough Richard and Butler had been. They had covered everything.

"You don't think we can hold off until spring?" she asked. "It gets cold out there—picketing in the snow." She forced a laugh.

"We'll get everyone thermal under wear," Richard said. He chuckled.

"One last thing Claudia, I know your relationship with Urho, and I'm glad for you, for the both of you. You are two good people. I'm being very honest. But I must have your word. Don't tell him about this meeting, about our plans to strike. Promise."

.There was a long pause on Claudia's end. She was being torn apart,

What could she do? She was really torn to shreds.

"Promise, Claudia?" Richard asked again.

Finally she said, "Yes."

CHAPTER 37

Urho had never fully anticipated the pressure, frustrations and complexities of being a publisher. There were a great number of important decisions and only he could make them. There seemed that there wasn't enough time to get the job done, especially now with the contract negotiations still going on.

And if he was hitting the bottle more than he ever had, it was understandable; sometimes a man had to relax—just take off his shoes, put his feet up, loosen his tie, have a drink and figure out where he was going next. And figure out Claudia. Lately why had she been acting withdrawn, confused? Was that why he was drinking? No.

This he knew. He was not going to pressure Claudia. She had enough on her mind, with the gifted book, and the deadlines at the Press. Then there was Jamie, her bright, talented youngster. Last, there was that damn union. He'd deal with that union, and he wasn't going to concede to anything that was not fair, fair for the employees and fair for the Press. Yes, he'd have to take care of business.

It was the middle of October, and the big Christmas advertising season was in the near future. Plans had to be made to publish extra color tabloid sections for Sunday's and Wednesday's editions.

Now at 1:45 p.m. the second Thursday of October, after working steadily all morning on the Christmas ad campaign, Urho left his office and walked to the board room to get ready for the 2 p.m. contract session with Butler. As usual the room was in disarray with stacks of newspapers yellowing in a corner, and old typewriters piled in another. Urho smiled thinking that Butler had all the genuine warmth, charm and charisma of a deadly rattlesnake. He was just the man to tame that snake.

After Butler and his two union representatives were seated, Urho rose to his feet and spoke. That put him on a higher, dominant level. He had learned that trick from his father. He laid it on the line to Butler and the others. He outlined his contract offer step by step and said that this was the best the Press could give. "I don't see any problems," he said, tossing the new contract proposal to Butler.

Butler paused to glance at the contract and then explained that in negotiations it was not wise to take anything for granted. One item in the contract might wipe out all the others, Butler added.

"There is no gap," Urho said. "Everything is covered. In the past, as you well know my father was opposed to a union in the Press. He alienated many of his employees. I've taken a different road and think the union and the Press can get along,"

Butler said, "You do?" He grinned.

The other two union men smiled.

Urho looked at them coldly. "What's so funny?"

"Liemus," Butler began. "You and the Press have put it on the line, true. But we're talking hard cash and good benefits, especially pension benefits. Are you willing to let it go down the drain by being soft on the pension issue?" He tossed the contract proposal back to Urho. "Because that is exactly what will happen if you keep knifing the union in the back."

"You're way out of line with this proposal," said one of the union men.

"Really?"

"Sure enough, you're out on a limb. And the union will saw it off," said the other man.

Butler said, "You have to do it our way, or no way."

Urho was silent.

"You and your Press lawyers," began Butler, getting angry now. "You sit in your plush office, wearing $500 tailor made suits, surrounded by great artists' paintings, antique furniture, and you don't know what the hell is going on in the real world, in your damn newspaper." Butler was just getting started. "And we're not going to lose to some schmuck who fell into it because his father owned the company." He slapped his hand on the old scarred board room table, sending up a cloud of dust. He glanced at the proposal. "This isn't what we want. It's shit."

"Is it?" Urho asked. Then he sighed. "Butler, you are a vulgar man. You are a vulgar opportunist. Whatever happened to decent men, men with refinement, wisdom, honesty?"

Butler said, "The Press had one. His name is Richard Lucavate, remember? Your father kicked that honest, decent man out on his ass. Now you have to deal with vulgar me." He laughed.

"You have no business bringing Richard into this."

Butler stood, and the other two men followed his lead. "We're getting nowhere with this session." He tossed the proposal across the table to Urho. "When you're ready to talk, really talk sense, and I mean outlining an adequate pension for your people, and other benefits, then we'll meet. Come on men, let's get out of here."

* * *

The next morning Urho received a call from Tessie. If he wasn't busy, she'd like to meet with him. It was important, she said. Minutes later there was a sharp rap on his door.

"Come in."

Tessie walked in carrying a file folder. Her red hair was pulled back and tied at the nape of her neck. A pale pink lipstick was the only make up on her freckled face. She wore a tight orange mini-skirt and a matching sweater.

Yes?" Urho scowled. His head ached. He was in no mood to chat with Tessie, who no doubt had some office gossip to relay.

"If you're not too busy," she said taking short steps and managing to walk closer to his desk. "I have some information, important news." She held the folder close to her, smiled, then licked her lips.

"Important news?"

"Yes."

"Sit down," Urho said. He touched his forehead momentarily. "You'll have to be brief, I'm busy."

"I know. That's why I brought you my folder, so I won't waste your time. I've been keeping notes ever since Labor Day whenever important meetings were held."

"What are you talking about?"

She pulled out some papers from the file folder. "Clyde has been my chief source. He goes to all the secret union meetings. They won't let me go because I'm non –union and proud of it. I'm for the Press. I believe what Mr. Liemus believed—I mean believes. It's that the union can not do anything for me. The union just causes trouble."

"All right, get on with it. I'm busy. What have you got?" He wondered why he was wasting his time with this gossip. Most of her information was worthless.

"I've written everything down, in code." She giggled. "I was being very careful. Besides Claudia and Bernie would let things slip out when they thought I wasn't listening. Bernie and Claudia talk about the union a lot. And my desk is right next to theirs—so it was kind of easy getting this information. Often, they let their guard down."

"Look," began Urho getting impatient. "I'm very busy, what have you got?"

Then Tessie began pulling papers out of her file, some spilling onto the floor. "I'm sorry."

Urho watched as she gathered up the papers. Tessie had an unusual job. Neil had hired her right out of high school. She was never given a real news story to write, never had a beat to cover and never wrote an in-depth feature. She was hired as a copy girl. Later she began writing obituaries, kept track of copy sent to the Detroit plant, cropped photos and wrote the cut lines. Now, Urho wondered, was another duty being added to her list of duties at the Press, the job of informer? And had Neil used her information in the past? Urho shook his head. He was tired of this girl-woman, this Tessie.

"Ah, here it is," Tessie said. She handed him a bulletin. The heading read, "OPERATION PRESS STRIKE—TARGET DATE December 7!"

"Where the hell did you get this?" Urho asked.

"I-I can't say. But it's true. That was the first meeting held, planning a strike vote. Richard was at the meeting."

"Richard?"

"Yes, and about twenty other staff members, including Freda, George, Bernie and Valley. And it was held at the home of –." As was her habit, she paused in mid-sentence.

"Strike vote eh? I guess that's why Butler was so eager to end the last contract talks."

"Oh?"

"What else have you got?"

Tessie smiled. She gushed as she spoke, eager to reveal all she knew. "I'd never strike. Your father was good to me. The Press has been good to me."

Urho nodded. He leaned back in his leather chair, his hazel eyes now inquisitive, seeking, fixed on Tessie's face. "So this was a secret meeting?"

"Yes."

"Where was it held?"

Then Tessie grinned. "It was at Claudia's house."

"What?"

"Yes, she even served doughnuts and coffee."

"Claudia's house? You're sure?"

"Very sure it was the first strike call meeting. They had another one since then. It was also at Claudia's house."

"Thank you, Tessie." Urho rose and walked to the windows, his back to Tessie. He stared out onto Main Street, watched the slow moving cars, wheels skidding, slipping, sliding on the snow-covered streets. It was an early snow, wet and heavy.

Tessie taking her cue from Urho got up and turned toward the door. "If there isn't anything else, I'll get back to the news room."

"Yes," he said, not bothering to turn around.

Tessie gathered her papers, put them back into the folder, placed the strike notice on his desk and let herself out.

"No, damn, I can't believe this." Urho said aloud to himself after

Tessie left his office. What is happening? he thought. He was not going to be defeated, not by Claudia, not by the union, not by Butler. If they wanted to play that game, then so be it. There were many with wants, hates, goals, needs and loves. He'd have to face it head on. Get to the truth, and there was only one way to do that, he'd make that call. He reached for the phone and dialed a number. "This is Claudia Kali, may I help you?" she said in a pleasant voice.

"I want to see you now." Then Urho hung up.

CHAPTER 38

Claudia presented a calm, steadfast manner when she entered Urho's office. If she was in an emotional turmoil, he would not know. No one would know, not Valley, not Bernie, not Matt, not Jamie, and certainly not Urho.

As usual his first question to her was, "How's Jamie?"

"Jamie's fine," she said. "She can't wait for Matt's gifted school to open." Claudia smiled. How she loved this man, she thought.

He closed the office door. "Claudia, there is something I have to ask you." Then he picked up the phone. "Freda, hold my calls, until I get back to you."

Then he turned to Claudia, the strike bulletin in his hand. "Look at this bulletin. Know anything about it?"

"Yes."

"I think I'm entitled to an explanation."

Claudia felt her face flush. She felt trapped, utterly defenseless. Why had she let Richard talk her into having those meetings at her house? Why had she placed herself in such an absurd position? Then her words tumbled out, racing, explaining, wanting to convince Urho that she was a pawn in this game. She tried to tell Urho that she did not want a strike. She wanted peace at all cost, a good contract for the Press employees. How did she get into this strike mess? Tears welled in her eyes. "I didn't want the meeting in my house, I swear, I didn't. Richard didn't force me he just thought it would be best. I don't know why I said yes."

Urho sat back in the leather chair, the chair that his father had sat in so many years. He listened, an unlighted cigarette in his hand, using it to gesture, make a point occasionally when Claudia paused. During her long explanation, Urho never stood, never reached out to touch her, never left his father's chair.

"Now, I know it was a mistake," she finally said. Outside it had stopped snowing. She could hear the sound of horns on Main Street, could hear a car racing its motor, and hear the shouts of children.

Then she stopped talking. Had she been running on, babbling? She was exhausted. She finally sat down across from Urho's huge desk. Did she tell him everything? Did she leave anything out, anything important? She pushed her hands into her jacket pockets, felt her amber beads, comforting beads. Then she gazed out the wide expanse of windows. At last her eyes fell on Urho, her love. Was he a clone of his father, from the tailored grey wool business suit to the perfectly groomed hair? Yes, he was her love, but now things had changed. She could see it in his eyes as he looked at her and said, "I'm disappointed in you, Claudia."

"I know." It was all she could say.

Finally he reached for the gold elephant lighter on the desk and lighted his cigarette, taking deep puffs, filling his lungs with smoke.

Claudia waited, sitting in the chair, her heart pounding. The bright lamp on his desk illuminated his face, his hazel eyes. How could she tell him? But she must. She had been living a nightmare long enough. It must end, now! She looked at him. "I've made a decision. I want to tell you about it. I've been thinking about it for a long time. When the union was voted in, and even when contract negotiations were going on. It's the only decision I can live with—."

Urho smiled, a tender smile, not the false one he often wore at staff meetings. At this moment Claudia wasn't sure she could tell him of her decision. But she must, she thought. If nothing else, she must be honest with herself. She could not go on like this a moment longer. "Yes, I have to tell you about my plans," she said.

"Your plans?"

"Yes, my plans." She looked down at her hands folded in her lap. He didn't answer immediately. She looked up and found him staring into her eyes. She said, "I'm giving you my notice. I'm leaving the Press."

"You're what? Why?" He slapped his palm on the desk top. "You can't!"

"Yes, I must."

He was up now, at her side, close by her chair, so disturbingly close. "What are you saying?"

"I must leave the Press, must leave—you." She stood beside him.

"What are you talking about? Don't you know I love you? You can't leave me." He grabbed her, hugged her, tried to kiss her. She turned away from him.

"Please listen, Urho. This union business is driving me crazy, I'm sick of lying, sick of this strike thing, sick of the whole business. You know that my life was a living hell when Alex was alive. I don't want to go through that kind of pain again with a strike. I can't." She began to sob.

"Claudia, my darling, please don't." He held her for a moment.

"Urho, I can't love you and plot to strike your newspaper. I can't."

"I'm not asking you to do that, quit if you must. But we must be together."

"We can't. I have to leave."

"I see." He was angry now. "What will you do? Where will you go?" He walked to his desk, sat down.

"My book is being published. I have that. And I'm planning to move to Chicago, to be near my mother, she needs me."

"What?" Then in an instant he flew around his desk, lifted her off the chair, held her in his arms, kissed her hard on the lips. "No, you're not leaving," he said. "You're staying. We are not through, we'll never be through, hear?"

"Urho, listen. Yes, we are through," she said abruptly, freeing herself from his embrace. She was sobbing now, searching in her pocket for a handkerchief. When he reached for his and offered it to her, she took it and dried her eyes, and numbly allowed him to lead her to the couch. While she cried, he waited patiently beside her. "Claudia," he whispered. "I love you."

Claudia felt the sweet hurting, agonizing pain grow inside her. "Urho, it's over. It's not that I don't love you. I think I always will."

"Then for God's sake, what is it? For the first time we can truly be together. I've paid the price, that's for sure. Don't do this to me—to us." He got up and began to pace.

"I can't—," she said. "I need a fresh start, no more battles. I'm tired of fighting, it's taking too much out of me. This Press contract and the possible strike are driving me crazy. I want some peace in my life. Is it too much to ask for a nice quiet normal life? Is it?"

"Maybe you're right," he said, resigned. "I can't get as angry as you about the conditions here at the Press. Sure, they need improving, but we're not running a sweat shop. And I'm not in this for the money, as many think. This is my life, now. As for pain, I think I saw too much in Korea and now with Neil that I have turned off my pain button for a while. Before you came along, nothing made sense, I was a very mixed up man. Am I making any sense?"

"Yes, you are. You're an honest man, a good man, too. And I worry about what the union will do to you. You don't think they will win, do you?"

"Oh, they'll win, but not everything. That's not the way things go in life, or in union life. The union will get some of the things they want, but there are issues that they will not get."

"What does that mean?"

"Everything can't be solved by striking. Things get worse before they get better. I've heard that when there's a strike and finally when it's settled the bitterness remains. There's the heartache and the memories that remain."

"That's why I'm quitting. I've had enough. And as for us—I'm so confused. I can't leave the Press and still love you although I always will. Does that make sense?"

Urho's temper was beginning to show again. "No, you don't make sense. You still love me, always will, but must leave me?"

"Yes. I want out. It's tearing me apart, but I must leave Pierre

Corners, leave Michigan. Once and for all, make a clean break, and try to forget, no Alex, no pain, no nothing." She stood up and paced back and forth, conscious of his gaze following her.

"Please Claudia, listen to me. I love you. I want to marry you. I'm not Alex." He grabbed her, forced his lips on hers, roughly. "Quit the Press! But when it comes to us, you and me it's different, I love you I'm not your enemy."

She pulled away from him. "Yes, you are, in a way," she said in a low voice.

"What the hell is that supposed to mean?"

"I don't know, can't understand it myself. But I know that deep down inside me I want to punish the Press."

"I love you," he said. He held her, close.

"No. Please let me go. I don't want to hurt you. And I don't want to change into someone I'm not."

"Hurt me? You're killing me," he said. He leaned over and touched her shoulder, gently. "Please, don't go."

"I have to." She looked at him and suddenly his face changed; she did not recognize him, he was another man, a stranger. Finally she walked toward the door.

"Very well," he said in a toneless voice. "I accept your resignation. Two weeks?" A slight shade of color, the palest pink crept into his cheeks.

"Yes, two weeks." She left, closing the door behind her. And then in the hallway she stared at the closed door with tears in her eyes.

CHAPTER 39

Where was it? Damn! Think! Think! Valley raced through the lounge of the Press. She rushed into the women's toilet area, looked at her reflection in the mirror. She smiled pleasantly at Valley LaPorte. Then she stuck her tongue out at her reflection and laughed hysterically. Was she looking at a drunk's face, all blood vessels, a heavy nose and watery eyes? Or was she looking at a beautiful woman with deep blue eyes, the bluest Neil had ever seen, and long blonde hair?

Enough of this shit, she thought. Where did she put her booze? Last night she had stalled Claudia, had told her she was busy, and the moment she left, Valley dashed into the lounge and hidden her bottle of vodka. So she was feeling good at the time. So she had a few nips during the day. So what? Why couldn't she remember where she put it? She had made a point of coming in early. Had she locked the door to the lounge? Quickly she checked. Yes, it was locked. She didn't want anyone sneaking in on her.

Pearl Harbor Day, today, nice day to start a war, isn't that what Bernie had said? Then she giggled. "We're going to war, Neil, and you're the target, the enemy!"

The battle soon would begin and she needed fortification to fight. That's why she was here, before eight in the morning, to gain her courage, and it was in that bottle. She moved to the small window looked out at Pierre Corners' icy Main Street, that had reduced the traffic to a crawl. Out of nowhere a cardinal lighted on the sill, beak open, searching for breakfast. Valley lifted the window a crack, and the red bird flew to a safer perch on the telephone wires. The cold wind had the bite of a Michigan winter. Valley shivered and closed the window. She took a deep breath, leaned against the tile wall. The question screamed in her mind. Where the hell did she put her booze?

She had to find it and get out, fast. There were more problems waiting for her. She could not face Urho, number one son. Oh, how she ached to talk to him, find out about Neil, find out about the baby, Dora's baby. But she couldn't. And at that last union meeting after the strike vote was taken, Richard had made a personal attack at her, calling her "a disgrace to the journalism profession" and "their greatest danger to getting a good contract." But what riled Valley the most was that Bernie and George agreed with him. George had been her long-time drinking buddy. And Bernie? Why, she and Bernie had worked together for ages. They both said they wanted to talk some sense into her. "Forget the bottle," they had said. "Screw them! Screw them all," Valley shouted to the walls in the lounge.

Of course they didn't realize how much clout she had at the Press. They didn't realize how important she was to Neil, and how important she was to Urho, number one son. And who the hell appointed Richard king of the mountain and her keeper? She drew a deep breath. It's too quiet in this room, she thought. She stared broodingly at the three sinks, the three toilet stalls.

"Eureka!" she cried. She remembered. She walked briskly to the first stall. For a long stomach-turning moment she clamped her veined hands on the tank's lid, lifting it carefully. "Easy does it now, gal." Then she slid one hand into the tank, into the cold water and wrapped trembling fingers around her bottle of vodka. "Oh, God, thank you!"

Her drawn face lit up and she nodded. "Thank you, thank you."

Instantly she uncapped the bottle and raised it to her lips. It was love. It was passion. It was everything, and much more. It was fire in her veins. It was her only need. It was the ultimate pain.

The first swallow made her more alert, more totally awake. Then she held the bottle close to her, smiled at it, patted it. She tried to convince herself that she really didn't need it. She just took the first drink because it was a habit. She could break that habit anytime she wanted to because she wasn't addicted to booze. She wasn't a drunk. Screw Richard! Screw them all!

In less than an hour she had drained the bottle and was sitting on the tile floor, her head resting on a bundle of old newspapers. She breathed in careful pants instead of lung-filling gulps. She tried not to make a sound. Urho might hear her.

She now could hear the soft knocking on the lounge door although it might have gone on for some time. She struggled to get up from the floor but she couldn't move. Then she heard a low voice. "Valley, are you in there? Open the door, we're ready." The voice was getting fainter, weaker more distant.

"Valley, open the door, please."

This time Valley clung to the tile wall. She must get up. She must unlock the door. It's time to start the war. And then instantly her legs began to tremble, violent tremors shot upward until they had her body in an arch and she slumped backwards, hitting her head hard against the porcelain washbasin. Then a cry, "Oh, God!" Then a burning sensation in her head exploded into deep pain. "Help me!" she cried as blood trickled down the back of her head. The knocking stopped. "Don't, please don't go away," she said.

She closed her eyes, panted, and tossed her head side to side. Her voice rasped at first when she tried to speak, "Damn it, somebody help me!" Suddenly the white tiles beneath Valley's head were red, wet and slippery. There was no strength in her anymore and her body sagged. She opened her eyes and they were large and bright, as if in surprise. This throbbing, this pain in her head would not go away, would not stop. She was tired, so tired, but she mustn't close her eyes, mustn't sleep. She had to do something, be somewhere. Where? Neil had warned her. "Don't you tell David about this, you hear?"

"I 'won't tell David, I promise," Valley cried out. Now thoroughly frightened and in great pain, she lay on the cold tile floor wet from her blood. Her face took on a grayish hew. She lay there stunned with her own rage. Then she said, "You son of a bitch Neil. You did this to me—you did."

CHAPTER 40

Claudia glanced out the back window and saw Richard lead the way, driving an unmarked van. Butler, a hundred yards back, drove a Jeep. Three union men were with him. Claudia knew they intended to take their time, it was still early. Strike time was scheduled for 9 a.m.. They had thirty minutes.

Claudia also knew that Richard's van held the picket signs and posters. What was in the Jeep was anyone's guess. Claudia suspected that Butler had brought along clubs, rotten eggs, smoke bombs and maybe a few explosives. Claudia wondered if they really would resort to those tactics, the first day of the strike. But then she remembered Bernie's comment, "It's war, we have to establish a beachhead."

It was 8:30 a.m. and Claudia heard a timid knock on the back door. She dashed to it. The face that peered in belonged to a young woman, the new dispatcher. She wore a leather jacket, black slacks, black shirt and combat boots. A brown wool stocking cap covered her long blonde hair. She hesitated before coming into the Press. "Brrrr, it's cold. Is it all right to drop off the galley proofs?"

"Come in. It's safe," Claudia said. She glanced at her watch. "You're bright and early, not like Bruce. He was always late. Maybe the Army will cure him of that habit."

"I'm sure they will, up at dawn," the dispatcher said. Then she leaned over and whispered. "Are you really going to strike?"

"I'm not. I'm leaving. But, yes, they really are going to strike."

282

She glanced at her watch. "In about twenty minutes."

"Is anybody here? I mean besides Mr. Liemus?"

"Sure. There's a skeleton staff, those who didn't want to strike. The strikers call them "scabs". And Freda's here, at the switchboard. I think her heart isn't in striking. And now that you mentioned it, I haven't seen Valley. Maybe she decided to take the day off," Claudia smiled. "Bad joke on my part. Have to get back to my packing— got to clear out of here before the fireworks start."

"Well, I'd better get these to Mr. Liemus and get out, too. I'm allergic to fireworks." And with that the dispatcher dashed to the elevator. She passed Tessie coming into the room. "Aren't you going to strike?" the dispatcher asked her.

"Are you crazy? I'd never strike, never in a million years." She smiled smugly, her too tight red sweater straining across her breasts. "What are you going to do, Claudia?"

"I'm leaving," Claudia said. Then the telephone on her desk rang. "Claudia Kali."

"Claudia, this is Urho. I've got to see you. I'll be down in a few minutes. Don't go until we talk, please."

"All right." Why was her heart thumping? Claudia rubbed her forehead and found she was sweating although the news room was cool. She pondered how she was going to handle this—this. Then the telephone rang again. This time it was Freda. "Claudia, where's Valley?"

"I don't know, why?"

"One of the counter girls tried to get into the lounge, and it's locked. Think she's in there? Think she's, you know, drinking?"

"I hope not."

"Listen, I have the master key. I'll get someone to relieve me at the switchboard. I'll find out why the door is locked."

"Freda, are you going on strike?"

"I don't know. I don't think so. I can't leave Mr. Liemus, and the press."

At about this time, Bernie dashed into the back door and raced to Claudia's desk. "Change your mind, Claudia, come on join us. I've got a picket sign for you."

"No, sorry, I'm almost packed, I'm leaving."

"You're going to miss a great war." He looked at her, face flushed. "We're going to stick it to Number One Son."

They stared at each other. Bernie was the first to look away. He shrugged and walked out to join the others lining up. Now there was just Tessie and Claudia in the news room. It was then that they heard Freda scream. She ran up to them, crying hysterically and grabbed Claudia's arm. "Come, please. Valley's hurt bad, hurry."

"Oh my God, Tessie, call an ambulance. I'll see what happened."

Minutes later Freda and Claudia found Valley. Freda hadn't touched her. She was still lying on the tile floor under the sink. Blood from her head wound had soaked through the bundle of newspapers where she lay. Claudia walked to Valley, shaking, crying. She kneeled beside the wounded woman, gently held her hand, spoke to her softly. "What happened, Valley? Hold on, we've called an ambulance. They'll be here real soon. Hold on." She watched her friend shiver, "Get something to cover her. Get some towels, a coat, anything. She's cold," Claudia said to Freda. "Where is that ambulance? We've got to do something to stop that bleeding." She could hear Valley's irregular breathing.

Valley's face was white, white as the tile. Then for a moment Valley's eyes opened. She was fighting to breathe, trying not to move. For when she moved that knife-like pain in her head got worse. There was more blood coming from the wound. Valley smiled at Claudia, a faint smile white with pain. She said nothing, just looked at Claudia. Freda came rushing in with a coat and towels. "The ambulance is coming," she said.

Claudia gently placed the towels beneath Valley's head and draped the coat over her. She turned to Freda. "Go, tell the ambulance medics where we are hurry." Freda raced out of the room.

Valley looked up at Claudia. "Listen kid," she whispered.

Claudia leaned closer to the older woman. "Yes, Valley, I'm listening." Valley's hand fumbled up Claudia's arm.

"Don't leave me kid."

"I won't. You're going to be all right."

"No, I'm not." Her eyes closed and her breath caught in sudden pain. "My God, it hurts like hell."

Claudia was sobbing now. "Oh God in heaven, oh merciful God, hear my prayers." She saw that Valley was dying, despite all that she could do, despite all the prayers.

Then Valley said, "I'm not going to die, kid. I'm tough, always have been." She took another deep breath. "I'm smart too. I fooled everyone, even Number One Son." She leaned against the blood-stained bundle of newspapers and towels, her blue eyes sunken, red rimmed.

"Valley, oh Valley." Claudia wanted to lift her old friend, run with her to the hospital. Instead she stroked her hand and prayed. When Valley opened her eyes again and moved her head, more blood soaked through the towels on the tile floor.

"It was our secret," began Valley in a whisper. " It was just the three of us." She gasped. "I knew we could do it, keep it quiet, right to the death."

"What are you saying?" Claudia asked.

"I got away with it," Valley whispered. "It took guts. No one suspected." Her voice was low now. "Pure guts."

"What?"

"Urho is my son. My Number One Son! I had to keep the secret. Neil threatened me. He's Neil's son too, of course. My husband, David killed himself when he found out I was carrying Neil's baby. He couldn't have children. That was too much for him. And that Greta, she stole my baby, my Urho."

"What are you saying?" Claudia said, shocked. "Why didn't you tell Urho?"

"Because Neil would kill me." The loss of blood had turned her face ashen.

Claudia was quiet with shock. She sat numb on the tile floor, staring at her friend. Urho was Valley's son? Another secret?

Valley whispered. "Neil warned me, he warned Greta. She got the best of the deal, my son to raise and clout with Neil's fortune, his land holdings. She held a sword over his head. I gave birth to Urho in New York and Greta came with me and brought the baby home to Michigan. She came back claiming Urho was her son. He's mine!" She paused, coughed. "We were afraid of Neil. He could be dangerous, we knew. We had to keep the secret. That's why I made such a mess of my life."

"Oh Valley," Claudia said. That was when she understood. She held her friend's hand and wept.

"We were constantly afraid someone would stumble on our secret. It was that story about prohibition and boot-legging in the Detroit newspaper that finally cracked Neil. He wasn't the same after that came out. But we did fool everyone."

Now Claudia remembered the old stories Valley had told her. She understood why Valley was always angry with Neil, why she called Urho, Number One Son.

Valley gasped. "The hardest part was seeing you and Urho so unhappy lately." She reached up to touch Claudia's face. "That was the hardest part. You have gone through enough grief in your young life."

"Valley, Valley," was all Claudia could say.

"I know what you're thinking, kid. But don't be afraid to go to him. He needs you, he loves you. Don't ever be afraid again. You went through hell with Alex." Then her head fell back, her eyes closed. Freda rushed in with the ambulance medics. She screamed when she saw Valley. A crowd had gathered in the lounge. Urho burst through the crowd. "What's going on here?" He pushed and shoved until he reached the wounded Valley and Claudia. "God, what happened?"

Valley was placed on a stretcher by the medics. Claudia could not stop trembling, her eyes glistened with tears.

* * *

Valley was taken to the hospital, with Urho and Claudia at her side in the ambulance. It was the same hospital where Neil had been earlier. And from which he had left to face a life in a mental hospital. But Valley would not leave. She died minutes later in the hospital emergency room. Claudia wasn't aware of it at the time, but the picketing and violence started immediately after the ambulance had left. Claudia and Urho were only grateful that the questions the police asked concerning Valley's death were brief. They answered them wearily, numbly. When the police finished questioning them at the hospital, Urho said, "Shall we go?"

"Go?" she asked.

"Yes."

Then Claudia made the mistake of trying to be cruelly flippant, a role to which she was not suited. "Where shall we go, to picket the Press, to take Valley's place on the line?" Then she burst into tears.

"I never expected that from you," Urho said. "What are you talking about? I just want to give you a lift back, so you can pick up your things— nothing else, no strings."

Claudia couldn't stop crying. She simply nodded. Urho hailed a cab.

When they entered the cab, they were silent. Then Urho said, "Why are you doing this?"

"I told you. I have to get away from all this, the union, the strike, the Press. I have to get out of this town, out of this state." Tears welled in her eyes.

Urho said, "Things will change, this strike will be resolved, soon. Do you understand what I'm saying?"

":No— I don't. We've changed too much. I'm not the same person you fell in love with, and you're not the same man."

"True, if I were, I'd be sharing a room with my father in the mental ward."

"What does that mean?"

Urho shook his head. "I had to change, to survive. This union thing, these talks with Butler have brought about the change. I had to get tough. I'm fighting for my life, Claudia. Is that straight enough talk for you?"

Claudia had been listening to him with tears streaming down her face. "Yes-s-s," she buried her head in her hands.

Urho grabbed her, held her close and kissed her. "I love you, love you, do you hear?"

"No, don't." It was all Claudia could say.

* * *

Back at the Press, the crowd of pickets had grown to at least fifty, with support from other unions. Policemen attempted to control the unruly demonstrations.

When Urho and Claudia pulled up in the cab, the mob surged forward, screaming obscene curses and brandishing picket signs. Eggs flew through the air; a few splattered on the cab's windshield as it took off. The police fought their way to Urho and Claudia. Finally an area was cleared and two policemen escorted Urho and Claudia safely to the Press building entrance.

A white-faced Bernie wildly waving a picket sign shouted to Urho, "You killed Valley—you son of a bitch!" He hit Urho with the sign before a policeman dragged Bernie away. Finally Urho and Claudia reached the Press building's entrance and rushed inside, safe from the angry mob.

A day later, a story of Valley's death appeared on the front page of both Detroit newspapers. Old photos were reprinted, old stories were retold. Claudia's only regret was that Urho got to Valley's side too late. Before she left the Press, Claudia told Urho that Valley was his real mother. That was the hardest part. Urho broke down and sobbed. Now he knew why Neil could not fire her. Now he knew why Valley drank. Now he knew why she called him her Number One Son. He knew many things, now, but it was too late to make amends.

* * *

Six months later, both Detroit newspapers headlined this story.

"LIEMUS PRESS STRIKE SETTLED

The Liemus Press and the newspaper union had reached an agreement and a two-year contract has been signed. Urho Liemus, publisher and owner of the Press, said he is pleased that a generous pension plan was in the package.

Richard Lucavate, former associate publisher of the Press, and one of the union negotiators for the contract, has been promoted to an executive post in the union's New York office.

CHAPTER 41

A year later, in September, the gifted book, called "The Neglect of a Valuable Natural Resource—The Gifted" was published and Claudia and Jamie moved back to Michigan. Now, Claudia stood gazing out the window of her new home on the Island. She unconsciously fingered her amber beads, the beads her father had given her so long ago. They felt so cool. Cool, alive, that's the way she felt and that's the way she was dressed, tan silk slacks, a matching silk blouse, an orange silk scarf falling in soft folds around her neck. She wore leather sandals. Little make-up, just a touch of lip stick and only the faintest perfume fragrance — roses.

She drew back the sheers and looked at the burning sun, the refreshing river, the sail boats, the motor boats. On Jamie's easel in front of the window was a watercolor of a Press dispatch boat. A blue ribbon was attached to the painting—"First Place—Gifted School Summer Art Fair."

Claudia thought, yes they were living a normal life in this new house. It was the house that Yiannis had build for them. She glanced at the pile of her books on her desk. She picked up one and ran her fingers down the dust jacket cover. Her book, she thought. Her name was on the cover.

She turned when she heard Jamie's voice, "Mom, where are you?"

"Right here, just signed some books. I'm waiting for Matt to pick us up. Can you believe I'm going on P. R. McMurray's Talk Show?

I'll be jabbering away about the gifted book. It was Matt's dream, my dream, and dreams do come true, don 't they honey?"

"Yes, they do," Jamie said as she entered the room. "Mine came true too, we're back in Michigan. And I'm going to the Gifted School."

Claudia put the book down and rushed to Jamie to hug her. "Yes, yes."

"Mom, I got a call when you were out. It was Urho."

Claudia held her breath. Was that what she wanted to hear? Did she give him up too willingly?

When Jamie spoke again her young voice was serious, "He heard we were back, he wants to see you."

Claudia ignored her daughter's remarks. "Did you know that the first time I met Urho, I wore my best navy blue suit? All business, nothing casual, like these slacks. I was a writer looking for a job. And I carried my worry beads for luck. But he didn't know that. Anyway I think he was impressed. And so was Richard. I mean with my work." Was she speaking too brightly, too easily? Was she talking nonsense?

"He was," Jamie said.

"I was hoping my appearance would convince Richard that I was a professional writer, and that he should hire me."

"He did, Mom."

She stood before Jamie. "Do I look all right, now?" She dangled her amber beads in her hand.

"You look great."

"Everything is all right now, isn't it Jamie?"

Jamie was silent. She leafed through one of the new books. Then she said, "No, it isn't all right. Urho wants to marry you, Mom. That's what he told me."

Claudia looked at Jamie— so trusting, so young. She's just a child. Then she said to her daughter, "Maybe it's too late, to go back I mean, to the way it was, months ago. I know Matt insisted we come back to Michigan to promote my book. He even arranged for this fine house that Yiannis built." She patted the book. "Remember this is Matt's dream too. But what if this whole thing fails?"

"It won't," Jamie said.

Claudia moved about the room, finally went back to the desk, to the books, leafed through one of them. "I want this book to work, to happen, and happen big, for Matt."

"It's going to happen- big, for both of you." Jamie rushed up to her and hugged her.

"Yes," Claudia said, her arms around her daughter. Then she released her and reached for her amber beads, again. Hadn't her father said they were good luck? Suddenly the sun glistened on the amber beads in her hand. And then she heard a car pull into the drive. "That must be Matt," she said.

"I've got to get my jacket in the bedroom. You go, I'll catch up." said Jamie.

"Okay, don't be long. Matt will be waiting for us," said Claudia.

Claudia flung open the door and saw Urho step gravely out of his Thunderbird. He smiled, a shy smile, and walked toward her. His smile was like his mother's, Valley. "Welcome back Claudia. There's been a change in plans, I'm replacing Matt."

She looked at him and caught her breath. "Urho," she cried. Racing down the driveway, as they both ran to meet each other, Claudia could not stop crying. When she reached his side, she went up on her toes into his waiting arms. " Oh my darling, I'm glad I'm back."

"You're back and you're not going anywhere without me. You hear?" He held her close and kissed her, hugged her.

"Yes, yes," she said.

From now on you will concentrate on me, Jamie and your other books."

"Other books?" She touched his lips with her hand, softly.

"Of course, you're an author now lady. What's the next book in the hopper?" Urho's smile held her close. "Now speak up my darling Claudia. Or should I say author?"

"My, you're fast. I can't think. Give me time to think. Another book—let me see. hmmmmm— I could write about a war, the Korean War, or the Forgotten War, as some called it. I have the perfect veteran to interview. He's very close to me."

Urho smiled, held Claudia's hands, kissed her tenderly. "Darling, I don't know if this veteran is ready to be interviewed. That war is still raw in his mind, in his heart, in his bones."

"Oh, my dear, of course it is. I will wait until the time is right."

"So what else have you got?" he asked.

"You're tough, really tough. Oh, now I have it. Of course, it's just a thought. Let me think. I have the perfect plot."

Urho said, "Okay, let's hear it."

"It will be a novel about a newspaper in a small town in Michigan."

"Really, a newspaper story, it sounds interesting, fiction, of course."

"Yes, and not only a newspaper story, but about a troubled family," she said.

"You mean two troubled families. Right? Well, what will you call it?"

"Too soon for a title, I have to give it a lot of thought. The idea is still working in my mind, it's still rough, I have to really think it through."

"Okay, no more questions. I'm glad I've got you now and forever. I love you, my Claudia." He paused for a moment, reached in his pocket. "Darling, will you marry me?" He opened the palm of his hand which held a diamond ring. "This is to make sure you don't run off to Chicago or points west."

Claudia gazed into his eyes, her own eyes filled with tears. "Oh my darling, yes, yes, I will marry you. And I will never run off, never."

EPILOGUE

Los Angeles—October 30, 1991 Afternoon

I slammed the phone down and yelled at my assistant standing beside me with a fistful of copy.

"Jamie, here's the copy," he said.

I grabbed the mock-ups from my desk, rechecked the copy he handed me. "No, this won't do. We need larger type. Don't forget this is an important ad."

He nodded, "Okay, I get it, I'll rework it." He took the mock-up, made some notes on it and left my office.

You might say I was a bit frazzled, deadlines and all. In a few hours I was headed for Detroit to attend the opening of the Liemus Press Museum. My mother and Urho were going to speak. Yes, it was a special event, even though I had my doubts about Neil and his legacy.

I glanced at the newspaper article my mother had sent me a while back. At that time a Dispatch reporter had called me for a quote. My mother mailed me the newspaper, in spite of being rushed on her book tour. This was her twelfth novel, all best-sellers. She had finally written the story she always wanted to do, about the Korean War, Urho's war. It was already on the New York Times best seller list as she finished two exhausting book tours in Chicago and New York. I smiled, proud of what she had accomplished. Then I reread the article.

DETROIT DISPATCH August 16, 1991

Pierre Corners—For almost a year, the Historical Preservation Society for the Liemus Press building has managed to raise $480,000 – to purchase and renovate the old historic building and now a construction company is in the final phases of restoring the building which is on the National Register of Historic Places. The new construction features casement windows, similar to the originals and tongue-in-groove hardwood floors and a leaded glass front door.

"It's more than just turning this building into a museum. It will regenerate Pierre Corners," said Lora Morrison, president of the Historical Society. "The contractor has done a splendid job of following the original plans. The group wants to take advantage of the location near the intersection of the town's major commercial thoroughfares. But money was a prime factor. Although the building is not finished, the group decided to schedule this dedication in October, according to the chairman.

"Now, is the ideal time for this museum, and to complete this dream will take an additional "$200,000." said the chairman. Ms. Morrison said they were now seeking additional funds from the U.S. Department of Housing and Urban Development.

If plans go as scheduled, the museum, although not finished, will have its dedication ceremony on October 31. At the ceremony will be Urho Liemus, former publisher of the Press, who took over after his father retired. His wife, Claudia Kali, best-selling author, worked at the Liemus Press as a reporter in the 1960s. Both will speak at the dedication cremony.

Liemus is now a noteworthy artist, his watercolors and landscapes are in several art institutes throughout the nation. Ms. Kali, recently finished her latest novel, "Not Forgotten." She said, "This time I've written an historical novel about the Korean War, or Police Action as President Truman called it, but it was known far and wide as the "forgotten war."

"Yes, I was in that one," added Liemus. "But getting back to the museum, Claudia and I have completed an illustrated book, a coffee table variety, abut Pierre Corners. I did the sketches and Claudia did the text. We highlighted the Liemus Press Museum. Copies will be available at the opening."

Also participating at the grand opening will be Ms. Kali's daughter, Jamie Kali, who is a graphic artist for a Los Angeles newspaper. Contacted in Los Angeles, Miss Kali said, "You might say my first job was at the Liemus Press. I was six at the time and did some art work in the ad department during a terrific snow storm."

The group chairman said, "I repeat, there are memories and a great legacy in this building that have to be preserved for generations to come."

But Mayor John Olson is not impressed. "The decay of the building makes it impossible to continue rebuilding the interior without a clean slate. However, we'll work with anyone who has the resources to build it from the ground up. Actually, I would like to see the building torn down and the site offered for new construction, or as a city parking lot," he said.

Parking lot, maybe the mayor is right, I thought as I put the newspaper down on my cluttered desk.. He certainly doesn't sound too keen about the renovation. What? Do I agree with him? Let it go! I told myself. Neil is in the past, the mad man that scared me.

He was a troubled soul, really three troubled souls —with Greta and Valley. Let it rest! And what about Neil's legacy? Let that rest too. It has to rest for my mother's sake, for Urho's sake. They have suffered enough.

My assistant rushed into my office with the revised mock-ups. "Well— is this better?"

I studied them and nodded. "Much better. I've got to get this wrapped up, because in a few hours I'm flying to Michigan. Tomorrow, I'm going to the opening of a newspaper museum and I'm one of the speakers."

"Sounds cool."

"As a child I lived through a 'so called' newspaper legacy. Now, I'm going back to see those memories showcased in the Liemus Press Museum, in Pierre Corners, Michigan. Did you say—cool?"

* * *

Detroit Metro Airport, 11 p.m. October 30, 1991

What a flight! No wonder they call it the red eye. I was tired, needed a strong cup of coffee or maybe a drink. I did not check my luggage, good thing, because there was a mob waiting for their luggage. So I pulled my carry-on to the nearest pub in the airport and sat down near a television screen. The news was on, so I ordered a glass of red wine and settled in. I was booked at a nearby hotel and looked forward to a good nights sleep before the big day at the Liemus Press Museum opening tomorrow. Before the grand opening, I was going to meet my mother and Urho for dinner in Pierre Corners.

I sipped my wine and glanced at the TV screen. The news was interrupted by a bulletin. Stunned, I listened and watched. The newscaster at the site hurriedly gave his report, a blazing building in the background.

The newscaster said, "Fire continues to consume the almost restored historic Liemus Press building on Main Street, in Pierre Corners. Fire Chief Clyde Gordon, said the building was fully engulfed in flames when they arrived on the scene and the blaze also destroyed the nearby coffee shop. Firemen from three cities worked to contain the blaze and protect other nearby structures."

Chief Gordon, with a microphone held by the newscaster said, "It appears the fire began between the walls near the switchboard. The cause could have been faulty wiring. I understand all the new wiring had not been completed. Once insurance inspectors investigate, we'll know more. Maybe faulty wiring, maybe – something else. As with all fires of this nature, an investigation is planned."

. "It appears that the blaze has destroyed most of the building," said the newscaster. "Oddly enough, a fireman found a metal pica ruler on what remained of the switchboard desk." The newscaster showed the metal ruler on the screen. "It's still usable," he added as he tapped it on his desk. "And that's the news. Good night."